THE KEPT WOMAN
A RITA Award finalist

HE LOVES LUCY

"A great romance…a top-rate novel…with its unforgettable characters, wonderful plot, and excellent message, *He Loves Lucy* will go on my keeper shelf to be read and re-read a thousand times…Donovan has proven that she will have serious star power in the years to come."   —*Romance Reader at Heart*

TAKE A CHANCE ON ME

"Comic sharpness…the humorous interactions among Thomas, Emma, and Emma's quirky family give the book a golden warmth as earthy as its rural Maryland setting. But there are also enough explicit erotic interludes to please readers who like their romances spicy."   —*Publishers Weekly*

"Donovan blends humor and compassion in this opposites-attract story. Sexy and masculine, Thomas fills the bill for the man of your dreams. Emma and Thomas deserve a chance at true love. Delightfully entertaining, *Take a Chance on Me* is a guaranteed good time."   —*Old Book Barn Gazette*

"Full of humor, sensuality, and emotion with excellent protagonists and supporting characters…a wonderful tale. Don't be afraid to take a chance on this one. You'll love it."   —*Affaire de Coeur*

"Impossible to put down…Susan Donovan is an absolute riot. You're reading a paragraph that is so sexually charged you can literally feel the air snapping with electricity and the next second one of the characters has a thought that is so absurd…that you are laughing out loud. Susan Donovan has a very

unique, off-the-wall style that should keep her around for many books to come. Do NOT pass this one up."
—*Romance Junkie Review*

"Susan Donovan has created a vastly entertaining romance in her latest book *Take a Chance on Me*. The book has an ideal cast of characters...a very amusing, pleasurable read...all the right ingredients are there, and Ms. Donovan has charmingly dished up an absolutely fast, fun, and sexy read!"
—*Road to Romance*

"Contemporary romances don't get much better than *Take a Chance on Me*... Such wonderful characters! You want sexual tension? This book drips with it. How about a love scene that is everything that a love scene should be? There's humor, a touch of angst, and delightful dialogue...*Take a Chance on Me* is going to end up very, very high on my list of best romances for 2003."
—*All About Romance*

KNOCK ME OFF MY FEET

"Spicy debut...[A] surprise ending and lots of playfully erotic love scenes will keep readers entertained."
—*Publishers Weekly*

"*Knock Me Off My Feet* will knock you off your feet... Ms. Donovan crafts an excellent mixture to intrigue you and delight you. You'll sigh as you experience the growing love between Autumn and Quinn and giggle over their dialogue. And you'll be surprised as the story unfolds. I highly recommend this wonderfully entertaining story."
—*Old Book Barn Gazette*

THE NIGHT SHE GOT LUCKY

SUSAN DONOVAN

St. Martin's Paperbacks

This is a work of fiction. All of the characters, organizations, and events portrayed in this novel are either products of the author's imagination or are used fictitiously.

THE NIGHT SHE GOT LUCKY

Copyright © 2010 by Susan Donovan.
Excerpt from *Not That Kind of Girl* copyright © 2010 by Susan Donovan.

Cover photograph © Jupiterimages / Getty Images

All rights reserved.

For information address St. Martin's Press, 175 Fifth Avenue, New York, NY 10010.

ISBN: 978-0-312-36605-6

Printed in the United States of America

St. Martin's Paperbacks edition / June 2010

St. Martin's Paperbacks are published by St. Martin's Press, 175 Fifth Avenue, New York, NY 10010.

10 9 8 7 6 5 4 3 2 1

This book is dedicated to my hardworking personal assistants, past and present: Marley, Murphy, Guinness, and Finnegan. True, you couldn't answer the phone, file, or fax worth a damn, but you kept my feet warm and protected me from the evils of the world, namely the UPS man, the FedEx man, and the mailman. Thank you, boys.

ACKNOWLEDGMENTS

The author would like to thank Dr. Richard Kramer, DDS, for information on oral surgery; Gail Barrett for assistance with Spanish translation; Arleen Shuster for help with German insults; and Teresa Barr for placing the winning bid at the 2008 Washington County, Maryland, Habitat for Humanity auction, allowing me to use her name for a fictional character.

This is a work of fiction. All characters and events are a product of the author's imagination.

The difference between dogs and men is you know where dogs sleep at night.　　　　—Greg Louganis

CHAPTER 1

Ginger perched on the edge of Mrs. Needleman's guest-room bed, wondering what the old woman wanted to discuss. Whatever it was, Ginger prayed it would be quick, because she was dying to get out of her brides-maid's dress. Josie and Rick had long ago departed in a shower of flower petals and good wishes, but Ginger's boobs remained squished in their pastel prison.

She tugged at the tight satin and tried to smile through her discomfort.

"You look simply lovely in that moss-green color," Mrs. Needleman said with a matter-of-fact nod, taking a seat in the antique boudoir chair across from the bed. She went on, "Contrary to popular opinion, not all redheads are flattered by green, especially women in their forties. But you have a rosy complexion, and I have to say your skin has held up quite nicely."

Ginger automatically raised a hand to her jawline and gave it a soft pat. "Thank you," she said, just before she realized she was offended. *What does this woman think I am, a 4-H farm animal? And why did she pull me into her room after the reception?*

The old lady looked Ginger up and down, smiling. "I wanted to prepare you for something, Genevieve.

Do you mind if I call you Genevieve? It's a mystery why you use a nickname in place of something so feminine and sensual."

Ginger squinted at the small, neatly dressed lady who'd officiated at her friend's wedding. According to Josie, Mrs. Gloria Needleman—a widow who fancied herself a matchmaker—had gotten Josie and Rick over their rough patch and to the altar.

"Prepare me for what?" Ginger crossed her legs and leaned her hands behind her on the mattress.

"A man, dear." Mrs. Needleman's eyes were warm and kind. "I thought you should know that there is a man waiting for you, as we speak."

Ginger looked around. Like all the guest suites at Rick's wine country estate, Mrs. Needleman's room was tasteful, comfortable, and fitted with valuable Victorian pieces, and Ginger hoped she would have time to feature the Sonoma Valley retreat in the *Herald*'s house and garden section before the newspaper went under for good. But a man? Waiting for her? Not unless he was hiding behind the shower curtain.

Ginger swung her foot back and forth, watching her silver-toned sandal dangle from her toes, trying not to sigh with impatience. "That's a sweet thing to say, Mrs. Needleman. Thank you."

"You think I'm a silly old lady."

Ginger laughed. "No, it's just that I'm not a teenager anymore. I stopped waiting for my knight in shining armor a long time ago."

"But look at Josie!"

Ginger smiled sweetly, happy that her thirty-five-year-old friend had found such a loving and devoted man to spend her life with. "I'm thrilled for Josie, of course, but that kind of thing is . . ." She paused. "It's so rare it's freakish!"

"Indeed," the old lady said, smiling. "And I insist you call me Gloria."

Ginger nodded, but was growing uncomfortable trying to keep eye contact with Mrs. Needleman, whose stare had intensified. What in the world did this lady want from her?

Mrs. Needleman sighed deeply. "You've given up on love, I take it."

"You could say that."

"Why?"

Ginger laughed, wondering how she could possibly sum up this tragedy for Mrs. Needleman, especially since it was a topic she and her friends had spent entire evenings—no, *years*—dissecting.

Mrs. Needleman stared, waiting.

"Okay, well, I recently turned forty, Gloria. I have two teenage boys and an ex-husband who behaves like one. The newspaper where I've spent my entire career is on the edge of insolvency. By this point—and I admit it's taken me long enough—I've learned a few lessons."

"I see."

"And I can assure you that if some man came up to me and told me he's been waiting for me, I'd dial 911."

Mrs. Needleman's eyes narrowed. "Tell me about those lessons you've learned."

Ginger looked up at the ceiling, silently pleading for patience. "Oh, you know—lessons about life. About *men*," she said, returning her gaze to her swinging sandal—anything to avoid the lady's laserlike eyeballs. "The difference between reality and fantasy, basically."

"Go on, dear."

Ginger shook her head, adjusting her bridesmaid dress to give her a little more room to breathe. She didn't want to be rude to Mrs. Needleman, because she'd been raised to respect her elders, but she certainly wasn't in the mood to be analyzed. All she wanted was to get back to her room in the guesthouse, ditch the increasingly tight dress, and chill out before they went to dinner. She was thinking shrimp linguine and a big, crisp salad.

"Here's what I'm sure of," Ginger said, finally returning the woman's gaze. "Ninety-nine-point-nine percent of the men in the world aren't worth my time, and I am done wasting my time; therefore, I am alone and prepared to remain so."

"That sounds awfully lonely."

"Thank God I have HeatherLynn."

Mrs. Needleman frowned. "Your daughter?"

"My bichon frise."

"Of course."

Ginger uncrossed her legs, slipped back into her sandal, and stood to go, aware that not everyone appreciated the deep love a woman can have for her dog. For many folks, the idea that a little white ball of fluff had saved Ginger from the depths of despair was laughable. Luckily, her friends Josie, Bea, and Roxanne understood perfectly. The three women in her dog-walking group had become Ginger's closest confidantes, and the group had walked and talked Ginger through the two roughest years of her life, dogs in tow.

"I should let you rest before dinner, Mrs. Needleman," she said. "I enjoyed our chat." Ginger had reached the door when the voice rang out behind her, clear and firm.

"He is out there."

Ginger spun, shocked that Mrs. Needleman had sneaked up on her. Looking into the woman's fierce expression, Ginger thought that Josie had been too kind in her description of her. "Odd" didn't do her justice. "Disconcerting" was better.

"Will seafood be all right?" Ginger was unsure how to wrap up this little get-together, but knew it was time.

"It's nothing to sneeze at, you know."

"Seafood?"

"No." Mrs. Needleman clutched Ginger's forearm. "I'm talking about that one-tenth of one percent of the male species you haven't yet written off. You could still get lucky, but if you spend all your time worrying that you're over the hill, then you'll miss your chance to be over the moon."

Ginger's eyes went wide.

"You must listen to your heart, Genevieve, not your fear. Do this, and you will find happiness."

"Super! Bye-bye now!" Ginger slipped out, closed the guest-room door, and stepped on to the patio. She raised her chin, shut her eyes, and breathed, damn glad to be out of that stifling room and into the fresh evening air!

A breeze brushed over Ginger's bare skin, followed by a strange electrical shiver that raced through her limbs. Ginger opened her eyes. She peered up the stone walkway leading from the main house to the guesthouse, squinting into the shadows. Her shivering intensified. She knew she wasn't alone.

"Is someone there?" she whispered. "Hello?"

There was a stirring behind the rose trellis. The wedding photographer stepped from the shadows. Ginger gasped.

His dark eyes smoldered. One of his hands fell comfortably at his side, and the other rested casually in the pocket of his impeccable suit. His lips parted ever so slightly as he smiled. In a heavily accented whisper, he said, "I have been waiting for you."

Ginger gasped again, but she couldn't seem to get any air.

"Me has robado el corazón."

Blackness flooded her vision. She knew she was about to faint. And as her knees buckled beneath her, Ginger had two simultaneous thoughts: *I really should have ordered this dress in a bigger size,* and *I sure wish I'd paid more attention in Spanish class.*

Technically, Ginger Garrison wasn't the first bridesmaid to faint into the arms of Lucio Montevez. That had occurred nearly twenty years earlier in Las Alpujarras, at Lucio's own wedding, when his young bride's best friend went into an apoplectic fit of jealousy. The girl had managed to call Lucio a hairy wild boar and pound her fists on his chest before she collapsed, which added some levity to the ill-fated event. Sadly, the last time Lucio returned to Spain, he'd encountered the onetime bridesmaid on the main street of his village. He said hello. She spat in the dirt near his feet and continued walking.

Ah, romance.

Lucio propped the most recent fainting bridesmaid against his chest, then reached up under a resplendent amount of green chiffon fabric until he found the back of her knees. He lifted her, pulled her close, and turned toward the guesthouse, where he'd learned she was staying. Lucio knew he should concentrate solely on the placement of his feet on the stone walk, but the allure of Señora Garrison's exposed bosom and satiny throat were impossible to resist. So he alternated. He looked at his feet on the stones, then at the glorious swells and slopes of the woman in his arms. He carefully placed his feet on the doorstep, then appreciated the graceful lines of her cheek. The stairs, her cute little nose. Kicking open the door, he admired her trim waist.

It was too much for him. The instant Lucio entered the upstairs guest room—even before he could place her on the bed—he lowered his lips to the satiny warm skin below her jawline. He kissed her there, gently flicking his tongue against her pulse. She would be fine, he knew. She simply needed to loosen her dress. So Lucio placed her on top of the coverlet, rolling her away enough for him to reach the zipper. Slowly, he pulled it down, and with the release of each stainless steel tooth, more of the woman's taut skin was revealed to his appreciative gaze. Lucio's breath quickened as the inches of flawless pink revealed themselves between her shoulder blades, around her ribs, along the straight, delicate spine, and lower, lower, to the top of what was proving to be perfectly rounded buttocks.

With great care—and an unexpected surge of self-discipline—he eased her onto her back, making sure the dress covered her bare breasts but did not hinder her breathing. He brushed her left cheek with the back of his fingertips.

"Te fuiste, mi amor," he whispered. "Wake up, love. You left me for a moment. Breathe now."

She stirred.

"That is good," he said, suddenly aware of a strange sizzle in the air, an electrical rush moving through his body. He glanced to check if a breeze ruffled the curtains. But there was nothing.

Then Ginger sighed, her dainty pink lips parting ever so slightly, and Lucio felt it again, stronger this time—a wave, a disturbance in the air, a question and its answer tucked inside a crackle of energy. Ginger's eyelashes flickered. His self-control had been short-lived.

"Forgive me," Lucio said as he lowered his mouth to hers. "But I must."

He kissed her. Her lips yielded to his gentle pressure, opening to him. Lucio groaned in bliss, the energy coursing through him, the kiss building, surging, growing hotter and hotter . . .

Until she struck him.

The thud of her palms against his chest knocked the wind from his lungs. Lucio prevented himself from falling off the edge of the bed, and managed a smile. "Sleeping beauty awakes!" he said, bowing slightly.

"You freakin' pig!"

With that pronouncement, Ginger sat up abruptly, her thick auburn hair askew, her dress falling far south of modesty. She choked in outrage, yanking the dress up past a set of stupendous breasts all the way to her clavicle. That's when she screamed.

In the two decades he'd roamed the globe as a nature photographer for *Geographica* magazine, he'd dealt with hysterical females of every size, shade, nationality, and demeanor. They'd cursed him in a variety of tongues—Mandarin, Punjabi, and Cajun French initially came to mind—and in a variety of exotic settings. The Nepalese highlands. Kenya's Rift Valley. Under a canopy of strangler fig vines over the Upper Amazon. But he couldn't remember any of them being as desirable as Ginger Garrison. There was something beguiling about the woman—quite tall but, oh, so feminine. He guessed she was in her mid-thirties, at the peak of mature beauty, with fiery hazel eyes and delicate hands, one of which was, at that very moment, flying toward his face, palm flat and open.

Thwack!

The guest-room door flew wide, and Lucio immediately recognized the cavalry as the other two bridesmaids in the wedding party, an older, mannish woman named Beatrice Latimer, and a little dark-haired cutie named Roxanne Bloom. Though he would have preferred it the other way around, Roxanne was in a bulky bathrobe and Bea was in a camisole and panties.

"What the fuck?" Bea said, balling her fists at her sides.

"Allow me to introduce myself." Lucio rose from the bed and headed toward the neutral center of the room. "I am Lucio Montevez, but those who know me well call me Lucky." The women did not seem impressed. "Your friend fainted on the walkway outside, and I brought her here to recover."

"We don't care if you're the pope!" Roxanne's eyes flew wide. "We heard Ginger scream and we're calling the police!"

Lucio tried not to laugh. "There is no need, I assure you."

"Really?" Bea took a step toward him, and by the looks of the woman's defined quadriceps, she meant business. "Because it sure looks like you just assaulted her." Bea pointed at Ginger. "Her dress is open. She looks unraveled. That scream was the real deal. Your luck has just run out, dude."

"Wait." It was Ginger. She fumbled with the dress, clutching it to her chest as she reached around her back to find the open zipper. Then she blinked, quickly shook her head, and touched her lips. Her eyes shot toward him. "I couldn't breathe. I saw you step out from behind the roses, then everything went black." Ginger's jaw slackened. Her hand fell to her side. And she stared at him in shock.

Ginger's friend had been right—the woman was

unraveled. Lucio certainly hadn't meant to unnerve her to this degree. It was only a kiss.

"You said you were waiting for me," Ginger whispered, horror in her eyes.

"I did."

"Then you said something in Spanish. What was it?"

"I merely explained that you'd stolen my heart."

Ginger's eyes went wider still. "You kissed me."

"I had hoped to revive you," Lucio said, smiling. "I am happy to see it worked."

"Ever heard of a cold cloth on the forehead?" Roxanne asked.

Lucio laughed. "This has been a rare pleasure, ladies. Please let me know if you should need further assistance."

He headed toward the door, looking back long enough to see the loathing in Bea's sneer and the distrust in Roxanne's narrowed eyes. Ginger, however, was once again touching a pair of lips that had drifted into a dreamy smile.

With a nod, Lucio headed down the steps and outside, a smile of his own spreading across his face. Without a doubt, loosening the dress of the hazel-eyed, auburn-haired Ginger Garrison had been the most pleasant surprise of the last three months, and Lucio decided he'd allow himself a moment to savor it. After all, he deserved a brush with beauty in the midst of all the ugliness that had recently become his life.

"Are you okay?" Roxanne rushed to the side of the bed and knelt on the rug, reaching for Ginger's hand. "Did he hurt you?"

Ginger blinked at her friend, feeling thoroughly stunned. Maybe the blackout had restricted the flow of oxygen to her brain! How embarrassing would that be, finding out from her doctor that cramming her size six body into a size four bridesmaid's dress had led to permanent brain damage?

"Ginger? Can you hear me?"

"Huh?" Ginger stared at Roxie until her friend's face came into focus. "Oh. Yeah. I'm fine."

With a loud sigh, Bea shut the guest-room door and began her commentary. "It simply fascinates me how men walk around this planet thinking they can just help themselves to women, like the female race is nothing but one giant sexual smorgasbord set out for their enjoyment."

Roxanne and Ginger stared at Bea in silence.

"I'm just saying that some men have a pathological sense of entitlement. It must arrive at the moment of conception, along with the DNA coding for testicles."

Roxanne laughed. "I think I'll make that my next quote of the day; would you mind?"

Bea shrugged. "Half the pearls of wisdom on your man-hating Web site are mine anyway."

"And I've always given you the credit you deserve."

Bea waved her hand. "More power to you." She sat on the edge of the bed. "So," she said, examining Ginger. "You look like you've been through the wringer. You sure you're okay?"

"I'm absolutely fine."

"So what the hell happened?" Roxanne asked.

"Pretty much what Lucio said. Excuse me just a minute."

Ginger pressed the loose fabric to her chest, rose from the bed, and retreated into the dressing room. She quickly changed into a short batik skirt, sandals, and a scoop-neck T-shirt. She brushed out her hair and checked her reflection in the mirror.

Not bad, she decided, considering her recent journey

to the brink. In fact—Ginger peered closer into the mirror to be sure—her eyes had a distinct sparkle to them. Her cheeks gave off a warm glow. Her lips were downright plump and rosy. It must be a hot flash, she decided, because she hadn't had a microderm abrasion since February, and hadn't yet gotten up the nerve to have lip augmentation. In fact, she hadn't touched her makeup for hours, not since she prepared to walk down the aisle ahead of Josie.

Ginger took one last glance in the mirror and let go with a contented sigh. Josie and Rick's ceremony had been the most beautiful wedding she'd ever witnessed, a real-life fairy tale. And, as she'd told Mrs. Needleman, she was ecstatic for Josie. Her friend had found true love with a truly good man, and there was no woman more deserving.

There is a man waiting for you . . . He is out there . . . You could still get lucky . . .

Ginger smiled to herself at the entertaining coincidence of it all. The old lady had said those words, Ginger opened the door, and a man named Lucky was out there waiting for her. But that's all it was. A coincidence. She knew Gloria Needleman was a peculiar old lady, and Lucky—no, *Lucio* was his real name—was just an old friend of Rick's who'd photographed the wedding. She wouldn't give it any more credence than that. Ginger didn't have time for a silly fantasy, no matter how tall, dark, and hot he was.

Or what a stupendous kisser he was.

Or how his accent melted her insides.

Or the way a strange crackle of electricity shot through her skin when he touched her.

Her friends were talking quietly when Ginger returned to the room, and by the way they abruptly ended their conversation, Ginger figured she'd been the topic.

"Are you sure you're all right?" Roxanne asked. "You want to file charges?"

Ginger shook her head. "My dress was too tight and I fainted. He came to my aid. There's no crime in that."

Bea rolled her eyes dramatically. "Looks like the buffet is officially open!"

"I can take care of myself, you know," Ginger said, shaking her head with amusement. "Besides, I thought we learned our lesson about butting into other people's business—our interference almost ruined Josie's life! And here you are, ready to do the same with me? Am I going to find you two under the tree outside my window, like we did to Josie?"

Roxanne's mouth opened, insulted. "You were just as much a part of that as we were, and you know we had only the best intentions."

"Yeah," Bea said. "And I still believe there's a fine line between butting into someone's business and making sure a dear friend doesn't commit the hugest mistake of her life."

"You're twenty years late on that one," Ginger said with a laugh, opening the door for them. "Where were you the night I met Larry Garrison at a fraternity kegger?"

Ginger's friends entered the hallway, but Roxanne turned around, narrowing her eyes. "You're going to go after Lucio, aren't you?"

Ginger shrugged. "If I happen to see him before we leave tomorrow, I'll thank him. But I'm not going to make a big deal of it."

"Oh, Lord," Bea said, rolling her eyes again.

Ginger smiled. "See you for dinner about seven."

Once alone, Ginger turned off the lamp by the bed and went to the open balcony doors. Evening had fallen. The breeze was cooler. The last moments of sunlight had cast a pale orange glow on the vineyards and gardens. Ginger stepped to the railing and inhaled the richly scented air. That's when she saw him.

Lucio stood quietly on the lawn near the stone wall, in profile, again with one hand in his pocket. He didn't move, but Ginger could tell by the set of his shoulders and the slope of his neck that he carried a burden. He looked worried—worried that she'd press charges, no doubt. Ginger decided to put the man out of his misery. She'd go down there and talk to him.

CHAPTER 2

Lucio had strolled across the lawn to the spot under the live oaks where, just hours ago, his friend Rick Rousseau had taken his wedding vows with a sweet and funny newspaper obituary writer named Josie Sheehan. It was a turn of events Lucio would never have predicted for his old running buddy, but, as he well knew, few things in life go the way we envision. His current situation was proof of that.

Lucio took a seat on the thick stone wall dividing the lawn from the gardens, then situated himself so that he faced west. The light here reminded him of home, the magical hills between Spain's highest mountains and the Mediterranean, with its fig trees and flowers, lemons and pomegranates, all that decadent bounty. He'd been gone nearly twenty years and had long ago acquired U.S. citizenship, but that sunny valley by the sea was the only true home he'd ever known, and would likely remain so. He'd used San Francisco as his base of operations for many years, but he was here so rarely it no longer even made sense to keep an apartment.

Lucio raised one knee and propped an arm on it, smiling to himself. Yes, Ginger Garrison was a beautiful woman, and it had been a real pleasure to have her in his arms and under his lips. But a woman was the last thing he should be concerned about. He'd come to San Francisco on the most serious of errands—winning back his reputation and rebuilding his career—and a woman could not possibly aid him in either pursuit. Wasn't his weakness for women at least partially to blame for his present circumstances?

Lucio shook his head. *Oh, how the mighty have fallen.*

He'd already been in town three months, sleeping on a friend's couch or in his agent's guest room until Rick blew him away with kindness and offered Lucio the use of his house in town while he and Josie were on their honeymoon. Then, just before the wedding earlier that day, Rick had told Lucio that the house was his for as long as he needed it, because the couple had decided to make the wine-country ranch their full-time home. Lucio had been speechless.

"Someday I will repay you for your generosity," he'd told Rick.

His longtime friend put his arm around his shoulder and said there was no need. "You were there for me when I needed you, Lucky. This is what friends do for each other."

Lucio recalled how touched he was by Rick's offer, and chuckled softly to himself. They were no longer the wild boys they once were, cutting a swath through the continents in pursuit of adventure and pleasure— and, for Lucio at least, an occasional paycheck. They had both made many mistakes in those years and the ones that followed. They had learned some hard lessons. And they had both come to appreciate the true value of friendship.

As it turned out, Rick's Pacific Heights home was

luxurious and convenient to everything Lucio needed. His agent lived only four blocks east in the same exclusive San Francisco neighborhood, much to the man's chagrin.

"I will do everything in my power for you, as always," Sydney Frankel told him the last time they'd talked. "But I am only human."

And the house was just a short trolley ride away from Lucio's friend and fellow photographer Piers Skaarsgard, who'd lent him his couch for weeks on end. It had been especially generous of Piers considering the fact that Piers's wife had died of leukemia just months before.

"It's good to have another beating heart in the place again," Piers had said to Lucio his first night in the apartment. "Stay as long as you'd like."

Lucio sighed. The rich and rewarding life he'd built for himself over twenty years was gone. It had collapsed—*se derrumbo*—that was the only word he could use to describe it. Instantly, he'd gone from the peak of his success to piecing together a day-to-day existence.

Just months ago he was finishing an assignment in the northern deserts of China, chronicling the effect of pollution and climate change on the region's wildlife. He had finalized travel plans for his next assignment, to Galápagos. And he'd recently learned he'd won the prestigious Erskine Prize for achievement in nature photography. He began to make travel plans to be in New York in December for the ceremony, where he'd be handed a check for a quarter of a million in U.S. dollars.

And then it all came crashing down.

First, some of his raw digital video went missing. Soon after, the U.S. embassy in Beijing sent word that

Lucio was in danger of being deported. The missing video had been leaked to the Chinese government, which found the images shameful, and in Lucio's opinion, they should have. At first, the Chinese claimed Lucio's work was hostile to the People's Republic. Days later, the Chinese amped up their claim, calling Lucio's work an act of espionage intended to weaken the country's international standing. Two additional details made the mess even messier: About fifty thousand in *Geographica* funds had been drained from Lucio's expense account, and word got out that Lucio had been bedding his official Chinese guide, the thirty-year-old daughter of a high-ranking government official, and the man went nuts over the "shame" his daughter had brought to him.

Days of in-person and Internet meetings followed. Lucio admitted it; he lost his cool a few times with the Chinese, the American consulate, and with his *Geographica* editors—but the accusations were pure insanity! Lucio vehemently denied charges of spying and stealing the money from his own expense account. It was all rubbish.

Nobody seemed to listen. Before he knew it, he was kicked out of the country and released from his *Geographica* contract, putting an end to a long and profitable professional alliance.

Piers encouraged Lucio to come back to San Francisco. That's what Lucio did—with his tail between his legs and his wallet open—ready to funnel every dime he had to his lawyer, who he prayed would untangle the string of misunderstandings. But that had been three months ago. With each day, it seemed to Lucio that the nickname he'd carried since childhood no longer fit him.

He shook his head and rose from the stone wall,

deciding to stroll into the heavily scented gardens of Rick's Sonoma Valley paradise. It was funny how life sometimes doubled in on itself. He was thousands of miles from the fig trees and strawberry patches of his childhood, but this place smelled much the same to him, and the scent had conjured up long-buried memories.

Alma had worn a simple ivory lace dress that fell to mid-calf, accented by an angry scowl. She carried a bouquet of wildflowers in front of her belly, camouflaging the baby that grew inside it. Lucio recalled how his throat had tightened at the sight of her—and it wasn't out of joy. Unlike Rick and Josie's ceremony, his own wedding hadn't been about love. Or even family alliances. It was simply the only choice given to two hormonal kids who'd shucked their common sense—and their clothes—on a hot spring night at the riverbank.

The truth was that when Alma lost the baby just weeks after the wedding, Lucio was relieved. She blamed him, of course. He was the one who had dragged her to the ugly, dirty, crowded city and was too busy with his studies to take care of her. Her brothers came to Seville to fetch her back to their village. The annulment papers came within a month.

At the time, Lucio felt as if he'd dodged a bullet. The life he planned would not have been possible with a wife and child.

But lately, Lucio would find himself stopping in the middle of a shoot or waking in the deep of night, overcome with the truth: If the child had lived, his son would be a man now. Lucio would be father to a tall, handsome, and ambitious young man, who might even have an eye for the light like his renowned father. But he would never know.

"Lucio?"

He turned, surprised to see Ginger Garrison approaching him in the twilight. She'd changed out of her satin and chiffon and into a pretty knee-length skirt and simple top. Her hair was down. She wore no jewelry, and she didn't need it. Her cheeks were flushed. Her pretty little toes peeped out of a pair of delicate sandals.

He stared at her. The strange energy he'd felt when he kissed her had returned, making his skin tingle. Lucio watched as the beautiful woman moved closer, her shoulder brushing against a stand of tall gardenias, releasing their perfume. Ginger smiled at him. It was a shy smile from a mature woman, and the beguiling power of that combination pierced his heart.

Nothing good would come of this. He was certain. The timing was all wrong. Holy Host! *He* was all wrong! Ginger Garrison deserved a stable man, a man with his own home and money in the bank, a man who wouldn't be on a plane to Galápagos the instant it became feasible.

But he returned her smile, because those details had never stopped him in the past, and they wouldn't now. As always, Lucio's only obligation was to issue his standard word of caution, leaving the woman responsible for her own fate.

"Unfortunately, I am no good for you, *guapa*."

Lucio's words stopped Ginger cold. She choked on her surprise. Did this man think she'd come down to the garden to hit on him? While his presumptuousness offended her, he probably had his reasons for saying it.

Lucio Montevez was an intoxicating man, a deadly combination of brawn and beauty. He had an edge Ginger imagined a bullfighter would possess—an intense gaze, perfect posture, muscles coiled and ready to spring to life—all while oozing the velvety charm of a gigolo. She could see this dichotomy repeated everywhere in him, each smooth and elegant thing about Lucio balanced out by something over-the-top macho. His big brown eyes were liquid and sultry, but they were capped by a thick, dramatic brow. His mouth was full and sexy, but framed by rough-looking stubble on his upper lip, cheeks, and chin. His wavy dark hair was long and thick, but combed back, close to his perfectly shaped head. He walked with grace, but was tall and muscular. Ginger figured all this would be too much for the average female to resist, and women probably lined up around the block to get a peek at him wherever he went.

Ginger took a moment to remind herself that she'd always been above average.

"I'm afraid you misunderstand me," she said, her voice as friendly as she could make it. "I just came to thank you for your help today and discuss with you when we might schedule the photo sitting."

"The what?" Lucio cocked his head quizzically.

"Before the wedding ceremony you told me you took nature photographs. I asked if you'd take a portrait of me and my bichon and you said you'd be happy to."

"I did?"

Was this some kind of joke? Ginger put her hands on her hips and frowned. "Yes, you did. You told me you were interested in expanding your business into weddings and pet portraits."

"Ahh." Lucio had up until that point kept his body turned to the vineyards while looking over his shoulder to address Ginger. He decided to face her square on, and a smile escaped his lips as he turned. "Of course I did. It's all coming back to me now."

Ginger rolled her eyes. "So that was just a crock of shit, some kind of pickup line you use?"

Lucio laughed. His laugh was hearty and loose, and it traveled up into the breeze. He was obviously a man who liked to laugh, and his enjoyment was contagious. Ginger would have laughed along with him if she weren't so angry.

"It is not a crock, precisely, but I must admit I stretched the truth in order to have a conversation with you."

Ginger sighed. She was getting a bad feeling about this guy. It was never a good sign when a man stretched the truth at the first meeting, since, in her experience, truth-stretching was only one tiny step away from outright lying. "So you're not really a professional photographer?"

He flashed a big, white smile. "I am, *bonita,* but my subject has been the larger scope of nature along with an occasional yak or Komodo dragon. The small domesticated lapdogs—not so much."

Ginger felt her blood rising. Not only was he messing with her, he was enjoying it. "Then why did you offer to take a picture of me and HeatherLynn?" She took a step closer, feeling the garden shadows envelop them. "And, better yet, why were you taking pictures of Josie and Rick's ceremony today? Sonoma Valley isn't exactly the yak capital of the world."

Lucio laughed again, holding out his hand to her. "Would you care to take a walk with me?"

Ginger stepped back instinctively. "I'm going to dinner with my friends soon."

"Ah, then we will make it a short walk."

"It's getting dark." She swallowed hard, feeling that strange pull of energy between them once more. It was almost as if she feared touching him again—because the spark would be impossible to resist.

Lucio smiled gently. "Please understand that when I said I am no good for you just now, I meant that I cannot recommend myself as a boyfriend."

Ginger's eyes went wide.

"However, I would never hurt you. You will be safe on a friendly walk with me." The warmth of Lucio's smile intensified as he continued to hold his hand out to her.

Ginger crossed her arms protectively over her chest. "I'm not in the market for a boyfriend, Mr. Montevez, and if I were, you would not be my choice. I try to avoid men who stretch the truth."

Lucio nodded silently. His hand fell to his side.

"Besides, I'm simply interested in having a professional portrait taken of me and my dog. I'll find someone in the Yellow Pages to do it."

Ginger was about to turn and go when Lucio stepped in close, his dark eyes shimmering with what little light remained. "I stand corrected then, Señora Garrison. Please forgive my insolence."

Ginger pursed her lips and tried to evade the pull of his dramatic eyes. "All right," she said.

"So, you will come with me now, yes?" Lucio's hand rose from his side once more, palm up, as if to show the harmless nature of his offer. "We will walk and I will tell you how I came to be taking pictures at my friend Rick's wedding, and you can tell me more about the charming and pretty Josie, his bride. And then we will say good-bye."

It was one of those moments that seemed disconnected from clock time. Ginger had no idea how long she stood there, her gaze alternating between Lucio's warm eyes and his outstretched hand, weighing the pros and cons of his offer. Who was she fooling? She already knew in her heart that this wasn't about a portrait sitting—this was about *him*.

She'd been fascinated by the man the second she'd spotted him milling about the lawn, taking candid photos of the wedding guests prior to the ceremony, pounds of heavy-looking camera gear slung around his neck and shoulders. He seemed dark and mysterious. Exotic. Languid and sexy, despite all the equipment. He had reminded her of a panther, sleek and dark, as he moved across the grass.

Dr. Larry Garrison he was not.

Ginger did not reach for his hand. She knew that if she did, there would be no turning back, that despite her above-average qualities, she would get sucked into the languid and sexy orbit of this dark-eyed panther man. And she couldn't possibly do that, because she was done being a fool. She was sick of being hurt. Besides, she had boys to raise, an ex-husband to rehabilitate, and a career to rescue.

Now was not a good time.

Lucio let his hand drop again. "I cannot blame you, *bonita*. When it comes to men it is always smart to err on the side of caution, and I see you are a very smart woman."

Ha! Now that was a word Ginger had not applied to her personal life in a long while. In recent years she'd come to doubt not only her intelligence but also her basic good judgment. In college, her mantra had been "Follow your bliss." These days it was "What the hell were you thinking?"

Ginger knew that if she were truly smart, she wouldn't have come out here to talk to Lucio. She wouldn't be standing here next to him in the low light of evening, aware of the closeness of his body, the scent of his skin, the weird energy bouncing around between them. If she were smart, she would have stayed away from him entirely. If she were smart, she would have ordered a size six bridesmaid's dress and avoided this entire dilemma.

And if she were really, really smart, she wouldn't do what she was about to do.

Ginger took a breath. She reached out a trembling hand. "Here is my card. My numbers are on the back."

Lucio took it, intentionally letting his fingers brush across the top of her hand. Ginger nearly jumped off the ground.

He raised a single dark eyebrow and gave her a tentative smile. "I am not sure what this means, señora."

"It means if you suddenly feel the need to photograph lapdogs, give me a shout. Good night, Lucio."

Ginger turned and walked away, leaving Lucio in the garden. She knew he was checking her out. She could feel the heat of his stare all over her legs and backside. But he said nothing. He let her go without a fight.

Ginger appreciated that he'd respected her wishes— for the most part, anyway.

It was hours later when the four women raised a glass to Josie and Rick and enjoyed a leisurely dinner at Carneros Bistro in downtown Sonoma. While they ate, Ginger got the distinct impression that Mrs. Needleman was taking Bea under her wing—to what end, she wasn't sure. Bea was an assistant sports editor at the *Herald* who spent most of her free time driving her Finnish spitz to West Coast dog agility contests. Bea was also a former Olympic swimmer—except that she had never gotten to compete in the 1980 games because of the boycott, a tragedy she'd just described to Mrs. Needleman in dramatic detail. Ginger couldn't imagine what Mrs. Needleman and Bea had in common, but their camaraderie was obvious.

Roxie seemed antsy all through dinner, and Ginger couldn't blame her. Her friend's life was in transition and she knew she just wanted to get home. Roxie had been the criminal courts reporter for the *Herald,* but just weeks after an ugly breakup with her boyfriend, the paper had canned her. Roxie was trying to make a go of a Web site called i-vomit-on-all-men.com, an online community where women shared boyfriend horror stories from around the world. She'd recently expanded into retail sales of hats, shopping bags, shirts, bumper stickers, and coffee mugs, and she was struggling to keep up with demand.

But the most immediate source of Roxie's anxiety was probably the phone calls she'd received from the kennel where her behaviorally challenged dog was being boarded. They'd informed her that Lilith was not socializing well with male dogs and male kennel workers. This was not a shocker.

Though Ginger had enjoyed the tasty seared tuna and the mixed green salad, she couldn't relax during dinner, either. Her mind kept wandering back to Lucio—the expression on his face when she gave him her card, that sly grin that revealed his amusement at her lack of willpower. All she'd needed to do was say good-bye and walk away. But she'd left the door open for Lucio when she gave him her card.

Why? Why? *Why* had she done that? She didn't need a man in her life. She wouldn't have the time or energy to deal with a man even if she had one. Especially a man who stretched the truth!

Which reminded Ginger of the main reason for her unease. Her boys were staying with Larry for the weekend, which was nothing unusual. But her ex-husband's attention span was growing increasingly short, and Ginger wasn't sure she could trust him to keep an eye on the twins, or, more specifically, Jason. She knew Joshua could take care of himself and most of the West Coast. But Jason needed eagle-eyed adult supervision, something that had recently proven too much for Larry.

In the last few months, Jason had been picked up for curfew violation, destruction of public property, and underage drinking—all while in Larry's care. In each instance, Larry admitted he'd been preoccupied with a girl, which wasn't a sexist comment because he clearly preferred the company of females under twenty-one years of age. Maybe he always had.

Ginger dropped her head to her hand, her brain heavy with the truth—if Larry continued to devolve like this, she'd have to go back to court to demand full custody. And that would require money, grief, and time she couldn't spare.

"Are you all right?" Bea tapped Ginger's other hand where it gripped the stem of her wine glass. Ginger jolted to attention.

"Just tired, I guess."

"It's been a whirlwind weekend," Roxanne said.

"So much happiness," Mrs. Needleman said, a devilish smile on her lips. "Now, which of you ladies do you suppose will be the next to marry?"

Everyone's jaw dropped. The silence fell on them with a thud. The busy restaurant buzzed around them, but no one moved.

Then Bea snorted with laughter.

Ginger and Roxie stole a quick glance at each other. Would this be the moment Bea chose to come out of the closet? Would she finally admit that the reason she never dated was that she didn't find men attractive? Would everyone finally get the answer to the question no one had ever dared ask?

"I noticed that Josie didn't throw her bouquet," Mrs. Needleman added helpfully.

"She knew it would've hit the dirt," Roxie said.

Bea smiled big. "Well, I think it's obvious," she said. "Ginger's our next vision in white!"

"What?" Once Ginger's eyeballs stopped throbbing, she gaped at her laughing friends. "That's totally ridiculous and you know it."

"Well, it sure as hell isn't going to be me," Roxie said, taking a sip of her pinot noir. "I haven't had anything close to a date in months, and, besides, a wedding wouldn't exactly be good for business, now would it?"

Bea chuckled. "You'd have to change the name of your site to 'i-vomit-on-almost-every-man.'"

Roxanne thought that was funny.

Mrs. Needleman shook her head. "Terrible. Just terrible," she muttered. "Such a thing would have been unspeakable in my day."

Roxanne took umbrage at that. "Really? Women didn't have man problems when you were young, I take it?"

Mrs. Needleman's shoulders moved up and down while she chuckled. "Of course we did!" The old woman's chuckle faded into a sigh. "Modern-day woman didn't discover the broken heart, my dears. As long as there have been men and women there's been drama, betrayal, ecstasy, hope, despair, and even, on occasion, *love*. But it's never been a cakewalk for any of us."

"So what's so terrible about my Web site, then?" Roxanne asked.

Mrs. Needleman didn't bother to hide her sadness, and her old eyes grew watery. "The sheer amount of *venom* oozing out of everyone these days—it's destructive to the spirit of the world." She pointed an arthritic finger at Roxanne. "You may think your business is tongue-in-cheek and harmless, but it's feeding the dragon, you see. If the world is to survive, we need women who are open to love, not hardened by bitter resentment."

Roxie laughed uncomfortably. "Hey, well, bitter resentment happens to be a growth industry. My retail sales are up four hundred percent since June!"

Bea snorted again.

Mrs. Needleman pushed her chair away from the dining table, piqued. "Only love attracts love. Distrust only creates more distrust. It's a universal truth." She lowered her eyes and in a whisper added, "I fear I'm running out of time."

Ginger was struck by the weight of Gloria's softly spoken words. It was almost as if the old lady thought the fate of humanity rested on her frail shoulders. Ginger reached across the table and touched the sleeve of Gloria's blouse.

"We'll get you back to the ranch for the night. You must be very tired."

"Oh, fiddle." Gloria waved her away. "I'm just a lonely old bat who talks too much when she gets a captive audience." She stood up from her chair and grabbed her handbag. "All right. It's settled, then."

"What is?" Bea asked.

"Ginger will be our next bride." Mrs. Needleman announced this with a matter-of-fact nod of her tightly permed head. "Now get me back to my room before I say something foolish."

* * *

The moon hung heavy and low in the sky. It peeked from behind the live oaks, spreading a pale blue glimmer over the gardens, the vineyards, and the bare skin of Ginger's legs. She pulled her wrap closer, shut her eyes, and melted into the Adirondack chair.

Tomorrow, she'd return to her real life. She'd pick up HeatherLynn from the kennel. Stop by the cleaner's. Get dinner ready for the boys. On Monday morning she'd go into a job that might not last the week, at a newspaper on its last legs. She'd call her lawyer about her custody concerns. She'd send out her résumé. She'd talk to the school counselor about Jason's grades and arrange for Joshua's learner's permit test.

But until then—just for the precious few moments that were left of this night—Ginger would let herself enjoy the soft, perfumed air and the warmth of the zinfandel coursing through her veins. Yes, she'd made some really big mistakes in her life. But every step she'd ever taken, every decision she'd ever made, had led to her being here, at this moment, in this place. That meant everything was right with the world, just the way it was. Just for this moment.

She laughed quietly to herself. *So this is the hard-won view from forty,* she thought. This was the half-way mark of a woman's life, a life half lived and half yet to come. Exactly who was she at that moment? Where was the girl she'd once been? How long would it be before she found the best version of herself?

Ginger raised her wine glass and toasted the moon. She believed there was still time to become a confident woman. She could call a truce with her changing beauty, her lost dreams, her rearranged possibilities. There was still time to be happy. She took a long, deep sip of wine and wrestled with the idea of calling for another Botox appointment. She'd have to keep it a secret if she did—Bea, Roxie, and Josie would only tease her again when she didn't go through with it.

Maybe this time she'd find the strength to resist the temptation altogether. Maybe this time she'd truly believe that Larry running off with a college girl wasn't an indictment of her beauty—it was an indictment of *him*.

She took another sip of the red wine and sighed. Just for tonight, she decided, she'd open her arms to the unlimited possibilities of her life right now, as it was. Where was the harm in that? It was permissible to let her imagination run free every once in a while, wasn't it? It was all right to let it out to play.

Even if it wanted to play with Lucio Montevez.

Ginger stretched out her legs and wiggled her toes in the moonlight. She fiddled with the hem of her skirt, feeling her fingers skitter across her thigh. It was still smooth and firm flesh, aching for a loving touch. Lucio had reminded her of that today. Melting under his caress, drowning in his kiss—it had flipped a switch inside her. She couldn't deny it another second. Her body was on fire for a man's attention. *That* man's attention.

It had been a long time since Larry had touched her with love. She couldn't even remember what it felt like. The last few years of her marriage had been confusing, hurtful, and lonely. Near the end, there wasn't a shred of devotion left in Larry's touch—just a cold, slimy guilt that he tried to cover up with words he knew Ginger longed to hear.

She held on to those words and pretended all was well for as long as possible. But she knew better, and it was a struggle to keep the truth pushed down inside her. She'd convinced herself that infidelity was something that happened to other couples, not them—not

Larry and Ginger Garrison, college sweethearts, good and decent people who worked hard to build a life together and raise their sons.

She'd held on to the ruse right up until the night she caught Larry with the boys' math tutor in the cargo area of the minivan. In her own driveway, for God's sake! Larry's bare ass was a ghostly white in the glow of the streetlights as it moved up and down. Up and down.

Right there and then, as Ginger watched her husband of eighteen years porking a college coed, her delusions were history. So was her marriage.

Ginger took in a shaky breath, counting backward, adding up all the months of disconnection and, then, separation. Could it be that she'd gone without a man's loving touch for *years*? She laughed bitterly. She'd been deprived. She'd become empty. And now she was starving.

Her fingers pushed up the hem of her skirt. With her eyes closed, she reveled in the feel of the night air on the exposed skin of her inner thigh. How would it feel? What would the sensation be like if, just now, Lucio Montevez were to come to her, kneel in the grass at her feet like the sexual panther he was, stretch her thighs wide and hook them over the armrests of this old Adirondack chair and touch her, wet and silky and so very, very needy.

Ginger sought out the satiny crotch of her panties and pushed it aside. Her fingers were immediately drenched in juices. Her own wetness startled her. Her legs trembled. She took one last fortifying sip of wine, and, with eyes still closed, she set the goblet on the grass. Her mind reeled. Her body was greedy.

It was well past midnight. The ranch was silent. Only Mrs. Needleman and the women in the bridal party had stayed overnight. She was hidden under the shadows of the old live oak. No one would see.

So Ginger did it. She reached under her bottom and yanked off her panties, tossing them to the ground. She took a deep breath and imagined him right there, on his knees before her. He would spread his big hands over the tender flesh inside her thighs and pull her open. He would lower his mouth to her.

"Lucio!" she called out in a ragged whisper.

Ginger squirmed. God, the man knew his way around a woman! He was teasing her, nipping and licking and biting everywhere but where she needed it most. He was really, really good at this. So good it was pure torture.

Ginger heard herself groan in frustration. She imagined his dark head hovering between her thighs. She imagined the heat of his breath so close, but not close enough.

Finally! He flicked his tongue around and across her enflamed clitoris. Then he drank from her. He used his tongue and teeth and lips to pull the juices from her body, pull her soul to the brink of orgasm. Oh! He was using those strong hands to adjust her, like she was a plaything, a doll—grabbing her by the ass and pulling her toward his mouth like he was a starving man at that sexual buffet Bea had described.

Ginger's head swam with the images—her body was the overflowing smorgasbord of lust and Lucio had already paid at the door. She wanted to feed him. He was a hungry man. *Everyone wins!*

Oh God, it felt so good, so real. Her hands fell away from her body, yet, somehow, the sensations continued to build. She imagined in detail how it would feel— she would reach for his long, thick hair, grabbing silky fistfuls as she pulled him tighter to her pussy.

That's right. *Pussy.* She never used that word. It was sordid, somehow. Daring. But wasn't that the whole point of a daringly sordid fantasy? So she let the word pulse through her. She was nothing but a lonely, dripping, needy *pussy.* And it was only for him. She was his pussy. Somewhere deep inside her she knew that she'd always belonged to him and only him, the sexual panther of the shadows.

"This is your pussy, Lucio," she whispered. "It belongs to you."

Suddenly, she threw her legs around his neck and convulsed wildly, the orgasm so deep and strong that it shot her into a swirling, black nothingness, then launched her back to consciousness with a flare of bright white light. Her body twitched and burned in exquisite pleasure. Her eyes flew open, and her vision was filled with the night sky and what was either the aurora borealis or one hell of a long, drawn-out orgasm.

Inexplicably, she felt as if she were rising from the chair, her limp body being taken up to heaven in the arms of God himself. She must have orgasmed so hard that she'd had a stroke, which would explain the aurora borealis.

God, no! I can't die! Who will take care of the boys?

It was a particular taste that brought her to her senses. The taste of herself. Soft, wet lips covered hers, sharing the tangy, salty taste of her own body. The mouth was covered in her juices and it pressed harder and harder against hers.

"My God, you are delicious," the lips said, an accent falling thick and hot in her ear, on her face. She was being carried up the lawn toward the guesthouse—*but how?*

"I will need more, *pelirroja,*" said the unmistakable voice. "I will be taking more of the redheaded pussy you say is mine."

Ginger stiffened, a lightning bolt of awareness hitting her smack between the eyes. "Ohmigod, put me down!" She tried to pry herself from Lucio's arms, but his muscles only contracted further. She was trapped against his chest as he climbed the walkway to the guesthouse. "I said put me down! *Now!* Are you deaf?"

Lucio ignored her. He plowed ahead, now almost at the guesthouse door. Ginger's pulse hammered wildly. She could hardly breathe. How in God's name had she ended up being carried to her door twice in one day by the same man? Had she fainted again? No, wait—he'd really had his mouth on her! It had all been real! This was awful—too awful to face.

"Put me down." This time her warning was delivered in a menacing whisper. "Put me down right this fucking second or I'll scream so loud you really will be deaf when I'm done."

Lucio's response was to reach around her face and cover her mouth with his big hand until they reached the guesthouse porch. Once there, he eased her down to her feet but kept her mouth tightly covered. He turned the doorknob with his free hand.

He pressed Ginger's back against the front of his body. Ginger wasn't stupid. Something big and hard was poking into the base of her spine, and she knew exactly what it was. She tried to squirm away.

Lucio whispered into her ear, his breath still infused with the scent of her body. "I will wait until I hear your door close and the lock slide into place. Then I will leave." He let his hand drop from her mouth and turned her toward him.

He flashed a smile. "Good night, my wild woman of the vineyards."

Ginger's spine stiffened. He smelled of her—her pussy! She'd told him—*out loud*—that it belonged to him! Her head pounded with confusion. Her limbs tingled with the remnants of the pleasure. What the hell had just happened? Had she fantasized so intensely that she'd conjured Lucio from the night shadows? Or had he been waiting for her, watching her—again? Either way, it had ended with her feeding her most intimate body part to a man she barely knew! And now he was seeing her to her room, as if the whole thing had been a non-event. Maybe in the world of Lucio Montevez it was, but not in her world.

"Do not look so perplexed, *guapa*." Lucio brushed the underside of her chin with his fingertip. "Back there, you called out to me. I answered. But it is late and you are not in your right mind at the moment, so we must stop."

Ginger's mouth hung open. "Whaa?"

"I do not wish to take advantage of you."

"Huh?"

Lucio's smile widened, and his teeth were blinding white in the porch light. "Loneliness and wine can make us do crazy things. So I will say good night." He reached for her hand and raised it to his lips. He kissed her knuckles. He kissed the fragile bones and tendons of her hand. Then he turned her wrist over and kissed the skin stretched over her wild pulse. It was all intensely sensual. Mind-numbingly sexual. Ginger tried to think clearly but failed. She was swooning! *Swooning!* Up until now she hadn't even understood what that word meant!

"What is happening?" She raised her gaze to his, whispering her question. Lucio's eyes met hers, endlessly deep and dark and probing. He really did possess the eyes of a sexual panther, but at some point he'd also acquired the manners of an Eagle Scout. Honestly, she'd never been more disappointed in her life.

"But you said you wanted more of me," Ginger said, the words so heavy with frustration it embarrassed her.

Lucio chuckled softly. "I must take a rain check." He pulled a pair of panties from his pocket and shoved them in her hand, adding, "You shouldn't leave these lying around just anywhere."

Then he turned her by the shoulders, gave her bottom a gentle pat, and sent her through the guesthouse door.

CHAPTER 3

Ginger stared at the stark white piece of *San Francisco Herald* stationery in her unsteady hands, perplexed. Why did they call it a pink slip if it wasn't pink? Not a shade of salmon, or rose, or even a soft coral. Her termination notice was in stark black and white, seventeen years of her life wiped off the map in two paragraphs.

"This truly sucks," Bea said, falling into Ginger's chair with a thud. "I have no other skills except sports editing. And only newspaper editing. I wouldn't even know where to start in broadcast or Internet journalism, or even Titterlating or whatever it's called."

"Bea!" Ginger snapped in annoyance as she folded the termination letter and shoved it in her bag. "This is *my* pink slip. Not yours. *I* just lost my job. Not you!"

Bea popped up from the chair, hugged Ginger quickly, then patted her back a little too hard. "Right. Sorry. Shit, Ginger. What are you going to do? Do you have any other skills?"

Ginger laughed. Of course she had skills—she was a divorced mother. She could do pretty much anything.

She could make a mean pot roast. She could iron a

man's dress shirt—including the heavy starch—in five minutes. She could paint a ceiling, transport a soccer team, change the oil in a lawn mower, and manage an investment portfolio. She could apply eyeliner at a stoplight. She knew instinctively which handbag went with which outfit.

Bringing home the bacon and frying it up in a pan was nothing—try bringing home an Associated Press First Place Award for special section editing and springing your kid from the juvenile detention center. Now *that* would put hair on your chest!

Ginger gasped, suddenly certain all the stress of the last few years had caused her to sprout chin hairs like the ones her grandmother Ola had. She reached a hand up to her jaw, finding nothing but smooth skin, and said a silent prayer of thanks. She might be an unemployed, love-starved woman, but at least she wasn't an unemployed, love-starved woman with chin hair.

"You look pretty freaked out by this," Bea said, concern in her voice. "What are you thinking?"

"Just that I could handle any job I'm offered," Ginger lied.

"That's the attitude," Bea said, giving her another slap on the shoulder. "Have you updated your résumé?"

Ginger bit her lip, knowing her résumé didn't reflect a wide range of abilities. In fact, it was downright one-dimensional, because she'd spent her entire working life at the *Herald*.

Ginger had started right out of school as a city desk general assignment reporter, working day and night to prove her mettle. After her maternity leave, she became a feature writer. And, for the last eight years, she'd been editor of the *Herald*'s house and garden section.

It was ironic. For nearly a decade now, Ginger hadn't

even needed to work. Once Larry had made it out of med school and his residency, he made good money as a private-practice urologist and medical school professor. They could have afforded to have Ginger stay home. But she chose to stay at the *Herald*. She never wanted to have to choose between her work and her kids. She wanted to build a career while she built a family, and saw no reason why she couldn't do both.

So when Larry had dumped her for a girl half her age, Ginger thanked the gods she'd remained in the workforce. At that moment her job became the longest-lasting relationship of her adulthood. But as of ten minutes ago, she had nothing to show for her wise decision except that familiar lump of rejection in her gut and a two-paragraph souvenir.

Ginger put her hands on her hips, scanning the chaos in the features department. She was one of six employees let go that morning, and there was a lot of crying and swearing going on, despite the fact that they'd all known it was coming, sooner or later.

"Let's go down to circulation and see if they have any boxes," Bea said helpfully. "I'll help you clean out your desk."

Ginger shook her head. "Don't bother. Misty told me there's been a run on cardboard boxes and they're out."

Both Bea and Ginger turned to watch Misty Mc-Ginty throwing the contents of her desk drawers into industrial-sized plastic garbage bags. The petite fashion and beauty reporter was working up a sweat in her designer ensemble, cursing loudly and with creative abandon. And she was naming names. Names that belonged to the managing editor. The publisher. Her immediate boss. Who cared? What was the worst that could happen to her—she'd get fired?

"Poor kid," Bea said.

"Poor everybody." Ginger sat on the edge of her desk, crossing her arms over her chest. "This is a damned shame."

Bea ran a hand through her short spiky hair in exasperation. "I'm worried about Josie. What if she gets back from her honeymoon and finds out she's been canned?"

Ginger looked at Bea like she was nuts. "Josie can do anything she wants with her life now, including nothing at all. She just married the gazillionaire CEO of a pet store chain!"

"This is true," Bea said, nodding. "I just wish they'd ax all of us at once instead of dragging it out like this, week after week. It's like eliminations on a bad reality show." Bea snatched a pen from Ginger's desk and pretended it was a microphone. *"Stay tuned to see which sorry-assed loser will be going home this week!"*

Ginger winced.

"Not you. I didn't mean you."

"Well, I'm taking my sorry ass home, and right now." Ginger rose from the desk and grabbed her bag. "It's like a funeral in here. I'll come back tomorrow with boxes from home."

Bea followed her out the double glass doors that divided the features department from the rest of the open newsroom. "But really," she said, nearly jogging to keep up with Ginger, "what are you going to do for a job?"

Ginger shrugged. "My job will be finding a job, like half the journalists in this country."

They headed up the center aisle of the newsroom. Ginger stopped to hug a few people and wave at a few others, but she was determined to get to the elevators before she shed a single tear.

When she reached Denise, a sweet girl raising three

little kids on a receptionist's salary, Ginger almost lost it. Because Denise was waving a white envelope. "I got mine, too," she said in a soft voice. "Hold the elevator and we'll all go down together."

HeatherLynn's shrill little bark meant the boys were home from school. Ginger decided to greet them in the foyer to lessen the shock. She was never home this early. She didn't want the boys thinking burglars had broken in during the day—and stopped to prepare homemade lasagna.

"Hey, guys!"

Jason and Joshua froze in the doorway, their eyes as big as blue plums, bookbags dropping to the floor.

"You got fired," Josh said, immediately assessing the situation. "Oh, Mom, I'm really sorry."

Jason pointed his nose to the ceiling and inhaled deeply. "How long till the lasagna's done?"

A third male figure popped up in the doorway, and Ginger groaned loudly, if only in her head. The boys' father laid a hand on each of his son's shoulders and peeked his head inside. "You made lasagna? Damn, I wish I could stay but I have a department meeting tonight."

"Bummer," Ginger said, waving the dishtowel to usher all of them inside. "How was your day, boys? Please shut the door. How's it going, Larry?"

Joshua, the youngest by two minutes, stopped to pick up HeatherLynn on his way through the foyer. He held her close and high on his chest, so the dog could tuck her head under his chin. "You doing okay, Mumu?" he asked, using his childhood nickname for her as he hugged her quickly. "You knew this might be coming, right?"

"I did, sweetheart. I'm okay."

Jason came up and kissed her on the cheek. "That sucks," he said, the identical sentiment expressed by Bea earlier in the day. Unfortunately, Bea's and Jason's vocabulary rules weren't identical. Ginger was trying to teach Jason how to behave like a gentleman, while Bea had long ago stopped caring about the rules of polite society.

Ginger sighed. "Jason, how many times have I told you not to use that word in the house?"

"Sorry, Mom." Jason flashed a charming smile eerily similar to Larry's. "You getting fired really blows."

Ginger raised an eyebrow, watching her sons stampede past her to get to the kitchen. Doors to the cabinets and the refrigerator were thrown open, and the makings of an afternoon snack began to pile up on the table—tortilla chips, leftover mashed potatoes, Oreos, roast beef, and kaiser rolls. Ginger was grateful for Larry's generous child support payments, if only because it cost a small fortune to keep the boys supplied with carbohydrates.

"Keep in mind we'll be eating dinner in less than two hours," she told them.

"Awesome," Jason said, his cheeks puffed out with the contents of his sandwich. "I'll be starving by then."

"Hey, you got a minute?" Larry hadn't fully entered the kitchen, but lingered in the foyer, looking sheepish. It had always fascinated Ginger how, after that night he got caught with his pants down, he'd instinctively stopped treating this house as his home. He'd left that night with a duffel bag, and hadn't slept here since.

"Sure, Larry." Ginger followed him into the living room. He took a seat in an armchair and she curled up on the sofa. It felt awkward to be with him here, in the living room they'd painstakingly furnished and decorated together, in a house they'd had custom-designed with every comfort and personal preference in mind.

It had always struck Ginger as odd how Larry turned around and bought a house just two blocks away, in the same development, and had it decorated in an almost identical fashion. Whatever made him happy, she supposed. And it certainly made it convenient for the boys, who split their time equally between their parents.

"So what are your plans?" he asked, resting his elbows on his knees and clasping his hands in front of him. He was sporting an unfamiliar platinum pinkie ring. "How is this going to affect our calendar?"

Ginger paused a moment, smiling at him sweetly. "Gee," she said. "I'm not sure I understand what you're getting at, Larry."

"Well, it's just that, you know . . ." Larry's pale blue eyes twitched nervously toward the kitchen, where they could hear the boys arguing and laughing—with their mouths full. "My plans. My schedule. How's this going to affect all that?"

She knew it! She knew he was going to go there! Ginger had just been fired from the only job she'd ever had—her world in turmoil—and Larry was worried how it might affect his freedom to shag every coed on campus. If only University Hospital's administrators knew how their chief of urology whiled away his free time.

"It's just that, you know, I'm planning on going away to Maui next week, remember? And I wanted to make sure any new job wouldn't, you know, conflict with my plans."

Ginger maintained her vacant smile as she put all of this in its proper perspective. Back in the day, during his first trip through adolescence, Larry Garrison had been a California fraternity hottie with a .359 batting average, a 130 IQ, and an unholy hankering for pretty girls. That's the man Ginger fell in love with. She knew what she was getting—a top-shelf guy who was a little on the selfish side. And today, deep in the quagmire of his second adolescence, Larry was a handsome and highly respected doctor with the same unholy hankering for the prettiest girls. And an ego that had swelled to the size of the North American landmass.

"I mean, have you thought about what kind of work you might do? What your hours might be?" Larry flashed her one of his toothy grins. "The boys are old enough to take care of themselves for the most part, obviously, but we will still need to make sure all the bases are covered."

Ginger sighed deeply, once again awed by her ex-husband's self-centered stupidity. HeatherLynn took that as her cue and toddled into the living room. Without a glance at Larry, she hopped into Ginger's lap, circled around a few times, then curled up in a ball. Larry frowned when he realized he'd just been dissed by his prized bichon.

Ginger stroked the dog's poofy white fur, immediately feeling her blood pressure reset to normal. It was as if her little dog knew exactly when she needed backup.

Ginger looked at her ex-husband and smiled. "You know what, Larry?"

"What?" He perked up.

"You're an ass."

Larry's hands rose in surrender, a stunned look on his face. "Was that really necessary?" he asked, his cheeks reddening.

She sighed. "I'm afraid it was, and I'll tell you

why." Ginger adjusted HeatherLynn and tucked her feet up under her, getting comfortable. "My career crashed and burned at about nine this morning, and it's not quite four in the afternoon, so it would be impossible to know how my new job might impact your social calendar, because I don't yet *have* a new job, you pompous douche bag."

Larry said nothing.

"Furthermore, our divorce agreement says that I have up to six months to find another job should I lose my current one, and, in the meantime, you have to increase alimony to replace my salary."

"What!" Larry stood up as if someone had stuck a pin in his butt cheek. "You're crazy."

"No, but as you know, I have an extremely good lawyer," she said, smiling again. Ginger had anticipated this. So she placed HeatherLynn on the sofa cushion and walked to the dining room table, where she'd left a file folder. She returned, opening the file to a copy of the settlement agreement. She'd already circled the pertinent paragraph with a yellow highlighter.

"Fuck." Larry slowly collapsed into the chair, running a hand nervously through his thick hair. Ginger watched him scan the pages, thinking that he was a lucky guy. What with all the other requirements of Larry's midlife crisis—the new sports cars, the too-young wardrobe, the spray tans, the hours in the gym—at least he'd never need a hair transplant. "I don't know how I'm going to swing this, babe," he said, shaking his head.

Ginger's toes curled. Why he continued to call her "babe" was anyone's guess. Ginger guessed it was because he'd forgotten her name. "I'm sure you'll manage," she said.

He peered up from the document. "Aren't you getting some kind of severance pay or something?"

"Yes," Ginger said. "I get a month's salary, which I will put into the college savings plan. If you look on page three, you'll see that your alimony goes up despite any severance."

Larry tossed the file to the carpet in disgust. "You just love busting my balls every chance you get, don't you?" He let out a nasty laugh, scanning her face with fake concern. "You want to know what I think?"

"No, but I'm going to hear it anyway."

"I think you're going to use your severance for that little nip and tuck you've been putting off, which would be a wise move. It's definitely time, babe."

Ginger's spine stiffened. Larry knew exactly where her buttons were, because the ones she hadn't inherited from her mother were installed by Larry's skilled hands. Throughout their marriage, Larry would imply that if Ginger didn't maintain her beauty she'd only have herself to blame if he strayed. Seventeen years of that crap had done nothing but deepen the crow's-feet around her eyes and the frown lines on her forehead. And the loneliness in her heart. Everyone else in her life—her friends, coworkers both male and female, her sons—they all told her she was gorgeous. Strangers in the produce section would stop and ask for her autograph, mistaking her for a celebrity. Everyone in her life knew she'd gotten her nickname as a teenager because of her striking resemblance to the glamorous Ginger on the vintage TV sitcom *Gilligan's Island*.

And hadn't Lucio called her *bonita,* which was Spanish for "pretty"?

Suddenly, Ginger felt dizzy. Just the thought of Lucio made her skin tingle and her breath come quicker.

How awkward! She was staring into the smirk of her ex-husband, yet she had to press her knees together with the thought of her sexual panther man. Oh, how Lucio had touched her! How he'd kissed her—*every-flippin'-where.*

Larry laughed. "Well, well. Looks like I hit a nerve." He swaggered through the living room to the front door and Ginger followed him, still in a daze. She'd have to remember to never—*ever*—think of Lucio while behind the wheel of a car.

"You leavin', Dad?"

Jason made his way into the foyer, a wad of Oreos in one hand and a glass of milk in the other. "We still goin' to the driving range this weekend?"

Larry suddenly looked nervous. "Uh . . ."

Ginger's heart sank to her feet. He was doing it again, despite his promise. He said he'd never again break a date with the boys, yet he was about to do it anyway! The worst part was that his excuses were often a lie. He'd tell them something had come up at work, and the boys would accept that, since they'd grown up with an absentee doctor as a father. But Ginger knew better. She knew Larry often traded the company of his boys for that of his latest barely legal girl.

"Sure, sure," Larry said, patting Jason on the back. "We'll touch base later this week. Say good-bye to your brother for me."

Jason grimaced. "Whatever," he said, shoving another Oreo into his mouth as he turned back to the kitchen.

"Larry—"

He cut her off. "I know. I know. I'll just have to do some juggling, is all. I'll make it work."

Ginger's whole body vibrated with anger. "Make it work? They're your sons!" Her voice had become high and squeaky, but she didn't care. "They are supposed to come first! All that other stuff is what you have to make work—not your own damn children!"

"Right. Of course."

Ginger lowered her voice to a seething whisper. "You're damaging your sons, Larry, and you'd better get yourself together or you're going to lose them, do you hear me?"

Larry shook his head as if he felt sorry for her. "What I hear is the menopause train coming down the track. *Woo, woo!*" Larry pulled his fist through the air a couple times, then laughed at his own cleverness. "Listen, babe, would you like me to write you a prescription? Something to take the edge off?"

Ginger moved a step closer to him, refusing to take his bait. "This is not about me. It's about Jason and Joshua."

Larry chuckled. "Josh is at the head of his class. A total Goody Two-shoes well on his way to being president of the United States, for fuck's sake! And Jason is a good kid. He's just got a bit of a wild streak, is all." Larry grinned. "It's perfectly normal."

Suddenly, HeatherLynn came around the living room archway like a demonic cotton ball, ears flying back, a menacing growl gurgling up from her throat, tiny little fangs exposed. Ginger was shocked—she couldn't remember ever hearing her sweet little girl actually *growl*. Maybe they'd been spending too much time with Roxie and Lilith.

Before Ginger could stop her, HeatherLynn leaped from the Mexican tile and nipped Larry right in the crotch. He screeched, more in surprise than pain. Then, just as quickly, the dog skittered back to the living room and dove under the couch.

Ginger's hand flew to her mouth in disbelief.

"That crazy little *bitch*!" Larry adjusted the zipper in his chinos and tried to brush away any dog hair that might be clinging to the spot of drool on the front of his pants. "I never really wanted her, anyway."

Ginger choked on her laughter, the tears forming in her eyes. "And that's why you spent twenty-five grand to fight me for her custody, right?"

Larry snarled. "Like everyone else around here, she's become emotionally disturbed without me as head of household. I could report her to animal control as a vicious dog."

Ginger laughed even harder.

"You think that's funny, but the city could put her in quarantine."

Still laughing, Ginger reached around her "*was*band" and opened the front door. "I'll drop a note to my lawyer about the alimony adjustment," she told him.

"Dogs like that can be put down."

"Good night, Larry." She turned him around and pointed him in the direction of his shiny new Porsche. "Too bad you can't stay for lasagna."

"How many days till they're home?" Bea tapped her thigh with Martina's leather leash as she watched her dog tussle with a pair of poodles.

"They fly in late Monday night," Roxie said.

"I can pick them up," Bea offered brightly.

Ginger smiled at her friends. She missed Josie, too. For the weeks Josie and Rick were on their honeymoon, the group had been getting together at six A.M. on Monday, Wednesday, and Friday—just as they had for three years now—but it wasn't the same without Josie and Genghis, her gregarious Labradoodle. The pair always made them laugh. Their mornings in the dog park lacked a kind of joy without them, Ginger decided.

"Teeny is picking them up," Roxie told Bea, which made perfect sense, Ginger thought. Teeny was Rick's best friend and business partner, and he'd been entrusted with Genghis and Rick's two other dogs while the couple was out of the country. The last time they'd talked to Teeny, he sounded exhausted. He was probably counting the hours.

"Cool," Bea said. "I sure miss her."

"God, so do I," Roxanne said, sighing. As close as the four women were, it was understood that Roxanne and Josie were best friends. They weren't far apart in age—Roxanne twenty-eight and Josie thirty-five—and they'd instantly clicked when they'd met at the paper on Roxanne's first day, six years ago now. By comparison, Bea and Ginger were recent add-ons. The four of them had met in the newspaper's break room and discovered they all had something in common—their love of dogs. That next day, they started their dog-walking group. It had been going strong ever since, through several nasty breakups, a divorce, job loss, family crises, and the death of Roxie's beloved old collie.

Four months ago, they'd made a vow to give up on men entirely and find happiness in the company of their dogs. Ironically, that's just when Josie met Rick. They were married three months later.

Ginger watched Roxie struggling with Lilith, a muddy-brown mutt who growled at every man and male dog to come her way. For months now, Roxie had been trying to "socialize" the rescue dog. So far, no luck.

"Have you made an appointment with that dog behaviorist yet?" Ginger asked Roxie. It was an innocent question, asked out of true interest for the well-being of Roxie and her dog, but her friend looked nervous.

"Why do you ask?" Roxie's eyes narrowed. "What are you getting at?"

Bea rolled her eyes at Ginger.

"Well," Ginger said cautiously, "I just know Rick introduced you to the guy at the wedding. Rick had just hired him as part of Celestial Pet's dog-training program, right?"

Roxie nodded. "Mmm-hmm."

"Okay, so spill it," Bea said, laughing. "You're already dating the guy?"

"What?" Roxie looked horrified. "Of course not. I'm not dating anyone. Dating is not part of my business plan."

Bea shrugged. "So have you started Lilith in his classes, or what?"

Everyone glanced down at the snarling Lilith, tugging desperately at the leash to get at a nearby dog, frothing at her muzzle the way she sometimes did.

"Guess not," Bea said.

Roxie did a little back-and-forth thing with her neck, then turned her attention to Ginger. "And how about you? Did you get your portrait taken by that Rico Suave dude yet?"

Bea chuckled, but Ginger didn't. It was happening again—the tingling, the weak legs, the flush of her chest, the smoldering low in her belly—all because the man was mentioned in passing. His actual name hadn't even been uttered! Ginger needed to get a hold of herself. The sad truth was that he'd never called to cash in his rain check and probably never would. It had been over two weeks since she'd laid eyes on him—and he'd laid his tongue on her—but her physical reaction to him seemed to be intensifying instead of waning. She didn't understand it.

"You okay?" Bea asked.

Ginger nodded. "Just another hot flash."

Both Roxie and Bea groaned loudly. "Would you *stop* with that garbage already?" Bea asked. "Seriously, Ginger, you're *not* going through menopause! Get it through your head!"

She nodded. In a soft voice she said, "Larry told me I needed a face-lift."

Roxie closed her eyes as if she were in pain. Bea puffed up her cheeks with air.

"I know. I know. He's a jerk, and he just tells me that to make me doubt myself." Ginger looked at her friends, hoping they would know she meant what she said.

"Ginger, you're damn lucky to have jettisoned that idiot," Bea said. "He spent nearly twenty years dragging you down. You deserve so much more."

Roxie touched Ginger's hand. "You are one of the loveliest women I've ever known, and I'm not bullshitting you. Ginger, you are a truly beautiful woman."

She nodded quickly, trying to hold back the tears.

Bea said, "Just please—*please*—don't tell me you're going to use this as an excuse to make another Botox appointment."

Ginger wiped her cheek. "Don't be silly."

"Thank God," Roxie said.

"I canceled it yesterday."

Ginger knew the whole thing was laughable. Since she'd found out that Larry had been cavorting with wrinkle-free girls, Ginger had been obsessed about her appearance—every fine line, every blotch, every pore. Her friends had watched as Ginger suddenly sprouted symptoms of menopause for which her doctors said there was no medical cause. They'd seen her make dozens of Botox appointments all over town, only to chicken out. Once, Ginger picked up a women's magazine in the plastic surgeon's waiting room and found an article that said research showed a possible link between Botox and brain tumors. She put the magazine down and walked out.

Her mother didn't help the situation. Teresa Barr, the former B-movie starlet, had become a cosmetic-surgery addict, and was hell-bent on getting Ginger hooked. Thank God she lived in Los Angeles and was afraid to fly. That meant she could only do her pushing on the phone.

So there Ginger was, well aware of what had rocked her self-confidence, but unable to find her balance. Unlike many other divorcees, her greatest challenge hadn't been loneliness or finances or that feeling of social limbo so many women talked about. Her challenge was being able to accept herself as she was. She had a hard time truly believing, deep down, that she was still vibrant and attractive, and that there was still a possibility for happiness, for love.

So she'd told herself and anyone who'd listen that she'd given up.

Ginger looked at the exasperation on her friends' faces and knew she'd tested their patience with all her nonsense. Frankly, she was sick of herself.

"You been talking to your mother again?" Bea asked.

"No."

"She doesn't need her mother—she's got Larry," Roxie said.

Ginger tossed back her hair and leveled her gaze. "Look, I swear to you I won't let Larry hurt me ever again. I know he's just lashing out because I got the house, alimony, *and* HeatherLynn. Oh! Which reminds me!"

She placed her sweet little bichon down in the grass, hoping she'd join Martina and the poodles. The dog looked tempted, hesitated, but eventually toddled out into the off-leash area.

Ginger made her announcement, filled with pride for her brave little princess. "The other night, when Larry came to the house, HeatherLynn jumped up and bit him in the crotch!"

She got the response she'd hoped for, including a few fist-pumping *whoop-whoops* from Bea. Roxie laughed until she doubled over. When she caught her breath, she asked if she could feature HeatherLynn on her Web site.

Ginger laughed and smiled, enjoying the moment to its fullest, not even caring how her emotion might accentuate her crow's-feet and frown lines. She was doing a fine job filling in for Josie, she decided. And it made her happy.

CHAPTER 4

Piers was late, which was the norm, and Lucio had been alone in his friend's apartment many times before. But on that particular day he felt just slightly awkward. The reason was the change in décor.

The one-bedroom apartment was filled with photos that hadn't been there just a few weeks before. The breathtaking landscapes for which Piers was known were exactly where they'd always been, plastered on every wall in the place. It was the addition of the photographs of Sylvie that surprised Lucio. They were hung on the walls, propped on the fireplace mantel, placed in frames, and arranged upon the side tables and the divider between the kitchen and living room. None of the photos had been on display in the weeks Lucio had called Piers's sofa his home. Obviously, Piers had put them away when Lucio moved in, and brought them back out the moment he was gone.

Lucio sighed. Despite Piers's assurances to the contrary, it seemed his friend had never completely let go of the past. Piers hadn't wanted Lucio to see all these photos of Sylvie, probably because he hadn't wanted their prickly history brought front and center.

Lucio walked toward the small room divider covered with frames. He barely glanced at the full-color wedding portrait he'd taken of Piers Skaarsgard and Sylvie Westcott all those years ago. It was the smaller photo next to it that fascinated him. It was a snapshot of the three of them, smiling in front of the tube station in Piccadilly Circus. They all looked so young. Unscathed. Filled with passion and plans.

A handwritten notation at the bottom right corner said, "London, 1992." The handwriting was Sylvie's. And, as Lucio well knew, the passion that burned in Sylvie's eyes that day had burned for him. All her plans had included Lucio.

His throat squeezed. Sylvie had been so very pretty, in that simple, unadorned way some women have about them. She could have been dressed in an old sweater and worn jeans—and usually was—yet she looked elegant. He'd always thought that it was due to her ridiculously correct English posture and her lithe, athletic frame, which seemed to make the freckles, the flyaway dirty-blond hair, and the slightly crooked teeth charming. He picked up the photo to look closer. It was unfathomable that this young, healthy, vivacious girl could be gone. But she was.

Lucio put the photo back in its place and ran a hand through his hair. He headed to the kitchen in search of wine, then stopped himself. Piers wouldn't have wine. He never had wine. What did Swedes know about wine? So he grabbed a cold Anchor Steam from Piers's refrigerator, then opened the patio doors that led to the balcony. He knew from past experimentation that if he adjusted the rickety wicker chair just so, he could see a blue slice of the bay from the fourth-floor flat. So he situated himself as such, propped up his feet, and set about the business of waiting.

Lucio smiled at the connectedness of it all. That

Piccadilly Circus photo had been taken by none other than Rick Rousseau. They'd encountered the American that very day, sitting alone in a corner booth at the pub that served as *Geographica*'s unofficial satellite office. The scruffy young man was eating his fish-and-chips in silence, but smiled and nodded politely when they glanced his way. Sylvie asked him to join them at their table. She was always doing things like that. And that's how Lucio's long—and fortuitous—friendship with Rick Rousseau began.

Chance meetings could change the course of your whole life, Lucio knew. But with one catch: You didn't get to choose which meeting would have the most impact. That unkempt American eating his fish-and-chips would become Lucio's travel companion and dear friend. Years later, Lucio would pull Rick from a street riot that erupted in Jakarta when the Indonesian government collapsed. And more recently, Rick would hand over his luxurious San Francisco home for Lucio to use for as long as necessary, which, at this rate, could be the rest of his life.

Though Lucio sat in a smattering of afternoon sun on an August day, he felt a hot shiver go through him. It made him sit up straighter, his body suddenly on alert. *Ah, of course.* Yet again he was thinking of his most recent chance encounter—with the beguiling Ginger Garrison. For more than two weeks now, her business card had been burning a hole in his wallet, while the memory of her—that taste, her scent, those legs—had been burning a hole in his trousers.

Of course he couldn't contact her. According to the old woman who'd officiated at Rick's wedding, Ginger was a newspaper editor and a mother of two teenage boys. She was also recently divorced from an unfaithful husband. Lucio knew he had no business bringing all his troubles into her normal, all-American life. It didn't matter how much he desired to cash in that rain check, how he longed to take her completely. For many nights now, he'd dreamed of doing just that. Lucio smiled to himself as he sipped his beer, knowing that the taking of Ginger Garrison would have to remain there, in his dreams.

The last thing that woman needed in her life was another man she couldn't rely on.

Lucio heard the apartment door open and close. He called out to Piers to tell him he was on the balcony. "You're late," he said, half over his shoulder.

When Piers didn't reply, Lucio swiveled around, seeing his friend motionless, his expression blank.

"You okay?" Lucio set down his beer.

"Sure. Sure." Piers joined him out on the balcony, sitting in the weather-worn director's chair next to Lucio. "I'm just a little embarrassed that you saw all the pictures of Sylvie."

"It's nothing to be embarrassed about," Lucio said, carefully studying his friend. As a rule, Piers didn't broadcast what he was feeling at any given moment. His pale mouth maintained a firm and straight line in most every circumstance. His small greenish-blue eyes were no-nonsense, designed to see the bigger picture of earth and sky, a talent that made him one of the most respected landscape photographers of his generation. Lucio had heard more than one person describe Piers as a cold fish, but he knew better. Piers was a serious man. Focused. Determined. Passionate. But to those who didn't know him well, he could come off as *un poco distante*.

"You know you can talk to me about her," Lucio

said, leaning toward him. "She was a wonderful person. I know you loved her more than anything in the world, and I am truly sorry she's gone."

Piers nodded so quickly it was barely detectable. He stared at the buildings of China Town between themselves and the bay. "She always thought fondly of you, Lucky."

Lucio sat back in his chair and stretched out his legs before he spoke.

"I have always considered her a dear friend." Lucio wasn't certain how far Piers wanted to go with this line of conversation, but he knew he needed to reassure him. They'd never once discussed what had happened in the months after Lucio left London for the Azores, leaving Sylvie with a shattered heart and Piers with the job of picking up the pieces. She'd married Piers eight months later, in the garden of her parents' Devon cottage. She'd been a beautiful bride. And she'd barely spoken to Lucio.

In general, Lucio wasn't proud of his record with women. In particular, he saw Sylvie as his most shameful offense. Lucio hung his head, wishing he could turn back time, make himself a more decent man with one wave of a magic wand. He would have gone about things differently. He would have let Sylvie down easy, taking more time to explain that she was a wonderful woman, but his only true love affair was with the camera, the light, the pursuit of the shot. Instead, he'd just left a note. He'd been an idiot. *¡Qué imbécil!*

And now she was gone forever.

"I put her pictures away when you were staying here because, well, I didn't want you to think I was living in some kind of morbid shrine to Sylvie." Piers glanced sideways at Lucio, a sheepish look on his face. "I didn't want you to feel uncomfortable, or unwelcome."

"I wouldn't have," Lucio said. "And it's not morbid. It's perfectly natural to want to surround yourself with her memory. She's only been gone a few months."

Piers nodded, then sighed. "Sometimes I don't think I can bear it without her."

Lucio placed his hand on his friend's shoulder. "I have always regretted hurting her the way I did. If she were here, I would seek her forgiveness."

The air whooshed in and out of Piers's nostrils. He nodded sharply and slapped his hands on his knees, as if declaring it was time to change the subject. Piers stood and smiled down at Lucio. "It was all a long, long time ago, my friend—part of another lifetime. We all have things we wish we'd done differently."

Lucio nodded, grateful for his friend's generosity.

"But we should get going," Piers said with a smile, extending his hand to Lucio. "A man in your position can't afford to keep anyone waiting."

"You're crazy if you think I'd do something that stupid!" Joshua stomped his foot on the asphalt of his dad's driveway and glared at his brother.

"Fine," Jason said, languidly placing his hands behind his head and stretching out on the hood of their father's new Porsche. "You don't have the balls for something like that, anyway."

Joshua shook his head in disgust. "You want to get yourself arrested again? Hey, go for it—drive Dad's brand-new car without a license. Whatever. Fine. I just won't be part of it. And I won't cover for you, either."

"You become a bigger nerd every day, do you realize that?" Jason yawned, as if the conversation were boring him. "It's embarrassing, really."

Joshua groaned in frustration. "If you had the least bit of respect for me as a person—for my dreams— you wouldn't do this kind of crap in the first place. I've told you a million times that the mistakes of a brother can taint a president's reputation. It's a historical fact!"

Jason closed one eye and leaned away, as if looking at his brother caused him physical pain. "What the fuck are you talking about, ass-face? You're never going to be president and you know it. Please—do us all a huge favor and let it go."

"Loser."

"Shut up, tardvark."

"Don't you know anything about history?" Josh's cheeks had reddened with outrage. "Billy Carter's alcoholism? Roger Clinton's drugs and disorderly conduct? You are my *twin*—and that makes it even worse! People will think we're wired the same! What *you* do will affect *my* ability to get elected and stay up in the polls!"

Jason hopped down off the hood of the 911, drilling a knuckle into the muscle of his brother's upper arm before he walked away.

Joshua yelped in pain. "Hey, I'm talking to you!" He ran after him. "What is your problem? What is it you think you have to prove? Is this about Dad?" He caught up to his brother and blocked his way, yelling in his face. "If you're doing this kind of stupid shit just to get his attention, then it's totally pathetic!"

"You're the pathetic one," Jason said, not looking at him.

"Our dad is a jackass," Joshua said. "He's a middle-aged sex freak and he's not worth ruining our lives for."

With that last comment, Jason spun around and punched his twin brother in the mouth. Both were shocked to see three small white teeth clatter to the bricks, followed by several plump drops of bright red blood.

Lucio felt confident when he arrived at his agent's office. Piers was with him, agreeing to vouch for him if needed, lend moral support, and voice a healthy dose of outrage as a fellow *Geographica* photographer.

The confidence didn't last long. Lucio got his first taste of bad news before the meeting even started. Sydney pulled Lucio aside and told him that the chairman of the Erskine Prize committee had called, and they had temporarily rescinded his award.

"What!"

"They will review the situation and decide by next month."

Piers overheard Sydney and shook his head sadly. "Oh, no. No. This cannot be."

Lucio was stunned. The Erskine was the biggest prize of them all, the ultimate mark of achievement in nature photography. He'd wanted an Erskine since he was twenty years old. He'd worked like a dog for it. He'd risked his life countless times for it. And it had a cash prize of $250,000, upon which his entire future now hinged.

"We have to—"

Sydney stopped Lucio by placing a hand on his arm. "No interference. They said if you or anyone else tries to lobby them about this, they would automatically pull the award. I am to notify them if your situation changes, but that's all."

"But . . ."

"Just sit tight," Sydney said. "The results of today's meeting might reassure everyone. Let's think positively."

Lucio sat on one side of the conference table along with Sydney, Piers, and Bill Voyles, Lucio's recently acquired—and very expensive—criminal defense attorney, who promptly passed his business cards to everyone in the room.

On the opposite side of the table sat two *Geographica* attorneys and a pair of underlings from the U.S. State Department.

Lucio's hopes for a hassle-free resolution were dashed within the first five minutes. The magazine's lawyers told him that *Geographica* had no interest in reinstating Lucio's current contract, nor would they be interested in any future partnership.

Lucio sat in silence, his blood hot and pounding.

Next, they went on to inform him that they had evidence linking Lucio to the missing fifty thousand in magazine funds.

"But I've already told you—I did not take that money!" Lucio waved his hands around in frustration. "I would never do that!"

As Lucio's lawyer whispered to him to keep his mouth closed, one of the magazine's attorneys produced a stack of papers, which he spread out on the table for inspection. In front of Lucio were sixteen completed expense reimbursement forms dated over a four-month period. The signature looked almost identical to Lucio's—*almost*.

The lawyers explained that all the forms had been couriered together from China to *Geographica*'s London office, where the requests had been approved and money had been wired to an anonymous personal account in the Bahamas. A routine audit had revealed discrepancies, and editors were alerted to the possible fraud.

"But that is not my signature," Lucio said, tapping

his finger on the black-ink cursive, the rage building in him as he examined a listing of hotel, food, transportation, and equipment expenses in southern China. "What is this garbage?" he asked, incredulous. "I don't even use this brand of diffusion filter and I certainly wouldn't be buying it in China! And I never set foot in the Jiangxi Province for that assignment."

"Exactly our point," the lawyer said.

"¡Es una trampa para incriminarme!" Lucio said, the realization slamming into him. He looked around the table. "I have been set up!"

"So this is not your bank account?" one of the lawyers asked.

Lucio looked again at the name of the offshore bank and the account number. "Absolutely not. For more than ten years I have used an account here in San Francisco—your records will show that. This is not my account."

One of the lawyers smiled as if he enjoyed the exchange. "Who would want to set you up as you claim, Mr. Montevez?"

"I do not know," Lucio said, trying to stay calm. "Just as I cannot explain how my rough video footage got to the Chinese foreign ministry."

The lawyer smiled again. "So you believe one person is responsible for both offenses—a conspiracy of sorts?"

"I suppose it is possible," Lucio answered. "I do not know what happened. That is what I am telling you."

"Hmm . . ." the lawyer said, his grin expanding. "So there is someone out there vengeful enough to go to all this trouble to damage your reputation? Someone who also happens to be knowledgeable of *Geographica*'s reimbursement procedure? Someone who can get a hold of the appropriate forms and then forge your signature?"

The heat of Piers's stare made Lucio turn toward his friend. Immediately, he knew Piers was thinking the same thing he was—*hell yes, such a person existed.*

Several persons, really. Several *women.* Lucio closed his eyes as he started to go down the list in his mind—Marina, the photographer's assistant in Belize; Hima, the freelance translator in Nepal; Julya, the documentary producer in Siberia; and, of course, Ilsa, the photo editor in Frankfurt. And that was just for starters. Like he'd done with Sylvie, he'd carelessly tossed them all aside for his only true love: his work. And each one had been quite unhappy about it. Ilsa, dramatically so.

"So where might we find this person?"

Lucio did not answer the lawyer, so Piers spoke in his defense. "Truly, this is a real possibility. My friend does not lie. There are many women who no longer think well of him."

"Give us their names and we'll begin an investigation."

Piers leaned close and whispered into Lucio's ear. "Remember what Ilsa Knauss said to you at the airport?"

Lucio nodded, sighing. "How could I forget?" he whispered back. "She threatened to cut off two critical parts of my anatomy! And then, there was the rat . . ."

Piers leaned into his ear again. "You really should give them her name," he suggested.

"But we haven't spoken in two years," Lucio said. "Don't you think she'd be over it by now?"

Piers looked at Lucio as if he were crazy.

"Yes, yes, all right," Lucio said. He supposed the gift-wrapped package that had awaited him upon his arrival in the northern Chinese city of Yinchuan nearly five months earlier was proof that she hadn't forgotten. "The thing was so . . . the word . . . ?"

"Desiccated."

"And smelly." Lucio swallowed, recalling how the accompanying gift card had been signed: "All My Love, Ilsa."

"Well?" One of the magazine's lawyers looked impatient. "I'm waiting."

Lucio nodded, but he took a moment to think this through. Was he capable of siccing investigators on Ilsa, or any of the women from his past? What if that just heaped further hurt onto innocent women who had nothing to do with this? But could Lucio live with the idea that he'd never get to the truth that would clear his name?

Before he could even confer with Bill Voyles, the magazine's lawyers shoved another document across the table. It was an agreement that *Geographica* magazine would forgo criminal charges if Lucio repaid the fifty thousand within ninety days.

"But I cannot," Lucio said, looking to Bill and then the magazine attorneys. To Sydney he said, "I won't get the Erskine prize money until December—if I get it at all."

"Would you consider six months?" Bill Voyles asked the lawyers.

"We're afraid this is the limit of the company's compassion," was the reply.

The rage built in Lucio's chest until he could not suppress it. *"¡Hostia! ¡Besa mi culo!"* he shouted, slamming his fist on the conference table.

The room got quiet. All eyes turned to Piers, who shrugged. "It means, 'The Host! Kiss my posterior!' "

Bill Voyles shook his head in disapproval.

"I did not take your damn money," Lucio said, pointing at the attorneys. "This is how you treat one of your best photographers? ¡*Absurdo!* ¡*No me jodas!*"

His lawyer elbowed Lucio in the side. When everyone's eyes turned to Piers for a clarification, he shook his head, opting not to translate "don't fuck with me."

"If you decline the offer, Mr. Montevez, we will have no choice but to press charges."

Lucio sat still for a moment, his mouth ajar with disbelief. Eventually, he looked into the faces of the lawyers and nodded. He would pay the idiots their money—money was not the real issue. The issue was that someone had ruined his reputation, and that was unacceptable. In silence, Lucio promised himself he would find out who had done this to him, no matter how long it took.

"Please relay to my former employer that their compassion overwhelms me," Lucio said, accepting a pen from his attorney.

He signed the agreement, then motioned to his handwriting. "And just for your jollies, you might want to compare my actual signature to those on the expense reports."

"We'll certainly take that into consideration," was their reply.

The State Department boys were next. They said a review of the facts in Lucio's case showed no merit to the charges of espionage—the only bit of good news Lucio had had all day. They went on to say that they believed the Chinese were only doing what they did best, diverting attention from a real problem with political posturing. In Lucio's case, the posturing was the spying accusation. The real problem was the environmental devastation caused by decades of unregulated industrial pollution. They assured him he was off the hook in that regard.

"Thank God!" he said with a sigh.

But he could never return to China, they added, and said he shouldn't bother trying to get his video footage back. Then they politely suggested that, from here on out, he might try to avoid sexing up the daughters of officials in communist, patriarchal societies.

Once everyone had filed out of the conference room, Sydney shrugged in Lucio's direction. "I think that was as good as you could expect under the circumstances."

Piers shook his head in sympathy. "How will you come up with fifty thousand in ninety days? Will you go to Rousseau?"

"Of course not," Lucio snapped. He could never ask Rick for money. He had *some* pride. He was already living in his wealthy friend's chic home and eating his food and driving one of his extra cars. There would be no begging for cash.

"It's not like he'd miss it," Piers said helpfully.

"I will not ask." Lucio turned to his agent. "Get me jobs, Sydney. I don't care what they are."

Sydney frowned, the expression on his chubby red face flustered. "What kind of jobs did you have in mind?"

"Stateside. West Coast if possible. Expenses up front. You know, tourism, travel, even commercial assignments—anyone willing to pay top dollar for my name and reputation."

Sydney cleared his throat. "Uh, I'm not sure who that would be right now, Lucky."

Lucio shifted his weight back on the heels of his

feet, surprised by his agent's lack of enthusiasm. "What are you saying?"

Sydney shrugged. "I'm saying that your target market is all but extinct—newspapers and magazines are washing up on the shore like dead fish every day. And even if the print market was flaming hot, your name and reputation stink like high tide." Sydney tilted his head, as if apologizing in advance for what he was about to say. "Your name and reputation are shit right now, Lucky. That's what I'm saying."

Lucio's mouth fell open. "But—"

"Even without criminal charges," Sydney cut him off. "The damage has been done. I'm sorry, but that's the truth, and I think you should save yourself some grief and just forget about the Erskine."

Piers let go with a pained sigh, turning his small, serious eyes Lucio's way. "That is not right."

Lucio shook his head. "No, it's not."

"We will find the woman who did this to you, all right?" Piers touched Lucio's shoulder. "We'll start with Ilsa. She won't be hard to track down. The last I heard she was still freelancing in Europe. I will help you."

Lucio appreciated the offer of assistance, but he knew he'd have to postpone traveling the world in search of Ilsa or whoever the guilty party might be. He could not afford it! Besides, Lucio could not help but feel he'd been lucky to escape the wrath of a heartbroken woman for as many years as he had. Perhaps, in some way, he had this coming. Perhaps he deserved it.

Regardless, he needed fifty thousand U.S. dollars, and fast. Lucio sighed at the enormity of the challenge ahead of him. He could not finance a project on spec, hoping to find a buyer. Nor did he have the time for that unpredictable process. He only had ninety days.

He shoved his hands into the pockets of his slacks, where he encountered his ever-thinning wallet. Heat burned his fingertips—he suddenly thought of the business card tucked away inside. He thought of Ginger Garrison and her lapdog. One eyebrow rose high on his forehead.

Perhaps he was going about this all wrong. Perhaps he needed to focus on what he *did* have as opposed to what he lacked. He had his talent, his imagination, and a treasure chest of top-of-the-line photo equipment. He also had the strongest motivation of all— self-preservation.

"I believe the answer is pet portraits, Sydney," Lucio announced.

His agent sucked in his cheeks and blinked. "Excuse me? For a second I thought you said something about pets."

Lucio laughed softly, because what was there left to do *but* laugh? He had become a penniless squatter on the verge of criminal prosecution, a globally renowned nature photographer who now needed to take pictures of poodles to pay his way. If he did not laugh, he would have to cry.

"Yes. Pets and their owners." He looked at Piers's and Sydney's equally shocked expressions. "Why do you look so puzzled? Think of it—an award-winning *Geographica* nature photographer is now available to take a portrait of you and your animal friend! Rich people will want to pose with their Chihuahuas and Siamese. I could even Photoshop in a variety of my own landscapes as backdrops—savannas, rain forests, the Himalayas, canyons and rivers, icebergs!"

The men were speechless.

"It will become the ultimate in status."

"Icebergs . . ." Sydney mumbled to himself.

"Little dogs! Big dogs!" Lucio waved his hands around, trying to drum up enthusiasm. "Parrots. Kitties. What do you call them, the little furry household rodents—*¡los jerbos!*"

Piers winced, then translated for a perplexed Sydney. "I believe Lucio wants to take pictures of gerbils."

Lucio tapped his friend's arm. "Now that is something I *will* ask Rick for. He could let me promote my services at Celestial Pet stores. That will bring in some business."

Sydney collapsed into his office chair, drumming his fingers on the desk. "How much do you suppose you can charge for this kind of job?"

Lucio looked to Piers for suggestions, but his friend shook his pale blond head, clearly having nothing to contribute.

Lucio felt himself break into a hopeful smile. "Thousands! *¡Todo es posible!*" He laughed. "I will make the most of these ninety days. Then I will win the Erskine. Is everyone with me?"

Piers produced a dubious glance.

Sydney bit down on the inside of his cheek.

"*¡Excelente!*" Lucio said. "I will begin immediately. I already have my first client."

CHAPTER 5

It had been easy to find her address, and Lucio used the brass knocker on the front door of the stately home. He heard a high-pitched yapping, followed by the slap of feet on a hard interior floor. A shadow passed across the frosted glass of the door just before it opened. And there she was.

Ginger Garrison was barefoot, her hair pulled up in a ponytail, wearing a pair of black stretch yoga pants and a tight, nipple-friendly piece of stretchy fabric Americans referred to as a sports bra. Despite the name of the apparel, when Lucio looked at that body—with its pale peachy skin, rosy red-painted toenails, the flat abdomen exposed by the low-waisted tights—sports were the last thing that came to his mind.

"We meet again, Señora Garrison," Lucio said. He reached for her hand and raised it to his lips, closing his eyes to savor for the instant his lips met her flesh.

She ripped her hand away.

Surprised, Lucio straightened. "I have come at a bad time, yes?"

The beautiful Ginger laughed. Her little dog—a puff of white with two tiny black marble eyes—began sniffing Lucio's shoe. "May I pick it up?" he asked, hoping that his obvious love of animals would soften whatever irritation he may have caused by arriving unannounced.

"HeatherLynn is not an 'it.' She's a 'she.'"

"Of course she is," Lucio said, feeling the now familiar hot shiver moving through his body. Why did this happen when in this woman's presence? Or even when he thought of her? Why did he seem unable to prevent it?

"Please come in."

Lucio did as he was told. He stepped inside the house, immediately aware of the shimmering dance of light from a skylight high above the foyer. It was a modern house, obviously custom-built, but had an agreeable warmth to it.

He returned his attention to the dog. "Ah, of course! I now see the full scope of HeatherLynn's feminine beauty."

"Right," Ginger said.

Lucio bent down and scooped up the hairball. He tucked its squirming body close to his side, realizing he hadn't held a dog since his tía Luisa used to shove her mutt with the runny eyes at him whenever he'd visit her at her home in La Valenciana. He hoped to the Host he was holding Ginger's little pet correctly.

"Why are you here?" Ginger was either not happy to see him or very successfully masking her pleasure. When she crossed her arms under her breasts, it only served to further enhance the mounds of creamy female flesh. He could not help but glance at her stupendous cleavage. He worried he may have just involuntarily licked his lips.

"Lucio?"

He looked up from his trance. "I am sorry, *guapa*. Did you say something?"

Ginger shook her head and returned her arms to her sides. It almost looked like she smiled, but he could not be sure. "Why did you come here?"

"Ah, yes." The dog had begun to lick his hand, a sensation Lucio found vaguely disconcerting, so he put the animal back on the floor. "I have come to discuss your portrait."

Ginger laughed again. "You don't say?"

"Yes. This is true. I would like to discuss appointment times, your preferences for the backdrop, and the costs."

When he got nothing but a blank stare, he continued. "Also, if you would be so kind, I would appreciate your sharing the names of any potential clients, friends or associates with pets you believe might be interested in my services."

"You're kidding, right?" Ginger balled up her fists and propped them on her perfectly formed hips.

Lucio's mouth went dry. He was coming unglued just looking at her, smelling her, feeling the energy vibrate between them. The desire to touch her was so great he feared his arms would begin to shake, revealing the effort it took to not reach out for her, pull her to him, and devour her with kisses.

It boggled the mind. When had a woman ever unnerved him so? When had a woman ever driven Lucio Montevez to such distraction?

And when had he ever put a woman's welfare before his own pleasure, the way he had that night he delivered Ginger Garrison to the guesthouse door? He'd shoved her panties in her hand and sent her to bed—alone! The Host! What had happened to him?

"No joke, señora," Lucio managed. "Current circumstances require that I branch out into pet photography, after all. I would be honored to have you as my first client."

Disappointment fell upon Ginger's beautiful face, clouding her hazel eyes. It was if a fire had been extinguished. She looked down and away in embarrassment.

Lucio tried to sort out what was happening here. Could it be Ginger had been hoping he'd come to cash in his rain check? The thought thrilled him. The thought scolded him, too. He was no good for this beautiful lady. There were many women who might recommend him as a lover, but of all the women in all the world, there was not one who would recommend Lucio Montevez as a partner. One of them had even tried to destroy him—and might yet succeed at her revenge.

"Unless you had other interests," he said.

Ginger didn't look up right away. And in those precious suspended seconds, he studied how the light from the skylight high above glimmered in her rich auburn hair and caressed the apple of her cheek. While he waited for her to say yes or no, he watched how the light gave contrast to her plump bottom lip and cast a shadow around her downcast eyes. He wanted to photograph her—in this precise moment—and he itched for the heft of his Nikon in his hand. But he wanted to capture more than just the play of light and shadow on a beautiful woman's face. He wanted to capture the woman herself. And he ached for the familiar feel of her body in his arms.

Ginger looked up then, a pained expression on her face. She shook her head. "Of course I don't have other interests. Let me get my calendar."

Lucio grasped her arm as she turned to go. Her head snapped around and her eyes burned into his. He saw it again—the same innocence and vulnerability he'd seen in her expression that evening in the garden. It had softened his heart then—and it stabbed his soul now. He wondered how a grown woman could have come so far in life and yet remain untouched in this way.

Then suddenly, he knew. It could only be one thing.

"You have never known a man's love, have you?" Lucio heard himself blurt out the words, and was surprised by the brutal honesty in them. But he knew he was on to something. "You have never been deeply and truly loved for who you are, have you?"

Ginger's lips parted. He could see her pulse banging in her throat. She said nothing, but her eyes filled with moisture and her cheeks with pink.

What was the meaning of this strange desire? It was as if Lucio had no control over his thoughts, his words. It felt as if he were guided by a force outside himself, beyond his understanding. He stepped close, held open his arms, and let the beautiful woman fall against him. She rested her head against his chest as she trembled in his embrace. Lucio's hands roamed all over the warm skin of her bare arms, her exposed lower back. His hands went to the base of her neck. He felt her body press closer to him, her firm thighs push up against him in need.

Clearly, it would not be enough to provide comfort to her. He wanted her. He had to have her. So Lucio raked his fingers through her hair, tore out the ponytail holder, and tossed it to the floor. In one motion, Lucio grabbed a fistful of all that fiery hair, tilted her head back, and claimed her mouth with his.

The power in that kiss left him dazed. It felt as if he had pulled her very spirit inside him and delivered his own into her. Their bodies melded. His heart melted.

They collapsed to the tile floor, where he cradled her in his arms.

It was not enough. He could not get enough. She was hot and sighing and pushing her breasts against him as they kissed with such abandon that Lucio felt a jolt of confusion. Where had this kind of need originated? Why had he never felt it before? Lucio thought he'd experienced all that sex had to offer!

"God. Take me." Ginger's breath was hot against the side of his neck. "I want it. Now. Please. Please don't make me wait another day for you."

She clawed at his clothing. He helped her unbutton his shirt, open his belt, pull off his trousers. With two smooth and economical movements, he had the sports bra up over her head and the exercise pants down around her ankles. She lay there before him in the glow of the skylight, wearing only a pair of the flimsiest, palest pink panties he'd ever seen. He could see her red curls pushing up against the crotch, her juices already darkening the thin strip of material. That thin strip was the only thing between him and her opening.

"*Joder!*" he hissed roughly, dragging his lips over her belly, her thighs, back up to her breasts and hard nipples. It was a beautiful realization—the soft pink of her nipples matched the soft pink of her panties. She was beyond beautiful. Her hands were in his hair.

Without warning, her body seized under his touch. She called out his name. She had come from the merest attention. He hadn't put his lips to her sex and just barely sucked on her breasts, yet she'd come in a fierce shudder.

How deprived she must be.

Suddenly Ginger sat up, her back straight, horror claiming her face. "Get up. Now. Get your clothes. *Go!*"

"What?"

She jumped to her feet, pulling up her pants. It was over! For some reason, Ginger had taken herself from him, and now she was ordering him to get dressed. He had not been intimate with many American women. Briefly, he wondered if this were a particularly aggressive type of foreplay.

"Get in the living room! Go! Here, take your clothes! Hurry!" Ginger shoved him toward the sitting room.

Lucio stumbled through the room and around the corner to the dining area, where he stood behind the wall as he dressed. This was not foreplay, he decided. This was him getting the boot.

"What is wrong? What is going on?" Lucio had seen women change their minds, most certainly, but never with this conviction and speed.

The little dog began to bark. Ginger had already pulled on the sports bra and was tucking her hair back into its holder when the front door flew open.

From his hiding place, Lucio saw two tall, towheaded young men. One opened a bloody mouth to show missing teeth. The other opened the folds of a towel, which contained the teeth.

"In the car. Now." The boys did as ordered. Ginger raced to the kitchen and back to the door in seconds. In one hand she carried a pair of athletic shoes and in the other a purse. Clenched in her teeth were a set of keys. With a panicked glance in his direction, she slammed the door behind her.

She was gone.

The dog toddled up to Lucio and sat at his feet, the very tip of her little pink tongue protruding from her tiny lips.

"Is it always so unruly here in the Garrison home?" he asked her. "Is this your natural habitat?"

She wagged her miniature feather duster of a tail, her tiny black eyes filled with anticipation.

"I suppose this is where I show myself out, yes?"

Lucio strolled through the sitting room and back to the foyer, the dog at his heels. He spied a telephone table near the door, where there was memo paper and a pen. He jotted down the phone number for Rick's Pacific Heights home and this message: *I will be waiting for you.*

He moved toward the door, almost stepping on the little white dog, which had placed itself between him and the exit. It was almost as if she wanted him to stay.

"Is there something you need?"

Those must have been magic words, because the dog popped up and toddled away, looking over her shoulder to make sure Lucio was following, which he was. Admittedly, he knew very little about domesticated canine behavior, but this struck him as unusual.

The dog went into the nicely furnished sitting room, and made her way to the far corner, near the fireplace. On the floor was a bed. A dog bed. Lucio cocked his head to make sure he was seeing what he was seeing—a creamy café au lait satin pillow, tufted. A matching little blanket, also satin. A bed ruffle, pleated. All on a raised platform about six inches off the carpet. The dog waited.

"I am at a loss, little one," Lucio said. "What is it I'm supposed to do?"

With that, the white fluff ball put her front paws on the edge of the pillow, glanced over her doggie shoulder, and waited. Lucio had seen that look many times in his life—it was the look of a woman who expected a door to be opened or a chair to be pulled out. There was no mistaking it.

Lucio took a few cautious steps toward the dog. He leaned down and picked up her hindquarters and scooted her onto her throne. The poofy-headed creature circled a few times before she settled in, resting her pointed little nose between her front paws. Then she turned her face away and closed her eyes.

Lucio laughed softly. He knew the meaning of that universal gesture, as well—he had just been dismissed.

He let himself out.

There were so many reasons Ginger was unhinged that she hardly knew where to begin.

Joshua was in oral surgery because his twin brother had punched him in the mouth, knocking out one top and two bottom teeth. Their fight had been over Larry, who was not answering his cell, his pager, or his hospital or private practice line. All the while, his nurse hadn't a clue where he was.

And there Ginger sat, outfitted in a sports bra and a bare midriff, an ensemble she hardly felt comfortable wearing at home with the blinds drawn, let alone in public. The man three chairs down didn't seem to mind her clothing selection, however, and Ginger clutched her bag to the front of her body, trying not to smear dried blood on the orange leather.

Worse yet, Ginger could not stop cringing at how she'd let a hot rush of insanity rule her the second Lucio Montevez walked through her front door. She'd never had such a ferocious sexual response in her life, including the night on the porch. Apparently that was just the way it was with Lucio Montevez. All he had to do was show up, and Ginger was stripping down. No one had ever done that to her. Just as no one had ever looked into her eyes and instantly known the truth.

"You have never known a man's love, have you?"

How could a stranger know this about her when she'd only recently acknowledged it to herself?

Ginger fidgeted in the plastic waiting room chair. It was horrible to admit, but it bothered her that she'd left Lucio in her house. Alone. She wasn't thinking he'd steal the big-screen TV, necessarily, but it did highlight an unsettling reality: She'd almost had sex on the floor with a man she didn't know well enough to leave in her home unsupervised.

What the hell was I thinking?

As all of this tumbled around in her mind, she had to wonder—maybe Lucio really was what Mrs. Needleman had warned her about. Maybe Lucio was *who* she'd warned her about. Maybe meeting him really was more than a coincidence.

Whatever it was, it was wild, and it scared her. She decided to call Mrs. Needleman the first chance she had.

Ginger squeezed her eyes against the throbbing in her head and waited for the pressure to subside. It didn't. But when a familiar melody began wafting down from the waiting room speakers, her eyes slowly opened in comprehension. The universe had chosen a soundtrack for her mental breakdown, and it was the Muzak version of the Clash's "Rock the Casbah," which meant that, in addition to everything else, she'd just learned that her high school prom theme song was old enough to become elevator music.

She laughed out loud. It was an unstable kind of laugh.

"Are you okay?" Jason sounded concerned.

"No. Of course I'm not okay."

"I'm really sorry, Mom."

That was the twentieth time her son had apologized in the last hour. Ginger tapped her fingertips against her forehead, hoping to loosen the frown lines that had probably become canyons in the last hour.

She turned to Jason, prepared to give him the lecture of a lifetime—he'd just caused grave injury to his brother! But when she looked at him, she saw how his blue eyes were filled with remorse. He looked almost meek. Frightened.

How could such a sweet boy be capable of such rotten behavior? Where had she gone wrong?

He'd been a joyous and happy baby, sleeping through the night by eight weeks, always wanting to be cuddled. Then he became a sociable toddler, fearless among the little ones in his playgroup—a natural leader. Next, he became a high-energy kid with a passion for baseball, like his father. And now . . .

Ginger studied Jason's face and saw the same boy she'd always known, intelligent and defiant. But he no longer liked to be hugged. There was blond stubble on his chin and upper lip. He was no longer interested in being a leader. And his passion for baseball ended last year, when Larry berated him for not making the traveling team.

According to the family counselor they'd been seeing, Jason needed to develop strategies for identifying and handling his emotions. In Ginger's opinion, her son's problem was far simpler than all that—he was so angry with his dad he couldn't see straight.

"I didn't mean to hurt him this bad," Jason whispered. "But he drives me nuts with all his insane whining about being president—I'm sick of it, Mom! You've got to get him to shut up about it. I can't take it anymore."

Ginger wouldn't go so far as to call it insane, but she did know that Josh had the tendency to grate on a person's nerves. He'd come home from his fifth-grade social studies class one afternoon and announced that he planned to become president of the United States. Everything he did from there on out, he said, would be with that goal in mind. Ginger and Larry had smiled and encouraged their sweet, idealistic son, knowing his attention would soon divert to cars or computers or the newest Xbox game. They'd been wrong. When Josh began working on the costume crew for his school's theater productions, they were thrilled, thinking maybe he'd found another passion.

He hadn't. Joshua stuck to his plan, making sure that every day was a steppingstone toward his eventual role of commander in chief. He'd joined the debate club. He'd volunteered for local, state, and national political campaigns. He'd helped with voter drives and the bloodmobile and environmental projects. And though he was now only in tenth grade, Josh had collected a hundred college catalogs and designed a complex spreadsheet comparing course offerings, Washington, D.C., internship opportunities, and famous political alumni. It made Ginger's head spin.

In fact, during their emergency dash to the dentist's office just an hour before, Josh had held the bloody towel to his jaw and said he worried the injury might dilute the photogenic quality of his smile, or alter his profile.

Ginger sighed. "I know Joshua can be annoying sometimes, but that doesn't give you the right to beat him bloody." She shook her head. "Besides, you already said this whole thing was about your dad. What did Josh say that made you so mad?"

Her son's eyes flashed before he turned away.

"Tell me what got you so upset."

Jason ignored her. Ginger was about to demand he answer her question when she felt the creepy stare of the guy three seats down. That was all she could take—she heard a distinct *snap!* inside her head. She knew it was the sound of her last nerve, now officially shot to hell.

Ginger swiveled her head to catch the man admiring her spandex-clad hips. She cleared her throat and smiled at him pleasantly. Then she spoke in a voice loud enough to be heard by everyone in the crowded waiting room and most of the office staff. "Excuse me—aren't you here with your wife?"

The man dragged his eyes from her butt and frowned. "Huh?"

"I thought so," Ginger said sweetly. "I am here with my son, who required emergency dental work."

The man seemed confused. "Okay," he mumbled.

"And I was exercising in the privacy of my home when he was injured, so I didn't have time to change."

His mouth fell open.

"Do you know where I'm going with this?" she asked, waiting for an answer that didn't come. "No?"

"Uh . . ."

"If you don't stop ogling me, I will march right in there and interrupt your wife's appointment and tell her what a sleazoid pervo scumwad you are. Don't think I won't."

The man stared at her, stunned.

Ginger pointed a French-tipped nail in his direction. "You picked the wrong damned day to mess with me," she hissed.

That's when the man gathered his *Sports Illustrated* and his wife's purse and moved to the other side of the waiting room.

Pleased with the results, Ginger returned her attention to Jason.

"Gee, Mom," he said. "That was kinda disturbing."

She laughed. "Oh, yeah? Well, the same goes for you, Jason. You've picked the wrong damned day to mess with me." Ginger lowered her voice. "It's time to spill it. What in the hell is going on with you, Jase? It's like you're trying to screw up your life just to make a point."

Jason remained silent.

"I'm so worried about you." Ginger tried not to allow her voice to break. "First the curfew violation and the drinking, then the destruction of property and the cheating at school. What's this about, honey? You can tell me. You *have* to tell me."

He shrugged and looked away, saying nothing.

"Answer me!"

He slowly swiveled his head in her direction. In a surly, exhausted-sounding voice, he said, "I'm a teenage boy, Mom. Get over it. So, is Dad coming or not?"

The dentist chose that unfortunate moment to enter the waiting room and motion for Ginger and Jason to join him. He escorted them to his office at the end of the hall, where Joshua waited, sporting a metal wire across his top and bottom teeth, much like the one he'd sported when he'd had braces.

"The teeth will reattach just fine," the dentist said. "But no solid food at all for about ten days. Just liquid. And after that only soft foods. He won't be eating anything like hard pretzels for about four weeks."

Ginger nodded, her brain frazzled.

"I'll need to see him back here next week."

"Okay," she said, her worried eyes darting from the dentist to Josh and Jason.

"Why isn't Larry here?" The dentist looked at all three members of the Garrison family for a reply. "Didn't you page him?"

"He's stuck at the hospital." Jason jumped in before

Ginger could think of how to respond. Clearly, her son was protecting Larry's reputation with a man who happened to be one of his dad's golfing buddies. "Medical emergency—you know how it is," Jason added, smiling.

"Sure." The dentist nodded. While writing out two prescriptions for Joshua, he added, "No more right hooks to your brother's face, got it?"

Jason swallowed hard. "Got it," he whispered.

The dentist looked up over the rims of his glasses. "Out in the real world, that's a felony. You know that, right? I'm sure your dad has explained that to you?"

Jason stared blankly for a second, then nodded enthusiastically. "Yeah. Sure."

At that point in the conversation, Joshua let out a distressed wail. All eyes turned to him. Then he said something that sounded like, *"What am I supposed to eat for ten freakin' days?"*

The dentist smiled. "I recommend milkshakes and smoothies. And I'm sure Jason would be happy to make them for you. Am I right about that?"

Jason sighed deeply. "I live to serve," he said.

"Here—have some more, my friend."

Lucio held out his wine glass and smiled. Sometime after the disastrous meeting, Piers had revealed the depth of his compassion and loyalty by going out—on his own, no less—and purchasing two bottles of Rioja from a little wine shop in the city. The gesture had required research, Lucio knew. Piers had gone out of his way for him. Lucio raised his newly refilled glass in gratitude. *"Muchisimas gracias, mi amigo."*

"De nada," Piers said, raising his glass in concert with Lucio. "So, go on. What happened next?"

"Where was I?"

"She had just run out the door with her purse."

"Ah, yes." Lucio had been rambling on to Piers for nearly an hour, describing the series of strange encounters he'd had with the delectable Ginger Garrison. Of course, he'd not gone into great detail. He'd skipped over how, the night of Rick's wedding, he'd drunk from Ginger's vessel of love right out on the front lawn of the ranch. He also left out how he felt inexplicably drawn to Ginger every time he saw her. In addition, he'd failed to mention the power of that afternoon's kiss, or how his heart had stopped at the vision of her stretched out on the tile in that see-through scrap of fabric that passed as underpants. He only wanted his friend's advice, and he could get that without stooping to locker room stories.

"Well, she runs out of the house and leaves me dressed in only my socks and shoes!"

"You mean that was it?" Piers looked disappointed.

Lucio shrugged, taking another sip of the rich red elixir and letting it mellow in the back of his throat. For a man who knew virtually nothing about wine, Piers had made a fine selection.

"But where did she go? How serious was her son's injury?"

"What do I know?" Lucio gestured to the world in general. "She has not contacted me since. I am concerned about her son—and I can only assume those were her sons—but what do I know? I know nothing!"

Piers grinned. "No time for formal introductions, I take it?"

Lucio laughed. "Perhaps we will save that for when I am clothed."

"And when no one is bleeding," Piers added.

Both men laughed.

"She is divorced. Did I tell you that?" Lucio went

on. "Her ex-husband was a dickhead. He still is, I hear."

One of Piers's blond eyebrows arched high on his forehead. "Rick told you that?"

"Oh, no, I believe Rick is still on his honeymoon. But I did have a lovely discussion with the lady who performed Rick's ceremony. She was an unusual old woman—quite an intense gaze for one of her age."

"What did she say?"

Lucio switched his wine glass to his left hand so he could gesture with his right. "It's a story we have both heard before. An unfaithful husband caught in the act. But in Ginger's case, she caught him in the driveway. In the back of the family minivan."

"You're joking!" Piers's lips parted in disbelief.

Lucio sighed with the burden of the truth. "But my point is this—I wonder, with all the lovely lady has gone through, whether perhaps I should leave her alone."

Piers's eyes widened.

"Perhaps I should never bother her again, yes?"

Piers thought for a moment, then gave him a confused look. "But didn't you say she was your first client?"

Lucio laughed. "Holy God, I forgot all about that! All I've been thinking about is Ginger the woman, not Ginger the paying customer!"

"Hmm," Piers said.

"But that is what she must remain—a customer. After all, I do not have the kind of stability a woman needs from a man."

"Unfortunately, you do not."

"I have no money. No career. No home. I'm a hairbreadth from prison. I would set a poor example for her sons, yes?"

"Yes."

"Today's events took a wrecking ball to my life!" Lucio's voice became louder and more excited, which he knew only intensified his accent. If he were having a conversation with anyone but Piers, he would fear he couldn't be understood. "Now I must pick up the bricks, one by one, and try to rebuild something, but I do not think my life will ever look the same!"

Piers nodded some more, propping his pale, sandaled feet to the balcony railing. "I know how you feel," he said.

Suddenly, Lucio had a brilliant idea: *The steadfast Piers Skaarsgard would make a much better match for a woman like Ginger.* He nearly made that observation out loud when something inside stopped him. He did not want any other man near Ginger Garrison. Not even a man of the most stable circumstances or unsullied history. Not Piers. Not anyone.

Lucio looked over at Piers, the glimmer of the city bathing Piers's white face and long, lean body in a pale glow. His old friend was six foot four, three inches taller than Lucio. He was his opposite in many ways, and always had been. Where Lucio had a tendency to be loose with his tongue and his anger, Piers remained stoic. Where Lucio went through women faster than rolls of film, Piers had only loved once— and it was Sylvie Westcott. While Lucio plunged headfirst into jobs, relying on gut feelings to guide him, Piers had always taken a studious and cautious approach to his work. Neither way was better. Just different. And both men had built formidable careers in a brutally competitive industry.

Lucio took another sip of wine, admitting to himself that this was the real reason he wanted the Erskine award. It wasn't just the money. It was the recognition.

The *honor*. Each November, every professional nature and wildlife photographer on the planet sent work to the Erskine committee in Stockholm. Then every March, they would await the announcement of who won, and in what category. This year would mark Lucio's first win. That is, if they chose to allow him to keep it.

Suddenly, Piers dropped his feet from the railing and doubled over, his head hanging to his knees. Lucio heard him cry.

The Host! Lucio set down his wine glass and turned his full attention to his friend. How selfish he had been—thinking only of himself and his ego when Piers was still filled with sorrow over Sylvie's death. It had only been six months. And to think, when Lucio had just complained about his house tumbling down, it had only been a metaphor. For Piers, the destruction had been literal. His home had collapsed when Sylvie died. He had lost his wife, his place in the world.

Lucio put a hand on Piers's bony shoulder as he cried. He did not know what to say. He hoped just being at his side was enough. It was the kind of support he should have offered six months ago.

Lucio was suddenly filled with shame, hot and heavy in his chest. He had learned about Sylvie's illness a year before she died, when he was on assignment on Easter Island. He'd sent an e-mail, but did not have the opportunity to speak to Piers and Sylvie for another three months. By the time he'd called, her leukemia had worsened, and Lucio was already on his way to Papua New Guinea with plans to move on to northern China.

He never made it back in time to say good-bye to one old friend and to comfort the one who remained. The truth hit Lucio hard—he'd had one chance to do the decent thing by Piers and Sylvie, and he'd blown it.

"I am so sorry I was not here for you," Lucio whispered.

Piers did not respond. His crying continued, and, out of embarrassment, Piers turned his head away and pulled his shoulder from under Lucio's touch.

So Lucio waited. He poured himself another glass of wine and kept vigil over his grieving companion.

Eventually, the sobs began to subside. When Piers straightened from his crouch, Lucio said, "I should have been here for you and Sylvie. I beg your forgiveness for my selfishness."

Piers nodded gently and wiped his eyes with his shirtsleeve. "Sorry for my outburst. The grief came out of nowhere and I could not fight it. It happens that way sometimes."

Piers raised his head and leveled his gaze at Lucio. Maybe the diffuse light of China Town was playing games with him, but Lucio could have sworn he saw peace in his friend's face. Piers looked almost serene. "I know you well, Lucky. And I know you would've been here if you were able," he said.

CHAPTER 6

"Ohmigod! They're here!"

Ginger swiveled her head to where Roxanne had pointed, past the palm trees and toward the northeast corner of Dolores Park. Sure enough, Josie and Genghis were heading up the sidewalk. Ginger got a lump in her throat at the sight of her smiling friend and her goofy Labradoodle.

It was awfully good to see her home safe.

Genghis arrived first. He bounded up the hill, tongue and ears flying, his dark brown eyes lit up with excitement. Ginger laughed, relieved to see that five months after Genghis's disastrous grooming, his coat had grown back to its normal disheveled and wild state.

HeatherLynn began wiggling in Ginger's arms, demanding to be put down. The instant the little bichon's paws hit the grass, she ran off toward her long-lost friend. In dog years, a six-week absence must feel like full-scale abandonment, Ginger decided, and Heather-Lynn was beside herself with delight.

"Josie! Up here!" Bea jumped up and down in her Reeboks as she waved.

Ginger watched Josie jog up the hill, her face as happy as her dog's. When she reached them, they fell into each other in a raucous group hug. They laughed and cried and screeched with joy. Eventually, Ginger held Josie out at arm's length so they could get a good look at her.

Her cheeks were rosy and her eyes sparkled and her gorgeous hair fell in soft spiral curls just below her shoulders. She looked fit and hardy. Relaxed. In love.

Yes, she was glowing.

So what if it was a cliché to say that a woman could be so in love that she glowed? The truth was the truth, and in Josie's case, there was no other way to put it. Josephine Sheehan had been glowing since the day she met Rick Rousseau. She'd glowed on her wedding day. She was glowing now.

Ginger kissed her glowing cheek. "Was the North Pole completely wonderful?" she asked.

"Are you exhausted from the trip?" Roxie wanted to know.

"So, are you pregnant yet?" Bea seemed shocked that her question would be met with bug-eyed stares of disbelief. "I have money riding on this, you know."

A triplet of car-horn beeps caused the group to turn toward the street. Rick drove by, waving and blowing kisses to the group. "Teeny will be back in an hour, baby!" he shouted out.

"Okay, Rick!" Josie returned his kiss and waved. When the newlywed turned back toward her friends, a distracted smile played on her face.

Ginger sighed, wondering how it would feel to be so outrageously happy, so delirious with love.

"He drove you into the city?" Roxie asked.

"Yeah. He's going to bring Genghis and me into town early on Mondays, Wednesdays, and Fridays so we can keep our usual walking schedule. Isn't that thoughtful of him?"

Bea lifted an eyebrow. "That's a damned fine man you got there, Joze."

She giggled. "Yeah. I know. He's incredible."

"Huh. Take a look at that, would you?" Roxanne pointed toward Lilith and Genghis. Everyone went still, afraid to breathe or move or do anything that might upset the delicate balance at work.

Genghis licked Lilith's face in greeting, while Martina and HeatherLynn stood nearby as witnesses. Lilith didn't growl. She didn't snarl. She wasn't frothing at the mouth. Instead, she was happily licking Genghis in return, as much as was possible through her muzzle. Lilith was wagging her tail! These were all new developments.

"Holy shit," Bea whispered. "I thought she hated anything with a penis—you know, as a matter of principle."

"Shush!" Ginger hissed.

"This is incredible," Josie said. "Did I miss something with Lilith while I was gone? Did you start those behavior classes with Eli Gallagher?"

Roxanne's eyes flashed. "No! Why? Did Rick say something about what happened with Eli and me?"

Josie squinted. "Uh, no. I was just wondering about the change in Lilith's . . . you know . . . *personality.*"

Bea leaned close to Josie for effect. "You wouldn't know this, of course, seeing that you were kind of busy getting married and all," Bea said, "but Ginger and Roxie made a couple of new friends at your wedding."

Josie's eyes went big.

"Roxie met Eli and Ginger met Rico Suave," Bea said, her shoulders bouncing as she giggled.

Immediately, heat spread through Ginger's body. It felt as if she'd caught fire from the inside out. Of course, part of it was because she was pissed at Bea for bringing up Lucio the instant Josie got home. But most of it was just her usual response—whenever she thought of him, heard his name, or pictured him in her mind, she heated up. She couldn't control it. The man lit a flame in her.

"No kidding," Josie said, smiling kindly. She turned to Roxie. "So what happened between you and Eli? Rick certainly didn't mention it."

Roxie interrupted Lilith's breakthrough moment with a jerk on her leash. "Forget it. Let's walk, okay? You only have an hour, right?"

"Hey, wait." Josie placed her hand on Roxie's tensed-up forearm. "Are you okay? What's wrong?"

"It's nothing," she said, shaking her head.

"Hey, Rox, seriously, I was just teasing." Bea added her hand to Roxanne's arm. "I didn't know something had really happened between you two."

Ginger stayed back, listening. She had been readying herself to field questions from her friends about Lucio and his trip to the sexual buffet, but instead, Roxanne was on the hot seat. Ginger didn't even know Roxanne had something to get hot about.

"I asked him to join me for lunch a couple weeks ago," Roxie said. "His answer was no."

"What!" Ginger was shocked at the sound of her own outburst. "I mean, really? You asked him out?"

Roxanne nodded. "Yeah. It was stupid of me. He just seemed really nice and I thought I'd try."

Josie frowned. "He really turned you down?"

"That doesn't make any sense at all," Bea said, leaning back in bewilderment. "I saw the way he looked at you during the ceremony—he was the dog and you were the bone."

Roxie offered a weak smile. "Yeah, well, that's

what I thought, too. But we were both wrong, obviously."

Ginger frowned; then, as if on autopilot, she tapped her fingertips against her brow creases. God, how she wished she could stop doing that! How could she fully embrace her mature beauty if one of her hands was always busy patting and slapping at her wrinkles?

"Was it because of your Web site?" Ginger asked.

"Surprisingly, no," Roxie said with a laugh. "He thought that was kind of amusing."

"Then what?" Bea asked. "Is he in a relationship?"

"You could say that."

Josie laughed. "Stop being so cryptic, Rox! Why did Eli turn you down?"

"Well, at least he was honest about it," she said. "He told me he planned to be in California for only about a year. He said he was here to deal with some unfinished business with his father and he wouldn't have time to date."

Bea snorted. "Sounds like a load of bullshit to me."

A sudden burst of barking and growling made everyone jump. Roxanne pulled a now-snarling Lilith off Genghis, who slinked away, wild-eyed from the sting of betrayal.

"I guess she'd had enough of being nice," Roxanne said with a sigh. "Can't say I blame her."

The women continued their walk. Ginger broke the news to Josie that the *Herald* had fired her from her editor post the week before. Josie asked Ginger if she was okay, and Ginger assured her that yes, she was. In a soft whisper, Josie admitted she'd been fired, as well. The certified letter had been waiting for her when she picked up her mail from the post office.

"They fired you while you were on your honeymoon?" Bea was incredulous. "How low can you get?"

"You know you're next," Roxie said to Bea. "Sports and comics may be the last to go, but they'll go. We might as well admit it—newspapers are dead."

The women walked a few moments in silence, and Ginger thought it felt like their own private memorial service for the *San Francisco Herald*. "She was a grand old lady," Ginger said. "That job ended up being the longest and most fulfilling relationship of my life."

"She's been awfully good to me, too," Bea said.

"I really loved my job," Josie added.

"Fuck 'em," Roxanne said.

Ginger then steered the conversation to the honeymoon, and Josie enthusiastically regaled them with tales from her trip. It had been Josie's dream to travel to the North Pole ever since she wrote the obituary for Gloria Needleman's adventurer husband, Ira. When she mentioned this dream to Rick, he made elaborate plans to take her there for their honeymoon.

Josie told them that once they were aboard the nuclear-powered icebreaker out of Norway, the captain and crew were shocked to hear it was the couple's honeymoon. "Why?" the captain asked, perplexed. "I hear Florida is really quite nice." Josie described the thrill of setting foot on the precise geographic North Pole and talked about their private flight to view ringed seals, polar bears, and arctic fox. She explained the odd glow of Arctic twilight and their four days of "luxury" in an ice hotel in northern Sweden. "You haven't slept until you've slugged four shots of vodka, then crawled under a stack of reindeer hide," Josie said, laughing.

"I think I'll pass," Ginger said.

"The vodka part sounds okay," Bea said.

Josie's attention eventually turned to Ginger. "So what's this about Lucky Montevez?"

"Oh, it's nothing," Ginger said, bending down to retrieve HeatherLynn, who immediately curled up in the crook of her arm. "He's branching out into pet photography and said he'd take a portrait of me and Heather-Lynn."

Josie's eyes got big. "Seriously? Pet portraits? Are you sure about that?"

"Yes. Anyone else interested?" Ginger looked around the group. "He said he would appreciate me hooking him up with other clients."

"Interesting," Josie said, swinging Genghis's leash at her side while her dog ran free, her brain obviously hard at work. "So how well have you two gotten to know each other?"

Ginger pursed her lips, trying not to let the panic show on her face. That was an interesting way to frame her dilemma, wasn't it? She didn't know Lucio Montevez at all, but, oh, did she *know* him.

"We're casual acquaintances," Ginger said.

Bea snorted again. "Except for the part where he ripped off your dress and kissed you senseless."

"Puh-leeze!" Ginger tried to shout over Roxie's and Bea's laughter. She immediately turned her efforts to reassuring a startled-looking Josie.

"There's a perfectly logical explanation," Ginger said, tossing back her hair. "I should never have ordered my bridesmaid dress in a size four. It was too tight. I blacked out. Lucky—I mean *Lucio*—carried me to my room and unzipped my dress so that I could breathe. It was nothing."

Josie tried very hard to look unaffected. "Oh," she said. "Okay."

"I'm pretty sure I read a paperback with that exact

plot back in high school," Roxie said. "My mom didn't want me reading trashy romances so I kept them hidden in a gym bag with my old soccer cleats."

"Was it *Breathless Passion in His Arms*?" Josie asked, excited. "I read that one, too! It was my favorite!"

"No, no, no," Bea said, hardly able to stop herself from snorting in advance of her punch line. "The title was *The Night She Got Lucky*!"

Everyone laughed. Everyone but Ginger, who was thinking that the girls had no *flippin' idea* just how lucky she'd been. And they'd never know the truth. They couldn't *handle* the truth.

When Josie stopped giggling she shook her head in wonder. "My God," she said with a sigh. "I go on one measly little six-week honeymoon to the North Pole and all hell breaks loose."

To celebrate the end of Josh's all-liquid diet, Ginger told him she'd make him anything he wanted for dinner—anything soft. He said he wanted chicken enchiladas with rice and beans.

It would be her pleasure, she said.

The boys retreated to the family room to watch the 49ers exhibition game while Ginger cooked. Their game-watching included bouts of arguing, but at least it was at the usual decibel level and there were no sounds of fists striking flesh. Ginger had to admit it had been nice to see Jason treat his brother with deference these past ten days. She didn't delude herself, however. The kindness wouldn't last, especially since Joshua had been determined to suck every drop of benefit from his brother's guilty conscience. For a week now, Jason had not only been whipping up his brother's made-to-order smoothies, he'd also been doing Josh's laundry and making his bed. But now that

Josh had gotten the word that his teeth were fine and he could go back to real food, Ginger knew things would return to normal.

She opened the pantry and cursed under her breath. She usually kept a couple cans of organic refried beans on hand, but she couldn't seem to find them. Josh strolled into the kitchen as Ginger began to pull out cans of soup and tuna and jars of peanut butter.

"What you looking for, Mumu? Need help reaching something?"

Ginger smiled at her son, the future president of the United States, whose speech was markedly less slurred. "Refried beans. I thought for sure I bought some."

"Oh," Jason said, entering the kitchen behind his brother. "I think I ate 'em last night."

Ginger frowned, not recalling that she'd seen him make a snack. "Both cans? When was that?"

Jason shrugged. "I don't know—one or two in the morning, I guess, whenever it was I woke up starving. I heated them in the microwave and scooped them up with Cheetos and saltines."

Ginger shuddered at the thought. At least he'd cleaned up after himself.

"I'll go get some," Joshua said. "Be right back."

He was back in about ten minutes, two cans of refried beans in his hands. "Here you go, Mumu. How long till we eat?"

"Thanks, honey," she said, immediately rinsing off the lids and sticking them under the magnet of the electric can opener. "By the time you guys set the table and get your drinks, it'll be time to eat."

The doorbell rang. Both her sons looked out to the foyer quizzically. HeatherLynn let loose with a series of high-pitched yaps usually reserved for the most special occasions, such as the arrival of the FedEx man.

"See who that is, please, Jason."

Ginger dumped the beans into a pot and set them on low. With a wooden spoon she stirred in some shredded cheese, diced jalapeños, and salsa to add a little zing.

"Hey, Mom?" Jason called from the foyer.

"Who in the world is *that*?" Josh mumbled from behind Ginger's shoulder.

"Who is it, honey?" she called to Jason.

"*Buenos tardes,* Señora Garrison," said the sultry voice.

She dropped the wooden spoon to the floor. Refried beans splattered everywhere.

Unexpected. Fun. Entertaining. Charming. Ginger leaned back in her dining room chair and tried to think of how she'd describe this impromptu dinner with Lucio Montevez as the guest of honor. She'd need to come up with something, because, without a doubt, she'd be telling Josie, Roxie, and Bea about it on Monday morning's walk.

She hadn't seen her boys this animated in *years*. Joshua had been pumping Lucio for details about his travels and the heads of state and foreign officials he'd met over the years. Jason grilled Lucio for information on lenses, filters, and tripods—things Ginger didn't even know he had an interest in.

HeatherLynn had curled up in Lucio's lap soon after they'd sat down at the table and she hadn't budged since. Lucio occasionally stroked her ears, her head, her back. The little dog looked like she'd died and gone to heaven.

Every once in a while, Lucio would pull away from conversation with the boys and give Ginger a smile or nod. She didn't know him well enough to be sure, but he seemed to be conveying to her that he liked her kids and was enjoying himself.

One thing Lucio didn't leave open to interpretation was his opinion of her cooking. "This is exquisite," he said, helping himself to a third chicken enchilada. "Do you cook this extravagantly every night?"

Ginger chuckled. She'd never seen canned beans and enchiladas made with grocery-store rotisserie chicken as extravagant. "What do you usually eat, Lucio?" she asked.

"Ah, well, that is not a simple answer." He thought about it as he served the boys an extra enchilada each. "I eat what is on the menu wherever I am. When I'm in San Francisco, that means anything and everything I want—Chinese, Greek, Spanish even."

"What about when you're on assignment?" Jason asked.

"Yes, well, then it can be a handful of nuts and a drink from my canteen if that's all that's available. Depending on my location, eating can be the biggest adventure of all."

"You mean you've eaten some weird shii—" Jason's eyes flashed toward Ginger as he stopped himself in mid-profanity. "You've eaten some weird stuff, right?"

"Oh, yes."

Jason propped his elbows on the table and leaned in, fascinated. "Like what? What was the strangest thing you've ever eaten? Pig brains? Goat feet?"

"How about refried beans and saltines?" Josh asked, laughing.

"I ate that last night," Jason explained to Lucio, looking embarrassed.

"Hmm." Lucio smiled at Ginger again and stroked HeatherLynn's fur. The bichon looked perfectly content. "Well, I remember that once on the island of Okinawa I ate a live octopus."

"Live?" Josh's eyes nearly popped out of his head.

"As I recall, it was more of a wrestling match than a dinner." Lucio laughed at the boys' horrified looks. "The creature bit my tongue on the way down. I'd probably do the same if someone tried to eat me alive."

"Whoa," Jason said, gulping.

Joshua's face lit up. "What else?"

"There were those bamboo worms in Laos," Lucio said, as if he were going down a checklist in his mind. "Quite crunchy, I recall. A hog-ear salad in Vietnam. Moose-bone soup in the Alaskan interior. Oh, and the reindeer herders of northwestern Russia make a mean ptarmigan stew."

Jason looked slightly green. "I don't even know what a ptarmigan is, and I'm afraid to ask."

"It's in the grouse family," Joshua told him impatiently. "Anything else?" he asked Lucio.

"Well, let me see . . ." He silently checked in with Ginger to see if it was all right to continue. She smiled at him, though she felt slightly green around the gills. Lucio seemed reenergized with the go-ahead. "Boiled fish eyeballs off the coast of Mexico. Ants in Zimbabwe. Fried sheep testicles in Iowa."

"Whoa," Joshua said.

"Okay, I think we get the picture," Jason said, swallowing hard.

Ginger sighed. "That certainly explains why you thought my enchiladas were extravagant," she said.

Everyone laughed.

The boys wanted to know more about Lucio's work

at *Geographica* magazine—where he'd studied photography, how he'd been hired, the kinds of stories he photographed, and his favorite adventures.

Lucio talked a long while before he told the boys he had a thousand stories, and that he'd share more later. But he said there was one thing he wanted them to understand. "The job of a nature photographer used to be to capture the wonder and beauty our world has to offer, but lately the job is to capture it one last time before it is gone forever. It is the only story worth telling these days, but still, few people want to listen."

"I do," Joshua said, his face solemn.

"Then we will have much to talk about," Lucio said, smiling at him.

"So why is it you came back to the States?" Jason asked.

With that last question, Ginger noticed Lucio's demeanor grow even more serious. His shoulders, usually level and held high, dipped under the weight of the topic.

"I ran into some legal and political problems in China, and had to come back to the States to try to sort it all out."

"What happened?" Ginger asked. Lucio shut his eyes, which made her momentarily regret her inquiry. "I'm sorry for asking that—it isn't any of our business. You don't have to answer."

Lucio's eyes opened and he locked his gaze on hers. His dark irises swirled with emotion. "Oh, but I have nothing to hide. I have done nothing wrong." He turned to the boys. "Someone took my raw video footage and delivered it to the Chinese government, then managed to submit several false expense claims on my magazine account. They even forged my signature."

Lucio shrugged and looked at Ginger again. "I was accused of spying and stealing. I got kicked out of the country and lost my *Geographica* contract."

Ginger's spine straightened. The boys looked excited.

"So you're a *spy*?" Joshua asked, practically drooling at the prospect of having a secret agent at their dining room table.

Lucio laughed. "I just take pictures. And I'm not a thief, either, though no one seems to believe me. So now I must pay back the money and start again."

"Do you know who did it?" Joshua asked.

"I have a few ideas, and someday soon my name will be cleared."

With that offhand comment, the events of the last few weeks began to make sense to Ginger. This was why Lucio had suddenly decided to switch to pet portraits—he needed the money. The concept may have originated as a pickup line at Rick and Josie's wedding, but now Lucio was desperate. That's why he had showed up at her house a couple weeks ago. It had nothing to do with her and everything to do with him making a few bucks.

Uggghhh. Ginger's tasty enchiladas had suddenly turned to rock in her belly. Men! Who was she fooling? Lucio Montevez was not one of the point-one percent of decent men left in the world. He was just like all the others.

Ginger began to stack plates and silverware to clear the table.

"I will do this," Lucio said. "Please, *bonita*. You have done too much already." She watched as Lucio took HeatherLynn in his arms and rose from his chair. He walked through to the living room and headed right toward the dog's bed by the fireplace. He placed her on her pillow, as if he'd done it a million times before.

How did he know to do that?

"We'll help," Jason said, and the boys jumped up and followed Lucio into the kitchen, stacks of dishes in their hands.

Ginger sat alone at the table, trying to get her mind to sort out all the inconsistencies. Okay, she could believe Lucio wasn't a spy or a thief. She'd give him that much. And she believed he was who he said he was, because Rick Rousseau was his friend, and Rick was the most stand-up guy she'd ever encountered.

And the boys sure seemed to like him.

And HeatherLynn obviously loved him.

But what, exactly, was happening between the two of them—Lucio and Ginger? That was where it got muddled.

She'd allowed herself to believe there really was something to the feelings she had for him. She'd let herself think his kiss and caress delivered such a thrill because he was special. She really thought all the heat and passion she felt were somehow linked to destiny. She'd considered the possibility that he'd been waiting for her, just as Mrs. Needleman had predicted.

But what if all that sexy sweetness was an act, a sales pitch? A sales pitch from a desperate guy prone to stretching the truth?

The sound of her boys' laughter jarred her from her thoughts. Ginger rose from the table and peeked around the pocket doors that were open to the kitchen. Lucio was elbow-deep in a sink full of suds, scrubbing out the casserole pan. The boys were loading the dishwasher, continuing their barrage of questions, including one from Jason about whether he could work as Lucio's assistant.

"I would be honored, if it is all right with your parents," he said.

"So if you got framed for spying and stealing, why did you get the nickname 'Lucky'?" Joshua asked.

Lucio's laughter rose up into the air along with the steam from the sink of hot water. He finished rinsing the pan and shook his head, still chuckling. "It is a very long story that will have to wait for another time, I'm afraid." He dried his hands on a towel. "I wanted to talk with your mother. Can you finish up in here?"

"Sure," Jason said.

"No problem," Joshua said.

Ginger rushed back to her chair and casually crossed her legs, trying to appear lost in thought. When Lucio entered the dining room, he was rolling down his sleeves and buttoning his cuffs. She got a peek of the dark olive skin of his forearms, the sprinkling of dark hair, the thick twist of muscle and bone.

The heat was back. In spite of everything—including the very real possibility that Lucio might have the personality of a used-car salesman—Ginger felt the heat flare inside her. The idea that she couldn't control her reaction to him made her frown. She reached up and patted her fingertips on her brow.

"Is something the matter, *guapa*?"

"No. Why?" Ginger stiffened.

"Because you are tapping your forehead. Is it a headache?"

Ginger ripped her hand away from her head and she shoved it between her crossed thighs. "I'm fine."

"I could not help but notice you have a lovely garden. Can we walk for a moment, do you think?" He held out his hand to her.

He must have seen her eyes dart to the kitchen because he said, "I will not keep you from your sons for very long, but there is something important I must discuss with you."

She looked up at him. His eyes were dark and his lids heavy. A gentle smile played on his lips. His cheekbones were bold and his beard stubble looked rough. Of course she felt heat in his presence. It was perfectly understandable. He was the sexiest man she'd ever laid eyes on in her life, and she might be forty, but she hadn't completely flatlined. Not yet, anyway.

Ginger let out a helpless little moan. She didn't intend to. When it came to Lucio Montevez, there were many things she didn't intend that happened anyway.

"Please. Come with me." His hand reached for her.

The offer was much like the one she received weeks ago in Sonoma Valley. She'd refused his hand that night. But tonight, in her home and with her boys in the next room, she knew she would accept. For reasons she could not even begin to fathom, the words of Mrs. Needleman began to waft through her mind. *You must listen to your heart, Genevieve, not your fear.*

"Oh, sure. Why not?" Ginger said. She reached up and Lucio was there to catch her hand. His palm was still warm and damp. His grip was confident but gentle. He pulled her to a stand, and her knees were so weak she nearly fell into him.

Swooning could do that to a girl.

CHAPTER 7

Lucio had not meant to take a meal with the Garrisons. He had not even known that Ginger's sons would be at her house that evening. Stupid of him! He knew nothing of the woman and her life, so he'd walked right into the middle of a cozy family evening. It was the last thing he'd expected, and the last thing he'd wanted. But his intentions no longer mattered. He'd ended up sharing a feast with the family, and now everything was far more complicated.

Lucio had long ago perfected the ability to manage garden-variety lust. It was simple, really. He just had to remain detached emotionally while hooking up physically. It required balance. Lucio would give the woman enough of himself that he wouldn't seem distant, and accept a large enough portion of the woman's affection so that she would feel needed. But no gifts. No promises for the future. No "I love yous." Certainly no meals with the woman's family.

And up until that evening, that was all Lucio had had with Ginger Garrison—lust. Granted, it was an unusually strong kind of lust. It was a lust so forceful it made his thoughts fuzzy and his blood hot—but, at its core, it had been only lust.

Until now.

Lucio had enjoyed himself thoroughly. He liked the Garrison twins more than he would have anticipated. They were spoiled American boys, yes, but they were smart and funny and interested in the bigger world. Lucio could work with that.

The meal was delicious. The home was comfortable and gracious. He'd laughed more that night than he had in many months. He enjoyed the way the little spoiled dog felt curled up on his lap.

And oh, how he liked sitting next to Ginger.

So it pained him to know what she was thinking. At some point during the meal, Ginger had decided his interest in her was only financial. He'd seen the realization hit her, taking the light right out of her eyes. She believed he was after her money to help repay the stolen funds and that anything else they'd shared was a ruse.

The thought was so wrong it was funny, but Lucio now had to decide if he wished to correct the misunderstanding. That was his problem, and it was a big one.

Lucio glanced to his side, just to watch Ginger walk. She created a pretty profile—a straight, small nose, a delicate chin, and lovely full lips. Her skin was much paler than his own, but tinged with a warm undertone and a few scattered freckles, especially on her chest. Ginger was long and lean and curvy in precisely the right places. She was a graceful woman.

He took a moment to really think this through: If Ginger thought he was only after her money, then she would hold him at arm's length. She would pay him his fee and might give him the names of potential clients and then leave it at that. And that's what he wanted, yes? He wanted to sort out his professional difficulties and resume his life. He was itching to get out of San Francisco and back on the road, yes?

Lucio peeked down at where Ginger's hand had slipped into his. Her fingers were long and elegant, like the rest of her. Like her arms. Her neck. Her—

"What are you thinking about, Lucio?" Her question jarred him from his private inventory.

"I am sorry, señora. You'll have to forgive me, but I am not like many men."

She chuckled. "No kidding."

He squeezed her hand and smiled. "What I mean is that I experience everything through my eyes. I understand my world by the light, the line, the composition and form. I was admiring how all those elements come together in you. It is pure pleasure to look at you. That's what I was thinking."

Her cheeks flushed. Their eyes locked. And suddenly, Lucio realized the woman at his side was nearly as tall as he was, that he could hold his head high and be looking directly into her eyes. He smiled.

"What are you, about one hundred eighty-two centimeters?" he asked.

Ginger's head snapped back. She looked offended. *"What?"*

"Your height. How tall are you?"

"Oh." She relaxed a little. "I'm pretty tall. About five ten without shoes, but I have no idea what the metric conversion is for that."

Lucio grinned, suddenly understanding what had made her uncomfortable. "You thought I had asked about your weight?"

Ginger shrugged.

"Bonita, whatever your weight is, it is perfect. Your height is perfect. Your body and face are perfect. Your hair is perfect."

She looked askance at him. "Uh-huh."

He laughed. Inexplicably, Ginger seemed uncomfortable with this line of conversation. It made no sense. How could a woman as exquisite as Ginger Garrison not want a man to admire her? In Lucio's experience, beautiful women of every culture couldn't get enough of that, unless, of course, they didn't believe it themselves.

That could not be the case with Ginger, Lucio decided. It would be ridiculous.

"You know you are a stunning woman, yes?" He asked this politely, without accusation. He wanted to see how she'd react. But she said nothing. "Ginger?"

She turned to him, a big smile on her face. "I love the way you just said that."

"Said what?"

"My name!" She laughed. "I don't think I've ever heard you say it before, because you're always calling me *señora* or *guava* or *peliglobo* or something."

It was Lucio's turn to laugh. "*Pelirroja*. It means redheaded. And it's *guapa,* which means 'lovely lady,' the same as *bonita*."

"Oh."

"But what is so funny about how I say 'Ginger'?"

She laughed again. "Your accent makes it sound like 'Jeen-jair,' is all. It's actually kind of cute."

Lucio frowned, not certain he liked the idea of sounding cute. He had never once aspired to be cute.

"My real name would probably be easier for you to pronounce," she suggested.

Lucio shook his head in confusion. "Ginger is not your real name?"

"No. Ginger is the same as 'Lucky' is for you. It's my nickname. My given name is Genevieve."

Lucio stopped walking. They had strolled from the

back patio down a flagstone walkway into what the Americans called "the yard," but he could not move another inch. He was astounded by that name—it suited her perfectly. So sensual. So regal.

"Genevieve," he said.

"Yes." She tilted her head and smiled. "Now *that* sounds very nice rolling off your tongue."

Lucio took a quick glance toward the house, trying to determine which windows might correspond with which rooms. He saw no youthful male faces pressed to the glass and decided he would risk it. He had no choice. He had to kiss her.

Lucio grabbed that beautiful, warm face in his hands and covered that mouth with his.

He gave himself wholly to the kiss and to the earnestness of her response. It was then that Lucio decided he might as well admit it to himself—there was something incredibly special about Genevieve Garrison. She fit him. She made him hum inside. She lit a fire in him the likes of which he'd never before experienced. He wanted to pull her so close and tight that there would be no space between them. He wanted to say her name over and over.

"Genevieve," he whispered, dragging his kisses over her nose and cheeks and chin. "Genevieve, Genevieve, *mi corazón*." When he kissed her throat she gasped.

"I don't know what is happening to me, Lucio," she whimpered. "What is this? Tell me what this is."

Lucio laughed, still planting kisses all over her face, in her hair. "Truly, I do not know. But it is something very powerful." He kept kissing. "I think we should pay attention to it."

"Me, too." She reached up behind his back and pulled his mouth to hers again. "Kiss me again."

"Wait. Stop. *Un momento.*" Lucio grabbed her by the shoulders and steadied her in front of him. "I need to tell you something before we go any further."

Genevieve's face fell. All the pleasure he'd seen there only seconds before had vanished. He did not even give her time to ask.

"No, no, no." Lucio shook his head, knowing what critical bit of information she sought. "I was married once, for three weeks, when I was still a boy. I have never been married since."

One of Genevieve's carefully groomed eyebrows arched high above a hazel eye. "All right. So you were going to tell me you're leaving the country next week."

He laughed. "Impossible."

Genevieve nodded slowly, as if further discussion were unnecessary. "Okay. So you want me to understand that if you weren't in trouble, you wouldn't even be here. Is that right?"

Lucio said nothing.

"You wouldn't be in San Francisco unless you absolutely had to be. You wouldn't have been at Rick and Josie's wedding. Or at my house tonight. I would never have met you if you hadn't had all those problems with the magazine."

"What you say is likely true."

Ginger chuckled bitterly, raking her fingers through her thick red hair. "Great. So you want me to understand that you'll take as many pet portraits as necessary to get your money, and then you'll be on your way."

He blinked.

"Ha! That's it, isn't it?" Genevieve pulled away from Lucio and crossed her arms protectively under her breasts. Whenever she did that it only caused Lucio's blood to boil further. What was he going to do with this woman, with everything he was feeling? How could starting a relationship with her possibly be good for anyone?

"You got me, Genevieve." Lucio smiled. "That was my initial plan."

She lowered her eyes to the ground.

"But no longer." Lucio tapped his fingertip against the underside of her chin, lifting her gaze to his. "I've changed my mind, *guapa*."

"Why?"

"Because of you. Because of how I feel whenever I see you. I cannot control myself. That is unusual for me."

Genevieve laughed. "It's unusual for me, too."

"But you feel it, yes? You feel something very strong between us, yes?"

"Yes," she whispered.

"Then we need to have a new plan." Lucio reached for her hand again, guiding her back toward the house. "I will court you, yes? I know this is not Spain. I know I've never before cared about going about things the right way. I know you're a grown woman in her thirties. But I would still like to ask your father for permission to court you. How might I reach him?"

Genevieve froze. She swallowed hard. "My father passed away a few years ago," she said quietly.

"I am so sorry, *mi amor*," Lucio said. "Your mother?"

Genevieve frowned. "Oh, boy."

"What?"

"My mother lives in Los Angeles, but trust me, she'd be thrilled that I was dating you. She might even try to steal you from me." Oddly, Genevieve began the strange tapping of her fingers against her brow again. He had seen her do this several times, and it baffled him.

"Something is wrong. What is it?"

"What?" She looked surprised, but continued to pat her face. "Nothing's wrong. Why do you say that?"

"Because of this *tap-tap-tap* you do on your face." Lucio mimicked her by patting his own forehead rapidly. "Is it a nervous tic of some sort? A disorder?"

Genevieve's hand fell to her side, her eyes locked on him but revealing nothing. "Just a second ago you said I was a woman in my thirties."

Lucio shrugged. "I am thirty-nine, myself, *bonita*. I was just guessing. You are obviously younger than me."

Again, her eyes revealed nothing. Her mouth was set firmly. Eventually she spoke. "Exactly how old do you think I am?" Genevieve waited for an answer, but by then, Lucio had realized he'd stumbled into the bramble bushes of the female ego. He decided it would be best to step away before he was scratched bloody.

"It does not matter, Genevieve."

"I'd like a number," she said.

Lucio laughed. "Why in heaven do you need a number? It isn't important, *guapa*! What are you afraid of?"

She said nothing, but her eyes narrowed ever so slightly.

"Ah. I see," Lucio said with a nod. "You do not wish me to know that you were a very young mother." He shrugged. "This is not a problem for me. All of us make mistakes when we are teenagers. I certainly did. There is nothing to be embarrassed about."

With that, Genevieve began walking again— marching, really—right up to the back patio door. As much as Lucio enjoyed watching Señora Garrison from behind, this was not the time to let her get away.

"Genevieve!" He ran to her side and grabbed her arm. "Stop! What is wrong?"

She turned to him then, her face twisted in sadness and streaked with tears. That familiar pang hit his heart. This grown woman had a child's sensitivity, a vulnerability he had yet to comprehend. He'd sensed that he'd need to proceed gently with her, but until that very moment, he hadn't appreciated how delicate an assignment it would be.

Just then, Lucio knew that when it came to Genevieve Garrison, he would need every bit of the expertise he'd amassed in twenty years of travel to unknown lands. It would take a sharp mind, a facility for diplomacy, patience, skill, and a sense of adventure.

"I am forty freakin' years old," she said in a tense whisper. "I am older than you, Lucio. I am going through menopause. Very soon now, things are going to start falling and stop working. I'm going to need a face-lift and an eye job and Botox injections. You should probably leave before it all goes to hell."

Lucio's lower jaw fell, leaving his mouth gaping open. So this was what the *tap-tap-tap* was about! This was why she was uncomfortable with compliments! It was shocking. "But—"

She didn't let him continue. "Forget it. You thought I was in my thirties. You were attracted to a woman you thought was still in her thirties."

"I am attracted to *you*—not your age." He said it simply, with no hint of reprimand. He only wanted her to believe him.

Genevieve closed her eyes.

Who could have put these ideas in her head? he wondered. It was a tragedy! What kind of monster could have convinced this magnificent woman that she needed to go under the surgeon's blade? Who the devil could have done her such a disservice?

"GINGER!"

Lucio watched her eyes fly open. "Oh, hell," she whispered.

The booming male voice echoed from the front of the house, followed by a door slam. Lucio heard the boys' voices grow louder as they came toward the kitchen.

"I need a moment to deal with this. Would you mind very much waiting out here on the patio?"

"Of course," Lucio said. "I will be right here if you need me."

"Thanks." With that, Genevieve turned, stomped across the patio, and flung open the French doors. Lucio took a seat in one of the outdoor dining chairs, and turned it so that he had a clear view of the kitchen interior reflected in the half-open door.

"Hello, Larry," he heard Genevieve say.

Clearly, the tall blond man was Genevieve's ex-husband and the father of her boys. Obviously, this was none of Lucio's affair, but he decided to observe, just as a precaution. The man had raised his voice, after all.

"You just don't know where to stop, do you?" the ex-husband said, pointing to Genevieve. "This is an outrage!"

She reached for her boys, who stared at their father in fascination. "Go to your rooms, guys. I'll deal with your dad."

"Hell no!" Larry shouted. "I want them to stay put so they can hear about how low you've stooped, Ginger. They have a right to know about their mother's deranged kleptomania!"

Nothing. That was what Lucio heard next—a whole lot of nothing.

"Have you completely lost it, Larry?" Ginger eventually asked. "You just barged into *my* home like a psycho and scared the hell out of everybody! Whatever your issue is with me, I'm happy to talk with you about it, but this is—"

"You're just never satisfied, are you?" Larry asked, interrupting her. "The alimony wasn't enough. The house wasn't enough! The money I set aside for the boys' education wasn't enough. The fact that I pay their health insurance wasn't enough! So you demand more and more and more and get your lawyer on my ass! And now, this! This . . . this . . . travesty!"

"I think you should go, Dad," Joshua said, taking a step closer to Larry.

"I'll walk you to your car," Jason said, reaching for his father's arm.

With a wild swing, Larry pulled it away from his grasp. "Get your hands off me!"

With that, Lucio realized the father was drunk. He jumped out of the chair and was headed to the kitchen where he planned to knock the fool silly and drag his ass into the street. Genevieve beat him to it, however.

Crack! The sound of her palm against Larry's face put an end to the man's idiotic ranting. Lucio knew from experience that her smack stung like the devil. He stepped to the side of the doorway, out of sight.

"Get out, Larry," Genevieve said between clenched teeth.

"You took my beans." The ex-husband straightened his shoulders when he said that, and sniffed in defiance. "You entered my house illegally and stole my canned goods."

Lucio watched Genevieve turn to her boys. The mother and sons stared at one another in silence, as if confirming that they'd all heard the same bizarre statement.

"What are you talking about, Dad?" Jason eventually asked.

"I am talking about the fact that your mother—whom I continue to support out of the kindness of my heart and to my own detriment—had the nerve to break into my home at some point during the day and steal two cans of refried beans."

Lucio almost laughed. There was something very odd about this conversation, but who was he to judge? It reminded him of when he was on assignment photographing the puberty rites of the Baniva people of the Orinoco River Valley. He hadn't understood their elaborate ritual, nor did he approve of it, but that didn't make it wrong. In the case of the Garrison tribe, Lucio knew nothing about the ex-husband, or his mental history, or his relationship with his ex-wife. As long as it didn't turn abusive, he had no right to interfere. But the fact remained that it was quite entertaining.

"Excuse me?" Genevieve seemed shocked by the accusation.

"You deny it?" Larry staggered around a bit, dipping his hand into his front pocket. For an instant, Lucio feared he was reaching for a weapon and prepared to rush inside to tackle the man, but Larry pulled out a set of keys. They looked familiar.

"I found your keys on my kitchen counter, Ginger. The pantry door was left open. I did an inventory. I am missing two cans of Annie's Organic Kitchen refried beans." With that, Larry jangled the keys in her face for effect. "Give me back my beans or I'm calling the police."

Lucio watched as Genevieve slowly turned to Joshua. Her son shrugged, looking guilty.

"I thought you went to the corner market for those beans, Josh," she said.

"Uh, no. I went over to Dad's. It's closer."

Genevieve rolled her eyes.

"That's sick," Larry said. "You would actually send your child to do your dirty work? Incredible! Beyond the pale!"

Genevieve grabbed her keys from Larry's hand. "Jason, get my purse. Joshua, get the cans out of the recycle bin and bring them to me. *Now*."

The boys did as she directed, scurrying off in opposite directions. While they were gone, Genevieve stood firmly in front of Larry and shook her head in disgust. "You're a mess, Larry."

"She left me," he mumbled, rubbing his hands through his mussed-up hair. "She was so young and so beautiful! She was so fun! So incredibly, unbelievably young!" He scowled when he realized he'd repeated himself. "I guess I was good enough to go to Maui with but not good enough to date once we got back to town! It's so unfair!"

"Gee, sorry to hear all that." Genevieve grabbed her purse from Jason as he ran up, holding it out to her. Joshua returned with the cans. "What is the price on each of those cans?" she asked him.

Joshua studied the labels. "Looks like one dollar and ninety-five cents each," he said.

Genevieve opened her wallet and pulled out a five-dollar bill, which she folded and stuck into Larry's front pants pocket. He looked confused.

"That will cover the cost of the beans with a little extra for your mental anguish." Then she grabbed the cans from Joshua and shoved them at her ex-husband. "Here you go. I wouldn't want to deprive you of your recycling refund."

Lucio lost his battle. He snickered. He could not help it. The dialogue was funnier than any BBC farce he'd ever seen.

"Who the fuck is that?" Larry pointed a can out toward the patio. "Who's out there?"

Lucio stepped forward, then moved inside the doorway to stand next to Genevieve and the boys. "Hello, Señor Garrison. My name is Lucio Montevez. I am a photographer here to take a portrait of Genevieve and her dog."

Larry scrunched up his nose and mouth, obviously having trouble processing the information Lucio had just shared. "Huh?" Larry asked. "Did you just call her *Genevieve*? What the fu—?"

"Let's go, Dad," Jason said, turning his father around so that he faced the hallway that would lead to the foyer and front door. "Lucio said I could work as his photographer's assistant. Isn't that cool?"

Larry spun out of his son's grip, then lurched toward Lucio. "You have no right to be in my home," he said, waving around one of the cans. "I didn't build this place from the ground up so that some greasy Italian pretty boy could come in here and put his hands on my wife and take pictures of my dog and pretend to be some kind of fucking mentor to my boys! They don't need a father figure! They have *me*!"

"Of course," Lucio said.

Larry was not done. "That's *my* dog you're talking about, Fabio! *My* wife! *My* boys! *My* house!" His face became flushed. "Just who the hell do you think you are? You'll never fit into Larry Garrison's shoes!"

Joshua went to his father's other side. Together, the teenagers dragged him down the hall to the door. Larry, however, wanted one last word, and managed to swivel free again. He straightened an arm and glared down the barrel of the empty can pointed directly at Lucio. "I've never trusted Italians," he said.

"I have always felt fortunate to be a Spaniard," Lucio said.

"Same thing," Larry said.

At that instant, little HeatherLynn decided to join the party. She toddled up to Larry, stretching out her front paws while raising her rump, then let go with a big, wide yawn.

"See?" Larry said, nodding toward the dog with pride. "She knows I'm her master."

With that, the little doggie sniffed at Larry's loafer, then squatted, shooting a hard and straight stream of urine directly onto the shoe's squared leather toe. Then she ran into the sitting room and dove under the sofa.

Larry was in shock. The only sound he made was a high squeak of disbelief as he raised his foot above the puddle. The boys turned him around and led him out the door and down the drive, walking right past a shiny new black Porsche convertible in the driveway. The boys were smart not to let him get behind the wheel.

"We'll be back in a few minutes, Mom!" Josh called out.

While they watched the boys navigate their father down the sidewalk, Lucio draped an arm over Genevieve's shoulder.

She sighed, curling her arm around his waist. "Well, you've just met my former husband, Dr. Lawrence Hutchins Garrison the Third. He's the chief of urology at University Hospital."

Lucio nodded. "In those shoes, he most certainly is."

She laughed. "You know, Larry's not a horrible guy . . . not all the time, anyway. He was in rare form tonight, and I'm sorry you had to see him like that."

Lucio leaned into Genevieve and hugged her tight to his side. "I have seen most of life's grand spectacle, *bonita*. I can handle one drunk and disorderly ex-husband."

She looked him square in the eye. "Are you sure about that?"

"I am sure."

"What about two wild fifteen-year-old boys?" Genevieve asked.

"They are good kids. I look forward to getting to know them."

"And a badly behaved bichon frise?"

"She has extremely good aim."

"And me? A forty-year-old, jobless, menopausal crone?"

Lucio would not laugh at her, no matter how preposterous she sounded. Ridicule was the last thing she needed. So he turned and gathered Genevieve into his arms, pressed her head to his shoulder, and held her tight against him.

"Be still, Genevieve," he whispered to her. "Lean against me and be still a moment."

Lucio inhaled the sweet fragrance of her hair, smiling to himself. Who, really, had he been advising with those words? Genevieve, or himself? Lucio felt her heart beat against him and her breath against his neck. Could it be that after all the years of adventure— all the exotic locations he'd seen and all the people he'd encountered—that he'd finally found a place where he wanted to be still? All he knew was there had never been a woman who touched his heart the way Genevieve had, or presented a challenge that called to him so clearly.

He could feel the upheaval as it swept through him. The elements of his universe were being jumbled, rearranged. Right at that moment.

Possibly forever.

Of course there would be his work. There would always be his work. He could not imagine a world without the light and the lens. There was his reputation to save, the Erskine Prize to hold in his hands, and money to make. And soon, he would track down whoever had messed with him and get the justice he deserved.

But all those things had just been bumped down in importance, replaced by this beautiful woman with the damaged spirit and two boys on the verge of manhood.

Genevieve's ex-husband had it so very wrong. Jason and Joshua *did* need a father figure in their lives—one who wasn't a self-centered buffoon. Genevieve most definitely needed the touch of a man who adored her, the encouragement of a man who believed in her. Perhaps then she'd be able to see her own strength and beauty.

But the last thing Lucio intended to do was step into Larry's pissed-upon shoes.

He would make his own way.

CHAPTER 8

About a half hour later, Lucio finished the last of his espresso. The sun had set, leaving the backyard in shadows. Ginger knew the boys would be busting through the front door at any minute and she was fidgety. She could barely look at Lucio sitting there, across from her at the outdoor patio table, his dark eyes penetrating her soul, his long and muscular body stretched out in one of her wrought-iron chairs.

"I really wish you didn't have to go," she told him, her voice sounding embarrassingly breathless.

"I don't want to go, but I think it's best if I don't force my presence on your sons. I don't want them to feel threatened in any way."

She sighed, knowing she should be grateful that Lucio was concerned about her sons' well-being. He was a sweet man. So kind. So understanding. So why did she want to scream?

Because if she didn't get his naked sex-panther body in her bed in the next five minutes she'd die.

No! Keep it together, Ginger. She ran a hand across her forehead in angst. How horrible would it be for her sons to come home and hear her squealing and panting in pleasure, behind her locked bedroom door?

Because that's what she'd be doing—no question about it. With Lucio Montevez, there would be plenty of squealing and panting involved.

She began to perspire. Another hot flash, no doubt.

"We have plenty of time, *bonita*." Lucio brushed his fingertip down her forearm. "We will take our time with each other, savor each other. The next time your sons are staying with their father, we will spend the entire day together—the entire weekend. We will start this right."

Naked. Hot and thoroughly naked and pushing up against her, nudging hard into her body.

Ginger let out a desperate little squeak.

"I am impatient, too," Lucio said, cradling her hand. "But how many times have we gotten started only to have to stop? The Host! If that happens one more time I think I will explode!"

Ginger swallowed. "Tell me about it. I'm afraid if that happens again something will break and it will never work right again."

Lucio laughed. The sound of his laughter was one of the most joyous things Ginger had ever heard. She wanted to wrap herself up in his laugh and roll around in it. Naked.

Stop!

She groaned in exasperation as she got up from the patio table. "Maybe you should just go." She gathered the demitasse cups and saucers and they rattled around in her unsteady grip. "This is torture. I'm coming unglued."

Ginger headed into the house, Lucio following. He held open the French doors for her, and she could feel the energy zapping from his body into hers, the way it did whenever he was close. And he was very close at that moment. Inches from her back. This was crazy, she thought. She walked faster. She reached the kitchen counter. He was still right behind her.

She set the dishes in the sink. He was on her. Up against her. She felt his hands cup her hips, then slide across her belly, his palms and fingers cradling her. She felt him, hard and long and pressing up against her bottom.

"I will say good night, then." He whispered into her ear. "I cannot have you tonight, but I want you to think of me as you fall asleep. I want you to dream of me. Can you do that, Genevieve?"

"Sure," she squeaked. "I'll give it a try."

He chuckled into her ear, and the movement of his body caused his erection to jump around on her butt. She could do nothing but lean her head back onto his shoulder in surrender. Her knees were wobbly again. Swooning was inevitable. The only thing that kept her upright was the pressure of his hands against her lower belly, and the support of his body behind her.

"I want you to dream of me being all over you, *pelirroja*. I'm going to gather you up, eat you, slurp you, kiss you, nibble on you, get my fingers and tongue up inside you."

She mewled.

"Then I'm going to take you, Genevieve."

Her knees began to give out. His hands caught her, grabbing hold of her breasts, and she slid lower.

"*Ohmigod,*" she breathed.

The phone rang.

Lucio helped her regain her footing. Ginger somehow managed to stumble to the cordless phone on the kitchen table. Her eyes flashed to Lucio as she picked it up and answered.

"Hello?"

"Mom, it's Jason."

"Hey, honey." She turned away from Lucio's dark stare. She couldn't take its intensity—both her breath and heartbeat were erratic. "Is everything okay with your dad?"

"He's passed out in bed."

"My God, is he breathing?"

"Snoring."

"Oh. That's good."

"So we were wondering, do you think we could stay over here tonight with him?"

Ginger spun around, catching Lucio staring at her ass. She didn't mind. Not one bit.

"Mom?"

"Uh-huh?"

"Is that okay? I know it's supposed to be your night, but Josh and I figured Dad should have someone with him. He's blubbering about some chick who dumped him."

Ginger's eyes went wide in comprehension. The boys weren't coming back tonight! She and Lucio were free to—

"Mom?"

Lucio swept his eyes up the front of her body, taking his time, then locked his gaze with hers. He smiled at her, sliding one hand into a front jeans pocket.

"Oh, yeah," Ginger whispered into the phone.

"Is everything all right? You sound kind of weird."

Lucio took a few steps toward her. She leaned back against the stove.

"Everything's fine," she said. "Great."

"Okay, so we'll see you tomorrow?"

"Sure. See you tomorrow."

Lucio immediately got it—the rules had just changed. His smile disappeared. His gaze darkened and his eyelids lowered to half-mast. He began to advance toward her, with a purpose. He was stalking her, his body coiled and ready, her own personal sexual panther about to move in for the kill.

"The next time you see Lucio, would you ask him when I can start as his assistant?"

Ginger gulped. "Absolutely," she managed, not sure for how many more seconds she'd be capable of speech. The pit of her stomach ached with need. She tingled between her legs. Her nipples were hard and poking at the fabric of her blouse. She'd begun to pant. She decided she might as well have been wearing a nametag that said, HELLO, MY NAME IS GINGER AND I'M IN HEAT.

"Are you working out on the treadmill, Mom?"

"Huh?" Ginger began to slide her bottom across the front of the stove, along the edge of the countertop, then around the corner into the dining room. She took a few steps backward, holding the phone to her ear with a shaky hand.

"Are you exercising? You sound out of breath."

"Yeah. That's great, honey. I love you guys and I'll see you both tomorrow." *Click.* She blindly tossed the phone behind her in the vicinity of the dining room table.

"¿Dónde está tu cuarto?" Lucio asked, his voice calm and low.

Ginger blinked. "Where's my *what*?"

He chuckled softly, stepping closer still. "Your bedroom. Where is it?"

"Upstairs," she said, hoping she'd remembered the layout of her home accurately.

"Are you ready for me?"

Her breath was coming way too fast now. She figured her heartbeat might be within the normal range for a hummingbird but not a human being. She couldn't answer.

Lucio's grin widened. "Do you want me, Genevieve? If you do not, just say so, and I will go."

She swallowed. "I want you bad," she said.

Lucio nodded. He held out his hand to her.

It didn't take long for Ginger to realize that Lucio's approach to sex was as foreign as his accent.

After all that heavy breathing and teasing and stalking downstairs, when they'd gotten upstairs he seemed distant. He'd told her to wait a moment and keep her clothes on, then disappeared into the master bath. That had been ten minutes ago. The whole time, Ginger had been sitting on the edge of the bed, wondering what was going on.

She heard water running and cabinet doors opening and closing, which indicated Lucio was taking a shower. There wasn't anything wrong with a man wanting to be clean before sex, she figured. She couldn't exactly fault him for having impeccable hygiene. Maybe it was a Spanish thing, though she'd never heard that Europeans were fanatical about personal cleanliness. But it did make her feel strange, just sitting there on the edge of her bed, waiting, fully clothed, her pulse restored to normal, the moment gone.

"Lucio?"

"Just another minute, please. Do not move, *mi amor*."

Ginger looked around her bedroom, feeling like a little girl who'd been put in the corner. "What are you doing in there?"

The bathroom door opened a crack. "You can come in now."

Ginger got up from the bed and walked across the room. He held the door open for her and she immediately saw what he'd been up to.

The Jacuzzi tub was filling with warm water and bubbles. The lights were off and every candle she'd stored in the linen closet was lit, its flickering reflected on the wall of mirrors over the double sink. The blinds were drawn.

"Oh," Ginger breathed.

Lucio chuckled, coming nearer. "What did you *think* I was doing in here, *bonita*?"

"I wasn't sure," Ginger said, embarrassed. Suddenly, she didn't feel like much of a seductress. She felt silly. Unsure of herself. It had been so long since anyone had gone to this much trouble to set the scene for her that it felt like overkill.

She looked around the bathroom, worrying she was in over her head. Maybe her initial hesitation had been wise—maybe she didn't have room in her life for a man who would, at best, end up disappointing her or, at worst, break her heart into pieces.

"Please do not do this," Lucio said, suddenly pressing against her arm.

"Do what?"

"Do not second-guess us before we even start." His breath was warm on the side of her neck. "There is only one thing I ask of you tonight. Can you give me this one thing?"

Ginger gasped at the feel of Lucio's lips on her throat, warm and soft. She involuntarily raised her chin to give him complete access. "Depends on the thing," she whispered.

Lucio's chuckle vibrated against her neck. His hands moved into her hair. His mouth continued its exploration of her throat, collarbone, shoulder . . . somehow he'd already begun to remove her blouse. He was good at this, she thought. Too good . . .

"Do not fight it. Just enjoy it. That is all I ask."

Ginger lowered her chin and grabbed Lucio's face, bringing him to eye level. When their gazes locked, she was startled by the complexity she saw there— tenderness and passion. Desire and caution.

"Lucio . . ."

She let her eyes drop to his lips, full and parted and revealing a hint of straight, white teeth. She watched as his tongue slowly emerged, spreading a sheen of moisture to prepare for the kiss she knew was on its way.

"I am going to make love to you, Genevieve," he whispered. His hands touched the bare skin of her upper arms. He stroked her. He gripped her. His fingers slid down her forearms and moved to her hips. The instant his mouth clamped onto hers, she heard her jeans unzip. She felt the air hit the bare skin of her bottom, her thighs, her calves. Her pants and underwear were already on the floor.

He kept kissing her. Her mouth opened to him. Her muscles loosened. Her eyes closed. Lucio deftly unsnapped the front closure of her bra. It, too, was gone.

Somewhere in the recesses of her brain, Ginger acknowledged that her transformation had been seamless—in less than a minute she'd gone from silly and awkward to desperate and naked.

How does he do that? Ginger marveled at his skill. It usually took her a while to warm up. Not with Lucio.

He slid his lips off hers, continuing to kiss down her chin, her throat, to her sternum. She braced her hands in his thick hair as he got to his knees, sliding his tongue across her nipples on the way, down the center of her belly, teasing her belly button and the crest of her mound. When he nudged her thighs open, she worried she might fall. She was about to mention this possibility when Lucio gently clamped his teeth onto her outer lips, and gave a delicate pull. The only sound she was able to produce was, *"Mmmmgggghhh."*

Lucio's hands clasped at her bottom, and he pulled her closer to his face. She had a flashback to the lawn at Rick's ranch, the night she'd said *out loud* that her pussy belonged to Lucio. It was true, she realized. Shockingly, she'd been dead on the money. How had she known? At that point she hadn't even said three words to the man, and it sure wasn't as if she went around saying she belonged to every guy she met. In fact, she'd never felt that way, certainly not with Larry. It occurred to Ginger that with Larry, she'd only allowed him to *borrow* parts of her body. And that was if he'd jumped through the appropriate hoops. And if she felt like it.

But not here. Not with Lucio. This was something new. It was something very simple and powerful.

She was his, and they both knew it.

After a few moments of licking and juicing her up, Lucio rose from his knees. Holding her hand, he took a step toward the tub and turned off the water. He swished his hand through the bubbles and looked up at her, smiling.

He let go of her hand and sat down on the wide ledge that surrounded the Jacuzzi, stretching out his legs. He leaned his head against the wall, still smiling, and began to study her at his leisure.

Ginger knew what he wanted. She stood completely still, the candlelight on her skin, her mind in a sex stupor, her body parts humming. She displayed herself for him as his eyes consumed her from her toes to her shoulders. His smile began to soften as his eyes grew pensive. Eventually, he sighed and shook his head.

"Genevieve," he whispered. "You are exquisite."

She sucked in a quick breath.

Lucio's dark eyes returned to her face. "You are beautiful, *mi amor*. You are a queen. You are what every man dreams of." Lucio lowered his chin, and in the light his eyes danced. He looked like a devilish little boy.

"Come." He patted the edge of the tub. "Come in and relax. Feel the warm water against your skin."

As Ginger approached the tub, Lucio stood, holding her elbow as she climbed in. He steadied her as she lowered herself into the bubbles, the hot water sending an immediate wave of deep relief through her muscles.

"There you go," he said, making sure she was safely situated, her back against the curved wall of the deep tub. Lucio bent down and pulled her hair up to the back of her head, gave it a twist, and secured it in place with a clip he must have found in the drawer. Ginger had to laugh. This man didn't miss a thing! Next, he placed a decadent, wet kiss on her lips. When he pulled away, it left her stretching out her neck for more.

"I have something for you, *guapa*," Lucio said, stepping back. "It is not perfect, but it is all for you."

With that, he crossed his arms in front of his body and whipped his shirt over his head. He let it fall from his left hand, flicking it atop Ginger's pile of discarded clothing.

How wrong he was, Ginger thought. If that wasn't perfection, nothing on God's earth could qualify as such. Ginger blinked, peering through a thin veil of steam from the bathwater, enjoying a slow visual tour of this beautiful man's body. Her hand unconsciously reached under the bubbles so she could touch herself. She'd seen him naked only once before, and most of that was the view of him as he ran into the dining room, still wearing his shoes and socks, clutching his pants and shirt close.

But now, there was no emergency. There was no reason to stop or hide or rush to get dressed before some door flew open somewhere. It was just the two of them. All alone. Two grown-ups with a very adult game under way. And he was unzipping his jeans, a wicked smile playing on his lips as he pulled them down, a pair of clingy boxer briefs going along for the ride. Lucio stepped out of the pants and used a toe to toss them onto the pile.

Ginger saw smooth olive skin. Dark chest hair that disappeared into a fine line slicing down the center of his torso. Maleness everywhere. Muscles that were long and defined in most places, with hard swells on his upper arms, chest, thighs, calves. And . . . *there.*

Oh.

Heaven.

Help me.

Ginger's eyes popped wide. Her head fell back against the tub so hard it hurt. She stared. Blinked again. She'd never seen anything like it. Unabashedly, her fingers tweaked her own nipples.

Lucio chuckled. "I am not . . . ah, the word . . . circumcised. I am exactly as God made me."

Ginger nearly choked. "Remind me to send him a thank-you note," she said.

Lucio laughed. "So it is all right with you, yes? Some women have worried it was too large." He shrugged, as if apologizing.

"We're good," she said, still staring.

Just as God made me. In Ginger's mind she saw how it must have been, Larry and Lucio in heaven before they were born, waiting in the same line, ready to get God's blessings before they began their earthly stay. Lucio received the Super Deluxe All-Inclusive Adventure Penthouse Package.

Larry got the junior suite.

Lucio's grin widened. "So, I will do, yes?"

Ginger nodded, and though she was soaking in a tub of water and her pussy was dripping, her mouth had gone completely dry.

Lucio tilted his head, looking quite serious. "Whatever you like about me, know that its only purpose is to bring you pleasure. I am for your pleasure."

Ginger tried to smile, but something profoundly sad had just occurred to her. Most men looked self-conscious standing naked in the middle of a room. Larry most certainly had. It was probably because he was always conscious of himself—to the exclusion of everyone else. Including his wife, the woman he claimed to love.

Not Lucio. He was as elegant and comfortable in his bare skin as he'd been in that stylish suit he'd worn at Josie and Rick's wedding. Maybe that was because his focus was outside himself. His focus was on her. He'd just said that whatever she liked about his body was *for her*.

The timing couldn't have been worse, but Ginger was unable to stop the wave of emotion that hit her. She had been so lonely for so long. Lucio's sweet spirit—the way he created this sensual setting and offered up his body as a gift—it was too much for her.

A sob escaped from her mouth. She turned away from him.

He was in the water in seconds, suds and waves splashing everywhere. He inserted himself between her and the wall of the tub, sliding his legs beneath hers. His arms went around her, and his hot whisper melted into her ear.

"Ah, Genevieve," he said. "You have much to tell me. I want to hear it all."

She sniffed, embarrassed.

"Take all the time you need, *mi amor*."

"I wasted a lot of my life on Larry," she whispered.

"Nothing is wasted if you find the lesson in it."

"I've had so many lessons lately I don't even know where to begin."

"Whatever you need to say will come to you when it is supposed to, and you can share it with me if you like." He nuzzled his rough cheek against her neck. "Everything comes when it is supposed to."

"Like you did," she said.

"Me?"

"You came to me right on schedule."

"Hmm." Lucio's chest vibrated against her bare back. "How do you mean?"

Ginger turned on his lap, so that the side of her body rested against his torso. She wrapped an arm around his neck and turned so that she faced him. Water dripped from her arm to his shoulder, and rivulets ran down his chest. Wiping the tears from her face seemed silly.

"Do you remember the lady who officiated at Rick and Josie's wedding? Mrs. Needleman?"

"Oh, absolutely," Lucio said, grinning. "How do you think I knew which guest room was yours? Or that you'd be chatting alone with her that evening? Or that you were unattached? Did you think I was psychic?"

Ginger's mouth fell open. She scooted around the rest of the way, spreading her legs so that she straddled

Lucio's lap. The feel of his erection startled her, and her train of thought was momentarily derailed. "Uh . . . what was I saying?"

Lucio laughed, spreading his fingers across her lower back, pressing her even closer. "You were talking about the strange old lady with the intense eyes."

"Yes! You noticed that, too?"

"Of course."

"Well," Ginger continued, "she told me about you, just seconds before we met on the walkway and I passed out."

Lucio tilted his head quizzically.

"She told me there was a man waiting for me. She told me I could still get lucky if I listened to my heart and not my fear."

One of his eyebrows popped up high on his forehead.

"I walked out, and there you were!" Ginger shook her head, laughing. "And your exact words were, 'I have been waiting for you.' And your nickname is 'Lucky'!"

"The Host!" Lucio let out a surprised laugh.

"I've wanted to ask you. What does it mean when you say 'the Host'? You say it a lot."

He shrugged, taking a wet hand and stroking her bare shoulder. "It is a Spanish curse, a very foul way of taking God's name in vain. It's a bad habit for a Catholic boy to have."

Ginger touched his cheek, then smoothed his dark hair away from his face. "Are you a good Catholic boy?"

He pursed his delicious lips. "I am no longer a boy, and I was never a very good Catholic."

"And do you have any other bad habits I should know about?"

"Not one."

They both laughed, and the sound echoed around the marble bathroom.

"Listen, Genevieve," Lucio said, the seriousness in his voice changing the mood instantly. "I want to know about you. I want to spend time learning who you are and where you have been and all the things you've been doing in the years before I found you."

Ginger smiled. Lucio's English sounded stilted sometimes, which she found charming. "I feel the same about you."

"But . . ." Lucio suddenly seemed nervous. He raked a hand through his wet hair, water splashing on both of them. "It is important that you know I am not skilled at this type of thing. I have never been the kind of man who spends a great deal of time with one woman, in one place. That is what I meant when I told you that I am no good for you."

Ginger wasn't exactly shocked by this confession. The life he'd described at the dinner table didn't sound like it lent itself to long-term commitments of any kind. What bothered her was that even as they sat naked together in a Jacuzzi, Lucio felt the need to issue another warning.

"Why are you telling me this?" she asked, her voice soft.

"I say this because I want you to know my intentions—they are good." Lucio's eyes filled with worry. "I have hurt many women over the years, but I do not want to hurt you, *bonita*."

Ginger shrugged. "Then don't."

Lucio chuckled in surprise.

"Just don't hurt me. It's that simple," she said. Ginger brushed her fingers along the rough stubble on Lucio's chin, studying those dark and liquid eyes. She was aware that, at that moment, her heart was in a shouting match with her fear, and she needed to decide which one she'd listen to. This was her chance to do what Mrs. Needleman had advised. She took a big breath.

"Lucio, I don't think it's important how we got here. We're here now. So let's concentrate on doing everything right this time around. Do you think that's possible?"

"Anything is possible, Genevieve."

"Good. Now, there's one little problem you should know about."

"Yes?"

"I don't think I'd survive another betrayal." The matter-of-fact way the words came out of her mouth surprised Ginger. But why not tell him the truth? The truth was from her heart, too. "You were right when you said that I've never known a man's love. I haven't, Lucio. I was married seventeen years and never managed to feel loved. That's quite a trick."

Lucio's dark brows knit together.

"And I want that before I get old and die," she whispered. Ginger lowered her gaze and let her forehead rest against his, aware that she wasn't strong enough to look him in the eye as she finished her thought. "I desperately need to be loved for who I am and to love back with the same certainty. Before it's too late. I really think this is my last chance. If it doesn't happen now, I'll be too scared to try again."

Lucio's hug was everything she needed—rock-solid strength and tender care, all inside the shelter of his arms. He pulled her naked flesh close to his and simply hung on to her. The water stilled around them. Their breathing synchronized. She gripped his waist with her thighs and held on tight.

"I will make a promise to you, Genevieve," he

said, his words delivered carefully, the embrace continuing. "I will stay put for as long as possible so that I can get to know you. I will tell you well in advance if I need to leave. I will be truthful with you, and I will be faithful. I will give you the best of what I am."

She nodded softly.

"I have never made such a promise to anyone. Ever."

"I understand."

"I have never wanted to."

Ginger slowly separated from him, straightening as she pulled away. "Thank you, Lucio," she whispered.

He chuckled softly, running a finger down the middle of her breasts, then teasing a nipple as it peeked out from the bubbles. "There is nothing to thank me for, love." He smiled. *"Yet."*

CHAPTER 9

They hadn't bothered to dry off. What would it matter? By the time Lucio was done rolling around with Genevieve in that giant bed of hers, they'd both be bathed in sweat, the sheets soaked, calling out to God. A few drops of bathwater would be meaningless.

So Lucio had carried Ginger directly from the tub to the mattress, his hands gripping her warm flesh, his mouth all over hers. And now, the feel of how she writhed beneath him—all of the wet, hot skin slipping and sliding against his own—it was maddening! She was driving him insane. His cock hadn't been this hard since he'd been a *bellaco* teenager—crazed with horniness. Something about Ginger made him feel as though he were touching, tasting, and seeing a woman for the first time.

Perhaps, in a way, he was. He'd just made a promise to her, after all. He'd promised he would stay put and spend time with her. Maybe knowing he had that luxury allowed him to savor every sensation in a way he never had before, pay attention to every small detail of the woman in his arms.

The odd thing was this: He hadn't intended to

make that promise to her. Even as the words escaped his lips, they astounded him. Those words were fully formed, born of thoughts from the deepest part of his heart, thoughts that had been stewing for a long time. But how had the seeds been planted? When? And by whom? Could it have been the handiwork of his own guilty conscience? The result of his old-fashioned father's years of reprimands? Was it a byproduct of Sylvie's untimely death? Were the words linked to his realization that he'd missed his chance to have a son of his own?

Lucio was nearly forty. He'd lived a charmed life. He'd been born in a time when it was possible for one man to see most of the planet, and, through the lens of his camera, to share it with all people for all of history. He'd become an expert at exploring the world, yet he was an amateur when it came to exploring his own heart.

Lucio looked down at the woman beneath him, trapped between his body and the damp sheets. "You are beautiful," he said, his hands buried in the tumble of her auburn hair. "I feel drunk on your beauty."

Genevieve's hazel eyes smiled up at him. Her countenance was one of complete openness, trust. It was the look of a woman who believed she would be well taken care of. Lucio closed his eyes for a moment, silently praying that his good intentions would make him man enough for the job. He did not wish to let her down.

Suddenly, a crackle of energy blasted through him, and his eyes flew open with surprise. By now, he'd grown accustomed to the electrical buzz he felt in Genevieve's presence, but this particular sensation was far stronger than any he'd felt before. It was stronger than when he'd laid eyes on her on the stone walkway. Stronger than the first time he'd kissed her or the first time he'd come to her home and attempted to ravage her on the cool tile floor.

"Did you feel that?" Ginger whispered, her eyes widening.

Lucio laughed. "You felt it, too?"

"I feel it whenever I'm with you, but I thought it was just me."

He brushed a fingertip along her bottom lip. "That time was different, yes?"

"Stronger," she said.

"Genevieve." Lucio moved a hand down the side of her body and took a handful of her slippery buttocks, pulling her tighter to him. He grabbed on, then rolled, taking her with him as they both laughed. When they'd come to a stop, Genevieve's hair hung down over them both. Her breath quickened.

"Mmm," she hummed, lowering her lips to the side of his face. She let loose with a steady rain of kisses, along his jawline, to his ear, forehead, eyelids, down again to his neck. She surprised him as she took his Adam's apple between her soft lips and sucked gently. That was something new and different.

Genevieve's mouth continued its journey, leaving warm licks and kisses on his chest, upper arms, the crook of his elbow, his wrists. She flicked at both his hard nipples with her tongue, making his dick twitch and, though he did not think it possible, grow even harder. He prayed it would not frighten her.

He raised his chin and hissed in pleasure as she slid her tongue down the center of his abdomen, into the bristly hairs at the root of his organ, and began kissing along the length of him. He watched her open her sweet soft mouth and search for the tip of his cock. She found it. He watched her pink lips open for him.

"The Host!" he hissed, closing his eyes, luxuriating in the pleasure that she gave him with her soft mouth, her tongue, her teeth. She was a wonder.

Inexplicably, she took her mouth away. "I'm sorry, but I don't know what I'm doing," she said, pushing herself up a little. "I've never met one of these that was still the way God made it."

Lucio chuckled, half in disbelief and half in amusement—how could this thoroughly sexual woman be apologizing for bringing him such pleasure? How in the name of God could she doubt her formidable skills?

"Larry always told me . . ."

Ah, yes. Larry.

". . . that I wasn't any good at this."

How much damage had that son of a thousand bitches done to her?

"You are magnificent!" Lucio hoped Genevieve would be reassured. He also hoped she'd continue doing what she'd been doing. He reached down and stroked the side of her face, still hovering near his now monstrous dick. Lucio had to laugh. "Can you not see how you please me? Isn't it obvious?"

He watched her eyes flick toward his organ. When she nodded, her hair brushed across its exposed and agonizingly tender head.

He wiggled his toes, hissing with the exquisite torture of the sensation. *"Joder!"*

"What does that word mean? You've said that before, too."

Lucio laughed. She was tormenting him! "Ah, *bonita,* it is a foul word and I apologize for using it around you, but it just comes out sometimes, like when you make me crazy with lust."

She squinted up at him. "So it means 'fuck'?"

"Fuck, yes, it does."

The instant she put her mouth back on him, the vibration of her laughter was almost too much for him to take. It had been many months since a woman's mouth had been on him, and even then, it was nothing like this. Everything Genevieve did was acutely satisfying, perfectly suited to his needs—her wit, her eagerness, her loving nature.

Her lips. They pushed down his sheath, taking his fully exposed organ into her mouth. She began to suck on him.

That was it. He could not wait another second. He would make sure she had every opportunity to explore his organ with her mouth at some other time, but at that moment, Lucio had to have her. He had to be up inside her, all the way.

With one hand, he gathered a fistful of her hair and gently pulled, getting her attention. Simultaneously, his other hand flailed around on the bedside table, rooting for the condom he'd placed there. It proved too much for him to handle in his agitated state, and he ended up knocking the foil square to the floor.

"I'll get it," Genevieve said, pushing herself up from his loins. She pivoted on all fours and, in profile, reached down over the side of the bed. The position revealed everything to his view. She was the juiciest piece of female he'd ever seen in his life. He wanted to take her in just that way, from behind. He didn't care if it was the least intimate position. There would be time for intimacy. Right now, it was all about taking her. He prayed she wouldn't mind.

"Got it," Ginger said, pushing herself up and extending her arm toward him, the condom trapped between two fingertips. The instant her eyes met his, she froze. *"Oh,"* she said.

The details of his wicked plan must have shown on his face.

"Stay right where you are, my wild woman of the vineyards," he said.

She giggled.

With impatient hands, Lucio managed to unwrap the condom and unroll it into place. He would have to warn his lovely Genevieve that she shouldn't get her hopes up. At this level of arousal, he would last about a nanosecond once he was inside her.

"Fuck me, Lucio," she whispered, looking over her shoulder. "This pussy belongs to you."

Lucio hung his head. He looked up after a moment of silence. "You are going to kill me, *pelirroja*."

She grinned at him and opened her legs slightly, exposing more of the most achingly perfect pussy he had ever seen, anywhere on the globe.

"I will not last. You are too much for me," he said, moving behind her. Lucio caressed her ass and her back and her hips, then used his hands to spread her thighs even more. "I promise that I will not always be in such a hurry."

He grabbed her, pressing the big head of his cock into her impossibly small-looking opening. The Host! She was tight!

He flexed his hips, held her steady, and tried to get more of himself inside her. It was then that the sad thought occurred to him—what if he could not fit into the pussy that belonged to him? What if he could not fit into the only woman he'd ever wanted to make promises to?

Suddenly, Genevieve's body received him. Lucio

slid deep into her, a journey made possible because she was so wet. But he still had a ways to go.

"Oh, oh, oh," she panted. "Don't stop. Please. Oh God, this is the most . . . *God!* More. Give it all to me, Lucio. *Please!"*

Of course he would. He would never deny her anything. He knew that now. Lucio lowered himself closer to her arching body, supported her belly with one hand as he grasped her shoulder with the other. He thrust into her in a long, slow drive. With his very life force he willed himself to hold off on his orgasm. Genevieve began coming so hard that he felt her body contract in waves. The sound she was making was one slow, continuous moan. Her juices had already coated the front of his thighs.

"That's what I wanted from you tonight," he whispered into her ear as he moved in and out of her. "I wanted to see you take your pleasure. Do not stop, *mi amor*. Take all your pleasure. Take it all from me."

Her body jolted. She screamed out, alternating her pleas for mercy between God and Lucio. He felt her twitch and spasm, which marked the beginning of the end for him, too. Lucio came so hard that the earth seemed to tilt on its axis. The heavens rained down and nature itself roared and rumbled as he emptied his passion into her.

After a few quiet moments, his body jerked involuntarily. Lucio groaned, resting his cheek on Genevieve's damp back, holding on to her tightly. He could feel her heart pound under his palm.

With a great exhalation, Genevieve hung her head, auburn hair spreading out onto the sheets before them.

"Bonita?"

"Hmm?"

He caught his breath. "Are . . . you . . . ?"

She had mercy on him, not requiring him to finish his sentence. "Yes," she said. "Are you?"

"Yes."

"Jesus, Lucio."

He made a noise somewhere between a laugh and a sob.

"That was . . ."

"Intense," he offered.

"Unreal," she said.

"Like nothing I have ever known, *mi amor*." Lucio began to straighten his body, pulling her with him. He wanted to remain inside her somehow. His plan was to bring them both to their sides, where he could stay inside her while they spooned. His plans changed the instant the bed began to shake. It occurred to him that for several seconds now, HeatherLynn's sharp little bark had been cutting through the night, and car alarms had been going off. Somewhere, glass crackled and rained down. Then the phone rang.

Genevieve stretched out her arm to answer it, pulling away enough that Lucio's cock slid from her body.

"Are you guys okay? Thank God. Yes, I'm feeling it. What? This is an *aftershock*? But I didn't even . . ." Genevieve spun around to look at Lucio, a smile breaking across her face. "I think we just made the earth move," she whispered.

Lucio smiled back. Their first time together had been an earth-shattering experience—literally—but they'd been so wrapped up in each other that they hadn't even noticed.

The bed rocked again, harder this time but only for a second. He saw a slight twinge of worry pass across Genevieve's face. "It'll be okay," she mouthed to him.

He nodded, trying to remain calm. There was probably worry in his eyes, too, but it had nothing to do with the moderate earthquake they'd just experienced. He'd just noticed the condom had broken.

Genevieve said good night to her sons and hung up the phone. She grinned at Lucio with pure delight, but when she saw he wasn't in the same jovial mood, she frowned. "What is it?" she asked.

"Ah, my love," Lucio said. "I'm afraid the earth wasn't the only thing that broke apart tonight."

CHAPTER 10

"I always do my best creative work in the middle of the night," Lucio said with a wink, flipping another pancake.

"Tell me about it," Ginger said, holding the coffee mug to her lips and leaning back into the kitchen chair. The moment was surreal. It wasn't quite five in the morning. A sexy, shirtless Spaniard was flitting about her kitchen, making enough food for several families, chatting away about his plans for his pet photography business. It was all very creative, indeed.

But her answer had been in reference to the imaginative nature of their six-hour sex-a-thon, which took place in her bed, on the floor, in the shower, and against the wall of the upstairs hallway.

Ginger was supposed to meet Bea, Roxie, and Josie at Dolores Park the next morning, as usual. But she might have to cancel. Because she might not be able to walk.

"How many of these do you think you can eat?" Lucio said, gesturing to the griddle full of blueberry pancakes.

She laughed. "Just a couple," she said, smiling, thinking it was a shame the boys weren't there. Lucio would have an excuse to make as many pancakes as his heart desired.

"We still need a catchy name for the company," Lucio said, heading across the kitchen toward Ginger, coffeepot in hand. "Do you need a little more cream, love?" he asked, taking her cup and refilling it.

"I'm good," Ginger said, watching his strikingly handsome face as he concentrated on pouring the hot liquid. She just couldn't stop smiling. She was being spoiled. Absolutely *rotten*. She glanced down at her little bichon, curled in her lap, and thought, *So this must be what it feels like to be HeatherLynn*.

"Sugar?"

"No, thanks. But I wouldn't mind another kiss."

Lucio leaned down, planting a sweet kiss on her lips as he caressed the side of her face. "You are exhausted, I know."

"Exhausted and happy," she said, straining her neck for another touch of his lips. Lucio seemed pleased to oblige. Before he returned to his duties at the griddle, he kissed HeatherLynn on the top of her head, too.

Lucio had been wonderful about the condom mishap. He gently encouraged Ginger to freak out if she needed to, then asked her to tell him everything. Where was she in her cycle? Did she want to get a morning-after pill? Why did she think she was going through menopause? Could she be sure she was no longer fertile?

Ginger wasn't certain about anything. In the last couple of years her periods had been more irregular than usual, which the doctor had told her was normal for her age. She'd never been a twenty-eight-day girl, but lately, it had been all over the map: a tiny spot one month and a heavy flow the next, coming whenever it felt like it.

So she told Lucio she wasn't too concerned and assured him he shouldn't be, either. Then she asked him if they could do it again. And for the next several hours he proceeded to show her everything she'd been missing out on for her entire adult life, careful not to break any more condoms in the process.

"We should think about how we'll stage your sitting," Lucio said from the griddle. "We will end up using your pose as an example of the kind of custom photography we offer, if it is all right with you."

Ginger grinned. She liked the way he'd been talking about his business as a "we" proposition. He'd included her in all his brainstorming. She was happy to help him get it off the ground. She was unemployed, after all. And the idea of spending lots of time at Lucio's side had a certain appeal.

"Do *you* have any preference?" Ginger asked Lucio. "What do you think would suit us? You're the expert."

He thought about that while he finished stacking the pancakes on a plate, which he then placed in the oven to keep warm. He ladled out a second batch. Who would eat them, Ginger had no idea. She could always freeze them, she supposed.

"You and your little fluffy dog are both very feminine," he said, waving the spatula around for emphasis. Ginger loved the way he used his hands when he talked, almost as much as she loved watching the muscles of his torso ripple as he moved. "I see you both in a . . . the word . . . *lánguido*?"

"Languid?" Ginger offered, laughing. "A languid pose?"

"Yes! Perfect. You are reclining. Something luxurious, yes?"

"Luxury always works for us," she said, raising her coffee cup in approval.

Lucio chuckled. "What are your thoughts, *bonita*? All those years as an editor have made you a visual artist in your own right, yes? So what do you see? How do you envision it?"

Ginger took a sip of coffee and cast her eyes downward for a moment. It was startling how Lucio so effortlessly described the essence of her work. Yes, she was a visual artist in addition to being a journalist—she had spent years designing pages and special sections, making words and images fit together in a way that would draw in the reader. What amazed her the most about Lucio's observation was that she'd known him for just weeks, yet he understood more about her job than Larry had in seventeen years of marriage. Ginger stroked HeatherLynn's poofy hair, thinking she liked having a boyfriend who was an artist, someone who could create something from nothing, the way she did.

She looked up. Lucio had been studying her.

"I am sorry, but I love looking at you," he said with a shrug. "I find I cannot take my eyes from you."

"What do you see when you look at me?"

"I see a beauti—"

"I know you think I'm beautiful, Lucio," Ginger interrupted, her voice soft. "And I can't tell you how much that means to me, because I've been struggling with getting older."

"I know, *mi amor.*" His smile was gentle.

"But what else do you see?" Ginger sat up straighter in preparation for his answer. "Can you tell me what else you see in me?"

Lucio flipped the pancakes even as he studied her.

"I see a mother who is raising two sons without any real help," he said. "A mother who can handle a crisis and juggle seven other things at the same time."

Ginger took in a breath of surprise. She was expecting him to mention something along the lines of her fashion sense or the way she styled her hair—not who she was at her very core.

"I see a strong and brave woman who did not fall apart when her husband left her. Nor did she fear that same man when he came back yesterday, angry and drunk and stupid as a rock."

Ginger's mouth curled into a smile.

"I see a tender heart, *bonita,*" he continued, touching a hand to his bare chest. "I see insecurity at times. I see a woman who does not truly understand how wonderful she is."

Ginger nodded, a huge lump in her throat.

"I see a flower in the peak of bloom." Lucio gave her one of his huge, bright smiles. "A rare and *beautiful* flower."

She was speechless. She sat very still in the kitchen chair, in awe of this man who seemed to have dropped down from the skies and landed smack in the middle of her life, already knowing her.

"I hope I do not offend you," Lucio said, stacking up another leaning tower of pancakes. He opened the oven door and tossed them onto the warming plate.

"Uh, no. You don't offend me," Ginger whispered, suddenly a little self-conscious. "You are very sweet to me."

Lucio tossed the spatula to the kitchen counter and laughed. Within seconds, he was in a squat in front of her. He gently gripped her thighs. "If Lucky Montevez sees it, it is there, my love. I am not being sweet when I tell you what I see, yes?"

Ginger frowned. Then she tapped her forehead to smooth the wrinkles. Then she immediately stopped tapping her forehead and just allowed herself to frown—*to hell with it*.

Lucio did not miss her little dance of anxiety and he shook his head, smiling. "You think I am only flattering you?"

"No. I don't know. Maybe."

Lucio patted her knee. "Do you know that every editor I've ever worked with has told me I had the best eye in the business?"

"Really?"

"This is true. I am known for being able to see what others cannot. I will tell you a secret—" He leaned closer. HeatherLynn's head popped up as Lucio came near her. She wagged her tail. "I sometimes suspect that I can see things an instant before they actually happen—you know, the lightning before it cracks open the sky, the very last sliver of a moon before it disappears, a single perfect snowflake before it falls in front of my lens."

Ginger nodded. "It's your gift."

He grinned. "Oh, yes."

"Is that why they call you 'Lucky?' "

Lucio laughed. "Ah, well, no. I got that name because I tend to survive dangerous situations. I've had the name since childhood, did I not tell you this?"

She smiled. "No, Lucio. I've got as much to learn about you as you do me."

"True." His eyes sparkled.

"Tell me some of the dangers you escaped."

He winced, sucking in air through his teeth. "Are you sure you want to know?"

She nodded, even as she acknowledged to herself that she might not like what he told her.

Lucio shrugged. "I fell off a roof when I was about seven. It was a game, you know, to jump from house to house while on the red tile roofs in my village. Two stories up, but I did not receive a scratch!"

Ginger's eyes widened, imagining how freaked out she'd be if she found out that was how Jason and Josh were spending their summer afternoons.

"Then, when I was twelve, I was pulled from the wreckage of a small European car after it had been hit by a logging truck. It was a narrow mountain road with many turns, yes? But I was not injured."

Ginger gasped. "Oh, my God, Lucio. Who was driving? Was anyone hurt?"

"My mother," he said, the sadness eclipsing his handsome face. She had never seen him sad, and it was shocking how it sucked the life out of his eyes. "My mother died," he said. "It was a hard time for me."

Ginger's hand flew to her mouth, hiding her moan of horror. She willed herself not to burst into tears, but the idea that Lucio had lost his mother so young— and in that way—was unimaginable. "I am so very sorry." Ginger reached out and stroked his hair. He leaned into her touch.

"Thank you."

"It must have been so painful."

Lucio nodded softly. "Yes." He took Ginger's hand from his face and kissed her palm, then set it down on her lap. "I do not mean to make you sad by going through my 'lucky' stories one by one."

"There are *more*?"

"Oh, yes. My first year with *Geographica* I got trapped in an avalanche in the Himalayas of northern India. I was the only person who lived."

"Holy hell!" Ginger's mouth hung open.

"And then, a few years later, I was on a barge in the Suez Canal when it exploded. I lost most of my equipment, but I had . . . the word . . . ?" He shook his head, annoyed that he couldn't find the English he needed.

"A lifeboat?"

"No—insurance! That's the word." He smiled. "You'll have to forgive me but sometimes I go blank on the English."

"Your English is phenomenal."

"Thank you."

"Well, that explains the nickname," Ginger said.

"But that is just the beginning. I've also survived a typhoon in Borneo and a bus crash in Cambodia and a few other things, but I won't go into the details."

"My God, Lucio," was all Ginger could come up with.

"So." He reached over and rubbed one of Heather-Lynn's ears. The dog's eyes rolled around in ecstasy. "For your portrait with the little fluffy Señorita Chiquitína here—any ideas?"

Yes, as a matter of fact, Ginger did have an idea. An image of HeatherLynn and herself had been stuck in Ginger's brain for years. She'd never shared it with anyone. Certainly not with Larry or the boys. Not even Bea, Josie, and Roxie. It was kind of embarrassing. But there had to be a reason she'd carried the vision around for all this time, right?

"I have one," Ginger said. "Do you promise you won't laugh?"

Lucio's eyes lit up. "I like it already."

Ginger smiled. "You might not feel that way once I'm done describing it to you."

"Let me worry about that," he said.

"In fact, you may not even know what the hell I'm talking about, because you're European."

The corner of his mouth hitched up. "Try me."

"Okay," she said, taking a deep breath and forging

ahead. "Have you ever heard of a 1960s TV show called *Gilligan's Island*? It's where this group of people go out on a three-hour tour and—"

Lucio laughed. "Of course! And I think I already know where you're going with this."

Ginger was almost disappointed. "But how could you know? I haven't even said anything yet!"

"That show is why you are called 'Jeen-jair,' yes?"

She laughed at how he'd overdone his accent. "I can't believe you figured that out."

"What is there to figure?" he asked, grinning. "You do resemble the red-haired actress."

"You've seen the show?"

He chuckled. "Of course. I have spent a lot of time here in the States, but even if I had not, you can see *Gilligan's Island* anywhere in the world. I once watched an episode in Kenya, inside a dung hut."

All right, she thought, *now he's truly messing with me.*

"No, my love. It is a fact." Lucio grinned. "Developing nations have turned into the dumping ground for worn-out U.S. goods—especially TV shows and secondhand polyester clothing." Lucio gestured broadly. "Africa may have started out as the cradle of civilization, but it is now the land of leisure suits!"

She laughed hard. "You're really funny, Lucio," she told him.

He rose from his squat, sighing a little as he stretched. "You have worn me out, *bonita*," he said, patting HeatherLynn's head before he stood. "And you have made me ravenous. Let's eat and you can tell me more about your island fantasy, yes?"

The front door flew open. It was Josh and Jason. Ginger figured she had about six seconds before they reached the kitchen, so it would have to be a quick inventory: Lucio was bare-chested and barefoot, but at least he was wearing his jeans; she was covered with a cotton knee-length robe and nothing else, but at least it was belted; there were no visible signs of their earthshaking sexual rampage, at least not in the kitchen.

God help her if the boys saw inside her bedroom.

"Hey, Mumu!" Josh waved at her as he lumbered across the foyer. The boys couldn't see Lucio, who was out of the line of sight, frozen, his eyes large.

Jason was right behind Josh. "I know it's early but Dad had us working all night, cleaning up from the earthquake. His garage was trashed and—"

This was the moment of truth. Ginger's boys had never seen her with a man other than their father. Not even a date to the movies or someone picking her up for dinner. But here she was, in the kitchen at five A.M., with a half-naked man who'd obviously spent the whole night in her bed.

What would her kids say? How would they react? Would they be angry at her? Would they feel betrayed or jealous?

"Lucio!" they yelled in unison, screeching to a halt as they cleared the kitchen doorway.

Lucio smiled at them. "Good morning, gentlemen."

As the instant of surprise passed, Ginger watched for how their expressions would change, what their faces would reveal. Her heart raced. A few more seconds ticked by.

Then Jason sniffed the air. He and Josh looked at each other like they couldn't believe their luck.

"Are you making *pancakes,* man?" Joshua asked, his head jutting out in front of his neck like a cartoon character.

"Blueberry." Lucio said. "Would you care to join us?"

The twins hooted, jumped, and gave each other a series of high fives and chest bumps, a ritual usually reserved for televised sports.

"Dude! Can you make some bacon, too?" Jason had already opened the refrigerator meat drawer. "Hey, Mom, do we have syrup? Should I go borrow some of Dad's?"

Smiling weakly, Ginger moved her gaze across the kitchen to Lucio. He looked at her over his shoulder, his dark eyes filled with warmth, humor, and something more.

Almost immediately, she felt it. The something more began to swirl in the air above them, invisible and silent as it looped through Ginger and into Lucio and back again. Lucio nodded gently, indicating he felt it, too.

It was all too much, she decided. It was way too soon. This was not what she'd intended and she was pretty sure it wasn't what Lucio expected, either. That soft smile on his handsome face had to be a mask for the panic he must be feeling. It was one thing to promise a new girlfriend that you'd stick around and get to know her, but it was a different thing altogether when the girlfriend's kids adored you and her dog worshipped you. Add to the mix one broken condom and the obvious fact that the girlfriend herself had fallen madly, deeply in love with you and never wanted you to leave her side, and you really had something to panic about.

Ginger squeezed her eyes shut at the realization. She'd fallen in love with Lucio Montevez, the shirtless, spatula-wielding Spaniard in her kitchen.

And he *knew* it!

Ginger opened her eyes and rose from the kitchen chair. She placed an excited HeatherLynn on the floor. She took a deep breath. "Wow!" she said perkily, addressing the crowd as she already started her exit. "I'll be back in just a jiffy, then!"

She raced up the stairs, telling herself she could handle this. She only *thought* she was in love. Yes! That was it! Obviously, it was hormonal. The beginnings of menopause had things jumbled up in there already, and then she went and surprised the hell out of her forty-year-old body by having the best sex of her life! At *forty*! She wasn't even sure that was medically advisable! Of course, now her brain was swimming in an unnatural hormonal soup. No wonder she'd convinced herself she was in love!

Ginger scurried along the upstairs hallway, planning her next moves. First, she'd get dressed. Next, she'd tidy up her bedroom. Then she'd get Lucio's shirt for him. All that activity would surely give her time to screw her head on straight.

CHAPTER 11

"Please, help yourself. Take anything that you think you might need." Piers picked his way through his crowded spare bedroom, eventually reaching the doors of the walk-in closet, which turned out to be stockpiled with even more lock stands, reflectors, light meters, old camera bodies, lenses, teleconverters, ball heads, filters, shipping containers, some of it remnants of a predigital age.

Lucio examined the contents of the shelves, then studied the room, piled to the ceiling in some places with photo equipment and accessories. "Have you never sold anything, Piers? Not given anything away? Do you still have every piece of equipment you've ever owned?"

Piers chuckled. "Well, you know, Sylvie and I have been in this apartment for ten years now. It's easy to become a packrat when you keep the same home base." Piers picked up an old handheld eight-millimeter camera and smiled sadly, turning it over in his hand. "Some of this stuff is Sylvie's, you know." He set it back down. "Like I said, help yourself."

"I cannot tell you how much I appreciate it, Piers." Lucio examined a large aluminum reflector that was folded down in a corner. "I am going to take pictures outside whenever possible, but I know I'll end up doing some studio work." He poked through the shelves, finding a few other things that might come in handy. "I will have to buy a decent high-key backdrop."

"I used to own one, but it's at Sylvie's parents' house in Devon."

"Ah, well. Like I said, I will have to invest in one." Lucio stopped his perusal of shelves when a huge padded shipping envelope caught his eye. It was addressed to Piers, in Piers's own handwriting, and the postal stamp was from January. It had to have been Piers's submission for the Erskine Prize, Lucio knew. The committee would review an entry and send it back when it did not place. Lucio knew all about the process. He'd lost fourteen years in a row before he ever won.

"May I look?" Lucio asked, tapping the package. It was a request he wouldn't have dared make with most other colleagues. Photographers could be a competitive bunch, and many would not be comfortable showing their contest portfolio to someone who took the same kind of pictures. But he and Piers had never had that barrier between them.

"Of course you can see it," Piers said.

Lucio pulled the leather-bound case from the envelope and opened it. Like his own portfolio, Piers's submission would have had to include ten pictures, one per category, representing at least ten of the fifteen categories determined by the board. The Erskine Prize was designed to show a photographer's range—from wide-angle views of an entire ecosystem to close-ups of plants, animals, and miniature landscapes as seen through a macro lens.

His friend's work was elegant and inventive. Lucio took a moment to carefully study Piers's submission in the category for naturally occurring texture, pattern, color, or form. "This is outstanding," Lucio said, admiring the complexities of the Gobi Desert at sunset. Piers's unusual perspective and precise timing had captured an illusion, where the rippling sand seemed to morph into the waves of an ocean.

"That was my only overseas trip last year," Piers said, his head nodding toward the photo Lucio held in his hands. "I could not travel much because of Sylvie's illness."

"Your stuff is top-level, as always." Lucio closed the portfolio and smiled at him. "I have always felt honored to have had the chance to work with you."

Piers stood quietly, his hand propped against the edge of a small desk. He smiled warmly at Lucio. "And I have been honored to work with you, Lucky."

Lucio shook his head and began to chuckle. "And now . . . now I will become a renowned pet photographer!"

The two of them shared a laugh. Lucio slipped the leather case back into the mailing envelope and returned it to the closet shelf that seemed to be the dumping ground for paperwork. Lucio smiled at the stacks of travel documents, visa applications, expense forms, receipts, and Piers's passport. Like Lucio's, the passport was thickened with the dozens of extra pages needed to accommodate his travel, and he let his fingers brush over the cover, a twinge of longing moving through him.

"Ilsa Knauss," Piers said out of nowhere, jerking Lucio's attention away from his silly sentimentality.

"Ah, yes," Lucio said. "I must admit I haven't had a chance to track her down."

"But I have," Piers said with a wiggle of his eyebrows. "She's in London. I e-mailed her a few days ago and she just got back to me. And guess where she was four months ago?"

Lucio's mouth opened. "China?"

"Even better—Jiangxi Province."

"You're joking."

"No. Let me show you our e-mail exchanges. I think it's enough to get the police involved." Piers gestured for Lucio to walk with him out the guest-room door. "So, do you really think this scheme of yours will work?" Piers asked.

Lucio saw the concern in his friend's frown. "The pet photography business? Yes! I do!" Lucio shut the closet behind him and followed Piers into the hallway. "Genevieve and I have been brainstorming. She's already got three of her friends and their dogs on the calendar. We even have a name for the company."

Piers raised an eyebrow. "Really?"

"Petography."

"Ah," Piers said with a nod. "Clever." They'd reached the living room and Piers sat down in his computer chair, turning on the power to the desktop.

"We will become San Francisco's only high-concept, fantasy photo studio for pets and their owners. Here." Lucio dug around in his back pocket. "Genevieve and her boys came up with this."

Piers unfolded the piece of printer paper with a mock-up of the company's Web page and began to read out loud. " 'Does your Maine coon cat have the soul of Cleopatra? Does your Akita possess the heart of a samurai? Does your pug parade around like a prince?' "

Piers looked up from the document, dazed, then

read the rest out loud. " 'Let San Francisco's only pet-centered fantasy photography studio capture your and your pet's unique personalities'." He handed it back to Lucio. "Impressive," he said. "Now, I must ask you something."

"Of course."

"Who the hell is Genevieve?"

Lucio laughed, plopping down in an armchair next to the computer desk. "I am sorry. Genevieve is Ginger Garrison. The same woman I've spoken of before. I discovered that Genevieve is her given name and, I have to say, it fits her better."

Now both of Piers's eyebrows were high on his forehead.

"Yes, well, we are seeing each other," Lucio told him. "I decided to find out if she is that special woman I think she might be. But, of course, I already know she is special. I only mean—" Lucio stopped, flustered. "You know what I mean."

Piers blinked a few times.

"I realize this is not my usual way of talking about a woman," Lucio said, taking note of his friend's stunned expression. It made sense—Piers had seen him with dozens of women over the years. And Lucio was fairly certain that Sylvie had revealed everything to Piers about her wild—but brief—affair with Lucio. It could not have been a flattering portrait.

Piers laughed softly, shaking his head. He clicked on a few keys of his computer. "When did all this happen?" he asked. "The last I heard you were going to stay clear of the woman. You said you didn't have the kind of stability she deserved—no job, no money, no home, a hairbreadth from prison, a horrible example for her sons . . ."

"The Host!" Lucio shouted in surprise, waving his hand in the air. "You make me sound like a . . . a . . . *vagabundo*!"

"Bum?"

"Exactly."

"But those were *your* words, not mine!" Piers smiled.

"Perhaps I was overly dramatic at the time." Lucio craned his neck to see the computer screen. "I'd like to come by with Jason to load up the equipment I'm borrowing. Just let me know when it will be convenient for you."

Piers grinned. "I won't even ask who this Jason person is."

"Oh," Lucio said, aware that he was smiling. "Jason is one of Genevieve's sons. He is almost sixteen. I have agreed to let him be my photographer's assistant."

Piers let go with a full-out belly laugh, the first Lucio had heard from his old friend since he'd arrived in San Francisco. The fact that Piers could produce such a guffaw was good. The fact that he was laughing at Lucio's expense was not so good.

"I am glad you find this so amusing," Lucio said.

Piers scrolled through his e-mail in-box, looking for his give-and-take with Ilsa. He turned to Lucio, shaking his head, still chuckling. "Please don't be offended, Lucky, but you have to admit it's bizarre. I have never heard you talk like this. In all the years I've known you, I have never heard you use the phrases 'seeing somebody' or 'somebody special.'" Piers shot a glance over his shoulder. "And this is surely the first time your assistant has not been gorgeous, starstruck, and *female*!"

Piers was right—about all of it.

"Are you sure you want to get chummy with her son?"

"You make it sound like a mistake."

"It's just a big step, that's all." Piers returned his attention to the computer. "Okay. Here. Take a look at this. I e-mailed her five days ago and she got back to me yesterday—then all this!"

Lucio scooted the chair closer to the screen and leaned forward to read. He wasn't exactly shocked by what he saw—Ilsa had most certainly called him a "bastard" and an "asshole" to his face that day at the airport, so why not say it again in writing? But the fact that she was still so livid surprised him.

Piers scrolled down to his first e-mail exchange between himself and Ilsa. She wrote: *Oh, by the way, while I was in China I had a chance to even the score with Lucky in a way that I'm sure has gotten his attention. Do you know if he got my gift? The next time you see him, please send him my regards. LOL!*

"*¡Hostia!*" Lucio stared at Piers. "The woman is unbelievable!"

Piers nodded. "In addition to the police, I think we should send it *Geographica,* the State Department, and the Erskine Prize committee."

Lucio ran a hand through his hair, suddenly agitated. "Jesus, Piers," he said, shaking his head. "Look, print out a copy of these, will you? I'll call Sydney and ask him what he suggests."

"No problem." Piers reached over and turned on the printer that sat on a shelf beneath his desk. "We finished off the Rioja the last time you were here, but would you care for a beer? Coffee? Tea?"

"No, but thank you," Lucio said, his mind elsewhere. "I need to get back."

"Hot date tonight?"

Piers had already gone to get himself a beer from the refrigerator.

Lucio frowned, impatient for the printer to warm up.

Piers returned from the kitchen, still chuckling, twisting off the bottle cap and taking a few large gulps. "Forgive me, Lucky," he said. "I can't help but tease you a little. You have to admit the turn of events is amusing."

"How so?"

Piers shrugged, leaning up against one of the pillars that separated the living area from his kitchen. "It almost sounds like you're ready to settle down with this woman, you know, actually take advantage of your U.S. citizenship and stay a while. I never thought I'd see the day!" Piers raised his bottle in Lucio's direction. *"Skål!"* he cheered. "To you and Genevieve!"

Lucio tried to smile, though aware of the irony that Piers had lost the love of his life just as Lucio had found his.

He felt his eyes widen. Is that how he saw Genevieve? Could she be the love of his life? Things had moved alarmingly fast, he knew, but maybe the old preacher woman had been right. Maybe Lucio had been waiting for Genevieve.

Perhaps he'd always been waiting for her.

"You sure you don't want a beer?" Piers asked, moving back to the computer and hitting the print key. "You look like you could use a drink all of a sudden."

"Ha! No." Lucio pulled himself together. "So when will it be convenient for Jason and me to stop by?"

"Tomorrow would be fine. If I'm not here, please let yourself in." Piers set down his beer and retrieved the pages from the printer. "Here you go."

"Listen, Piers—" Lucio had already headed to the

door but turned back toward his friend. "We are having a get-together Sunday evening at Rick Rousseau's home in Sonoma. I would love it if you could join us."

Piers seemed surprised by the invitation. "What's the occasion? Who's coming?"

"We're having a launch party for Petography. You can meet Rick's wife, Josie. And Genevieve will be there. I'd love for you to meet her. And Genevieve's friend Roxanne . . ."

A tiny crinkle formed between Pier's eyebrows. Lucio immediately regretted mentioning Roxanne, knowing his friend was notoriously uncomfortable in social situations and certainly not ready to meet someone new.

Piers quickly changed the subject. "I haven't seen Rick since the funeral. Did I tell you he traveled to England for the service?"

No, Piers had never mentioned that, and the subtle dig was not lost on Lucio. "I know Rick would love to see you," he said.

"I'm leaving for New York on Friday, unfortunately."

"Really?" Lucio smiled, knowing the trip likely meant a new assignment for Piers. "Anything you want to tell me?"

Piers laughed. "Not quite yet," he said, grinning. "What I'm saying is that I may not be home by Sunday. But if I am, I will try to make it."

Lucio thanked him for the e-mails. They shared a hearty embrace and he told Piers he'd see him Sunday, though he knew he wouldn't show.

Ginger met up with the girls Wednesday morning. As predicted, she'd canceled on Monday. She'd been a disheveled, exhausted wreck, and besides, she really did end up walking kind of funny. The last thing she needed was for eagle-eyed Bea to make an issue of it.

So Ginger spent Wednesday morning getting caught up with everyone. The earthquake had thrown books from the shelves at Bea's place. Roxie lost a few wine glasses and Lilith had freaked out. But Josie and Rick had felt nothing up in Sonoma.

"Teeny had to take a couple Valiums, though," Josie said of Rick's best friend, a former Syracuse cornerback with a big heart and a fear of earthquakes.

"Poor baby," Bea said. "I'm looking forward to seeing him Sunday. It's been too long."

Ginger smiled. It amazed her how her circle of friends had instantly expanded to include Rick and Teeny. She could hardly remember a time when they hadn't been part of their group. While Josie and Rick were on their honeymoon, Teeny even joined the women for a drink once a week. They'd made him an honorary member of their girls-only club, a distinction Teeny embraced as only an openly gay man could.

"Good news," Bea announced. "I have at least ten more people from my canine agility organization interested in photos."

"That's fabulous!" Ginger said. "Lucio will be thrilled."

"Rick said he's talked to a few customers about the pet photography idea and they've been enthusiastic," Josie said. "He's just waiting on the posters."

"Excellent!" Ginger said.

"How long have you been sleeping with him?" Roxie asked.

Ginger stopped walking. So did everyone else.

"Seriously, Ginger, you didn't think we'd miss that

development, did you?" Bea gave her a crooked smile. "I'll try not to be indelicate here, but you have the blissed-out look of a woman who's just hit the fucking *mother lode.*"

Roxie shook her head. "Good work, Bea. That wasn't indelicate at all."

"My God," Josie whispered, grabbing Ginger's arm. "That was fast."

Ginger winced, wishing she could disappear. She'd thought her best friends wouldn't notice anything different about her. How stupid could she have been?

"You're even walking funny," Bea added.

"All right," Ginger said, trying to gain control of the conversation. "Can't I have a smidgen of privacy? I mean, *really*! I am an adult woman with my own life to live!"

Josie shook her head to the contrary. "Privacy didn't even enter into the equation when I was getting to know Rick." She narrowed her eyes at Ginger. "At least *we're* not spying on *you*!"

Ginger truly regretted doing that to Josie, who had a valid point.

"So?" Roxie asked impatiently. "What's the story with Rico Suave?"

Oh, boy. Ginger had no idea where she'd begin or how much she'd reveal to her friends. It wasn't like she was obligated to tell them anything. Just because they'd invaded Josie's privacy didn't mean they could turn around and do the same to her—two wrongs and all that.

"I really wish you wouldn't call him 'Rico Suave,'" Ginger said. "He's not a cartoon character. He's a remarkable man—creative, funny, charming. He just happens to look like a sex god. And the boys love him.

And he's the best damn—" She paused. "Anyway, I think I'm already—"

Ginger stopped herself, suddenly aware of the astonished expressions around her. My God! What had she been about to say? Out loud? For everyone to hear?

"You're already *what*?" Bea asked, her neck ratcheting forward. "What? What? *What*?"

There had been no closure for Ginger, so she really had no definitive answer for them. Once Lucio and the boys had devoured pancakes, bacon, and eggs, her new boyfriend had helped clean up and made his excuses for a rapid departure. He kissed Ginger on the cheek, right in front of the boys, and told her he'd talk to her later.

Lucio had called that night. They'd talked briefly, mostly tossing around ideas for the photo business, the boys hanging on her every word and making their own suggestions. He phoned once on Monday and again on Tuesday, but Ginger didn't pick up. She couldn't help thinking that Lucio was calling so he could say he did, though he was just as conflicted as she was. She sent her ideas for the Web page to him in an e-mail instead. She needed a little time and space to regroup, to let the hormonal chaos subside.

Unfortunately, there had been no subsiding. She would be seeing Lucio on Friday for the photo shoot, if not sooner, and she wasn't anywhere near her usual clearheaded self.

"Ginger?" Bea was still waiting for an answer.

"You weren't about to say that you've already fallen in love with him, were you?" Roxanne looked worried.

Josie patted Ginger's shoulder. "I'd be the last person to judge someone for falling in love too fast. I sure could have used your support while it was happening for me, but I just didn't think I could share it with you guys at the time."

Ginger nodded. That must have been hard for Josie, falling in love with Rick immediately after their little group had made a solemn vow to be done with men forever and be content with their dogs.

Josie smiled sweetly at Ginger. "But the situation is different now, right?" she asked. "We've promised not to hide stuff from one another again. We're here to help you, Ginger. We are your friends. Right?"

Ginger nodded, the emotion rising up from her chest and into her throat. Maybe her pals really could help her sort out all these contradictory feelings. Maybe she'd be a fool to not take advantage of their collective wisdom.

She looked at the faces of her friends. They had circled her protectively as Dolores Park came to life, more dogs and owners showing up as the sun rose in the sky.

"All right," she said, taking a deep breath for courage. "It's a long story. Remember the night we went to dinner with Mrs. Needleman? Well, when I got back, Lucio . . . we . . . I . . . well, it started when I went out to sit in the dark and look at the moon. I guess I got a little tipsy."

"Let me get this straight," Bea said, looking incredulous. "You went out there—alone—to get drunk and howl at the moon?"

"To *look* at the moon," Ginger said. She was about to assure Bea that there'd been no howling that night, but that wouldn't have been entirely truthful. "And I was only a little, you know, *uninhibited* at the time."

"Who cares about the moon?" Roxie said, bugging out her eyes. "What happened with you and Lucio?"

Ginger sighed. "Well, remember the sex buffet Bea talked about?"

Bea's eyes widened.

"Day-um," Roxanne whispered.

"No!" Josie yelled, clearly confused. "I have no idea what you're talking about! What sex buffet? I don't even know what a sex buffet *is*! Somebody fill me in!"

At that moment, a guy walked by with his border collie, chuckling to himself.

"Keep it down, will you?" Ginger groaned, flipping her hair away from her face. "Maybe we should just go get a cup of coffee. That way the entire San Francisco dog-walking community won't have to hear the lurid details of my outrageous sex life."

"I'll meet you at Starbucks," Bea said, who clucked for Martina to heel and turned to leave the park.

"But you hate Starbucks!" Roxanne called after her. "What happened to the whole 'global enslavement through caffeine intoxication' theory?"

Bea shook her head but didn't look back. "Fuck that," she mumbled. "I'm going to need to alter my brain chemistry in some way before I hear the rest of Ginger's story."

The other women gathered their dogs and followed after Bea.

"It's not really *that* bad, is it?" Josie's hopeful face scanned Ginger's as they headed to the park exit.

Ginger tried valiantly to smile, but gave up. "God, Joze. I can't lie. It's pretty bad. Or good. However you want to look at it."

Roxie frowned at her. "On a scale of one to—"

"Sixteen," Ginger interrupted.

"But the scale only goes to ten."

"Sixteen," Ginger said.

"*Day-*um," Roxie repeated.

"But what do I know about sex, really?" Ginger let loose with a desperate laugh. "I have no idea what I'm supposed to do now that I've had sex like that! I have no frame of reference for what's happened to me in the last few weeks! I'm realizing that I've been cheated my whole life, that I didn't know the first thing about sex or love while married to Larry. I had no idea it could be the way it is with Lucio!"

"Whoa," Josie said, bringing Ginger to a stop. "Take a breath, sweetie."

Ginger waved her hands around frantically, tears filling her eyes. "I don't want to breathe! I want to scream! For twenty years Larry's been telling me I was dining on chateaubriand and now I find out that it was freakin' Spam the whole time!"

Roxie and Josie stiffened and leaned backward, as though they were being hit with gale-force winds.

"You know who I feel like?" Ginger continued to wave her hands around, a lump of desperation growing in her chest. "I feel like that woman in the vegetable juice commercial, you know, the one who smacks herself in the forehead and says, 'I coulda had a V8!' only I'm a lot more pissed off about it than she was!"

Roxanne and Josie exchanged glances. "*Day-um!*" they said in stereo.

"I'm going home to take an extremely cold shower now," Roxie said, sighing.

"I really need to call Rick," Josie said, squirming.

"I should go to work," Bea said, checking her cell phone for the tenth time.

Because Ginger's friends were trying to avoid eye

contact as they sat around the sidewalk table, she knew she'd been smart to leave out most of the details from her and Lucio's sexual smackdown. The general overview had left them plenty uncomfortable.

It wasn't as if the group didn't discuss sex—they did. Often. But Ginger knew her story of lust on the lawn and panties in the pocket and getting naked on the foyer floor and bubbles and candles and earthquakes had left them a little shaky. She knew how they felt.

Ginger sighed, noticing how Roxanne had started wiping her overheated forehead with a Starbucks napkin. Josie was fidgeting in her chair and stroking her neck. Bea just looked smug, no doubt mulling over the information Ginger had shared about Lucio's steady diet of world travel and brief encounters.

"Don't even think of saying it, Bea," Ginger warned, pointing in her direction.

"What? You mean I shouldn't say 'I told you so'?"

"Lucio is *not* the biggest mistake I've ever made in my life," Ginger said. "I don't know what he is—yet. He might turn out to be the best thing that's ever happened to me."

"Or, not." Bea shrugged.

The four women sat in silence for a while, their dogs asleep at their feet. They'd been talking for nearly two hours. The conversation may have been hot, but Ginger's latte had long ago gone cold.

"Well, what does everybody think?" Ginger asked. "You now have a pretty good idea what I'm dealing with here. What do you think I should do?"

Everyone looked blank.

"Should I listen to my heart and not my fear, like Mrs. Needleman said? Or should I just chalk this up as a once-in-a-lifetime bit of insanity and get out before my heart gets flattened—like Bea thinks it will?"

"I never said that." Bea folded her hands on the tabletop.

"But you want to," Ginger said.

Roxie shook her head slowly. "Look, I can't tell you what to do, but I'll tell you one thing—I'm not getting within a hundred yards of that crazy old Mrs. Needleman again. She's put some kind of weird mojo on you and Josie, and I want none of it."

"Let me ask you this," Bea said to Ginger, her voice quite serious. "What exactly is your biggest fear about Lucio?"

Ginger fiddled with the cardboard coffee sleeve on her cup while she thought that through. "Oh, you know—that he'll leave," she said with a shrug. "That one day he'll fly off somewhere, the way he's done all his life, and I'll be left here insanely in love with a man I can never have." Ginger looked around the table. "That scares the hell out of me."

"And rightly so," Bea said with a nod.

"But he made a promise to you, didn't he?" Josie bit her lip before she went on. "He promised he'd stay here long enough for the two of you to get to know each other. He said he wouldn't go unless he talked it over with you."

"He did," Ginger said with a bitter laugh. "But all that means is he's willing to give me a heads-up before he disappears!"

Bea laughed, too. In an overexaggerated Spanish accent she said, "*Adios*, señoreeeta. I will be sure to send a postcard from *Arr-ghhhhhen-teena*."

Ginger rolled her eyes.

"But do you trust him?" Josie asked.

"With what?"

"With everything—your kids, your dog, your heart? Do you trust him?"

"Actually, yes," Ginger said. "That's another scary thing—there's no real reason for me to trust him, but I do. I don't even know his whole story yet. But somehow, trusting him feels right. *He* feels right. I can't explain it."

"I think that's what Mrs. Needleman was getting at," Josie said, smiling wistfully. "It was the same for Rick and me. I had to decide if I trusted him. I had to listen to what my gut was telling me."

"I hate to be the one to add some reality into this conversation, but someone has to do it," Roxanne said, ending a long stretch of silence. "Here's the deal, Ginger. Sometimes it's hard to tell the difference between gut feelings and below-the-belt crazy-monkey-lust, do you know what I'm saying? So just be sure that when you're listening to your gut, it isn't some other organ doing the talking."

Bea wagged an eyebrow and chuckled.

Roxanne continued. "In my experience, the hotter the sex, the harder the fall." She tilted her head to study Ginger. "And sooner or later there's going to be a fall. Trust me on this one—you can't have great sex and a great relationship with the same man. You're going to have to settle for one or the other. It's a universal law."

Bea nodded in approval.

Ginger burst out with a laugh. "Or, you can be married to Larry Garrison and have neither! Woo-hoo!"

"That's complete garbage!" Josie's sharp reprimand was directed toward Roxanne, and the two friends stared at each other in silence. After an awkward moment, Josie turned her attention to Ginger. "Listen to me when I tell you that you really *can* get it all in one place. I'm living proof. And if it could happen to me, it can happen for you or Roxie or any woman."

"That's exactly what Mrs. Needleman said!" Ginger sat up taller in her chair.

"I've had all the Mrs. Noodle-brain I can take for one morning." Roxie rose from her chair and pulled a sleepy Lilith to her feet. "I won't be able to make it Friday—I have an early appointment with my Web designer—so I'll see you guys at Josie's on Sunday. Want to drive up with me, Bea?"

"Sure."

Roxie's eyes flashed briefly at Josie and then moved on to Ginger. "Just protect yourself."

Ginger nodded soberly. "We're using condoms."

Roxie laughed, but a sadness crept into her eyes. "I was referring to the emotional kind of protection, but condoms are always a swell idea." She fiddled with Lilith's leash, her gaze softening. "The only thing worse than having a guy abandon you has got to be having a guy abandon you when you're pregnant with his kid. Nobody wants that."

Ginger gasped, suddenly panicked. "I'm not going to get pregnant! That's ridiculous!" She looked at Bea and Josie for confirmation. "I'm in the beginning stages of menopause, you know."

"Ppphhhhtttt!" Bea said, dismissing Ginger with a flap of her hand. "Even if you were, which you *aren't,* that doesn't mean jack. Just ask *my* mother."

"What do you mean?" This was new information for Ginger, and she didn't much like it.

"Imogene Latimer never planned on having children, right? I'm her only spawn. She's ninety-eight years old, and I'm fifty-three. You do the math, girls."

Ginger gulped.

"See you Sunday, Rox!" Josie called out as Roxanne turned to go.

"See you guys Sunday," Roxie said, not looking back.

CHAPTER 12

Ginger knew exactly what she was looking for. She even knew in which large green plastic storage tub it was buried and in which section of the attic. Of course she hadn't labeled and alphabetized the contents of her storage areas—that would have been neurotic—but Ginger was no slouch when it came to household organization.

"That one," she said to Josh, pointing to a top shelf. "Can you grab it for me?"

Joshua reached high and pulled it down from a shelf against the eaves. "Where's it going?" he asked, carrying the container across the wood plank floor.

"My room. On the floor by the bed would be great."

"What's in here, anyway?" Josh headed down the steep, narrow attic stairs.

Ginger followed him. "Just a bunch of Grams's old clothes. Stuff from her Hollywood days."

"Cool. Can I see it?"

Her son's interest in fashion made her smile. She wondered if it would be possible for Josh to be both the leader of the free world as well as a personal shopper.

"Sure."

Josh let the box drop to the floor of Ginger's room,

then bent to pry open the lid. "What are you looking for, Mom?"

"Well . . ." Ginger laughed a little to herself, knowing that once she told Josh what she was up to, she'd never hear the end of it from her boys. "Grams's old bikini, you know, from her beach-blanket B-movie days."

Josh narrowed his eyes.

"And there's a big floppy sun hat in there, and some big white sunglasses."

"You going on vacation?"

Ginger laughed loudly. "No, sweetie. It's for my photo with HeatherLynn. Lucio and I thought it would be fun for me to pose like—"

"Like Ginger from *Gilligan's Island,*" he cut her off, smiling. "That'll be awesome!"

Yet again, her idea hadn't been a surprise. She was disappointed.

"Mom, c'mon! It's a no-brainer," Josh said. "What's HeatherLynn going to wear?"

That was something Ginger hadn't yet figured out.

"Wow!" Josh tossed the lid aside and the clothes began flying out of the storage container, landing all over the floor. Josh threw the bikini pieces toward Ginger, then the sun hat and glasses. Eventually he pulled out what had piqued his interest. "There's a cover-up!" He held the blue tropical-print robe above his head. "I can make HeatherLynn a little matching bikini with this!"

He could? Ginger was baffled. "You can do that?"

"Sure."

"You know how to sew?"

"Sure," he said, shrugging. "That's what I do on the costuming crew at school, Mom. I've been doing it for two years."

Her mouth opened. "You have?" Ginger suddenly felt guilty. She should have known this about her own kid! "Why didn't you tell me? I thought you just helped with costume rental."

"That, too, but I also make stuff. It's no big deal." He folded the fabric and shoved it under his arm. "I'll work on it after school tomorrow. When's Lucio taking your picture?"

She smiled involuntarily. "Friday night."

"I can do it by then," he said, bending down to place a kiss on her cheek.

Ginger brought her hand to her face in astonishment. Once her son, the designer, had left the room, her gaze fell to the pile of clothes on the floor, and she was hit by a stroke of genius.

"Lucio! C'mon in!"

The fact that Jason opened the door for him with such enthusiasm was Lucio's first surprise. The second came when he nearly tripped over a large green storage container in the middle of the foyer. The third surprise was how Josh enthusiastically volunteered to load the container in the car for Lucio, while Jason invited him to have a seat in the living room and relax. "Mom will be just a minute," he said.

Lucio sat awkwardly on a chair, aware that things were stranger than usual in the Garrison habitat. Just then, HeatherLynn came careening around the corner from the dining room, headed right for Lucio. She stopped at his feet, placed her cute white paws on his knees, and wagged her feather-duster tail. He picked her up and she began licking his face.

"Care for a cocktail?" Jason asked. "Martini? Whiskey sour? Gin and tonic?"

Lucio tried to pry the dog off his face while scanning

the room, half expecting to find video cameras trained on his every move. "You know how to prepare cocktails?"

Jason laughed. "Not really. That's just what people are always saying in those old movies from the sixties—you know, 'Would you care for a drink?'" He laughed some more.

"Ah." Lucio nodded, as if he now understood everything.

Josh returned to the living room and sat next to his brother on the sofa. It was the first time Lucio had seen them at ease, relatively still, so close to each other. They were identical twins, yes, but they were not identical human beings. Jason's left eye sat just slightly lower than his right, while Josh's were more symmetrical and closer-set. When Josh smiled his lips went decidedly crooked, while Jason's were straight. Jason seemed a little more muscular than Josh, and Josh was probably about a half inch taller than his brother. They were Larry Garrison redux, only with a more delicately shaped nose that they'd inherited from their mother. They were handsome young men.

And at that particular moment, both looked as if they were ready to bust out laughing.

"What's going on, gentlemen?" Lucio asked. "What's the big secret?"

Josh punched Jason in the leg. "You *told* him Mom has a secret?"

"No, piss-face! I didn't say anything!" He punched Josh back, harder.

Lucio laughed a little, still wrangling Heather-Lynn. He hadn't had the burden—or the pleasure—of growing up with a sibling. He could not imagine what life was like for Genevieve's two boys, who faced the world every day as a team.

"Then why did he ask what the secret was?" Josh yelled.

"I don't know!" Jason yelled back.

The boys abruptly stopped their arguing and turned to Lucio. "Hey, uh, can I start tonight?" Jason asked.

For a second, Lucio had no idea what the kid was talking about, but then it dawned on him that he was referring to his duties as photographer's assistant. Yes, Lucio did look forward to introducing Jason to the world of photography and getting to know him better. But tonight? No. It would not fit in with what Lucio had planned for the boy's mother.

"Doofus," Josh said to Jason, shaking his head. "Tonight is more of a *date* than a photo shoot! Didn't you see how Mom's getting all dressed for—" He stopped himself.

"I'm the doofus?" Jason asked, looking to the ceiling as if asking God to give him strength.

Lucio buried his face in HeatherLynn's soft fur, hiding his smile. So that was the big secret. Genevieve was getting dressed up to come over to his place. He'd mentioned they'd be having a bite to eat before he took pictures, but he didn't expect her to go to any trouble. She'd have to change into her costume eventually, after all.

"Next time, yes?" Lucio nodded to Jason. "Did you read the book I suggested?"

"Yeah," he said. "I have a million questions about lenses and exposure and shutter speed, though."

"I hope I have a fraction of the answers," Lucio said.

"Here's a question for you," Joshua said. "Are you and my mom, you know, *together*?"

Lucio leaned back in surprise.

"We know that has nothing to do with photography,"

Jason said sheepishly. "But it's something we were wondering."

Lucio nodded, impressed and touched by the protective streak coming out in Genevieve's sons. "It is my hope that we are," he said. "I would like very much to be your mother's man. I offered to ask her father's permission to court her, but she told me he had passed away."

The boys nodded sadly. "When we were in fourth grade," Josh said.

"So I offered to ask her mother."

Josh and Jason looked to each other and promptly cracked up.

"What is so funny?"

"Well, it's weird enough that you'd want to ask permission to date a grown lady, but it's even weirder that you'd want to ask Grams. She's, uh . . ." Josh paused to find the right words.

"A man-eater," Jason said. "She's had five husbands."

"I see."

Josh nodded in Lucio's direction as if he were sharing a private joke with him. "Mom's not exactly interested in her advice when it comes to men. After all, Grams absolutely *loved* Dad. She still does."

"Ah," Lucio said, biting down on the inside of his cheek.

"But you can ask *us* for permission!" Josh suggested brightly. "Yeah! Ask us!"

Jason stared at his brother in horror. "What are you, brain-damaged? Lucio doesn't have to ask us—we're fifteen and he's probably, like, fifty or something!"

"Actually, I'm quite close to your mother's age, and asking your permission is a very good idea." Lucio put HeatherLynn on the floor. "You are the men of the house, yes? I would like to know your opinion."

"Uh, okay," Josh said.

"How do you feel about me dating your mother?"

After exchanging a quick glance with his brother, Jason shrugged. "Fine, I guess. You're really cool. So, you know, as long as you're good to her and everything, I don't see any problem."

"I am happy to hear it."

Joshua tipped his head and studied Lucio. "So what *are* your plans for Mom?"

Lucio didn't bother trying to suppress his smile—it would have been a losing battle. "I only have the best intentions," he said. "I plan to stay here in San Francisco and spend as much time with her as possible. I think your mother is a very special woman and I want to know everything about her."

Jason squinted. "Seriously? *Everything?*"

"Yes."

"Like how many layers of antiwrinkle crap she puts on her face before bed?" he asked.

"Uh . . ."

"Or how soy milk gives her hives?" Josh asked.

"That is all quite interesting, but—"

"Or how she goes totally psycho if we're at a restaurant and the waiter comes over and squats by the table?" Jason said, giggling.

"She really, really hates that," Josh said. "She made us leave an Outback Steakhouse once because the waiter got to the table and squatted to take our drink orders. And my mouth was watering for their onion rings!"

"So if you make her dinner or something, don't squat by the table, whatever you do," Jason added helpfully.

Lucio was thoroughly puzzled. Squatting waiters? He'd never heard of such a thing! "I appreciate all this help, but I was thinking more along the lines of your mother's favorite flower, or her favorite music, or who the lucky man was who got to give your mother her very first kiss."

The boys stared at each other, their brows furrowed.

"Hydrangeas," Josh said.

"Nirvana," Jason said.

"But you're on your own with the kissing thing," Josh added.

"Thank you for your help, gentlemen." Lucio chuckled softly to himself as he checked his watch. "Do you know how much longer your mother might be?"

"Hold on. I'll check." Jason twisted his body around and leaned over the back of the sofa. *"MOM?"*

Lucio heard Genevieve's voice upstairs. "Yes?"

"Lucio's waiting!"

"Okay! Be right down!"

Jason flopped back around on the couch, smiling at Lucio. "She'll be right down," he said, as if Lucio had not heard the exchange—as if anyone in the Bay Area had not heard it.

"Thank you."

"Wait till you see her. You're going to love it," Josh added conspiratorially.

"I know I will."

"But you're going to be sweet to her, right?" Jason asked. The worry Lucio saw in his face was touching.

"You won't make her cry or anything, right?" Josh added.

"You have my word," Lucio said. "I—"

The moment Genevieve appeared at the foot of the stairs, Lucio jumped from his chair, forgetting what he was about to say. If anyone had pressed him at that moment, he would not have been able to remember his own name.

"Whoa," Josh whispered.

"See?" Jason said, pointing toward his mother. "Didn't I tell you?"

"I was the one who told him!" Josh said, punching his brother's arm.

Lucio stared.

Genevieve had poured herself into a vintage cocktail dress and was now a cross between a Bond girl and a living, breathing Vargas pinup. Her auburn hair had been flipped up at the ends and teased a few inches at the top. She'd applied black mascara and thick eyeliner in a provocative upward sweep at the edge of her upper lids. Her lips glistened in a shade of light pink. She'd added a small, dark beauty mark just above and to the side of her mouth.

And her skin! Lucio ran a hand nervously through his hair as he noted how her skin gleamed against the pale olive silk of the dress, her bosom full and succulent as it rose above the low, square neckline.

Lucio's gaze continued on to appreciate how her firm upper arms looked restrained by the tiny cap sleeves. The sight of that made him flare his nostrils. And he stared at how her waist was nipped by the darted silk, how her hips, belly, and thighs were accentuated by the tight, shiny fabric. Lucio did not think it would be possible to shove a single sheet of paper between Genevieve's body and that dress.

Which did not matter, of course, because the only thing that would be shoved in that dress tonight would be his hands.

"Me dejas sin palabras," Lucio breathed. "Truly, you leave me speechless."

Genevieve gave him a knowing little smile, then she pivoted on a pair of pointy-toed black pumps, providing the view from the back. It was all Lucio could do to keep his composure in front of the boys. He stood stock-still, his breath ragged, his instincts telling him to get down on his hands and knees and crawl to her like a well-trained dog.

The Host! He had begun to sweat! That dress was cut all the way down to her lower spine. The entire back was open. He had to get her out of this house—now—before he went back on his promise to the boys and began to behave in a decidedly *un*sweet fashion toward their mother.

Lucio took several controlled steps in Genevieve's direction. He kissed her cheek chastely and offered her his arm.

"Shall we?" he asked.

"Yes, let's," Genevieve said, her eyes never leaving Lucio's. "Please remember to lock up when you leave for your dad's," she added without a glance back.

They'd reached the door when the boys began to laugh. They turned to see Josh holding the satin pillow and Jason holding HeatherLynn's leash. The dog herself sat patiently on the carpet, her tiny pink tongue poking out, waiting to be picked up.

"Aren't you forgetting something?" Josh asked.

Lucio was thoroughly embarrassed that they'd forgotten the pet that would be required for the pet portrait. "Of course," he said, accepting the leash from Jason. "Thank you for all your help tonight, gentlemen."

Josh leaned close and whispered, "Looks like you're going to need all the help you can get, dude."

"I believe you may be right about that," Lucio whispered back, giving the boys a wink.

* * *

"I must ask—where did you get the incredible dress?"

Ginger smiled to herself as she pushed around her salad with a fork. It was a pity that Lucio had gone to all this trouble with dinner when she didn't feel hungry. He'd tidied up Rick's lovely home and lit candles on the table. He'd poured wine. He'd pulled her chair out for her.

"It was my mother's," she said. "She had roles in a bunch of low-budget movies in the mid to late sixties, and I think this may have been a costume from one of them, though I can't be sure. She's given me a bunch of her old clothes over the years."

"But it fits you perfectly. Did you have it altered?"

Ginger laughed. "No. I barely had time to have it cleaned. And it's a little tight around the hips."

"I do not mind that at all," Lucio said.

She laughed. "Somehow, I knew you wouldn't."

"But I do not want any other man seeing you in that dress, all right?" Lucio's dark eyes sparkled.

"Why is that?"

"Because any man with the gift of sight will try to steal you away, *mi amor*. I will have to fight him off with my bare, bloodied fists!"

Ginger laughed. "The poor guy could try all he wanted, but I'm only interested in you, Lucio."

"I cannot tell you how glad I am to hear it." Lucio placed his elbows on the table and folded his hands, studying her. "But I see that you are not at all interested in *la tortilla de patatas y la ensalada*. You've hardly eaten a thing."

"No! It's very good, actually. You're an excellent cook." Ginger looked down at her lap, smoothing the napkin out over her dress, wondering how she'd tell him she didn't feel like eating.

"Then why are you not enjoying it?"

She looked up. Lucio was obviously puzzled, and she supposed the truth was the only way to put him at ease. She'd had sex with the man—and it was the best sex of her entire life—so why shouldn't he know where she was in her menstrual cycle?

"I'm a little sick to my stomach," she said.

Lucio's eyes flew open. He looked scared to death.

"I'm fine!" she added, laughing in surprise at his reaction. She reached out to touch his clasped hands, his knuckles now white with tension. "I just finished my period today, is all. It's nothing, really."

She watched Lucio's body nearly melt with relief. He hung his head and slowly shook it side to side, exhaling deeply.

"Bonita," he said, looking up, his eyes wide. "I was certain you were going to tell me you were pregnant."

Ginger stiffened, balling up the linen napkin in her lap, stung by how happy he seemed. But of course he was happy. *She* was happy! They were both damn happy that the whole broken-condom incident hadn't put an end to life as they knew it.

"Looks like we dodged that bullet," she said, trying to sound lighthearted.

He reached for her, cradling both her hands in his. "I see that my reaction hurt you. I did not mean to. Of course I am relieved, but if you were pregnant, it would not be a catastrophe, yes?"

Ginger kept her face expressionless. She willed herself not to cry. What was wrong with her? Why had Lucio's reaction stung so? Did she *want* to be pregnant? Did she expect him to be crushed that she wasn't? What was her *problem*?

Right then, Ginger decided she didn't care what the doctors said. She really was going through menopause. Her period had lasted just two days and barely warranted unwrapping a tampon. And now she felt as though she had a raging case of PMS. Maybe, in her case, the acronym stood for "Pretty bad Menopausal Syndrome."

Ginger took her hand from Lucio's and placed the wadded-up napkin on the table. She stood. She walked from the huge open dining area of Rick's modern house and went into the living room, now Lucio's studio. She hadn't been here since the night all hell broke loose—the night Josie got kidnapped by crazy Bennett Cummings.

Tonight felt much the same, since all hell was breaking loose in her heart.

"Please tell me what's wrong." Lucio had come up behind her. He placed his hands on her hips and breathed onto her neck.

"I don't know what's wrong," she said. "I feel ridiculous for being so emotional. I know you probably hate it. Larry always hated it when—"

"I am not Larry," Lucio said, spinning Ginger around so that she faced him, his equal in height in those heels. "I want to know all the little things about you, yes? All the hidden corners in your mind and heart. Do not apologize for them and do not assume I will react like Larry did when you allow me to see them."

Ginger's mouth fell open.

"You understand, yes?"

"I guess," she said, baffled.

"Share it all with me, Genevieve. That is what I ask." Lucio leaned forward and kissed her forehead, then smiled at her. "If you get moody in your cycle, so what? Who cares? It's natural! And if you aren't hungry for my famous potato omelet? We'll wrap it up for later. It doesn't matter. But if you are angry with me because I am relieved you aren't pregnant—then you must tell me you are angry. Share it with me, *bonita.* This is what I want."

Ginger swallowed hard. "Seriously?"

Lucio laughed. "Seriously." He reached for her and drew her close to his chest, though Ginger could tell he was being careful not to smear her makeup.

Suddenly, it all made sense to her. "This is what happened to you before, isn't it?" Ginger asked, still wrapped in his arms.

"Before?"

She slipped from Lucio's embrace and stood before him. "Is that why you had to get married when you were young? Was she pregnant? Do you have a child in Spain?"

Lucio shook his head. "No, *guapa.* It has never happened before. She was pregnant, yes, but I was seventeen and ignorant and I did not even bother to use a condom at all."

Ginger was shocked. "So you *do* have a child! Why didn't you tell me?"

"There is no child," Lucio said abruptly. He ran his hands through his hair. "She lost the baby three weeks after the wedding and immediately asked for an annulment." He shrugged, a faint shadow of sadness falling over his face. "It seems so far away now that it is almost like it never happened."

Ginger did not know how to respond to that story. "I am sorry about the baby," was all she could come up with.

Lucio tried to smile. "I believe that things happen for a reason, yes? I have often thought that God or the universe or whatever you want to call it actually wanted me to have the life I've had. Perhaps God knew I'd make a better photographer than father." His voice was soft as he brought his face to hers. "All I know is I could not have accomplished all I have if there was a child and a wife in my life."

Ginger understood. On good days, she could see her years with Larry in the same light. If she hadn't met him in college then she wouldn't have Jason and Joshua—an unthinkable possibility.

"It must sound harsh to hear me say that, but it is true." Lucio let his forehead rest upon Ginger's. She felt his hands stroke her back. "I have never told anyone this, but there are times I truly believe that I would trade all my adventures and success to be able to know the child who was never born."

"Lucio . . ."

"He would be a grown man now."

Ginger put her arms around him, holding him tight.

"And your boys—" Lucio made a sound somewhere in between a laugh and a sigh. "They are a funny pair, yes? And I watch them and I can't help but think of my own son. I know that dwelling on this is . . . ah, the word . . ."

Ginger smiled, now accustomed to the pause that occurred when Lucio couldn't come up with the English needed to finish his thought. "Dwelling on it is sad?"

"Yes, but that is not the word I was thinking of."

"Pointless?"

"Almost."

"Maudlin. Morose? Self-pitying?"

Lucio laughed. "You know too many words, *pelirroja*. But you do understand." He tightened his hold on her and adjusted his head so that he could rest his cheek against hers. "What I am trying to tell you is that I am relieved you're not pregnant, it is true, because I do not know if I could be a good father right now in my life. But it is not so simple. I often wonder about it, what it would be like to have a child."

Ginger closed her eyes and inhaled the scent of him. It was spicy and clean and delivered a shot of heat through her veins. She'd missed him—his voice, his touch, his scent—over the last week.

He pulled his cheek from hers and steadied her in front of him. "I have something I need to ask you."

Ginger smiled. "You can ask me anything."

"You have just finished bleeding. I understand this. And you have taken great care with your hair and makeup and it is all so perfect for the picture. But none of it can deter me. I want you."

Ginger swallowed hard.

Lucio ran his fingers inside the low, square neckline, brushing a fingertip just above her nipples. She gasped, trembling under his touch.

"The moment I saw you in this dress I was . . . the word . . . yes! I was *reduced*! Reduced to my most base self. All I wanted was to throw you down in the sand next to the bamboo hut you share with MaryAnn."

"Oh, *reeelly*?"

"I wanted to rip the dress off you, muss up your hair, and get inside you." Lucio's grin widened and he cupped her face with his hands. "Do you have any idea how sexy you are dressed like this, Genevieve? Do you have any idea what you have done to me tonight, how you have made a ruined man of me?"

Ginger tilted her head back and laughed at Lucio's speech. "Wow," she said, catching her breath. "So this is your way of telling me you've always had a thing for the girls of *Gilligan's Island*?"

"What normal man has not?" he murmured, nuzzling her ear.

"But which one really did it for you, Lucio?" Ginger captured Lucio's earlobe between her lips and sucked gently. "Tell me who you liked the best."

"Ginger, of course." When Lucio chuckled it tickled her neck. "For me, it has always been about Ginger."

CHAPTER 13

Modeling was more work than she ever imagined. Lucio had prepared the studio beforehand, bringing in real sand and spreading it on the floor of the plain white backdrop. He'd also acquired a lifelike palm tree, a beach umbrella, and a few coconuts. The rest of the island paradise would be added on the computer using his own stock photos of Tahiti and a little bit of digital magic, he explained.

Lucio posed her on her right side, propped her on her elbow, and began flashing light meters all over the place—next to her face, her belly, and her legs, then adjusted the aluminum reflecting panels and light stands. While all this was going on, HeatherLynn curled up on her pillow, attired in her bikini. Josh had done a spectacular job of mimicking the design of the vintage swimsuit but still making it comfortable for the dog. Ginger smiled at HeatherLynn, knowing that years of being groomed, fussed over, primped, and attired in various sweaters and coats had left her perfectly willing to don a bikini when called upon to do so. She'd even been willing to have the fur on the top of her head teased and sprayed, a little blue bow holding her bouffant in place. The girl was a trouper.

The infant-size sunglasses were going to be another issue entirely, however.

"I have not done much studio work so we will have to learn together, yes? We will experiment."

Ginger smiled, watching how Lucio's brow creased as he fiddled with his lens. He popped his head up. "Do you have the doggie treats?"

"Hidden right behind my behind," she said.

"And what a very fine behind it is," Lucio said, smiling. "It is crazy, you know—how you resemble her! But I must say, your face is prettier, softer."

Ginger rolled her eyes. "I already agreed you could make wild passionate love to me when we're done. There's no need to go overboard with the compliments."

He let go with a laugh as he reached into his camera bag for something. "All right, we are going to take a couple shots of you alone before we try to add Señorita Chiquita, yes? I need to make sure the exposure is exact."

Ginger held her chin high, hoping to God that the lights didn't accentuate any pulling skin at her throat or lines around her eyes. She prayed that the veins in her legs didn't look like a roadmap highlighted in green marker. And what if she appeared bloated because of her period? She made a point to pull in her core muscles.

"Relax, Genevieve. Get those ridiculously negative thoughts out of your head." Lucio kept the shutter whirring and clicking.

"How did you know what I was thinking?" she asked.

"It is broadcast all over your face," he said, continuing to take shot after shot. "I know what to look for now. All those times you were doing the tap-tap-tapping you had that exact look in your eye."

"What look?"

"Worry. Fear. A little sadness. I think maybe Larry put all that rubbish in your head, am I right?"

"Ha!" Ginger said, moving a shoulder forward in the hopes it would accentuate her collarbones. "I had no idea I was so transparent."

"You are sweet is what you are. Sweet and sexy and a joy to be around."

Ginger smiled, licked her lips, then tried to shake her hair provocatively, forgetting that there was so much hairspray on her head that there would be no movement whatsoever. Gilligan's Island would have to be hit by a category 5 hurricane for that to happen.

"My God, Genevieve. Looking at you is making my cock as big as a telephoto lens."

She laughed, having fun with him, knowing he was teasing her, trying to get a reaction he could capture with the camera.

"How do you say 'cock' in Spanish?" she asked, giving him a devilish smile.

"Do not move!" Lucio popped up from his crouched position and went to get HeatherLynn. She seemed pleased to see him.

"Here you go, you cute little girlie girl, you." He set the dog in front of Ginger, near her knees. "Get a treat ready, Genevieve. I am going to put the sunglasses on her face and you will try to keep her still with the treats. You must continue with that sexy little smile of yours while keeping her still, yes?"

"Yes, yes," she said. While Lucio perched the tiny sunglasses on HeatherLynn's snout, Ginger tried to reassure her pretty girl by stroking her ears, cooing, and baby-talking.

"What a good little doggie she is," Lucio whispered, steadying the sunglasses. Within seconds he was back at the camera.

Ginger fed the dog a steady stream of treats and sweet talk. Through it all, she tried her best to smile but knew she probably looked stiff and fake.

"There are many ways to say 'cock' in Spanish, *bonita*," Lucio said, out of nowhere.

"Really?" Ginger tilted her head in curiosity.

Click.

"I know you ask me that because there are certain things you long to say to me in Spanish, certain dirty things."

Ginger laughed. "I do?"

Click. Click.

"Oh, yes. You long to tell me how you need more of my cock. That you dream of it at night. That you love the way it feels all hard and silky inside your mouth."

Clickclickclickclickclick.

"And there are many ways to say 'pussy' in Spanish."

"There are?"

"Oh, yes, *bonita*."

"But there is only one language to speak of the pussy and the cock."

She let out a little groan.

Click. Click. Click. Click.

It had to be the accent, Ginger decided, because if Larry had murmured these same words to her she'd be laughing at how ridiculous he sounded.

"The only language we need is the language of the body, of passion. No words are needed, yes? Just the lips and the tongue and the teeth and the fingers and the skin."

Click. Click. Click.

"That's it, my sweet Genevieve. Feed the doggie her treats. Later you will feed me your pussy, yes? Your pussy will be my treat."

Click.

"So you will allow me to love you tonight? You will give yourself to me?"

Ginger was shoving the treats into HeatherLynn's mouth faster than the little dog could gobble them. "God, yes, Lucio," she breathed.

"Go a little slower, *mi amor*. I need to capture the seconds in between the treats, yes?"

"Oh. Sorry."

"Look at the camera."

"Okay."

"I'm going to fuck you so good tonight."

Click. Click. Click

"You will take all of me up inside you. You will be hot and slick."

Clickclickclickclickclickclickclickclick.

"Oh, my God."

At that point, HeatherLynn apparently reached her limit for dog treats and dirty talk. She raised a paw and knocked the sunglasses off her nose, then ran back to her pillow.

Ginger was panting. She felt a light sheen of perspiration all over her body, and she knew it wasn't from the harsh lighting.

Lucio said nothing. He went about switching off the lights and putting away his equipment. Ginger sat up in the sand, crossing her legs and reaching above her head to stretch.

"Did we get enough pictures, do you think?"

Lucio didn't answer her.

"I've always thought you had to take thousands of pictures to get one really good one," she said.

He chuckled softly. "It is often the case, yes. But sometimes, you take one shot, you nail it, you know it, and you pack up and go home."

"Did you nail it?"

Lucio looked at her, his eyes smiling. He said nothing, just continued with what he was doing.

Ginger watched every move he made. There was an intensity to Lucio when he was sexually charged. Sex was serious business to him. His sentences were shorter. His eyes grew darker. He became the aggressor. Ginger could tell that even as he worked, he was seriously aroused.

It made her breathless to think of what would come next.

Suddenly he stood above her. Lucio reached his hand down for her and pulled her to a stand. Her heart was pounding.

"Open your mouth just a little bit for me," he said. She did what he asked, thinking maybe he was planning ahead for another picture. Lucio slid his middle finger between her lips.

Her eyes flew wide. She let go with a moan that felt like it started from the soles of her feet.

"You make me insane," he whispered, leaning close, adding his tongue alongside his finger. After a moment of this, he placed his lips over hers, continuing to invade her mouth with tongue and finger.

Ginger shivered. She'd never felt anything so erotic in her life.

She reached out, placing her palm flat on his chest. She felt his heart racing. She felt the heat of his body through his shirt.

Without a word, Lucio ended the kiss, the tonguing, and the fingering. "Come," he said, guiding her toward the bedroom.

"I'm covered in sand," she whispered. "I've got fake eyelashes on, and way too much hairspray."

"None of it will matter," he said.

Lucio marched her right on through the bedroom and into Rick's palatial master bath. Lucio opened the doors to the huge slate shower and started the water. Hot streams shot out at every angle, from a dozen showerheads.

He turned to her, a pensive smile on his face. "Something very strong happens when I'm with you. The word . . ." He shook his head.

"Potent," she said.

"Exactamente." He reached around her chest and unclasped the old-fashioned hook-and-eye closure of the bikini top. "The animal in me comes out, Genevieve. My male animal. I feel dominant. I know I will take what I want from you, and I know you will give it to me."

Ginger nodded slowly, trying to swallow. He slipped his fingers into the sides of her bikini bottom and pulled them down her thighs, past her knees, down her calves, and to the floor. She stepped out of them.

"Does it bother you that I become so forceful when I want you?" Lucio traced a fingertip down the side of her face. "Does it scare you? I do not want to scare you, *mi amor.*"

"I'm not scared."

"Does it arouse you?"

"Oh, hell yeah."

"I will never do anything you do not like." He kissed her gently on the lips. "The sex talk in the studio—I saw how it lit up your face, how your skin grew flushed. I took advantage of that. I trust it did not offend you."

Ginger shook her head. "The only thing that would

offend me is if you used the same technique with Roxie and Bea and everyone else you photograph."

Lucio laughed softly. "I do not foresee that happening."

"Then we're good."

"Will you undress me now, Genevieve?"

She nodded, giving him a shy smile. Ginger reached out for his belt, pulling it through the buckle. She unzipped the fly of his jeans and watched as the pants slipped down his slim hips. Ginger grabbed the edge of his casual cotton shirt and yanked it over his head. Lucio got to the boxer briefs before she could, pulling them off his body with impatience.

Ginger gasped. She hadn't forgotten what he looked like, of course, because the vision was forever burned into her memory. But seeing him in front of her made her heart skip and her hands shake. Lucio Montevez was the most beautifully masculine thing she'd ever seen. She ran her hands over his biceps and then his forearms, feeling the steely flesh and the hard bone. She traced her fingertips over the muscular ripples of his abdomen, the swell of his hard ass as it flared just slightly from his lean waist.

"You make me insane, too," she whispered, leaning forward to flick the very tip of her tongue on one of his nipples, then the next.

She let her tongue slide down the center of his chest, down to the narrow dividing line of dark, silky hair, to where it disappeared into the swell of his pubic bone.

She fell to her knees. She wanted to worship him, show him how much she desired him, how glad she was to have found him.

"You've changed everything for me, Lucio," she said, brushing her fingers along the root of his hardening cock. "You bring out something I never knew I had inside me."

His hand fluttered against her cheek. "What is it?"

"My sexual self." Ginger leaned closer, running her tongue back and forth at the base of his shaft. She could feel him growing in girth and length. "The male in you brings out the female in me."

"That is how it should be, my love."

Ginger placed her lips around the head of his cock and sucked him softly. With her hands she lightly teased the rest of his shaft. She rubbed her hard nipples against the front of his thighs.

She looked up. Lucio had his head thrown back, his eyes closed, his lips open slightly. A thrill coursed through her knowing how she pleased him.

"Ah, please stop, *bonita*. You will make me come."

She smiled up at him. "You don't want that?"

He laughed, looking down at her, his eyes black with desire. "I do. I want to come while I'm inside you. So please . . ." Lucio reached down and supported her under her arms, bringing her to a stand. "Step into the water with me. Let me wash the sand off you."

She entered the huge shower, Lucio behind her. She heard the door close just as she felt him press up against her back.

"Feel the water come down on you," he said, pushing her forward, grabbing her hips as the hot water soothed over them both. She felt his hands in her sticky hair, slowly massaging the water into her scalp until the hairspray began to dissolve. Ginger closed her eyes and was enjoying the pure decadence of his touch when she smelled something faintly minty, herbal, and she knew he'd opened a shampoo bottle.

"Allow me," Lucio said from behind her. His hands lathered the shampoo as he massaged and rubbed, gently making sure the suds reached everywhere. She heard him pull out a handheld nozzle, then shuddered at the pleasure of the hot water hitting directly on her scalp, his hand running down the length of her hair.

"I love your hair, *mi amor*," he said. "The color is exotic. It is the color of desire, did you know that?"

"Uh-uh," Ginger managed.

Lucio chuckled, opening another bottle Ginger could only assume was shower gel. It smelled fresh and light and she moaned out loud when a soft sponge touched her shoulders, back, bottom, and her thighs and calves. Lucio asked her to turn toward him so that he could soap her feet. Ginger had to giggle at all the attention he paid to her toes, feet, and ankles. It made her feel like a princess. Next, he continued the sensual massage of the shower gel into her legs, thighs, belly, arms, breasts.

"Let's get you rinsed off, my love."

Only then did Lucio touch her between her legs. Ginger knew he'd find a very swollen and slick pussy.

"You are very wet, *mi amor*," he said. He moved her long hair to the side and kissed the side of her neck.

Ginger's knees began to buckle, but Lucio caught her. "Sit with me," he said, gently guiding her to a large seat built into the wall of the shower.

Lucio sat down first, then pulled her into his lap. She straddled his thighs and lowered herself, the sensitive outer lips of her pussy opening and pressing down onto the light curly hair of his legs.

Lucio's hands were all over her back and ass, massaging her flesh as the hot water continued to rain down her skin. The pleasure was intense. The physical joy she felt nearly made her cry.

"Give me your mouth," Lucio said, pressing the back of her neck toward him until her mouth touched

his. Ginger felt every muscle in her body release, un-
coil, melt. Lucio's kisses were not just about the lips,
they were an all-body contact sport. His tongue and
teeth played with her, his hands gripped and caressed
and slid all over her, his thighs spread apart, which
opened her legs further.

How could she have lived without this? How could
she have gone twenty years without knowing how this
felt? He was kissing her, stroking her, when she began
to cry.

"Oh, oh . . ." Ginger gasped, taking her mouth away
from his in surprise. Lucio's fingers had just entered
her engorged vagina. His touch was so soft, so loving
and careful, but the sensations built in her fast and
hard. There was no way to stop the orgasm taking
her over.

She clamped down on his fingers and came almost
immediately, her cry muffled by Lucio's tongue, which
he'd returned to her mouth. His free hand caressed
and moved her bottom, lifting her up as his fingers
continued to play inside her. Somewhere deep in her
brain, Ginger knew he was adjusting her position so
that he could impale her, even before her orgasm
could subside.

With her last functioning brain cell she thought
about a condom. She was about to interrupt the moment when she glanced down at him, only to find he
was already sheathed. He must have done it while her
back was turned—Lucio was a consummate pro.

Suddenly she was lifted higher, pulled forward,
and pressed down. Before she knew what was happening, Lucio had replaced his fingers with his cock,
which penetrated her in one long, hot slide of pleasure.

"¡Que Dios me ayude!" he groaned as he entered

her. The outburst was followed by a torrent of Spanish she could only guess was the equivalent of her own English babbling.

"Oh God, yes," Ginger cried. "This is so good. Don't stop. I didn't know, Lucio! I didn't know it could be so good!"

"Genevieve. You are mine." His hands cupped her breasts. His dark eyes demanded she look at him.

"I know I am," she whispered. "I've wanted to be yours forever."

"And I am yours. Do you understand? I belong to you just as you belong to me."

She laughed suddenly, the intensity of the physical pleasure and the emotional closeness almost too much to process. "I know you're mine, Lucio. I've wanted you all my life."

"And now you have me." He hissed, gritting his teeth. "Ah, *bonita,* now you really are going to make me come."

She pushed down onto him, feeling him go deeper than he'd ever been before—deeper than anyone had ever been. She braced her hands against the slate wall and rode him, squeezing and squirming as she moved up and down. Lucio let his head rest against the wall, his eyes focused on hers.

"I wish I had met you sooner," he whispered.

"I wish the same," she said.

"I would have wanted to make a child with you. Of all the women in the world—" Lucio stopped speaking. He closed his eyes for a moment, then shook his head. "I wish it could have been you."

That's when he grabbed her hard by the hips and thrust into her with all his strength. Ginger screamed, the rush of joy sharp and clean. Lucio groaned out to God, in both English and Spanish.

Many long minutes went by. The two of them stayed exactly where they were, their bodies fused, the hot water running down their skin.

Ginger was overcome with a deep comfort. She never wanted to leave this place, his arms, this moment. She rested her cheek on Lucio's shoulder.

"Thank you, Genevieve," he whispered.

She kissed his damp skin. "For what?"

"For this. For you. For everything."

She nuzzled his cheek, then dragged her lips to deliver a gentle kiss upon his lips. "I really am yours, you know," she whispered, studying the tender look in his eyes. "That night on the lawn? When I told you I belonged to you?"

"I remember." Lucio produced the smile of an exhausted—but happy—man.

"It was the truth," Ginger said, her voice catching. "I didn't even *know* it at the time, but it really was the truth."

Lucio nodded slowly, raising a finger to her heart and tapping lightly. "But you knew it inside here, yes?" he said.

She smiled at him. "I suppose I did."

"That is the only place we ever know anything, my love." He wrapped his arms around her and held her close. "Everything else is just a guess."

CHAPTER 14

Ginger knocked on the blue door of the little blue house on Cayuga Street, trying not to judge the monochromatic color scheme Mrs. Needleman had chosen for the exterior paint job. Ginger liked powder blue as much as the next person—just not slapped on stucco, shutters, windowsills, trim, concrete steps, *and* the front door with the same heavy-handed exuberance.

She might no longer be employed to evaluate home and garden design for the *San Francisco Herald,* but old habits were hard to shake.

"Genevieve!" The small woman reached out her wrinkly arms and wrapped them around Ginger's waist. "It is so lovely to see you! I was thrilled when you called! Come in, come in. Would you like some tea?"

Ginger had to blink a few times to get her bearings. Most of these Cayuga Terrace houses were built right around World War II, and by the looks of the living room, Gloria Needleman hadn't bothered to redecorate since. The only striking features of the small room were the top-quality hardwood floors and a hideous sparkly gold couch that was wrapped in clear plastic. Ginger decided it looked like a giant Twinkie still in its wrapper.

"Thank you for agreeing to meet with me," Ginger said, being ushered into the home. "I know it was last-minute."

Mrs. Needleman smiled, and Ginger noticed how cute she looked—even with the intricate web of wrinkles that decorated her face. It had to be the little old lady's beady brown eyes, she decided—they burned with a zest for life. As Ginger lowered herself onto the crackly plastic seat, she realized she'd never before allowed the words "cute" and "wrinkles" to coexist in the same thought.

"How do you like your tea?" Mrs. Needleman asked, already scurrying toward the kitchen. "Oh, fiddle. I'll just bring out cream and sugar and you can serve yourself."

"Thank you," Ginger said, sighing, reevaluating why she had decided she needed to come here. She was a grown woman, after all. She really should be able to sort out her emotions on her own.

"I must say, you look quite well, Genevieve!" Mrs. Needleman called out from the kitchen. "Bright-eyed and glowing! You must be getting extra sleep these days."

Not exactly, Ginger thought to herself. In fact, she'd been getting more than enough fabulous sex and not enough shut-eye. She knew she was doing a bang-up job making up for a lifetime of sexual deprivation but might never catch up on her lost sleep. In fact, she'd been utterly exhausted the last few days.

"Here you are, dear," Mrs. Needleman said, handing Ginger a circa 1950s china cup and saucer.

"Thank you so much," she said, inhaling the comforting aroma. "This looks like the real thing, like my grandmother Ola used to make."

"Oh my, yes!" Mrs. Needleman took a seat next to her on the sofa, a loud crunching noise filling the room when the petite lady's bottom hit the plastic. "I think half the world's troubles would disappear if we'd only just slow down enough to make a real cup of tea. How long does it take to boil water on the stove, pour it in a teapot, and steep the leaves? About fifteen minutes—enough time to let the mind and soul rest."

Ginger nodded politely and took a sip of the strong black tea. Truly, it did taste a lot better than her usual tea bag in a mug of microwaved water, but she wasn't sure it was the secret to life.

"Now," Mrs. Needleman said, setting her cup and saucer on the coffee table. "What is it you wanted to talk to me about? Did you ever find the man who was waiting for you?"

Ginger laughed, shaking her head, placing her cup next to Mrs. Needleman's. "I do believe I have." She kept her eyes focused on her clasped hands in her lap. "But I need some advice, and I don't know who else to ask."

"I see," Mrs. Needleman said, patting her hands. "Have you consulted with your mother?"

Ginger looked sideways at Mrs. Needleman. "Uh, no. My mother has better taste in shoes than she does men."

"All right. And what about your wonderful friends?"

Ginger nodded, pursing her lips. "Well, I've asked them, but I'm not sure I'm getting an accurate read from any of them. I mean, Josie is living on Planet Bliss right now. She's like an Amway salesman for true love. I'm not sure she sees my situation clearly."

"You don't say? What about Roxanne?"

"Roxie? Please! She *wants* me to fall flat on my

face, just so she can prove her point! She's Rush Limbaugh and I'm President Obama!"

"Ah," Mrs. Needleman said. "And Bea?"

Ginger blinked a couple times, then fell back against the couch, her hair picking up static from the plastic slipcover. "Look, I love Bea. I do. She's always been there for me. But the truth is, she's had about as much personal experience with romantic love as the Dalai Lama."

Mrs. Needleman giggled, her narrow shoulders moving up and down in her short-sleeved polyester blouse. "But you know, part of the Dalai Lama's wisdom comes from the fact that he's not in the thick of things. Maybe Bea's objectivity can be helpful to you. After all, no one can see the whole battlefield if they're down in the trenches."

Ginger laughed. "Bea sees the battlefield all right, and in her opinion, it's nothing but wall-to-wall land mines."

Mrs. Needleman giggled again. "Bea is a special person. We've been spending quite a lot of time together."

That surprised Ginger—Bea hadn't mentioned she'd been socializing with Mrs. Needleman. Somehow, Ginger couldn't picture what the duo would do for fun—run five Ks together? Play a little one-on-one basketball? Tackle a new agility course with Martina?

"We discuss the whole gamut of things. Philosophy, spirituality, fate. We debate the limits of science and the realm of the unexplained."

Ginger's eyes popped wide. "*My* Beatrice Latimer?" She laughed uncomfortably. "Are you sure we're talking about the same person? The *Herald*'s assistant sports editor?"

Mrs. Needleman smiled sweetly. "You know, Genevieve, it could be that you are only acquainted with one side of Bea."

Ginger shrugged. "Maybe."

"It could be she only shares one part of herself with you, Roxanne, and Josephine, because it's what you've come to expect from her. People are often a lot more complex than we give them credit for."

Ginger felt herself frown. It was true that she'd never been to Bea's home. She'd only met Bea's mother once, and that was more than enough. In all the years she'd known Bea, she'd never once had the courage to come right out and ask Bea about her sexual preference—she'd been waiting for Bea to have an epiphany and share it with the group.

For the first time, Ginger considered the possibility that Bea had always known exactly who she was and didn't give a damn what anyone else thought. Maybe she didn't feel the need to explain herself.

"That's an interesting theory," she told Mrs. Needleman.

"All I'm saying is that you might give Bea a little more credit." Mrs. Needleman gave her a pensive smile. "In the meantime, what can I help you with?"

Ginger crossed her arms over her chest, crossed her legs, and swung her foot back and forth.

"You are nervous, Genevieve."

"No."

"Yes."

Ginger turned her head toward Mrs. Needleman and sighed. "Look, I know you set us up."

Mrs. Needleman looked surprised.

"Lucio told me how you gave him the scoop on me at the wedding. You told him that I was divorced, that my husband had cheated on me, that I had two boys, what I did for a living, and that I was staying in the upstairs bedroom of the guesthouse."

Mrs. Needleman shrugged, but said nothing.

"And you told him to wait for me outside your guest room that night."

Mrs. Needleman took a sip of her tea.

"So? Did you?"

The old lady sighed and set down her teacup. "Perhaps."

Ginger laughed. "Here's the deal, Gloria. At this juncture, I've got it bad. I'm in deep doo-doo here and I'm scared to death. I'm already in love with him. So, since this is all your doing, you could at least tell me the truth. Did you arrange for us to be together? Did you set us up? And, most importantly, *why*?"

Mrs. Needleman held her hands out in the universal gesture of mea culpa. "So shoot me," she said. "Sometimes fate needs a little kick in tuchus. What can I say?"

Ginger's lips parted in amazement. "That's it? That's all you have to say?"

Mrs. Needleman shrugged again. "Was I wrong?"

Ginger blinked. A low-frequency buzz started between her shoulder blades and spread through her arms and hands, her chest, her belly, and her legs. It was as if her body were reminding her of the charge she felt in Lucio's presence, the power of their connection.

"No. You weren't wrong."

"Finally—we're getting somewhere."

"But you don't understand," Ginger wailed. "It's so intense and deep that I don't know what end is up. I feel lost in him, part of him already, like I've just been sitting around for forty years, killing time until he dropped into my world and pulled me to his side and said, 'This way, Genevieve.'"

"That's very poetic," Mrs. Needleman said with a smile.

"It's more neurotic than poetic, I hate to tell you."

The old lady giggled again, patting Ginger's tensed-up shoulder. "My dear, we are right back to where we started, are we not?"

"How do you mean?"

"You sit here, your arms and legs all twisted up like a pretzel, your foot swinging back and forth, scared to discover what life has to offer you."

Ginger's mouth fell open. "Pardon me?"

"Does the intensity of your love frighten you?"

Ginger pursed her lips. "Somewhat."

Mrs. Needleman laughed quite loudly. "So we could say that the intensity of your passion for Lucio has you scared *somewhat* shitless?"

Ginger gasped, not even sure an eighty-something-year-old lady should be using that kind of language.

"The important thing to realize is that you weren't just sitting around killing time, as you put it. You were growing, Genevieve. You were maturing. You were collecting the life experiences that would open you to Lucio when he finally arrived. And, all the while, he was doing the same—preparing his heart for you!"

Ginger tilted her head, listening.

"That process was not wasted time, on your part or his." Mrs. Needleman smiled warmly. "What we're dealing with here is fate, my dear. The grand plan. Do not be afraid."

Ginger felt her eyes sting. Suddenly, she was over-whelmed with a surge of emotion. She didn't know where it came from or how long it would stay, but it packed a wallop. "I apologize, but I don't know what the hell's wrong with me lately. Was menopause this rough on you?" Ginger was embarrassed to look at Mrs. Needleman with tears dropping on her cheeks.

Mrs. Needleman chuckled. "Soon you'll understand everything, my dear girl. Now, look at me and listen very closely, Genevieve." The old woman scooted closer on the plastic couch, taking both of Ginger's hands in hers. "Just because a relationship feels more intense or powerful than you're accustomed to, it doesn't mean it's something to fear."

Ginger wanted to wipe her eyes but Mrs. Needleman had her hands locked in a viselike grip. "Okay," she whispered.

"I've always thought that romances were like food—every dish and every relationship has its own distinct flavor—a flavor that's produced by the chemical reaction of the ingredients."

"Uh . . . what?" Ginger wasn't following her.

"Some romances are oatmeal. Some are five-alarm chili."

Ginger laughed.

Mrs. Needleman smiled. "And what do you think you have with the handsome photographer?"

She managed to free a hand so she could wipe the tears from her face. "Is there a six-alarm?"

"Why not?" Mrs. Needleman reached into the front pocket of her jumper and handed Ginger a clean, pressed handkerchief. "Here. I can see all those hot peppers are getting to you."

"Yeah," Ginger said, dabbing her eyes with the crisp linen. "But that's what I'm worried about—a six-alarm fire can't burn forever."

"Ah."

"Roxanne tells me I'm headed for a fall."

Mrs. Needleman nodded. "But it can be a controlled fall, my dear. Even the hottest spices mellow over the years. It's the way of things. The taste will deepen, become more complex and satisfying over time." Mrs. Needleman winked.

"Oh, God," Ginger said, sighing loudly. "That's the problem! Lucio's never stayed in one place long enough to simmer over a low flame, if you know what I'm saying."

Mrs. Needleman placed her hand on Genevieve's arm, her eyes fierce. "A man's past does *not* always determine his future."

"I try to tell myself that."

"Keep doing so," Mrs. Needleman said. "Everything will work out for the best, just you wait and see. It's a good thing you came to see me today."

Ginger nodded.

"But may I be frank about something?" Mrs. Needleman suddenly looked quite concerned.

Ginger had to laugh. "You mean you haven't been frank yet? My God, I don't think I want to hear this next part."

The old woman giggled, too. "I just wanted to tell you to hold on tight, my dear girl—your journey will be bumpy before it becomes smooth."

Ginger scowled. "Bumpy?"

Mrs. Needleman smiled. "The important thing to know is that your little family will come out just fine. Never doubt it."

A few minutes later, Ginger backed out of the drive of the powder-blue stucco house on Cayuga Street, double-checking that her seat belt was fastened. Mrs. Needleman's last few words had left her scared somewhat shitless.

* * *

"Ach, nein!"

Despite everything, Lucio had to laugh. He hadn't heard Ilsa Knauss's German-flavored groans of displeasure for more than two years, and it brought back fond memories. He'd always liked her. She was a perfectionist and a control freak, but she'd been a whole lot of fun when she wasn't working.

Lucio had debated with himself whether to call her, but he knew it had to be done. He could not sic the police on her unless he was sure she was responsible. He needed to hear her admit it. Thanks to the Internet, it had taken him less than five minutes to find her London phone number.

"Ah, Ilsa, surprised to hear from me?" he asked her.

The long-distance phone line was silent. For a moment, Lucio feared he'd lost the connection.

"What do you want, you *schmutzige Hund?* Please tell me you're not in the U.K."

"Uh, no. I'm in the U.S."

"So? What do you want? I'm busy."

"It's the middle of the night in London."

She was silent again, then said, "I'm hanging up."

"Don't!" Lucio called out. "Look, I need to talk to you about what happened in China. It's important we discuss this—get everything out in the open so that we can put it behind us."

He heard her giggle. "Did you like your little rat friend? I thought he bore a striking resemblance."

Lucio sighed.

She chuckled again. "Are you calling from jail, Lucky? Because the last I heard, your ass was headed to prison. And what a shame about the Erskine—sucks for you, eh?"

Whatever sentiment Lucio felt at the beginning of this call had disappeared. "How could you do this to me, Ilsa?"

"Because you deserved it, *Schwein*! I woke up and you were gone and all I got was a note on the kitchen table." Lucio heard Ilsa breathe heavily, as if she were overcome with emotion. "I had to chase you down like a dog at the airport! You humiliated me! And I really cared for you, you heartless, bastard *Scheissekopf!*"

Lucio dropped his head, truly ashamed of his behavior. Maybe if he'd apologized earlier, he wouldn't be in this mess. Better yet, he could have had the decency to sit down and talk with Ilsa before he left. Why had such basic kindness been impossible for him?

"I hurt you, Ilsa. I was wrong. I apologize. But your revenge has been over the top. You've succeeded in ruining my career."

"*Mein Gott,* you are such a crybaby!"

"I saw the e-mails you sent Piers."

"Piers Skaarsgard? That oaf? So what? I was sorry to hear about Sylvie, though. That was extremely sad."

"You deny you e-mailed Piers about how you got your revenge on me in China?"

Ilsa laughed. "So what if I e-mailed Piers? Look, Lucky." She sighed loudly. "You deserve whatever you got. It's karma. Now, fuck off."

She hung up.

Lucio stared at the phone and shook his head. All right. Fine. He could now give her name and a copy of the e-mails to Sydney, the lawyers at *Geographica*, the State Department, and the police without missing any sleep. Maybe somehow he could find a way to get the information to the Erskine Prize committee without it looking as if he were begging.

Regardless of the outcome, at least he had the relief of knowing the truth. That was a very good thing, yes? But it did not feel good. It was awful to think that a woman he once slept with could hate him so much, call him such horrible names.

No wonder it didn't feel like much of a victory.

CHAPTER 15

Lucio thoroughly enjoyed the drive up to Sonoma. Back at Genevieve's place, she'd tossed him the keys to her Volkswagen and slid into the passenger seat with a smile, comfortable with Lucio being behind the wheel. Josh and Jason took up residence in the back, Señorita Chiquita on her satin pillow between them.

The boys chatted the whole way, regaling him with stories of their own life adventures, including the time Josh almost fell off a scenic overlook into the Grand Canyon, the night Jason got thrown in juvenile detention for underage drinking, and Josh's elaborate plans to become president of the United States.

"You can take my official portrait when the time comes," Josh told him.

"It would be an honor," Lucio said.

Next the boys told a revealing tale of their grandmother's weeklong stay while their parents' divorce was finalized.

"We don't see Grams a lot, so it was kind of weird having her stay with us," Jason said. "She was a Hollywood actress, did Mom tell you? And she's still kind of glamorous-looking, even though she can't move her face so good anymore."

Lucio frowned. "She had a stroke?"

"She had Botox," Josh said. "Lots of it."

Jason jumped in. "And a chin lift and something that yanked up her eyelids so much that she always looks like she's just seen somebody get ax-murdered, and a bunch of other shiii—" He stopped himself before he cursed in front of his mother. Good for him, Lucio thought.

"She's had a few too many procedures," Ginger explained, clearly uneasy with the subject matter.

"How many?" Lucio asked.

Ginger let go with a tired sigh. "She's been under the knife more times than a sheet cake at a kid's birthday party."

The boys laughed. Genevieve shook her head and looked out the window. Lucio nodded slowly, grateful for another piece to Genevieve's puzzle.

"Yeah, and she's always telling Mom she needs 'work done,' too." Joshua leaned closer to Lucio's headrest to whisper theatrically into his ear. "Maybe you could tell her she doesn't. Maybe she'll listen to you."

"That's enough, guys," Ginger said.

"Well, you won't listen to anyone else," Josh said.

Lucio glanced at an annoyed Genevieve in the seat next to him. "Please, do not do it, *mi amor*," he said, watching her frown. He noticed that she did not succumb to her usual *tap-tap-tapping* of her forehead, however, and that impressed him.

He tried to keep his eyes on Route 37 North, but it was difficult. The sun was hitting Ginger at an angle that transformed her hair into ribbons of coppers, browns, and golds, with just the tiniest hint of silver threaded throughout. Her hazel eyes shimmered, despite the frown.

"Nature has already done all the work you need,"

Lucio told her. "You are the rarest wildflower, at the peak of her splendor."

Ginger tried to hide her embarrassed smile. There was no comment from the back, at least not right away.

"Okay, that was awkward," Jason said.

Lucio laughed, checking in the rearview mirror on the teenagers, who didn't look like they felt the least bit awkward. They were grinning, in fact. They looked relieved that someone might have talked some sense into their mother—or simply lavished her with the kind of praise she deserved.

"I Googled you the other day," Josh said. "You're one of the most famous photographers in the world."

Lucio chuckled. "I would not go that far."

"But you are, man," Jason said. "Your pictures have been on the cover of a bunch of magazines like *Geographica* and *Smithsonian* and *Nature*. You were even in a PBS special. We watched it on YouTube!"

"Ah, yes." Lucio nodded, thinking back to the documentary that Sylvie Westcott had produced in the late eighties—when she first met up with Piers and Lucio. "That was a very long time ago."

"God, it had to be," Josh said. "You looked young!"

Jason smacked his brother on the shoulder. "You're a complete jacktard," he told him. "No, wait—pardon me—you're president of the Jacktards of America!"

Lucio looked to Genevieve in bewilderment.

"You don't want to know," she said, shaking her head. She raised her voice to add, "And that's the last time he'll ever hear that expression used by either of my sons, isn't that right?"

Silence had returned to the back seat.

"Isn't that *right*?" Genevieve repeated, threatening to turn all the way around in her seat.

"That's right, Mom," Jason said, his voice soft.

"Ass-wipe," Josh said, smacking his brother in retaliation.

"Joshua Franklin Garrison!"

"Okay. Okay, Mom."

The last ten miles of the trip were much quieter, but as they pulled up to the gates of Samhain Ranch, Genevieve smiled shyly at Lucio. He knew exactly what she was thinking, because he was thinking of it, too.

"I haven't been here since the wedding," she said.

"Me, either." Lucio could not hold back. He reached for his wild woman of the vineyards and brought her hand to his lips. He didn't care if the boys saw. He had nothing to hide, nothing to be ashamed of. He was going to do everything right when it came to this woman. He would not give her anything less than the best he had in him.

Genevieve did not pull her hand away. Her smile grew and she let out a little laugh of pure pleasure. And the second his mouth brushed the top of her fingers, he knew it would be pointless to avoid the truth any longer—he loved her. He wanted to be with her, always.

Finally, after more than twenty years of roaming, Lucio had found his home.

"Wait! Wait! I have it!" Roxie jumped from her wicker chair on the front porch of Rick and Josie's ranch house, suddenly inspired.

"What'd you decide?" Josie asked. She'd just come back from the kitchen with another platter of chicken and steak taquitos with all the trimmings—guacamole, sour cream, fresh salsa, tomatilla sauce. Lucio beat even Josh and Jason in the race for seconds.

"I am picturing a rain forest setting," Roxie said,

looking out onto the vineyards, reaching out like a movie director framing a scene. "It's kind of surreal, maybe mists rising from the ground, mountains, waterfalls, a jaguar or two pushing through tall grass in the background."

Rick wagged his eyebrows at Lucio and raised his glass of lemonade in a toast. "I hope you've got Photoshop," he said, and they both laughed.

"I hope you've got dry ice," Bea said.

Roxie's eyes shone. She raised her chin and put her shoulders back. "And I'm standing there, an Amazon woman, full of my own glory and power—a true queen."

Lucio finished his taquito. "That would make a grand statement," he said.

Roxie wasn't done. "And I'm holding a spear that's way taller than I am and wearing some kind of headdress with plumes from exotic birds. My midriff is bare but my breastplate is ornate."

"Well, duh," Bea said dryly. "Those plain ole breastplates are so *yesterday*."

"Shhh, Bea," Josie said, giggling as she snuggled into her spot next to Rick on the white wicker love seat. Lucio smiled as he watched his friend casually put his arm around his wife and grin at her. All evening, Lucio had been entranced by how perfectly the newly married couple complemented each other. They hosted this party like they'd done it a thousand times, though it was their first official get-together at the ranch since the wedding. Rick's face was perpetually lit up, like he'd discovered the key to everything.

It looked to Lucio like Josie and Rick had been designed for each other. They fit—their personalities, their spirits, their physical bodies. And the ranch fit both of them. Even their three dogs seemed ecstatically happy with the arrangement. From where Lucio sat, it appeared the universe had settled down around the couple with a great sigh of relief, everything in place, just as it was supposed to be.

Lucio watched Rick kiss the tip of Josie's nose. It was so innocent and so tender that it sent a pang of need through him. Lucio's eyes went to Genevieve in her chair, legs crossed casually, a sweet smile pasted on her face as she watched the newlyweds. She must have been thinking the same thing.

Her eyes found his. Her cheeks flushed, embarrassed to have been caught gawking at the couple, but Lucio reassured her with a smile of his own.

Perhaps they wanted that same kind of comfort, connectedness, and love for themselves. There was no shame in that.

Lucio could not help but sigh. As much as he was enjoying the company and the good food and wine, he suddenly wished that it were just Genevieve and himself here—alone. He wanted to lift her in his arms once more and lay her down in the grass, or on the porch floor, or the great big leather sofa inside in the main room of the house, or upon one of the dozens of antique beds on the property.

It didn't matter where, really. He just wanted to lay her down, to cover her with his body and his passion.

In what seemed like slow motion, Genevieve batted her eyelashes at him. The desire rose in him so fast that Lucio had to adjust his trousers, a move that HeatherLynn didn't much like. He reassured the little dog in his lap with a pat to her head.

"Go on, Rox," Teeny said, raising his wine glass. "I'm on the edge of my seat over here waiting to hear about your choice of footwear."

"Right," Roxanne said, nodding seriously. "It's gotta be some type of thigh-high animal-hide boot, you know? It needs to be laced up the front."

"Sounds like Pocahontas on steroids," Bea said.

Teeny's laugh was so loud the whole pack of sleeping dogs raised their heads to make sure all was well. It wasn't until that moment that Lucio realized the evening had been spent in the company of six dogs of varying breeds and temperaments, ranging in size from Rick's huge mutt, Chen, to little Señorita Chiquita in his lap. Then there was Rick's small yappy terrier mix, Tara, and Roxanne's muzzled brown dog, who looked like she wanted to relax but didn't know how, growling at poor clueless Chen for no reason at all. Rounding out the canine crowd was Josie's fun-loving Genghis, and Bea's Martina, a sleek and intelligent animal with better manners than most of the humans he'd run across.

Truth be told, Lucio had never been interested in socializing with dogs—unless they were pulling his sled through the tundra. The only purpose for this particular pack of canines was the joy they brought to their humans. He had to admit the arrangement wasn't bad.

"You're just jealous," Roxanne reprimanded Bea, laughing. "My idea puts yours to shame."

Bea waved a hand through the air, then casually scratched Martina behind her ears. "Mine's more practical. More people can relate to it."

Lucio had to agree. Bea had asked for a photo of dog and owner on the tennis court, Martina photographed in midair, jumping over the net to catch a tennis ball in her mouth. Lucio thought it sounded fun, and knew the perfect setting would be Rick's tennis courts, right here on the estate, at sunset.

"Besides," Bea continued. "Where are you going to find an Amazon Woman outfit on short notice?"

"I know where," Josh said matter-of-factly. "Our drama club rents from this costume warehouse in the city—they have everything, I'm telling you. Batgirl. Nefertiti. Slutty nurses."

Lucio started laughing before anyone else, mostly because of the horrified look on Genevieve's face.

"Dear God," she said under her breath.

"Sorry, Mom, but you can't protect us from the world." Josh shoved another taquito into his mouth and swallowed it whole. "That freaky stuff is everywhere in society today—especially in San Francisco. But don't worry, we know how to keep it in perspective."

"You just have to trust our judgment," Jason added with a reassuring nod.

"That's exactly what I was thinking," Genevieve said, trying to smile over clenched teeth.

Josh finished wiping his mouth on a napkin. "I can give you the name of the place," he said to Lucio. "I'll even volunteer to do all the costuming for the photo shoots. I've worked backstage at our school's theater productions for years!"

"Wonderful," Lucio said, reaching across to give Josh a high five.

"And I'll do the rest of the Web site design and get it listed with search engines," Jason said. "Once we get some sample portraits we'll be ready to go online. I'm working on the MySpace and Facebook sites, too."

"Great!" Lucio high-fived Jason, as well.

"As soon as your posters are ready, I'll make sure they're up at all the stores," Rick said.

"My thanks to you, as always," Lucio said, bowing as deeply as he could manage with a small dog in his lap.

"My pleasure."

"We have our idea, too," Josie said from her nest under Rick's arm. She looked quickly to Rick, who nodded for her to do the honors. Josie sat forward on the love seat.

"Rick and I are on the Harley, right?" When everyone started to chuckle, she smiled. "We've decided to go totally over-the-top with the black leather stuff. Chains, shades, and tattoos. Well, mine will be fake."

Teeny laughed.

"And the three dogs—they'll be dressed exactly like us. Little helmets, sunglasses, vests, the whole deal."

Bea shook her head. "Good luck pulling that off."

Rick gestured to the haphazard pile of dogs on the porch floor near his feet. "Our pack is pretty mellow. They spend all day running the property, so with Lucio's expertise I think they'll be able to sit still long enough to get the shot."

Lucio nodded in approval. So far, the ideas from the group had been outstanding. But no one had even inquired about Genevieve's pose with HeatherLynn, and Lucio was itching to make the big reveal.

He was about to toot his own horn when Bea, bless her, barged in. "How about your shoot, Ginger? How did it go?"

Genevieve gave Lucio a sheepish smile. "I'll let you be the judge."

"You brought it?" Josie said, scooting to the edge of the love seat.

"Mm-hmm," Genevieve said. "Be right back."

Lucio watched as she rose from her wicker chair and headed for the front door of the ranch house. He couldn't help himself—he admired her tall elegance, the sweet indentations at the back of her legs, her soft heels, the swish of her lovely ass. Lucio felt Rick's eyes boring into the side of his head, and knew he'd been caught.

He turned, nodding ever so slightly to Rick, hoping his friend would see that he was pleading guilty to being crazy about Genevieve.

Rick's eyes got big and he dropped his jaw. "Damn," he whispered, shaking his head.

"What?" Josie asked her husband.

"That was incredibly fast," Rick said. When he noticed the strange looks from the crowd, he amended his comment. "The photo," he said. "What I meant was that Lucio sure got that picture together fast."

"Everyone ready?" Genevieve stood before the group on the front porch, the blank side of the large poster board visible between her shapely, long legs. The only sound was the *slap!* of the screen door as it closed behind her. Everyone was frozen in quiet anticipation.

Genevieve flashed her eyes at Lucio for the go-ahead. "Whenever you wish," he said, smiling at her.

"Ta-da!" She whipped the horizontal eleven-by-seventeen glossy blowup from behind her back, flipping it so the image was on display for all to see.

Lucio was thrilled. The reaction was precisely what he'd hoped for. There were a few seconds of complete silence, followed by dropping jaws, then an outburst of laughter, surprise, and squeals of delight.

Bea was on her feet. "Look at you, girl!" she said, laughing. She then made a few *whoop-whoop-whoop* sounds while pumping her fist through the air.

"Awesome, Mom!" Josh called out. "And look at HeatherLynn's little beehive! It's perfect!"

It really was, Lucio had to admit to himself, smiling. Somewhere in the stream of treats and titillating

talk, he'd captured one single perfect image: Heather-
Lynn's face pointed right at the camera, her little pink
tongue licking her lips, while Genevieve lay stretched
out on her side, all long and languid curves, a few
sand grains stuck to the glistening pink of her flat
belly, her eyes simmering with the kind of overt sexu-
ality the original 1960s TV Ginger could never have
gotten away with.

Everyone got to their feet and crowded around the
print. Teeny took it from Genevieve's hands and held
it in the middle of the huddling group. "Unbelievable," he breathed. "Wow! Ginger—you're amazing!"

Josie looked up from the image, her eyes huge.
"Good God, Garrison," she whispered. "I think you
missed your calling!"

Rick nodded slowly. "Nice, man," he said to Lucio,
chuckling in shock. "Real nice."

"You sure you want this on the Internet?" Roxie
asked, her brow furrowed. "You don't know who
might see it. I mean—" Her eyes darted to Josh and
Jason, then back to Genevieve. "It might attract the attention of one of those 'he was a quiet man and mostly
kept to himself' serial killers prowling the Web for his
next victim!"

Lucio laughed, as always, amused at Roxie's worst-
possible-scenario view of anything related to man-
woman relationships.

"Well," Josie said, sitting back down. "You've set
the bar pretty high, Ginger. The rest of us have our
work cut out for us."

"You're going to make a ton of money, Lucio," Bea
said, walking over to slap him on the back. The
affectionate tap nearly caused him to spill his wine all
over HeatherLynn, who was still asleep in his lap.
"Every dog owner I know is going to want one of these.

I hope you're ready for the demand you're going to unleash."

Lucio looked around at his crowd of friends and raised his glass in thanks. "Thanks to all of you, I most certainly am."

"I owe you one, Genghis," Lucio mumbled, watching as the fun-loving Labradoodle ran off with the last intact shuttlecock on Samhain Ranch. Blessedly, the badminton tournament had come to a standstill.

"I'll check in the barn again," Teeny said with a great sigh. "I swear there's some more in there somewhere."

"Have mercy on me, Teeny," Lucio whispered in his teammate's ear. "Come up empty-handed, I beg of you!"

Teeny laughed as he jogged off to the barn.

"We're gonna take you down, *sucka!*" Joshua said, making theatrically threatening hand gestures from the opposite side of the net.

"Yeah," Bea called out, laughing. "Is that all you got for us, pretty boy?"

Lucio chuckled as he wiped the sweat off his brow.

"You are a far better woman than I, Bea. I need a break."

She laughed again, giving her teenage teammate a victorious high five.

Smiling, Lucio strolled across the lawn to the shaded stone wall, where he ditched the badminton racket. He surveyed the ranch for any sign of Genevieve. Josie and Jason were still on the front porch, talking about her trip to the North Pole. Rick and Roxie had taken the horses out for a ride. Teeny was running toward the barn. Lucio was puzzled. Granted, it was a huge property, but Genevieve was nowhere to be seen.

He decided to try to find her. Lucio took a path through the gardens, remembering that first night they'd spoken, when he'd advised her that he'd be no good for her and, with a trembling hand, she'd given him her card. It was just two months ago, but it seemed like another lifetime.

He'd been filled with self-pity that night, ruminating over how he was nothing without his career. It made Lucio smile to think how drastically his perception had changed. Now, he knew how much he had missed when his career was his only passion. He walked farther, noticing the tall gardenias to his right, recalling how Genevieve's shoulder had brushed against the flowers as she approached him, sending their scent into the evening air. He reached toward the flowers, cradled a single blossom in his hand and inhaled. It was a fragrance he'd always associate with her. He picked the bloom to take along with him, sure that Rick and Josie wouldn't mind.

Lucio continued his stroll through the gardens, stopping long enough to nibble on a few ripe raspberries before he turned onto the crushed-stone path that would eventually take him to the pool and tennis courts. This entire area of the ranch was bordered by a row of tall, flowering hedges that filled the air with a light, intoxicating perfume.

He stopped in mid-stride. In a thick carpet of grass in the shade of the hedges, Genevieve was curled up, asleep, HeatherLynn in the crook of her knees. The dog heard Lucio approach and her tail began to wag, but Lucio put his finger to his lips, knowing she'd understand. Silently, he drew near, then lowered himself to the grass right next to Genevieve. He tucked the hollyhock blossom into HealtherLynn's pink leather collar, then gently adjusted Genevieve so that her head rested in his lap.

Lucio didn't speak. He didn't move. He fought back the desire to touch her silky hair in exchange for the pleasure of watching her sleep. HeatherLynn stretched and yawned, then toddled off across the lawn, flower in her hair, swinging her little fancy dog butt. Lucio chuckled to himself.

He looked up to the evening sky and could hardly believe where he found himself—the woman, the boys, the dog, good friends, the city of San Francisco. It was shocking to think that just two months ago, none of these things were as important to him as clearing his name and getting his *Geographica* contract reinstated. Everything had changed the night Genevieve Garrison fainted in his arms. Ironically, now that he'd taken steps to clear his name and put the blame where it belonged, it didn't seem all that important anymore.

She stirred. Her lips parted and she absently rubbed the tip of her nose, still not fully awake. Lucio leaned down. "*Te amo,* Genevieve," he whispered, just before he kissed her tenderly.

She kissed him back, which meant she'd either been awake to hear his profession of love or had woken up in mid-kiss, oblivious to his confession. Lucio realized that either way was all right with him. There was nothing he wanted to keep secret. He loved her. That was a fact.

"Please don't tell me I fainted again," Genevieve whispered.

"And the kiss was merely my attempt to revive you, Señora Garrison."

She giggled, adjusting her head on his lap. She brought a hand up to softly stroke his thigh. "You really did, you know. You revived me."

"Hmm, that is a nice way to see it. Very romantic."

"Extremely."

Lucio allowed his hand to play in her hair. He noticed that she felt warm to the touch. "Are you feeling all right, *bonita*?"

"Sure, just tired. I came out here to sit a minute and was lulled to sleep by the perfume of the bushes—isn't it glorious?"

"It is."

"Lucio?"

"Hmm?"

"I heard what you said."

Lucio's heart began to thump wildly. He had never told a woman he loved her—and actually meant it. Early on, he told women he loved them as a matter of strategy. He'd told Alma to see if it would convince her to take off her panties. It worked like a charm, and within three months she was his child bride. Lucio told a few girls he encountered early in his career that he loved them. He'd said it to Sylvie, knowing that he was an insincere cad. It was shameful to recall. He told Sylvie he loved her, and then he left. The cowardly act ate away at his soul for years, but at least it cured him of ever doing it again. And if there were just one mistake he could take back—in a lifetime of them—hurting Sylvie would be it.

But with Genevieve, it was so different. Lucio was a grown man. He had known many women. But he had never known a woman who made him laugh like Genevieve, made him look forward to each regular day like Genevieve, made him a slave to his passion like Genevieve. It was a curious thing, this love he had for her, because it had given Lucio permission to simply *be*. With this lovely woman at his side, he was able to fully experience the present moment, instead of plotting his next move, his next trip, his next challenge.

Genevieve sat up, her hair falling across her face as she climbed up to sit fully on his lap. He put his arms around her waist as she wrapped hers around his neck.

"I love you, too, Lucio," she whispered. "I love you with all my heart."

He nodded, swallowing back a surge of emotion he'd not expected and didn't know how to handle. It would not do for him to cry, of course. He had not cried since his mother's death.

"Then it's official," he said. "We love each other."

"It's been official for a while now," Ginger said, a touch of humor in her voice.

"It has?"

"Sure. Roxie, Bea, and Josie figured it out a couple weeks ago."

Lucio chuckled. "And Rick figured it out today, on the porch. He caught me staring at you."

"And if Rick knows, then Teeny does."

"And how about your boys?" Lucio asked. "Do they know?"

Genevieve unlocked her arms from his neck and straightened, looking down into Lucio's eyes. Her face was so beautiful. It was the center of his world.

"Of course they do, silly," she said, smiling. "Even HeatherLynn knows."

Lucio laughed. "How could she not, after your photo shoot?"

Genevieve laughed. It was a heartfelt and joyful sound. And as she laughed, every glorious wrinkle, every lovely furrow, every one of her crow's-feet came to life on her face.

Lucio grinned. He'd seen so much of the world—the frozen cathedral of Mount Everest, the impenetrable tangle of life along the Amazon, the awe-inspiring mystery of Machu Picchu—and all of it had stirred his soul, most certainly. But it wasn't until right then that he'd discovered his favorite spot on earth, the place that afforded him the single most spectacular view available on the planet.

It was the happy face of the woman he loved.

CHAPTER 16

"Sit, sit. Coffee?"

"No, thanks." Lucio took one of the chairs in the sitting room of Sydney Frankel's downtown office, a little annoyed that his agent had insisted he take time to visit him in person. He'd told Lucio he had an "intriguing idea" to discuss with him.

"Am I getting the Erskine? Did they change their minds?" had been Lucio's first question.

"No, unfortunately. Their decision to rescind the award was final."

"But *why*? Didn't they care that we had proof that Ilsa Knauss set me up?" Lucio was dumbfounded. "*¡Hostia!* What do they want from me?"

"I'm sorry," Sydney said, looking down. "Their decision was final. They'll be announcing the new winner any day."

Lucio fell back into the leather chair in Sydney's office, crossing his legs, though he knew he'd never be comfortable. He was too angry to be comfortable.

"It is unfair," Lucio said, shaking his head. "That is my award."

Sydney nodded. "There is always next year."

Lucio looked away, staring out the window. "Any word on who's getting it?"

Sydney sighed softly. "The rumor is Kieran O'Shaunessey, but it's not official."

"Ah," Lucio said, still looking out the window. "He's young, but he's good."

"Yes," Sydney said.

The two men sat in awkward silence for a moment, until Sydney cleared his throat. "Well," he said, his voice noticeably brighter. "You're certainly looking well, Lucky." His agent took the seat opposite him.

Lucio said nothing.

"So," Sydney said, chuckling. "I've got to tell you, those pet portraits you've got up on your Web site are absolutely top-notch. They're funny and sophisticated and—I suspected this might happen because I know how good your work is—my wife wants one taken of her and her moronic Maltese."

Lucio cracked a smile, finally turning away from the window. "So you called me down here to try to get a discount?"

Sydney roared with laughter. "I wouldn't dare. But, since you brought it up, how much is something like that going to set me back?"

Lucio snickered. "It depends on how elaborate the owner wants the setting or backdrop to be. The more props and costumes, preparation, or digital enhancement a picture needs, the more expensive it gets."

Sydney's bottom lip protruded the way it always did when he was running numbers in his head. "Ballpark?" he asked.

Lucio shrugged. "I've been charging anywhere from one to five thousand, U.S."

Sydney's mouth fell open. "You're shitting me."

"No. And I am booked for the next six weeks. I am enjoying myself, though, and I've got a terrific staff. I am on my way toward paying off *Geographica* in ninety days."

"You've got a *staff*?" Sydney looked shocked.

"Mostly volunteer, but I'm paying my girlfriend's teenage sons a little for their work. They've been doing costuming, Web design, and one of them is working as my assistant in the studio and the field. My girlfriend has been doing most of the scheduling, billing, and sales. She's phenomenal."

Sydney's left eye squinted. "You have a studio?"

Lucio nodded.

"You have a *girlfriend*?"

Lucio nodded again.

"Well." Sydney slapped his palms on his thighs and took a deep breath. "Sounds like you might not find my news as exciting as I'd assumed you would."

"What news?"

"I have to be honest with you, Lucky—I truly never thought I'd see the day."

"The day for what?"

"I swear it sounds like you're settled, like you're planting your ass right here in town and you're fine with it."

Lucio was preparing a response to that when the left pocket of his trousers began to vibrate. "Ah, *un momento, por favor.*"

As Lucio fished for the cell phone Josh and Jason had convinced him to purchase for the business, Sydney's eyes got big.

"It is a text message." Lucio squinted at the tiny screen and tried to decipher the strange code the boys used to convey information: *c u @ 7 yr crib game at 8 imo we shld order za.*

Lucio laughed, thinking Jason had just told him they'd be at his place at seven P.M., that the game started at eight P.M., and that they should order pizza— but Lucio could not be certain. He stuffed the phone back in his pocket.

He noticed Sydney gawking at him. "The boys are coming over to my house tonight to watch American football. The 49ers are playing the Seahawks," he said.

Just then, his pants vibrated again. "I am so sorry, Sydney." He fished out the phone and saw that Gene-vieve was calling. *"Dígame,"* Lucio answered. "Can I call you right back, *guapa*? Gracias." He snapped the phone closed, then laughed at Sydney's increasingly stupefied expression. "New phone," he said, holding it up before he shoved it back in his pocket.

"Since when do you have a cell phone?"

"Three days ago."

"My God."

Lucio dismissed Sydney's reaction with a wave of his hand.

"You're in a relationship, Lucio. You're in love!"

"Yes, I am."

"You're buying phones and hanging out with the woman's kids!" His agent's face was red with the effort it took for him not to burst out laughing.

"I am." Lucio recrossed his legs, bothered by Syd-ney's level of amusement. It was almost worse than Piers's.

"Well." Sydney got up and paced his office for a moment. He went to his desk and hit the intercom but-ton. "Bernice, can you bring in that contract for Lucky Montevez?"

Lucio's fingers gripped the chair's leather armrest. "What contract?"

"Yes, well, that's why I asked you to stop by.

You've just been offered a field assignment for *Nature* magazine. It's a four-week gig in Mauritius. They're doing a piece on pollution, deforestation, soil erosion, and the island's growing list of endangered species. It's the same sad tale you've told a hundred times from a hundred different locations."

Lucio refrained from any type of reaction, because he didn't know what kind of reaction to have. One part of him wanted to hear more. The other part of him wished he hadn't heard a word of any of this. Sydney was staring at him, waiting for a response.

Bernice entered the office with the papers, giving Lucio the few seconds he needed to get himself together.

Sydney glanced over the pages as Bernice left. "It's a forty-thousand-dollar job," he said. "As usual, they're offering a decent daily stipend with a bonus if you get the cover. The budget isn't enough for helicopters locally, so it looks like it will be private planes, off-road vehicles, and shoe leather, but they usually take pretty good care of you."

Lucio tried to get comfortable in the chair, which was proving to be a real challenge, since he didn't even feel comfortable in his own skin at that moment.

This one job would be almost enough to pay off his debt to *Geographica*. He would be in the clear, and could come back and pick up where he left off with Petography. But, of course, he couldn't take the job. He couldn't leave Genevieve and the boys and his business. He did not want to. The idea was preposterous.

"They'll give you ten thousand more as a signing bonus if you take the job today."

"I cannot take the job today!" Lucio said, shaking his head. "I cannot take the job at all!"

Sydney placed the contract on the glass-topped

coffee table. "I'm sorry—I just thought I heard you turn this down outright."

"At the very least I need some time to discuss it with my girlfriend."

Sydney laughed. "I've never heard you utter those words, and I'm especially surprised to hear them now."

Lucio frowned.

His agent balanced his elbows on his knees and peered at Lucio like he'd lost his mind. "This is Lucky's lucky day, right?" When Lucio didn't say anything, Sydney huffed in frustration. "Look, I know we've nailed Ilsa Knauss for all that business in China, but she hasn't been charged with anything yet, so you're still on the hook for the cash."

"I realize that," Lucio said.

"And I know you just started a little side business and you've got a new girl in your life, but if you take this field assignment, you're back in your element. Once you take this job, the whole China debacle will recede into the background and you won't be walking around with 'bad boy' tattooed on your forehead anymore. This is the break you've been waiting for."

Lucio nodded. "I said I needed some time to think it over." He got up to leave.

Sydney stood, as well. "Hey, why don't you see if the new girlfriend wants to go along? You'll have to cover her air and hotel, of course, but if she's the adventurous type it might be fun for her."

It was a romantic notion—taking his love to an exotic island paradise—but he doubted Genevieve would appreciate the reality of the flying and crawling insects, dripping humidity, poverty, poisonous plants, and scorching sun. He could set her up at the new Four Seasons in Anahita, but she'd still be left alone while he traipsed through the jungle.

"How soon do they need an answer?" Lucio asked.

"This week."

"I'll get back to you." Lucio reached for the door-knob.

"I have to say, Piers didn't expect this reaction."

Lucio turned around. "Piers? What does he know of this job?"

"Well, they offered the assignment to him first, but he declined, suggesting they give it to you. We just got the offer yesterday."

"Really?" Lucio was shocked. "Why would Piers turn down such an assignment? He needs the work as much as I do."

Sydney shrugged. "I didn't ask. But apparently, he lobbied pretty hard for you. I think he just wants to help."

"That is extraordinary," Lucio said, shaking his head. "I am surprised, but maybe I shouldn't be. He has always gone out of his way to help me."

"Those kinds of friends are one in a million, Lucky."

"Indeed." Lucio stood in silence for a moment, letting the situation settle in his brain. Truly, he didn't understand why Piers would do such a thing, and it bothered him. "Thank you, Sydney," he said, letting himself out. "I'll get back to you soon."

By the time Lucio made it to the underground parking garage where he'd left the car, he knew the reason Piers's intervention was so puzzling: Piers knew all about his feelings for Genevieve. He knew that Lucio was trying to start a relationship with her. So why would Piers be working behind the scenes to get him a job that would send him so far away from her, for such a long time?

Was this jealousy? Was this about Sylvie, somehow?

Lucio turned the key in the ignition, shaking his head at his new level of paranoia. He could not let what happened in China make him doubt everyone in his life. If Lucio allowed that to happen, then Ilsa Knauss would have inflicted a fatal wound.

He picked up his new cell phone and, for the first time, appreciated the convenience. With two clicks of a button, he was ringing Piers's flat.

"*Buenos dias, mi amigo.* Would you mind if I stopped by?" he asked.

Piers opened the door to his apartment with a huge grin, his eyes shining with excitement. Lucio immediately saw that Piers assumed he'd come to thank him. It was the happiest he'd seen Piers in months.

"Come in! Come in!" Piers said. "I've been looking at your Web site! What fun you must be having!"

"Absolutely," Lucio said.

"Please, please. Make yourself comfortable. I picked up another bottle of Rioja, thinking we might have something to celebrate. Would you care for a glass?"

Lucio laughed. "Sure, Piers. That would be nice."

He followed his friend out to the balcony, the spot that had become their private outdoor watering hole.

"To new beginnings," Piers said, touching his wine glass to Lucio's.

"*Salud,*" Lucio said, taking a sip and leaning back in the chair. He sighed and propped his feet on the iron railing, absently looking out over Green Street four stories below, with its string of Italian restaurants, and on to China Town a few blocks beyond.

"So, have you just come from Sydney's?" Piers asked, his grin still as wide as when he answered the door.

"Yes," Lucio said. "It was quite unexpected."

Piers laughed. "I thought it would be more fun for you, finding out that way. Do you have any idea how hard it's been for me to keep my mouth shut all these weeks while *Nature* made their decision? You know how nitpicky Marco LaGuardia is."

"He's one of the best photo editors I've ever worked for," Lucio said.

"So? Did you sign today?"

"Ah," Lucio said, setting his glass down on the balcony's concrete floor. "I did not sign. I wanted to stop by this afternoon and tell you that I won't be signing at all."

The light left Piers's face. His mouth collapsed and drew in tight. His eyes went flat. "But *why*?"

"Look, Piers. I appreciate you thinking of me." Lucio touched his friend's trousers, feeling a bony knee beneath the cotton. "But the reality is, I do not want to leave. I am happy here. I am not even certain I will accept any more out-of-country field assignments, ever."

Piers cocked his head in surprise, then leaned back in his chair, speechless.

Lucio laughed, a little annoyed by his obtuseness. "Piers, just a few weeks ago you were toasting me and Genevieve, wishing us happiness. And then you went right out and tried to have me sent away, halfway across the world?"

Piers's mouth fell open. "Sent away? Since when does Lucky Montevez see an assignment as a *problem*?" He looked mystified. "It pays extremely well, and you need that money. Plus you have a good chance to make the cover, which will put you right back into the game. I do not understand."

Then Lucio saw it—Piers truly did *not* understand.

His anger left him. "Piers, I wasn't joking when I told you how I felt about Genevieve."

Piers sputtered, then shrugged. "I just—well, Lucky, if I may be blunt, it never occurred to me that you were serious when you said that. I mean, when have you ever been committed to a woman? I just assumed . . ." He ran a hand over his chin nervously. "My God, Lucky," he whispered. "None of this is what I intended. I owe you an apology."

He watched as Piers hung his head and shook it back and forth. Lucio gave him a moment to compose himself. He retrieved his wine glass from near his feet and took a couple sips. "It is all right," Lucio said.

"No!" Piers jerked his head up and looked toward Lucio with a pained expression. "I am such a poor friend! I did not listen to you. I did not *believe* you. And now I have caused you grief." He got up from his chair and leaned over the railing.

Piers was so tall and so much of his torso rose above the wrought iron that Lucio feared he could topple right over. Four stories wasn't a skyscraper, but it was enough to crush every bone in his body.

"It is nothing. Forget it," Lucio said. "It was a misunderstanding. Just tell Marco that you want the job after all. Tell him you mistakenly assumed I was available but I am not."

Piers looked over his shoulder and down at Lucio. "You wouldn't mind?"

"Of course not," Lucio said, waving his hand around. "They wanted you in the first place! It was your job from the beginning. Take it. Get back to work, Piers. It will do you good."

Piers nodded slowly, then turned his gaze out toward the city. "I haven't accepted an assignment since Sylvie died."

"I know, *mi amigo.*"

"I just realized something," Piers continued, chuckling softly. "Maybe all that altruism was just a way for me to avoid facing my own fear. I was able to tell myself I was doing you a favor, when really, I was just afraid to get back into the world."

Lucio nodded, touched by his friend's introspective honesty. "It could be."

"Forgive me, Lucky." Piers let go of the railing and fell back into his chair. "I can be so stupid sometimes."

"There is nothing to forgive." Lucio laughed a little.

"What is so funny?"

"Ah, it's just that maybe I should be asking for *your* forgiveness."

"You?" Piers seemed baffled. "Why on earth?"

"Because I think I am more shaken up by that whole mess in China than I have led myself to believe. Knowing what Ilsa did to me has made me a bit paranoid. I even thought—for just a moment—that you, well, were out to get me."

Piers's mouth went wide, then he laughed. *"What?"*

"I know, I know," Lucio said. "But just for an instant I worried you had arranged for me to go to Mauritius to take me from Genevieve. That you might be a little jealous because you've lost Sylvie and I've just found Genevieve."

Piers closed his mouth with an audible snap of his lips. "I see," he said, looking away.

"And that is why I ask for your forgiveness."

Piers nodded, but didn't say anything for a long moment. He sighed as he returned his gaze to Lucio. "I know it must sting to know that someone you once cared about could treat you so badly. Ilsa tried to destroy your life. It must weigh heavily on you."

Lucio shrugged. "Yes and no," he said, sipping his

wine. "I know she's under investigation and the whole thing will be cleared up eventually, but the more I fall in love with Genevieve and enjoy my pet portrait business, the less it enters my thoughts. Sometimes it feels like China was part of someone else's life. Even losing the Erskine doesn't seem like a fatal blow anymore." He looked up at Piers. "Does that make any sense?"

Piers offered a small smile. "Sure."

"I suppose it is no longer about how others perceive me. I am more focused on being true to my heart, being a good man to Genevieve, and being *happy*." Lucio noticed the incredulous look on Piers's face and they enjoyed a laugh together.

They wrapped up their visit a few minutes later, and Piers gave Lucio a big hug at the door. It had taken a while, but Lucio had convinced Piers to join him for dinner at Genevieve's the next evening.

"Fine. I will come," Piers said, looking nervous.

"You will love her," Lucio said.

Piers laughed. "That's a given! But what if she despises me? You know I'm not good at socializing."

Lucio shook his head and chuckled. "Relax, Piers. Genevieve is a good judge of character. She'll love you right back."

He settled back into the comfortable sofa in Rick's den, stuffed to the gills with greasy pepperoni pizza and chicken wings. It boggled Lucio's mind to see how much food Josh and Jason could consume in a sitting. Lucio knew he'd had a healthy appetite as a teenager, but perhaps not *this* healthy. He did not recall ever eating an extra-large pizza by himself.

"A flag? What the— *Holding?* The ref is out of his mind!" Jason turned to Lucio, slack-jawed, tomato sauce on his chin. "Did you see that?"

Lucio smiled. "I did. But I am not an expert with American football. I'm more of a soccer man."

"Sure," Josh said. "Football in Europe is soccer, right?"

"Right."

"Did you ever play?" Jason asked, wiping his hand over his chin, which only served to spread the tomato sauce up his cheek.

"I had no choice," Lucio said. "My father was a professional soccer player when he was young—a goalkeeper for the team in Seville. He also made it to the national team a few times."

"No way!" Josh said.

"Sounds like me," Jason said, tossing a half-eaten slice back into the box. "Dad was a big baseball star in college and he pretty much forced me to follow in his footsteps, but he freaked out on me when I didn't make the cut on the traveling team."

Lucio nodded. "The same happened to me. My talent was behind a camera, not in front of a soccer goal. Unfortunately, it just gave my father another reason to make things difficult for me."

"SOML," Jason said, shaking his head.

Lucio frowned. "I'm afraid I do not understand."

"That's text talk for 'story of my life,'" Josh said, scrunching up his nose as if he smelled something bad. "Jason likes to use expressions he thinks make him cool."

"A year on Antarctica wouldn't make you cool, Josh."

Lucio grabbed his beer to hide his smile.

"So do you still hang with your dad? Does he still live in that area of Spain you're from?" Jason asked.

Lucio nodded. "He still lives in Las Alpujarras, but

we have not spoken for twenty years, I am sorry to say."

"Dude!" Jason said. "Seriously?"

"I am afraid so," Lucio said. He leaned forward, resting his arms on his knees and pressing his fingers together as he considered how to frame this story for the boys. "We did not get along very well. He was . . . I cannot find the word . . . anyway, he was up and down all the time with his moods."

"Unpredictable," Jason said.

"Volatile," Josh said.

"Oh, yes." Lucio paused a moment, not wanting to say anything negative about their own father, but knowing his story resonated with them.

"Dad's like that sometimes," Jason said. "It's frustrating, because I don't know which Dad I'm going to get when I go over there—the fun and nice one or the complete wack job."

"It depends on how the ole in-and-out is going for him that week," Josh said.

Lucio coughed, nearly choking on his surprise. It was a shock to hear how jaded the fifteen-year-olds sounded. It was extremely sad.

Josh continued. "Dad really thought his new pussy-puller would be drawing them in like flies, but it isn't working. At least the flies don't fly around for long."

After blinking a few times, Lucio knew he had to ask. "What is a . . . uh, what is this puller you mention?"

"The Porsche 911," Jason said. "That's what Dad calls it. I guess it's supposed to help old guys attract young girls." Jason reached for his half-eaten pizza slice, and in three huge bites it was all eaten.

The Host! Lucio let his forehead drop to his hands.

It was a complete mystery how Genevieve had remained married to that man for so long.

"So have you found out who did all that crap to you in China?" Joshua asked, trying to change the subject. "Do you have any suspects?"

Lucio looked up from his hands, seeing the curious faces of the young men. He chuckled with the realization that Josh had not succeeded in changing the subject in the slightest.

"There were quite a few suspects."

"Really? Who?" Jason asked.

"A few women," Lucio said. "Unfortunately, for much of my life I did not treat women very well. I left many of them angry with me."

"What did you do to them?" Josh asked, frowning.

"I was not very kind or respectful. I had a reputation for leaving without saying good-bye."

Jason's eyes went huge. "That's cold!"

"And wrong," Lucio said. "I have learned my lesson. The way you treat others will surely become the way you get treated."

Josh looked worried.

"I would never do anything to hurt your mother," Lucio said. "She is my heart."

Joshua squinted at him. "So one of these girls decided to make your life miserable?"

"It looks that way. She told my friend Piers what she did. I called her a couple weeks ago, and she admitted it to me."

"That's the guy whose place we went to for all the photo equipment, right?" Jason asked.

"Yes. He's coming over to the house for dinner tomorrow night," Lucio said.

"Cool," Jason said.

"So why was this chick so mad at you?" Joshua asked.

Lucio smiled, amused by Joshua's dogged pursuit of the truth. "We had dated for a few months while we worked on an assignment together. I left her a note saying I was leaving the country, but she followed me to the airport. She cursed at me in front of many passengers, and told me that one day she'd make me pay."

"So she ripped you a new one right there in public?" Jason asked.

Lucio chuckled. "I'm afraid so. And she could curse in several languages."

Josh nodded. "She had to be really smart to pull off all that stuff in China, with the paperwork and the bank account and giving your work to the Chinese government."

Lucio nodded. "Yes. She is a smart woman."

Josh blew out air, his face looking slightly pale. "Well, thanks for that life lesson," he told Lucio.

"How do you mean?"

"Dude, I'm going to try my best to never piss off a smart girl."

Lucio smiled, wishing someone had taught him that lesson when he was fifteen.

CHAPTER 17

Ginger pushed her chair away and began to clear the dishes from the outdoor table.

"Absolutely not," Piers said, placing a large pale hand over hers. "This has been such a wonderful evening and you've already done so much to make me feel welcome. Let me do this, please."

Her eyes shot to Lucio, who produced a warm smile. "You know, it's funny," she said to Piers. "Lucio made that same offer the first night he ate dinner with us. Are all European men this gallant?"

Piers and Lucio looked briefly at each other and then howled with laughter.

"The short answer would be no, *guapa*," Lucio said, coming over to her chair and kissing the top of her head. "And just you wait—twenty years from now I will have forgotten all of my manners. I will be throwing my drawers around and picking my teeth with twigs."

Josh and Jason thought that was hilarious, but Ginger didn't believe it for a minute. Lucio was the most conscientious person—man or woman—she'd ever known. And his good habits had most definitely rubbed off on her boys, who, at that very moment, were helping to clear the table without being asked. But what resonated most in Lucio's joke was the reference to twenty years in the future. The idea of a lifetime with him at her side sent a shiver of pleasure through her.

"Do you need a sweater, my love?" Lucio asked.

"I'll get it, but thank you." She placed a tender kiss on Lucio's lips before she headed for the patio door. The boys had become used to their kisses and caresses, though she and Lucio had been careful to create a PG-13 environment around the house—the last thing they wanted to do was turn the place into a replica of Larry's Barely Legal Love Emporium three blocks away.

But one look at Piers and Ginger knew he'd been surprised by the kiss. Piers stopped stacking dishes and stared at her and Lucio, his mouth slightly open.

She smiled at him, and he smiled back, clearly embarrassed.

Piers was an odd bird, she had to say. As Ginger walked upstairs she thought of how awkward he seemed when he first arrived with Lucio that evening. Shy and stammering, he needed some time before he relaxed, but once he did, he had the boys enthralled with stories of his mishaps and misadventures. He and Lucio got into a rhythm with their storytelling, and Ginger had been charmed by how Piers sometimes finished Lucio's sentences when his friend struggled to find the correct English, just as she and the boys sometimes did.

She could see how close they were. She understood that they knew each other well and respected each other immensely. Ginger knew all about their past, how Lucio left the heartbroken Sylvie in London for

Piers to deal with. She knew how sad Piers had been after she passed away. It had been Ginger who suggested Lucio invite him over.

It was nice of Piers to offer to pick up Jason after school tomorrow and show him his work.

Jason asked specifically to see his passport. "Is yours as sloppy and overstuffed as Lucio's?" he asked.

Piers had laughed. "His is tidy compared to mine."

Ginger had almost reached the top of the stairs when her head suddenly felt funny. She had to brace herself against the banister. She stumbled up the last two steps and kept a hand on the wall as she ran toward the master bathroom, not sure she'd get there in time. The sickness hit her with almost no warning, and it left her weak and dizzy.

After a few moments, Ginger made it to the sink. She washed her face with cold water and rinsed out her mouth, staring at her reflection in the mirror.

"No way," she whispered, examining the rosy flush of her skin. "There is absolutely no way this can be happening."

Ginger's hands gripped the bathroom counter. She needed to calm down. It didn't have to be that. It could be a virus, or something she'd eaten. It could be menopause! Of course!

But what else did she need to consider?

Well, how about the fact that the condom broke the night of the earthquake?

How many weeks ago was that?

But she'd had her period.

She'd had two periods, even!

But they'd both been lighter than usual, and shorter, with the spotting in between. And there were days when she was just bone-deep exhausted for no reason.

"Oh, God!" She knew if she weren't careful she'd start to hyperventilate. She didn't want Lucio to find her passed out on the bathroom floor, now did she?

Oh, crap. Lucio! He'd been so glad she wasn't pregnant!

Ginger ran a brush through her hair, willing the tears to stay put in their ducts. She applied a little lipstick. She took a slow and deep breath, deciding that for the rest of the evening she'd just relax. Maybe she'd skip that second glass of wine, fine, but other than that, it would be business as usual. Then tomorrow, after she got back from her morning walk with the girls, she'd stop by the drugstore and pick up a test kit. She'd make a point of stopping at a pharmacy on the other side of town, where no one knew her.

"Oh boy, oh boy, oh boy," she said, turning, taking a moment to catch her side view reflection in the mirror. She smoothed her skirt across her belly. She sucked in and held her breath.

She wondered exactly what she was seeing—one too many waffles that morning or a baby?

A baby she'd made with Lucio. A baby growing inside her.

Oh, Lord, what had she done?

This wasn't supposed to happen to her.

For God's sake—she was *forty*!

Lucio and Ginger said their final good nights to Piers and shut the front door. The boys retreated to the family room, hoping to catch the end of the game.

"All right," Lucio said, leading Ginger to the sofa and gesturing for her to sit. He plopped next to her. "Let's have it."

Oh, damn. She thought she'd done an excellent job

of pretending she was carefree. Relaxed. Not pregnant. "It's nothing," she said. "Really."

"*Genevieve.*" Lucio shook his head, scolding her. "I meant it when I said I want to know everything that's going on with you. Please don't try to hide it from me. I can tell when there's something wrong."

She gave him a halfhearted smile.

"You do not like Piers, is that it?"

"Ha! No. I mean yes. I like him. He's shy but sweet. That's not it."

Lucio frowned at her. "You didn't eat much at dinner. No dessert. You were quiet the last part of the evening, too. Is your stomach bothering you again?"

"A little. I think I'm just tired." Genevieve tried to rise from the couch, but he grabbed her arm, gently pressed her down on her back and stretched out her legs. He got on top of her.

"*Guapa,*" he whispered, brushing her hair away from her face so that he could kiss her forehead, her nose, her cheeks, her chin. "I worry about you, yes? I think you should see your doctor. It could be something serious."

Ginger was overwhelmed at the concern she saw in his eyes. She truly loved this man. He was everything she could ever hope for. But how would he react if she really *was* pregnant? He'd been so happy when she told him she wasn't! And later he'd said he might have been open to the idea if he'd met her earlier!

But it wasn't earlier. It was *now*. And he'd already told her he didn't think he would be a good father *now*.

Ginger kissed him sweetly on the lips and ran her fingertips down his rough stubble. She knew there was no point in freaking him out tonight. She would tell him when, and if, she had news to tell.

"I'll make an appointment," she told him. "But please don't worry. It's probably nothing."

The crease between his dark eyebrows deepened. "I . . . I love you with all my soul, *pelirroja*. I have never loved anyone before you. How can I not worry?"

"I love you, too, Lucio," Ginger said, raising her mouth to his. "I know everything's going to be fine."

"I'll be damned—it's official." Bea stood at the top of the hill at Dolores Park early the next morning, obviously near tears. She let Martina off the leash as they approached, whipping out the folded newspaper she'd been holding under her arm.

She held it up. A twenty-four-point bold headline ran the width of the front page, just below the masthead. It said simply:

GOOD-BYE, SAN FRANCISCO

"Aw, man, that's so incredibly sad," Josie said, scowling. "How long have you known?"

Bea laughed bitterly. "Are you kidding? I *didn't* know. Nobody did! They didn't bother telling those of us who were still employed."

"You're kidding?" Roxanne said.

"I'm not. I just pulled this out of the newspaper box at the corner of Market and Sixteenth!"

"It was bound to happen," Ginger said, her voice quiet. "At least you were one of the last few people in the newsroom."

"Doesn't make it hurt any less," Bea said.

Josie patted her on the arm. "Have you been thinking about what you might like to do?"

Bea nodded. "Actually, I've been thinking about

getting into canine agility training as a profession. I'd need to get certified, but that wouldn't take too long."

"Hey, and you could use your Petography picture on your business cards!" Roxanne suggested.

"I could!"

Suddenly everyone turned to Ginger, who had been unusually quiet. She looked down at her shoes.

"I didn't think you'd take this so hard," Bea said. "I know you miss the paper, but you've been enjoying your work with Lucio, right?"

Ginger looked up and tried to smile. "I'm having more fun than I ever imagined I would."

Bea looked baffled. "Then why the long face?"

Ginger took a second to look into her friends' eyes, one at a time. "This is a little embarrassing to tell you."

"Uh-oh," Roxanne said.

"What's wrong?" Josie asked, stepping close.

Ginger wrapped her arms around her ribs, as if she were trying to prop herself up. "Well, it's just that I've got a really bad feeling about something and I was wondering if you guys would let me vent for a minute."

"Uh-oh," Roxanne said again.

"I might need your help with something this morning, is all I'm saying. Is everyone free?"

Bea laughed. "Can't get much freer than the four of us. What's going on?"

"Wait. Let me guess," Roxie said. "You think Lucio's going to dump you and you want us to help you spy on him!" She pounded her fist on her thigh and shook her head in disgust. *That low-down, dirty, no-good, chicken-shit motherfucker!*

After a stunned moment of silence, Ginger said, "Uh, *nooo.*"

Bea looked impressed. "That was a Pulitzer Prize–

winning spew of obscenity, Rox—how long you been waiting for the perfect moment to unleash that puppy? Is it on the Web site yet?"

"Not yet," she answered, smiling big. "I came up with it just a couple days ago. It's great, isn't it?"

Josie clucked her tongue in annoyance and turned to Ginger. "What's wrong?" She touched Ginger's shoulder. "Is Jason in trouble again?"

Ginger smiled. "No, in fact, it's the opposite. Since Jason's been helping Lucio, he hasn't had one truancy issue or curfew violation and his grades are getting a lot better."

Bea leaned back and examined Ginger studiously. "So did Lucio take off with your credit cards? Steal money from your checking account?"

"What?" Ginger's mouth fell open. "God, no!"

"Savings?"

"No, Bea! Good Lord! He'd never steal money from me!"

"You think he's stepping out on you?" Josie's eyes were huge.

"No, no, no, no, *no.*"

"Then it can only be one thing," Roxanne said, reaching for Ginger's hand. "He's going away on assignment, isn't he?"

"He is?" Ginger's pulse spiked.

"I don't know, I'm asking *you!*" Roxie said, rolling her eyes.

"Okay, girls, this is ridiculous. Just cut to the chase, will you, Ginger?" Bea's voice suddenly grew soft. "You're starting to scare me."

"Okay. Okay." Ginger took a deep breath. "Look, it could be nothing. It may be that I really *am* starting menopause. But I've got all this weird spotting going on and nausea and I'm exhausted all the time."

Her three friends said nothing. Roxanne looked like she'd stopped breathing.

"Oh my God," Josie said, her hand flying to her mouth.

"Yeah," Ginger said with an uncomfortable laugh. "That's what I said."

"What the fuck?" Bea looked frantic. "I don't have the slightest idea what you're all so freaked out about. What's going on?"

Ginger sighed. "I think I'm pregnant."

"She's still holed up in the bathroom with Josie," Roxanne said, opening the door to Ginger's home, ushering Bea and Mrs. Needleman inside. Bea transferred the old lady to Roxie's care, and Roxie guided her through the foyer and into the living room.

"They've been in there the whole time?" Bea asked, incredulous.

"Yeah," Roxanne said. "She says she's never coming out and she won't let Josie out, either."

"Well, this is just hellish," Bea said, throwing her car keys onto the front hall table.

"You doing okay, Mrs. Needleman?" Roxanne made sure she was seated comfortably on the sofa.

"Oh, stop fussing over me. I'm fine. It's Genevieve I'm worried about." Mrs. Needleman set her big square handbag on the floor by her feet. "Now, you go up there and tell her enough is enough."

Roxanne's gaze traveled to where Bea stood in the foyer, arms crossed and eyes rolling toward heaven.

"Who, me?" Roxie asked.

"You and/or Bea. It hardly matters," Mrs. Needleman said. "Just go up there and tell her that I am an eighty-four-year-old widow and I'm in no position to climb up all those steps, and, since she asked for me, the least she can do is be courteous enough to come downstairs."

"I'll do it," Bea said. She ran up the steps, taking two at a time. She called out to Josie and Ginger once she got to the upstairs hallway, not certain which bathroom they'd been using as their positive-pregnancy-test fallout shelter.

"We're in here!"

Bea followed Josie's voice and stood in front of the door of the master bathroom. She tried the knob. It was locked.

"Okay, girls. Open up." Bea listened as Josie tried in vain to get Ginger to agree to leave the bathroom. Bea heard Ginger crying, then the sound of the lock disengaging from the other side of the door.

Josie opened it a crack. "Is Mrs. Needleman here?" she asked.

"Downstairs," Bea answered, poking her head inside to see Ginger huddled on the floor next to the Jacuzzi. "And she said she's too old and frail to get up the steps. She said if Ginger didn't put on her big-girl panties and get down there in two minutes, she'll be leaving."

Ginger looked up, her eyes red and swollen, the test stick dangling from her hand. "She really said that?"

"Yes."

"Really?" Josie asked, looking doubtful.

"Okay, not the part about the big-girl panties. That was my contribution." Bea walked toward Ginger and held her hand down. "Come on, little mama. You can't spend the next nine months cowering in the bathroom."

"Seven months," Ginger said, taking Bea's hand

and allowing herself to be pulled up. "I'm two months pregnant."

"Those tests tell you all that?" Bea asked, impressed. "I always thought it was just an on/off kind of result."

Ginger shook her head. She ran cool water over a washcloth and dabbed her face. "The test doesn't know—*I* know."

"Well, I hate to tell you this," Bea said. "You've got a whole lot less than seven months to get your act together, because your boys are going to be home from school in about an hour."

"Oh, no, that's right!" Ginger straightened up and smoothed out her shirt. "And Piers is coming over to pick up Jason at five. I need to get a grip."

Bea steadied Ginger's elbow and led her and Josie into the living room. Bea delivered Ginger to the spot next to Mrs. Needleman on the sofa.

"You have a lovely home, dear," the old woman said to Ginger.

"Thanks."

"Just think how fortunate you are! Think about all you will have to offer this blessed child of yours."

No one said anything. Josie left the room and came back with a handful of paper napkins from the kitchen, shoving them at Ginger.

"You have already proven that you are a loving mother," Mrs. Needleman said. "You have a man who adores you, two nearly grown sons who will be devoted big brothers, and a thriving business concern."

Ginger blew her nose into a napkin.

"Genevieve, do you remember what I told you when you came to my home?"

"Yeah. You told me I was in for a bumpy ride."

"Yes, but what did I say after that?"

Ginger took a deep breath and folded the napkins

into a neat pile in her lap. "You said *my little family* would come out just fine. But I didn't know you meant I was about to have a new little family member!"

Mrs. Needleman patted Ginger's hand. "Do any of us ever really know what is around the next bend?" She looked at the three women gathered near the sofa.

"Josephine, a year ago could you have even imagined where you are now?"

Josie laughed. "Hell no."

"But is your life now better than ever?"

Josie's smile was huge. "I guess, though some days I really miss Lloyd."

"For God's sake," Roxanne said. Everyone else laughed, remembering the last of Josie's ex-boyfriends.

Mrs. Needleman turned to Bea. "Do you know where you'll be a year from now, Beatrice?"

She chuckled. "Collecting cans?"

"I think you will be pleasantly surprised."

Mrs. Needleman turned to Roxie next. "Think back to a year ago, Roxanne. Could you have envisioned your life as it is today?"

"No," she said, shifting her weight from foot to foot. "A year ago I had the job of my dreams and a man I thought was the love of my life."

"So it can all change in an instant, can't it?" Mrs. Needleman asked.

"Absolutely."

"Keep that in mind, my dear," she told Roxanne.

"And Genevieve, how much has your life changed in, say, the last three years?"

Ginger let out a combination groan and laugh.

"And looking back, can you say that there was a reason for all these changes?"

Ginger peered up from her napkin collection and nodded at Mrs. Needleman.

"Tell us about that."

She looked into the faces of her friends and gave them a sad smile. "It's nothing everyone hasn't heard a hundred times."

"Refresh our memories," Mrs. Needleman said.

Ginger took a moment to collect her thoughts. "Well, I guess you could say I found Larry doing the math tutor in the driveway because I needed to know the truth about my marriage. I guess I wasn't brave enough to see it without, you know, a few audiovisual aids."

Bea snorted.

"Nicely put." Mrs. Needleman patted Ginger's hand in delight. "Anything else?"

"Well, I guess you could say I was at Josie's wedding to meet Lucio."

Everyone nodded.

"And that Lucio got thrown out of China so that he would be here in San Francisco to take pictures at Rick's wedding, so he could meet me."

More nods.

"And I became friends with Josie, Rox, and Bea so that I would be a bridesmaid on that day," Ginger said.

"And we became friends because we all had dogs," Bea added.

"And we all had dogs because we thought they were more reliable than men," Josie said.

"And I was so vain and self-centered that I ordered a size four bridesmaid dress, which cut off my air supply and caused me to faint, which meant Lucio had to carry me to my room and kiss me."

"Which means this could go on forever," Roxie said, looking bored.

Mrs. Needleman giggled and her narrow shoulders bobbed up and down. She clapped her hands in delight.

"That was your whole point, wasn't it?" Bea asked.

"Absolutely correct, my brilliant friend." Mrs. Needleman turned her attention to Ginger. "Now, with that kind of cosmic context in mind, how in the world can any of us see this baby as a mistake, or a problem? Everything in Genevieve's life has led up to this moment—this child. There is a reason. There is always a reason."

Bea sniffed, wiping a tear from her eye. Josie put her arm around Bea and pulled her close. Roxie cracked her neck.

"Well, then, I guess my next step will be to tell Lucio," Ginger said, her voice getting stronger. "Then together we'll tell the boys. And I guess—wow—we're going to have to tell Larry."

"*Ooh, ooh!* Can I watch?" Bea asked, clearly over her moment of sensitivity.

"I just hope to hell it's a girl," Roxie said.

"I didn't even think of that!" Ginger straightened from her slump, suddenly brightening. "I'm so used to having boys that I just assumed I had another one in there! But what if it really *is* a girl?"

"What would you name her?" Josie asked.

"HeatherLee?" Bea suggested. "HannaLynn?"

Ginger shook her head, laughing. "I'm sure that together we'll all come up with the perfect name."

"Hey," Josie said, smiling shyly. "Do you think you guys can help me come up with a name, too?"

Everyone stared in silence.

"My sister named Genghis, so I'm damn sure not asking her for suggestions when it comes to a baby."

"*What!*" Roxanne clutched at her heart.

The next five minutes were nothing but screams of happiness and jumping around and Bea letting loose with a few *whoop-whoop-whoops* of joy.

"Does Rick know?" Ginger squealed.

"No. I'm telling him tonight," Josie said. "So nobody—I mean *nobody*—can say a word to anyone, all right?"

"Same goes for me, actually," Ginger said. "This is all just between the four of us—" She stopped herself, turning toward Mrs. Needleman. "I mean the five of us."

"The seven of us," Bea said, pointing at both Josie's and Ginger's bellies.

Mrs. Needleman giggled.

"Come on up here," Bea said, walking over to the sofa and helping the older woman to her feet. "We have a little ritual that we do. Maybe you'd like to be part of it."

"Well, I'll certainly try my best," she said, joining in the circle.

"Pile on, girls," Bea said, shoving her hand in the center, palm side down.

Ginger put her hand on top of Bea's. Roxie put hers on Ginger's. Josie took hold of Mrs. Needleman's arthritic hand and placed it gently over Roxie's, then put hers on top.

Josie went first. "I pledge to enjoy every moment of this next phase of my life, to be open to all the adventures that lie ahead, no matter what is around the next corner." She winked at Mrs. Needleman.

Bea went next. "I vow to provide rides to doctor's appointments or Lamaze classes or run out for pickles and baklava or anything else you girls might need in the coming months. Plus, I will learn everything I can about babysitting. But I won't make a pest of myself. Plus, I swear I won't tell Teeny about any of this."

"You better not!" Josie said.

Roxie looked at Mrs. Needleman, who nodded for

her to go next. Roxie sighed before she made her contribution. "Okay," she said. "I give my word to all of you that I'll refrain from bad-mouthing men during your pregnancies because, well, men are how you got that way in the first place."

Everyone snickered.

"And if they turn out to be boys I'll love them anyway," she added.

"Thank you for that, Rox," Josie said.

They all turned to Mrs. Needleman, who giggled again. "Is it my turn?" she asked.

"Yes!" they all said together.

"Can I say anything I want?"

"Of course!"

"All right, then." She cleared her throat. "I promise to watch over each and every one of you, forever." Mrs. Needleman's eyes sparkled. She took her free hand and placed it on Ginger's belly, bending slightly to address whoever lurked inside. "And that means you, little one." Then she touched Josie's stomach. "And you, too, my dear."

Mrs. Needleman straightened and her eyes filled with happy tears. "You have no idea how much joy you've brought to this little old woman," she said. "I treasure you all."

By the time the boys got home, Ginger had showered, fixed her hair, got something in her stomach, and made herself presentable.

The boys didn't notice that anything was amiss. Of course, they were distracted by the bag of Doritos, the leftover apple pie, the frozen miniature bagel pizzas, and the half a gallon of orange juice they were hauling out of the refrigerator.

Josh ripped the foil cover off the pie tin, perplexed.

"Hey, how many pieces of this pie did you eat last night, Fatty McFatface?"

"Shut up, Faggy McFagtard," Jason said. "I had one piece last night, like everyone did."

"But there's only one piece left! Who's going to get to eat it?" Josh moaned.

"Ever heard of fractions, President Pissbrain?"

Ginger sat down at the kitchen table, putting her hands in her lap, thinking back to when her boys didn't insult each other twenty-four/seven, to when they didn't have armpit hair, or Facebook accounts.

She remembered when she was pregnant with them. She loved being pregnant. She'd been equal parts thrilled and terrified. She'd read everything she could get her hands on, and knew on any given day what exact stage of development the babies had reached. She remembered feeling as if she were the center of the universe, the only woman who had ever been pregnant. She'd felt more special—and more beautiful— than at any other time in her life.

This time around, she would be less terrified and more knowledgeable. She would savor it instead of wishing the time would race by. She would feel even more special, because this baby wasn't planned. This baby had arrived in her life unexpectedly, just the way his or her father had.

Suddenly it dawned on Ginger that Josh and Jason would be well over sixteen when the baby was born. She gasped. They'd be thirty-four-year-old *men* by the time the baby graduated from high school! And she'd be fifty-eight!

"What are you thinking about, Mumu?" Josh asked. "You okay?"

"Yeah," Jason said, putting the pizza bites in the microwave. "Dad told us you were going through the change and that we could expect to see you freak out on a regular basis. So is that what you're doing now?"

Ginger laughed at the irony. Just a couple months ago she was worried about whether to get a glycolic acid facial. Now she was worried about getting enough folic acid. Back then she was booking appointments with plastic surgeons who could make her look younger. Now she had to book an appointment with an OB who specialized in older moms.

She smiled at her boys. "I'm going through a change all right, but not the one your dad thinks."

Jason shoved a wad of Doritos in his mouth and looked at her for a minute, as if he were weighing her last statement. "You know, Dad said he didn't appreciate all the time Lucio was spending with me. He said he thought Lucio was just pretending to like me and Josh so you'd let him move in here and sponge off your alimony."

"He called him a freeloader," Josh said.

"And a gigolo," Jason said.

"And Dad said your work at Petography wasn't a real job," Josh said.

"And he said he's going to come over here one day and kick Lucio's ass," Jason added.

Ginger began laughing in earnest. It was just too hilarious. Here she was, knocked up with the disingenuous, freeloading gigolo's baby and not even gainfully employed! Was Larry going to have a field day with that, or *what*?

She was laughing so hard she didn't hear the doorbell.

CHAPTER 18

Piers stayed for a quick cup of coffee, talking with the boys about his work. Eventually he told Jason they should be going. "Do you mind if I speak with your mom for a moment?" he asked Jason.

"Sure," he said. "Let me get my backpack from my room."

Piers opened the patio doors and gestured for Ginger to walk with him outside. HeatherLynn was right at her heels. It was a cool October day, and Ginger pulled her cardigan close.

"Is everything all right?" she asked, noticing a nervous energy in Piers.

He laughed a little. "That's what I wanted to discuss with you."

Ginger stopped walking, and placed her hand on Piers's forearm. "Is it Lucio? Is he all right?" She couldn't prevent the horrible thought from racing through her head—something had happened to him before she could tell him about the baby!

"He is fine, physically. That's not it." Piers pulled out a chair for her at the outdoor table. "Maybe you should sit down."

She did, yanking the sweater tight across her chest,

suddenly shivering. HeatherLynn put her paws on her shin, whimpering to be picked up.

"I don't know you very well, Ginger, but you seem like a very nice woman, and so I believe it is my duty to tell you that Lucio may not be exactly what he seems."

Ginger's heart thudded. For a second, the blood pounded so hard in her head that she couldn't hear.

"I don't understand," she whispered.

Piers looked racked with uncertainty. "I love him. He is like a brother to me," he said, now near tears. "But I can't just sit by and watch him do this to you, the way he's done it to so many women."

"Do what?" Ginger asked, her head suddenly clear, the blood rushing to her limbs. She knew she would have to fight the instinct to run away—that was how much she did not want to hear what was coming next.

"You know, Lucio is not very good at keeping relationships going. He left his home in Spain and has had no contact with anyone in his family. It's sad."

"I knew that," Ginger said.

"And he's walked away from every woman he ever professed to love. One of them was so mad she had him tossed out of China and let go from his *Geographica* contract as her way of getting revenge."

"He has told me all about this."

"And my late wife, Sylvie? He crushed her heart into a million pieces."

Ginger didn't like how this sounded. It was as if Piers were trying to poison her view of Lucio.

"Unfortunately, that approach even spreads to his friends," Piers went on. "When Sylvie died, he didn't even bother coming to the funeral."

Despite the fact that her hands were tucked under her arms, she felt them begin to shake.

"What I need to tell you is that Lucky has taken an assignment very far away and plans to leave any day."

No.

He wouldn't do that.

HeatherLynn suddenly jumped from her curled-up position in Ginger's lap, letting loose with a string of high-pitched yips. Ginger's throat tightened. She began frowning. She ripped a hand free so she could tap her brow.

"The assignment is in Mauritius. Are you familiar with it?"

Did it matter where the hell it was? she wondered. If the man was leaving for *Sacramento* it would be a deal-breaker—simply because he hadn't told her in advance.

HeatherLynn would not stop barking. *"Shush!"* Ginger hissed.

"It's an independent island nation off the coast of Africa, in the Indian Ocean. It is famous for being the home of the dodo bird."

Ginger almost laughed. As Bea would say, *What the fuck?* Why did this guy feel compelled to give her a geography lesson when her world was falling down around her?

But wait.

Ginger leaned back in her chair and took a deep breath. She studied Piers's pained expression, his downturned mouth. She didn't really *know* Piers Skaarsgard. But she knew Lucio, and she loved him with everything in her. There was no way she would think the worst of Lucio simply because a near stranger told her to.

"I don't believe you," she said. Ginger pointed her finger at him. "Look, Piers, I don't know what game you're playing here, but Lucio wouldn't do that to me.

I'm sure of it. I can only assume that you're trying to get back at him for something, but it's not going to work." Ginger adjusted the direction of her point, gesturing to the backyard gate that would take him to the driveway. "You need to leave now."

Piers cast his eyes down and shook his head. He reached in his jacket pocket. "Look at this first," he said, pulling out a folded document.

Ginger didn't reach for it. "Whatever it is, I'm not interested."

Piers sighed. He unfolded the legal-size sheets of paper and held them in front of her. Ginger couldn't help it. She looked. It was a contract between *Nature* magazine and Lucio. She grabbed it, flipped through pages, and found where Lucio had signed and dated it. She threw it at Piers.

Lucio was leaving her. Just as she feared. And she was pregnant with his child.

HeatherLynn wouldn't shut up.

Inadvertently, Ginger let out a tiny mewl of agony. Piers did not miss it.

"I am so sorry to cause you pain by telling you." He reached out, stroking her cheek with his long, cool fingers. HeatherLynn growled and then snapped at Piers's hand. He pulled away quickly but not quickly enough—Ginger saw a flash of red blood on his knuckle.

"I need to go lie down," Ginger said, putting Heather-Lynn on the patio. She didn't apologize for her dog's behavior. Part of her was glad HeatherLynn bit the messenger.

Piers briefly scowled at the dog before he returned his attention to Ginger. "You have no idea how I debated whether to tell you. It has been eating me alive for days. I have been lost."

"You knew about this last night?"

"Yes," he said.

Ginger thought of how sweet Lucio had been the night before, offering to get her sweater, clearing the table, holding her in his arms before he left, telling her he worried about her health, that he loved her with all his soul.

Ha! No wonder Piers had stared at them when they'd kissed at this very table last night. No wonder he'd looked surprised! Piers knew! He knew Lucio was about to break her heart, the way he'd broken Sylvie's heart and the hearts of who knew how many others?

Ginger felt as if she were going to be sick.

"Oh, my God," she whispered, bringing a hand up to her shaking lips. What had Roxie told her last month? *The only thing worse than a man abandoning you is a man abandoning you when you're carrying his baby . . .*

And just that morning, Roxie had called Lucio a *low-down, dirty, no-good, chicken-shit motherfucker.* And Ginger had defended him!

"Perhaps I've made a mistake telling you."

Ginger snapped to, noticing Piers sitting next to her. She'd almost forgotten he was there. "No. I needed to know."

"Maybe I should show Jason my work some other time."

Just then, Jason poked his head out of the patio doors. "We going?" he asked.

Piers looked to Ginger, his eyes full of sorrow.

"No. Go ahead and take him. Can you bring him back by nine?"

"Sure."

Ginger got up from the chair. She nearly tripped over HeatherLynn, the dog was sticking so close to her feet.

"Have a good time, Jase," Ginger said, trying to pretend as if her world had not just spun off its axis as she walked them to the door. Next, she poked her head into the family room to see Joshua watching TV. She went up to her room and collapsed on the edge of the bed. HeatherLynn leaned against her ankle, looking nervous. Ginger picked up the phone and called Bea.

"I need you guys." Ginger began to cry. "I need help."

"Seven at Starbucks," Bea said, not even asking what had happened.

"Great," Ginger said, knowing that it wasn't great. Nothing was great. And she knew there was no way she'd be able to keep it together until seven.

"Fuck that," Bea said abruptly. "I'll pick you up in a half hour. Hang on, Ginger. I'm on my way."

She smiled, the relief flooding over her. Mrs. Needleman had been right about Bea. She was something else.

"You've got a cool apartment," Jason said, looking around at Piers's place. He'd seen it before, when he was here with Lucio getting the equipment, but he thought it was the polite thing to say. Besides, he hadn't really had much time to wander around while he was here with Lucio—they just got the stuff and left.

Jason's eyes scanned all the large photographs on the walls.

"Your pictures are totally ridonkulous!" Jason said. "All of these are yours, right, man?"

"Every one of them," Piers said, following Jason as he went from picture to picture. "This is the aftermath of the Exxon *Valdez* disaster. These are sandhill cranes on the Butte River here in California. This a juvenile Kodiak bear on the Kenai River of Alaska."

"God! That fish is flying right into his mouth!" Jason said, amazed.

"It's a salmon."

"That is the coolest picture I've ever seen. How did you get it?"

Piers laughed. "By lying on my belly in the muck for six hours, waiting for the sun to rise and for a bear to show up."

"No way." Jason couldn't believe it.

"That is half the job of being a photographer—waiting around, getting filthy, and staying awake for that second that makes it all worth it."

"Dude," Jason said. His eyes scanned the dozens of other photos in the room. "Hey, that's Lucio!" Jason walked over to the framed photograph on a ledge that separated the kitchen from the living room.

"This must have been right around the time you guys did that documentary together. We saw it on YouTube."

"Really?"

Jason bent to look closer. He looked up at Piers. "Is that your wife?"

Piers blinked. He shoved his hands in his pockets. Jason stood up straight, knowing he'd said something wrong. Piers's face had gone completely weird. It looked like he'd turned to stone.

"Yes. That's Sylvie."

"Oh. Okay." Jason felt awkward. "Does she live here, too?"

Piers looked directly into Jason's eyes. "She's dead," he said.

"Oh. Sorry." Jason took a step back, then turned on his heel to pretend to be looking at other stuff. He felt really stupid asking that because now he had a vague memory of Lucio telling him that Piers's wife had died of cancer or something.

"Have you eaten?" Piers asked, suddenly cheerful again, already in the kitchen.

"Uh, no. Not really. I mean, I had some leftover pie from dinner last night and a bunch of bagel pizzas and some Doritos and stuff after school, but no meal or anything. What you got?"

Jason could hear Piers laugh, and that made him relax a little.

"I thought I'd make us some chicken and dumplings. Have you ever had that?"

"Not sure. Is it good?"

Piers smiled at him. "One of my favorites."

"Great. Yeah. That's cool." Jason wandered around a few more minutes in silence, looking at Piers's photographs. As Jason strolled around, he noticed how the pictures would make him feel sad, or happy, or excited, or angry—and he figured that's what Lucio meant when he'd talked about Piers's talent. Lucio said Piers's pictures always managed to tell a story while they captured an image. Jason had nodded, figuring this Piers dude might be kind of nuts but he was a great photographer.

"You can go look around in the spare room if you want. Remember where you got the equipment?"

"Oh, yeah. The place was a mess."

Piers laughed again, cutting chicken into pieces on a cutting board. "There are a bunch of portfolios of my work lying around and some loose prints on the desk in there. I'll join you once I get the chicken going."

"Cool."

Jason opened the door and giggled to himself—there was more crap in there than in his dad's garage.

He ran a hand over the tripod stands, a whole pile of lighting equipment, packing crates, and what looked like the kind of trunks a roadie for a rock band would wheel around. There were stacks of photos leaning against the wall and even more hanging. Jason opened the closet and laughed—it was worse than *his*.

He peeked into boxes that held camera bodies and lenses and little gadgets he had no idea of the name of. Piers had a bunch of papers jammed in there, loose and in files. Jason noticed the telltale blue of a U.S. passport sticking out from a stack of stuff.

He yanked on it. That's when half the stack of crap fell off the shelf. When he reached down to gather up all the paper he saw something that didn't make sense—Lucio's signature. On a *Geographica* expense report. Jason felt a stab of fear go through his body, followed by a slow and sickening understanding.

The smart girl didn't set Lucio up—his friend did.

Jason got out his cell phone and sent a quick message to Lucio. Then, as fast as he could, he sorted through the other papers—there were a whole lot of forms with Lucio's signature. Jason's hands began to shake.

He grabbed the passport and started thumbing through to the last pages. It was hard to think straight, but he tried his best to figure out exactly when Lucio was in China. He'd been in San Francisco for about six months, and six months ago would have been late March or early April. So if he saw that Piers was in China at that time, they had a situation.

And there it was—the immigration stamp showed that Piers entered China on March 15 and left the country on April 3.

Jason was so nervous his fingers could hardly hit the buttons of his phone. He sent another text and prayed Lucio would get it right away.

"What are you doing in there?" he heard Piers ask. "You're awful quiet."

Jason threw the passport back on the stack and texted Lucio one last time. "HELP" was all he had time for.

"Hey, Lucio, what's up?"

Lucio strolled into the foyer, giving Josh a high five and then a hug. "It is a beautiful day, yes? Where is your lovely mother?"

"I think she went upstairs."

"Where's Jason?"

"Piers just picked him up."

"Oh? That's great."

Both Lucio and Josh looked to the stairs, hearing the skittering sound of small paws racing down plush carpet. HeatherLynn bounded up to Lucio, barking, pawing his leg, her tail spinning around over her back.

"What is all this, *nena*?" Lucio leaned down to pick her up. She licked his face desperately, whining, wiggling in his grasp. Lucio looked at Josh. "Is there something wrong with little Miss Bichon today?"

Josh shrugged, then his head turned toward the door. He chuckled. "Maybe she's just excited 'cause *Dad's* here!"

That's when Lucio heard the unmistakable sound of a Porsche turbo engine winding down in the driveway. He sighed, not really prepared for a heart-to-heart with Larry, but knowing it was inevitable.

HeatherLynn squirmed and barked until Lucio put her down, but instead of running to the door she ran back upstairs. She sat on the landing, her dark little marble eyes looking down on the foyer.

The front door flew open. Larry sneered at Lucio.

"Hello," Lucio said.

Larry laughed. "Oh, so this is your place now? You're doing the meet-and-greet duties around here, big man?"

Joshua took a few steps toward his father. "Give it a rest, okay, Dad? *Please*."

Larry put his hands on his hips and tightened his mouth. "Where do you get off disrespecting me like that in front of a stranger?"

Josh stepped back. His eyes flashed and he shook his head. "Lucio is not a stranger. I see him more than I see you. And if you were someone I respected, then maybe I'd treat you that way."

Larry's face went scarlet with rage.

"Hey, hey," Lucio said, putting himself between Josh and his father. "Listen, Josh, that was no good. You need to apologize to your father."

"Sorry," he mumbled.

"Why don't you take a breather in the family room?" He walked the teenager to the kitchen and whispered, "This is more about me than you, so give me a few minutes to calm him down, yes?"

Josh's eyes were big with uncertainty, but he nodded and headed toward the family room.

Lucio took a deep breath, turned, and found Larry inches behind him.

"You really think you're the shit, don't you?" Larry laughed sarcastically.

"Why don't we sit down and have a talk," Lucio suggested.

"There's nothing to talk about. You're my wife's Eurotrash boy toy—her last desperate attempt to prove to herself that she's still attractive—and you're trying to turn my boys against me. End of discussion."

Lucio could not believe this man. He did not appear to be drunk and he could not smell alcohol on his breath, but he was behaving the way he had the night of the refried-beans incident. Lucio said, "She is no longer your wife, Dr. Garrison. And the reason she is now your *ex*-wife is because you regularly belittled her, and after you committed adultery here in your home, she divorced you."

Larry looked offended. "Nothing happened in this house. It was outside in the driveway."

Lucio could not contain his laughter. "What do you want, Larry?" he asked, still laughing. "Why did you come here tonight?"

"Oh, so I need to book an appointment to come talk to my own children now?"

"Of course not, but each time they see erratic behavior like this they trust you a little less. You confuse them."

"Excuse-fucking-me?"

"All I am saying is you need to examine how you have chosen to live your life and ask yourself how it is affecting your sons."

Larry took a step closer, his eyes menacing. "And you are their hero now? *You* are their good example?" He laughed in Lucio's face. "Come on, now. I found out a little bit about you. It wasn't hard. You're a notorious no-good horn dog with a checkered professional reputation, and that's putting it kindly."

The text message alert went off on Lucio's new cell phone again, the second time in the last minute. He wanted to take it from his pocket and make sure all was well with Jason, but he didn't have that luxury, not with Larry breathing like an angry bull, puffing up his body in preparation for attack.

"I do not wish to fight you, Larry," Lucio said. "If you are smart, you do not wish to fight me, either."

"Ha! You think I can't take you down, big man? Is that what you think?"

Lucio bit his tongue. It was not easy when he would rather give the *idiota* a tongue-lashing.

"Answer me. Is that what you think?"

Genevieve's former husband was a schoolyard bully in a middle-aged man's body—not an attractive combination. "I refuse to play this game," Lucio said, his voice calm and soft. "You should go."

Larry's eyes burned. "You think you're a badass, don't you? *Don't you, punk?*"

Lucio sighed, knowing it was time for Larry to hear the truth. "What I think, Dr. Garrison, is that you are having the midlife crisis from hell. I think you are setting a terrible example for your sons, who are on the verge of becoming men with only you as their guide—a man who fucks anything that moves, flies off into rages, and cares more about his car than his children. Having a father like this does not bode well for them, I am afraid."

Larry's jaw dropped.

"I think you are an egomaniac," Lucio continued. "And I think you are a coward and a brute for treating Genevieve the way you have through the years, not to mention being the world's biggest idiot for letting her go—though I do thank you for your idiocy."

After the stunned silence continued a moment more, Larry tilted his head back and let go with a roar of laughter. He wiped his eyes and sighed when he was done. "And you have become an expert in marriage and child rearing . . . *how,* exactly?" Larry balled his fists at his sides. "How many diapers have you changed, Ricky Ricardo? How many five-hour T-ball games have you sat through? How many god-awful elementary-school band concerts have you video-taped? How many boys have you taught how to catch a pop-up, or drive, or shave?"

When Lucio did not answer, Larry felt free to continue. "And how many women have you been married to for seventeen years? How many times have you had *that* gem of a life experience? Because from where I stand, it looks like you don't have a fucking clue what you're talking about, and you sure as hell don't have the right to tell *me* how to do any of it."

Lucio nodded, about out of patience. "It is true. I may not be a parent, but I was a boy once, and I had a father much like you, whom I have not spoken to in twenty years. Is that the kind of relationship you want with Josh and Jason?"

The corners of Larry's mouth pulled down.

"I also happen to be the man who loves your ex-wife and cares deeply for your boys. I am the man who stepped into the giant pile of doo-doo you left behind and has begun to clean it up."

Larry's nostrils flared.

Lucio gestured graciously to the front door. "And now, I must insist that you leave."

HeartherLynn started barking from the top of the stairs.

Larry's right arm swung out in a wide arc, his elbow cocked, his fist flying right at Lucio's head. Lucio ducked and Larry's fist went swishing by. Then Lucio blocked an uppercut coming from the left, and a right headed for his chin. After a few more moments of such ridiculousness, Lucio realized that Larry had no intention of stopping his flailing. That left him with no choice.

HeartherLynn continued her barking frenzy.

Lucio popped Larry right between the eyes.

The doctor cried out in pain. His fists ceased swinging and he cupped his palms under his nose to catch the blood. But the fury still burned in his eyes, and Lucio suspected that a broken nose was not enough to stop him. He braced himself as Larry lowered his head, turned his shoulder, and prepared to inflict a full-body slam.

"Stop it!" Joshua screamed, running into the hallway from the kitchen. "Dad! Stop it!"

Ignoring his son's plea, Larry charged Lucio, who avoided the onslaught with a simple sidestep. Larry head-butted into the wall with a thud.

"God, Dad!" Joshua went to his father, who was lying in a heap on the tile, blood still flowing from his nose. Larry moaned. "Get up," Josh said, with more annoyance than concern in his voice.

Lucio helped Josh pull his father to a stand and walk him into the kitchen. Once Lucio saw that Josh was doing a fine job settling his father in a chair, he went to the freezer for some ice.

"Why did you have to do that, Dad?" Josh collapsed in the chair next to him and handed him a wad of paper towels. Larry tipped back his head and stuck the paper to his nose.

"Where's your mother?" Larry mumbled.

Lucio handed Josh a plastic bag filled with ice and stepped away, leaning up against the stove out of Larry's view.

Josh nodded his thanks to Lucio. "She's upstairs getting dressed or something." Josh held the ice to his father's upturned nose.

"Go get her. I need her to see this," Larry whined. "I want her to see the handiwork of her new boyfriend. I want her to see with her own eyes the difference between us—that I am a healer and he is a destroyer."

Josh glanced at Lucio and rolled his eyes. "You started it, Dad. I saw the whole thing," Josh said. "Lucio didn't want to fight you. He was only defending himself."

Larry tried to laugh but just ended up gurgling his own blood. "The man is a fraud," Larry said, pointing over his shoulder, well aware that Lucio stood behind him. "He's a thief and a liar and maybe even a spy."

"Yeah," Josh said. "We know all about the trouble he's been in."

Larry peered over the ice bag at his son. *"You do?"*

"Of course," Josh said. "He told us all about that stuff the first night we met him."

Larry's shoulders hunched over. "Oh," he mumbled.

"None of it is true, Dad," Josh said, gathering the bloody paper towels and tossing them in the trash can below the sink. "The State Department has cleared him. There were no criminal charges. And Lucio found out who set him up in the first place and there's going to be an arrest."

Larry's eyes traveled to Lucio, leaning back with his arms across his chest. Even from under the ice pack, Larry was producing a sneer.

Since it looked like Josh had the situation under control, Lucio excused himself. "I'll go get your mother," he said to Josh. Then he nodded in Larry's direction. "You might want to get that nose checked out."

"I'm a physician." Larry took the ice from his face and glared at Lucio. "I know what I need to do," he said, the blood dripping down his chin.

Lucio shrugged. "Suit yourself."

He found Genevieve sitting on the edge of the big bed, slipping on a pair of shoes, listening to a CD with the volume turned up high. No wonder she hadn't come running downstairs when Larry cried out in pain.

Lucio stood in the doorway a moment, simply

watching her. He loved the graceful arch of her foot, her slim ankle, the delicate bones at the top of her feet. His chest tightened at the sight of her arm extended its full length, fingers stretched to buckle the strap.

She was so beautiful. He loved her so much.

"I think I broke Larry's nose," Lucio confessed.

Genevieve's head snapped up. She blinked at him, surprised to see him there. "Really?" she asked. Genevieve didn't look very concerned.

"Yeah. He went crazy on me. I had no choice."

She shrugged, then stood. She grabbed her bag from the coverlet. When she raised her eyes to his, Lucio was stabbed with the knowledge that something had changed in her. Her coloring was high. Her eyes were brighter. Genevieve's expression seemed to hold a subdued peacefulness he hadn't noticed before.

"Are you all right?"

She nodded, taking her eyes away.

"Genevieve?"

She turned quickly, her hair flying around her head with the movement. Tears welled in her eyes. "I know," she said. "I know you're leaving. Piers told me all about it."

Lucio's body tingled. He straightened from his casual pose against the doorjamb, and stared at her. Why would Piers tell her such a thing? He knew Lucio had no intention of taking that job. They'd talked all about it!

And then, seamlessly, everything clicked in Lucio's head. The paranoia he'd felt leaving Sydney's office wasn't paranoia at all—it was his intuition. Piers getting him that contract was underhanded and mean-spirited. It was not the act of a friend. It was an attack from an enemy, and the wound was intended to be fatal.

"Joder!" he hissed.

"Don't use language like that in front of me," she whispered.

It was then that Lucio realized Genevieve's expression wasn't peaceful at all. She looked defeated. Devastated.

"I was offered a job, yes, but—"

"How nice for you." She clasped her hands to the front of her belly, the small bag dangling by its strap. She looked at him with sarcastic enthusiasm. "And how was I going to find out about this little trip? By postcard?"

"I did not take the job," Lucio said, a lump of sorrow filling his gut. "I planned to tell you all about it tonight. I was going to let you know I was offered a contract but did not accept it."

"I see."

"I am not going anywhere, *mi amor.* Please believe me."

She did not respond.

"Genevieve, my agent called me to his office two days ago to tell me I'd been offered an assignment. That is all."

She said nothing. She hadn't moved.

He reached for her, cradling her upper arms in his hands. *"Guapa—"*

"Cut the Spanish endearment shit," Genevieve said, slicing her hands straight up to knock his grasp away. "That's enough. I've had enough of your Rico Suave act. And that's all it has been—all along—an *act!*"

The knife of her words cut to his heart. An icy fear ripped through the center of him. He was so stunned that he could hardly speak. "I do not understand," he said. "Why would you say that to me?"

Genevieve let loose with an embittered laugh. "Please," she said. "I can't hear any more of this. I told you that I couldn't survive another betrayal, that all you had to do was not hurt me and everything would be okay. You said you wouldn't, but that was a lie! You betrayed me and you hurt me anyway."

Lucio raked a hand through his hair in frustration. Genevieve had not heard a thing he said! It was like she'd already written him out of her life!

"If I go anywhere, I want you with me."

"Mauritius? The independent island off the coast of Africa known for being the home of the dodo bird?"

"Well, if that is what you wanted," he said, a little confused by her flippant response. "It would not be first-class travel the whole time, but you would get to see the world the way I see it. You could watch me work—get to know me better by seeing how I've lived my life."

She stared at him, her eyes steely and steady but revealing nothing.

"Genevieve, is that what you want?"

"Not hardly."

He reached for her hands.

"Don't touch me."

A wave of nausea flooded through Lucio and he stumbled back from her. What had Piers done?

"I couldn't go there even if I wanted to," she said. "It wouldn't be safe."

Lucio's attention returned to her face. She looked stricken, afraid. "You mean being away from the boys? Leaving them with Larry?"

She laughed nervously. "That's always a concern, but that's not what I mean."

"What do you mean, then?" It occurred to Lucio that a chasm had formed between them. Untruths and doubts had created a vast, dark separation between them. They weren't communicating. They could not read each other's hearts. It had happened fast. It was the ultimate injury.

"It doesn't matter," Genevieve said. "Nothing matters anymore."

"Where are you going?"

"Nowhere."

"Genevieve!" Lucio blocked her way out of the bedroom, unsure how to proceed but certain he had to get to the bottom of this. How he longed to touch her! "Please do not leave."

Genevieve's chin trembled with the effort not to cry. "Piers showed me your contract, okay? Let's just be real here. I saw it. I know. There's nothing left to say."

Lucio felt the blood roar through his brain. "No, *mi amor*. There is no contract."

"I saw your signature, Lucio!"

The bad taste in Lucio's mouth had a familiar tang to it. Suddenly, for the very first time, *he knew*. He knew everything, the whole picture.

Ilsa may have sent him the rat, but the real rat was Piers. Piers had probably doctored those e-mails from Ilsa. And, of course, Piers knew how to fill out a *Geographica* expense report—he'd done it as many times as Lucio had! And he'd certainly seen his signature enough to do a decent job of forging it, on an expense voucher *and* a contract! Setting up the anonymous bank account? It would be a snap for Piers. Getting the video to the Chinese? A minor errand.

Oh, Mother of God. How could I not have seen this?

Lucio froze where he stood. Whatever was displayed on his face caused Genevieve to raise an eyebrow in curiosity.

The stupid cell phone in his pocket buzzed once again. Why on earth had he let the boys talk him into getting one?

"Aren't you going to see who that is?" Genevieve asked, walking around him to get to the door.

Lucio yanked the phone out of his pocket to turn it off, but the small screen announced that Jason had sent him three messages.

"It's Jason," he said, clicking on the button that would bring up his messages. Even before the words appeared on the screen, Lucio was filled with a horrible dread.

"I hope he's learning a lot from Piers," Genevieve said, swinging her bag onto her shoulder. "He'll probably be spending quite a bit of time with him once you're gone."

The bitterness in her voice barely registered with Lucio, because he was focused on the terrible words now appearing on his cell phone.

The first message from Jason read, *Smthin's f'd up ovr here.* The second read, *Saw P's passpt was n Chna sm tm u were girl didn't do it cm get me NOW.*

And the third message said only one word—*HELP.*

Lucio looked up. He shoved the phone in his pocket, his breath shallow and fast.

"Is something wrong with Jason?"

"I have to go." Lucio turned, but Genevieve grabbed his arm.

"What's going on?" she yelled. "Is he okay?"

"I don't know," Lucio said. "Wait here. I'll go get him."

He raced down the stairs but Genevieve was right behind him, yelling for him to tell her what had happened to Jason, demanding she go with him.

When they hit the bottom of the stairs, Josh and his

blood-soaked father waited for them.

"What the hell is going on?" Larry asked.

"God!" Genevieve said, seeing him.

"Your boyfriend beat the crap out of me," Larry said.

Josh gripped the stair railing, looking to Lucio and then his mom. "There's something wrong with Jason, isn't there?"

Lucio flung open the front door, his mind racing with all the worst possible thoughts: Piers was unstable and would hurt Jason—even kill him—to get one last jab at Lucio. He couldn't let that happen. *He would not.*

"*¡Coño!*" Lucio hissed, seeing that Larry had blocked his car with the Porsche. "We have no time. Give me the keys to your car." He shoved his hand toward Larry. "Now, *gilipollas!*"

Lucio could barely think over the dog's incessant barking.

Larry fumbled in his pocket and pulled out the keys. "You are not touching my car," he said, his announcement muffled by the towel. "I will drive."

Josh ripped the keys from his dad's hands and tossed them to Lucio. "You can't even see, Dad! Your eyes are swelling shut!"

Lucio was already running across the lawn to the car. By the time he got the door open and got behind the wheel, it was clear that whatever kind of mission he was on would not be a solo one—Larry and Josh had already crammed themselves into the back half-seat of the Porsche and Genevieve was sliding in beside him in the front.

He groaned in frustration and gunned the car into reverse, squealing as he made his way through the neighborhood. It was barely sixty degrees Fahrenheit, but Larry had the top down on the pussy-puller! There was no time to fiddle with niceties—it would have to stay down.

How could he have missed this? Lucio slammed his palms against the steering wheel. He'd sensed it! But he'd ignored it! *¡Estúpido!* And now the crazy son-of-a-thousand-bitches had Jason!

CHAPTER 19

Lucio took a quick glance at Genevieve next to him. Her red hair was flying around her face. Her mouth was open in shock and her eyes were huge.

Lucio would give anything to save Genevieve's son. He would give *himself* for the boy's safety, and might yet have to. And to think—this had nothing to do with Jason. It was Lucio's battle, Lucio's problem, Lucio's past that had brought all this on. But the innocent boy might end up paying for Lucio's selfishness with his life.

If something happened to Jason, Genevieve would never forgive him. He would never forgive himself.

"Tell me!" Genevieve screamed over the wind and the sound of the high-performance engine. "What's going on?"

Lucio shook his head, dreading having to say it out loud. "The best thing you can do is call the police," he told her, his voice calm. "Piers's address is 890 Green Street, number eight."

Genevieve had her phone out, already dialing 911. Tears were rolling down her face. "Do you think he's hurt? Has there been an accident?"

Lucio took a corner way too fast, and the screech of the tires had other drivers pulling to the curb.

"What are you doing to my fucking car?" Larry screamed from the back. "Where are we going? What's wrong with Jason?"

"I don't know!" Lucio yelled over his shoulder, taking the entrance ramp to the 101. "I just pray we're not too late."

Lucio heard Genevieve screaming into the phone that she believed her son was in danger, but that, no, there was no fire, no medical emergency, or crime that she was aware of.

"Just tell them there's been a break-in!" Josh called out from the back. "A man with a gun! Give them the address!"

She did it, groaned in frustration, then hung up.

"This is a nightmare!" she yelled. "I think I'm going to be sick."

Lucio felt his cell phone vibrating in his pocket. He took one hand off the wheel and fished it out, tossing it to Ginger. "What does it say?" he shouted.

She clicked on the phone, turning slowly to Lucio. "It says, *All is well. No need to come.*"

Genevieve was not the only one on the edge of being sick. "Are the words spelled out?" Lucio shouted.

"What?"

"The words in the message—are they spelled out instead of . . . the Host! I do not know the word!"

"Abbreviated?"

"Yes!"

Genevieve looked again. "It's all spelled out. No abbreviations. Why?"

He shuddered. That last message had been from Piers, not Jason. He was sure of it. And it had been a warning to stay away.

"Tell me now!" she screamed. "What does this have to do with my son?"

"No! Stop! *Please!*"

Piers had him by the hair. With one hand, he dragged Jason backward through the living room, through the kitchen, and toward the balcony doors. With his other hand, he pressed the barrel of a gun into Jason's skull.

Jason didn't know which sensation was worse—the searing pain he felt from the way his hair was being pulled or the press of the gun against his head.

"Please don't do anything to me!" Jason said, gasping for air, struggling in vain to find a foothold that would support some of his weight. "I'm a kid! I haven't done anything!"

"Shut your fucking mouth," Piers said, his voice soft and cold. "If you do not shut your fucking mouth I will cut out your tongue." At that moment, as he dragged Jason past the kitchen counter, Piers grabbed a serrated kitchen knife from the cutting board and shoved it in his belt loop, then put the gun back to his head. "Do not think I won't."

"I'm sorry. I'm sorry. I know I shouldn't have been looking through your stuff but you said I could go in there! You told me I could see your passport!"

Piers yanked harder on his hair.

"Whatever happened between you and Lucio, you can work it out! Lucio will understand. He's your friend!"

Piers made a grunting sound. "He is not my friend. I despise him for what he did to Sylvie and me. He is a selfish, foul excuse for a human being." Piers unlatched the glass sliding door to the balcony and flung it wide.

"I don't understand," Jason said. He raised his

hands to his hair, trying to pull in the opposite direction to reduce the pain. "What did he ever do to you?"

Piers slapped Jason's hands away with the gun. "Shut up."

Jason knew Piers had begun crying. He heard a low weeping sound and he felt how the man's body jerked—he felt it all the way to the roots of his hair.

"Help me, Piers," Jason said, thinking he had to find some way to distract him. "If Lucio's such a rotten guy, my mom needs to know, right? I need to stop him before he hurts my mom."

"She already knows," was his reply.

The heels of Jason's athletic shoes got caught in the metal doorframe to the balcony. To dislodge him, Piers pulled on his hair so hard that some of it tore from his scalp.

"Ahhhhh!" he cried out.

Piers threw him against the railing and hit him across the face with the butt of the gun. A gash opened up across his cheek and brow and it hurt so bad that Jason thought he would pass out.

"Please, please . . ." Jason sobbed.

"It wasn't enough that Lucio poisoned every day Sylvie and I had together," Piers whispered, bending close to Jason's face. "He even ruined the last few seconds we had on this earth. He left me nothing—*nothing*—I could call my own. He left his stink on everything! For twenty years I've been living with the rotten stink of Lucky Montevez!"

Piers pulled Jason's hair again, then shoved his face into the concrete floor. Piers put his big foot on the back of his head, and pressed the gun into his neck.

"Please don't hurt me," Jason repeated. He felt dizzy. He couldn't think right. "I'm just a kid."

"Sylvie was only forty-two, and she is dead."

"I'm sorry she died," Jason said, gasping for air. Then he heard the click of the gun. That's when he knew he was going to die, too, unless he did something immediately.

"You can't shoot me, Piers," Jason said. "This is a crowded neighborhood. Everyone will hear it. You'll get the chair."

"Who said I planned on shooting you?" he asked, laughing.

That's when Jason felt his body being hefted off the concrete. Suddenly, he was on his feet. But he was so dizzy. So dizzy . . . and then he was being bent backward over the railing. All he saw was the blue of the sky, the edge of a few buildings, and an upside-down piece of Chinatown way off in the distance.

"We cannot wait for the elevator." Lucio ran through the first-floor lobby, using a key to open the glass doors to the inside of the apartment building. Josh was right behind him, and he held the door for Ginger and Larry. They began to race up the stairs, but Lucio got ahead of all of them.

"Hold up, for God's sake!" Larry complained, last in line, struggling to keep the ice on his face while navigating four flights of steps.

"I will go in alone!" Lucio ordered, now a full flight ahead of Ginger. "Do not come in after me. Just keep calling the police. I need to deal with Piers alone!"

"That's my fucking boy up there!" Larry said, nearly stumbling as he rounded a landing, his hand slipping from the banister. "I'll do whatever I want!"

Ginger breathed hard. Her legs burned. She had forgotten how drastically her body could change once a tiny life began to grow inside her.

She knew Lucio had reached Piers's apartment,

because the pounding sound of Josh's and Lucio's foot-steps had stopped. Once she reached the top floor, she saw them huddled in front of a door, listening. Lucio had the key in the lock. She tiptoed toward them.

Lucio placed his finger to his lips and then pointed at Josh and Ginger. "Stay here," he whispered. "Do not come in, whatever happens." He stopped for a fraction of a second. "Keep your mom safe," he told Josh.

"I will," he said.

"I love you," he told Ginger.

Then he went inside.

She put a hand over her mouth in fear. She closed her eyes and said a very short prayer: "God, let them be okay—let Jason and Lucio be okay."

Josh steadied Ginger and propped her against the hallway wall. "Give me the phone, Mom. I'm calling the police again, tell them what's going on."

Crack!

Ginger's eyes flew wide. Her heart was pounding so hard she was afraid it would pop through her ribs. "Was that a gunshot?" she wailed.

Josh nodded, looking scared to death. He yanked Ginger down to the floor and began to dial 911. His fingers were trembling. "Gunshots fired at 890 Green Street, number eight! Hurry!"

They heard another shot, followed by the shatter of glass. Ginger screamed and covered her ears. She clenched her eyes shut. Her entire body began to shake in terror. *This can't happen! Please, God, don't let this happen! Not my boy! Not Lucio!*

Strong hands pulled her up. She opened her eyes, hoping against hope that she would see Lucio, alive and well . . .

It was Larry. He hovered over her with his eyes

swollen into slits and his face puffed up and crusted with blood.

"Don't worry, babe," he said, gulping down air. "I'm going in."

Lucio had opened the door to Piers's apartment and slid into a small alcove just inside, where he could remain hidden for a few seconds. He hadn't heard anything—no voices, no sounds. So he slowly peeked around the corner. No one was in the living room or kitchen. Had Piers taken Jason somewhere? Oh God, no! That possibility hadn't even occurred to him! Where could they have gone?

Suddenly, Lucio saw movement beyond the kitchen, out on the balcony. For an instant, he didn't understand what he was seeing—Piers had his back to him. He seemed to be leaning over in some way—over the railing? Where was Jason?

Lucio ran. He knew that Piers would hear him coming but decided he had no choice. If Piers was doing what Lucio feared he was, there wasn't a second to spare.

Lucio dove through the open balcony doors. As he flew through the air, Piers turned, aimed a gun, and Lucio heard a loud *pop!* as a jolt of pain raced down his right leg. He landed on Piers with a thud, and locked his arms around his neck.

Piers's arm waved around wildly, and the gun went off again, shattering the glass door.

It was then that Lucio had a chance to look down. He was greeted by Jason's terrified eyes staring up at him. There was a bright red gash over his brow and cheek and his hands gripped the wrought-iron spindles of the railing. He was dangling four stories above the street by sheer determination.

"Hang on!" Lucio called to him. "I will get you."

Piers swung his shoulder and elbowed Lucio in the gut. Lucio hit the balcony floor with a thud. He knew he'd been shot but couldn't spare a second to find out how bad it was.

Piers aimed the gun at him again, but his entire arm was shaking. The big man looked as terrified as Jason.

Lucio used his uninjured left leg to kick the weapon from his hand, and watched it skitter across the concrete and fall over the edge. Then Lucio popped up to a sitting position and shoved his hand up into Piers's crotch. He twisted and pulled until Piers's face was purple.

Then Lucio punched him in the stomach.

Piers hit the outside wall of the balcony and slid down. Lucio got up, hopped on one leg, and leaned over the balcony railing, holding an arm down to Jason.

"Listen to me," he said calmly, despite the fact that he was anything but calm—Lucio knew his body was going into shock. "Take my hand." Instantly, Jason let go of the iron bars with his right hand and clasped onto Lucio. Then he did the same with his left.

Lucio hooked the foot of his uninjured leg under the railing to provide leverage. "Good," he said. "Swing your foot up to the edge of the balcony. I'll pull you—"

A crushing pain went through Lucio as his chest was smashed into the iron rail. Piers was on him like a wild animal—kicking, howling, doing his best to gouge out Lucio's eyes. Unfortunately, Lucio had just gripped Jason's hand and was in the process of pulling him up—he could not let go. If he did, Jason would fall.

"Grab the bars again!" Lucio screamed.

"I can't!"

Piers delivered a blow to Lucio's arm, right at the elbow. Lucio felt the bones break. He lost his grip on Jason.

"Noooo!" Lucio screamed.

Jason managed to grasp a single iron bar, and he swayed violently, his fingers slowly separating, loosening . . .

"Help me!" he called out. "Oh, God!"

Everything happened at once. Lucio heard the unmistakable sound of a damaging uppercut hitting bone. Piers fell away from his body, giving Lucio the single instant he needed to lean far across the railing and grab Jason's wrist—just as the boy's fingers lost their hold. Lucio had him, but he'd lost his foothold. With a broken arm and a bullet in one of his legs, he didn't have the strength to stop from sliding over the railing himself.

"Lucio!" he heard Ginger scream.

"Jason!" he heard Josh scream.

Police sirens were wailing louder and louder.

"Do not let go of my boy," Larry said, his arms seizing Lucio around the waist and slowly, carefully pulling him back over the rail.

"Here!" Josh said, offering Jason his other arm. His brother grabbed it.

"I've got him now," Larry said, once Lucio was upright. Lucio watched Larry grab Jason's other wrist while simultaneously grabbing the boy by the shirt collar. Josh and Larry had done it—Jason was saved. His mother was holding him and crying with relief.

Just then, the pain slammed into him. Lucio staggered backward. Larry grabbed him by the shirt as he began to fall and slowly lowered him down into Genevieve's waiting arms.

She cradled his upper body as he lay on the balcony floor. "You've been shot," she said. "Oh, my God, Lucio. Don't die!"

"I'm not going to die, *guapa,*" he told her, hoping to God he was correct. The entire right side of his body throbbed. He was on fire with the pain.

"You can't die," she whispered to him, stroking his head, kissing his hair.

"I will not leave you," he whispered, feeling his strength begin to fade.

"You can't leave our baby," she said.

Lucio tried to sit up but his body seized in agony. "What?" he gasped, pulling Genevieve down closer. "A baby?"

"Yes, Lucio. I just found out. I'm pregnant. The night of the earthquake . . ."

Lucio's body was racked with pain and joy at the very same instant. All he could do was pull Genevieve to him and kiss her. "I am so happy," he whispered. "You have made me so happy."

"Oh, shit."

The flatness in Larry's curse made Lucio's blood run cold. He raised his head enough to see what had happened. Jason was fine, sitting on the concrete on the other side of his mother, Josh holding him. Larry was standing near what used to be the sliding glass door. But Piers was standing on the thin iron railing, arms stretched out to his sides, precariously balanced. He stared down at Lucio with crazed grief in his eyes.

"Please don't," Lucio croaked out.

"Do you know what Sylvie said to me just before she died?" Piers asked, his eyes wild, his balance growing unsteady.

"Come on down," Larry said. "We'll figure all this out. Don't do this."

"If you come an inch closer I will jump." Piers glanced down at the sea of emergency vehicles pulling up to the apartment building and let out a bitter laugh.

"Picture this, my charming friend," Piers said, staring directly at Lucio. "It was the middle of the night. The lights were off. It was just Sylvie and me, in the glow of all her machines. I hadn't slept for three weeks, at her bedside every day, all day. Her eyes suddenly opened. I moved up to put my face next to hers. I put my lips against her cheek. And do you know what she said to me?"

Josh had left Jason and was crawling across the balcony floor. He got a few feet behind Piers and went into a crouch, ready to spring.

"What did she say?" Lucio fought to hold on to consciousness, trying to keep him talking.

Piers got a peaceful look on his face. Lucio had seen that look one other time, when he had sat on this very same balcony with him, talking of Sylvie.

"My wife looked me right in the eye. She smiled and whispered to *me,* her *husband*—'Is that you, Lucky? Have you come back to me?' "

No one breathed.

"And then she died," Piers said. He began to sway. Tears rolled down his face.

"Piers, please. No," Lucio said.

"You left me nothing, Montevez. I have nothing."

Josh leaped to grab Piers's legs, but he'd already begun to fall backward, eyes to the sky. Lucio watched Piers extend his body in a graceful arc, offering himself to the nothingness.

Then he was gone.

"No, no, no," Lucio moaned.

Instantly, Larry was at Lucio's feet. "Listen to me,

Montevez." Larry's eyes were steely behind their swollen lids, and a deep frown of concentration dominated his face. "Your friend is gone. But we've got another problem right here and I'm afraid it can't wait."

Larry's face began to wash out as Lucio's vision faded. He turned to Ginger. The last thing he saw was her beautiful hazel eyes, filled with fear and love. The last thing he heard were the words "femoral artery" and the sound of his jeans being ripped to shreds.

CHAPTER 20

Ginger took one last glance at herself in the full-length mirror and grinned at what she saw.

She was big as a house. Her cheeks were chubby and her ankles had morphed into cankles and she was happier than she'd ever been in her life. Lately, she wasn't sure the world was big enough to hold all her happiness.

Today was her wedding day.

"Psst."

Ginger looked up to see Josie sticking her curly head in the door. "Are you ready?"

Ginger nodded.

"Are you okay?"

Ginger nodded again.

"Are you sure?"

She held out her hand. Josie came to her, arms outstretched, and hugged her tight. They both began laughing.

"We have to stand five feet apart to hug these days," Ginger said.

"Between the two of us, we're twelve months' pregnant!" Josie separated from her friend and smiled at her, touching her cheek. "Ginger, I have never seen you more beautiful."

She reached for Josie's hands. "I remember the first time I did this, I was a nervous wreck. It was such a huge production. My mother and my father had to be separated because they hated one another. Larry was hungover from his bachelor party. I'd practically starved myself to squeeze into my wedding gown. I couldn't get my hair right. It was raining and I was supposed to have an outdoor reception . . ."

Josie grinned. "But this time?"

Ginger glanced to the French doors that looked out over the snow-covered vineyard. "This time I'm just happy. That's it. I'm not worried about anything. I'm forty and pregnant and getting married in a freak snowstorm and I'm happy about it!"

Josie went to the dressing table to retrieve Ginger's bouquet just as there was a knock at the door.

"You decent in there?" Bea asked, sticking her head in before Ginger could answer.

"I'm an unwed mother, but other than that, sure," Ginger said.

Bea laughed. "Just for another ten minutes or so, babycakes."

Roxanne came in next, smiling broadly. "Everything's ready in the main house. Mrs. Needleman is getting antsy and your mother is still hitting on Lucio's dad, who doesn't understand a freakin' word she's saying but sure seems to like looking down the front of her dress."

Bea snorted. "Maybe she's finally found her ideal man!"

"Please, *please* don't make me laugh," Ginger said, holding her belly.

"So you don't ruin your makeup?" Roxie asked.

"No! So I don't wet my pants!" Ginger said. "My bladder is the size of a raisin these days."

"Tell me about it," Josie said. "Just you saying that and I've got to hit the powder room again. Don't leave without me!"

Before Josie toddled off to the bathroom, she tossed the bouquet to Roxie, who looked like she was going to keel over in horror. She stared at the red roses in her hands for a second, then flipped them to Bea.

"Remember the last time we were all in this room?" Roxie asked cheerfully, making sure no one said anything about what had just happened.

"Absolutely." Ginger's gaze drifted to the guest room bed. "You guys were worried that my honor was being compromised."

"Silly us!" Bea said with a snort.

Josie's voice echoed from the bathroom. "Compromise can be a good thing! Sometimes all it takes is a little compromise to make your dreams come true!"

Roxie rolled her eyes. "We better get moving," she said. "Lucio shoveled the walkway so you wouldn't get snow on your shoes, but if we wait much longer he'll have to do it again."

Ginger sighed. "That was sweet of him."

"Josie, would you hurry up in there!" Bea walked through the dressing room and toward the bathroom. "We don't want Ginger's kid to be born out of wedlock, do we?"

"Coming, coming."

Josie opened the door and waddled past Bea, shaking her head. "You're such a bossy thing."

Bea's hand flew to her mouth and her eyes bugged out. Then Roxie did the same. That's when Ginger saw what they found so hilarious. Josie had tucked the back of her maid-of-honor dress into her panty-hose.

"Hey, Joze," Bea said. "You know how you're al-ways telling me to mind my own business?"

Josie spun around. "Yeah." She spun back around when she heard Ginger and Roxie snicker. "What's so funny?"

"Look, I hate to 'butt' into your personal affairs." Bea could hardly contain herself. "But you should know that your entire booty is exposed."

Josie fumbled around behind her and gasped.

"I'll get it, Joze." Ginger yanked up on the ruby-red satin until it was unhitched, then smoothed it out to where it fell at mid-calf. She smiled at her friends. "You all look gorgeous," she said. "Thank you for be-ing my bridesmaids. Come here a minute."

Ginger motioned for everyone to stand with her in front of the huge mirror.

With her dark hair and pale skin, Roxanne looked stunning in the three-quarter-length-sleeve wrap dress. Bea looked downright sophisticated. She was even wearing small diamond stud earrings and a touch of lip gloss! Josie looked adorable, with her pink cheeks and all those glossy curls brushing her shoulders. Ginger had asked the seamstress to adjust the cut of the dress to accommodate Josie's growing bump, and the result was perfection.

Maybe Josie was right—maybe Ginger had never looked more beautiful than she did right then. She wore an ivory silk sleeveless dress that fell just above her ankles. The retro style of the gown was accented by elegant elbow-length gloves. Ginger's hair had been pulled back into a French twist, and she wore her mother's matching pearls and earrings.

She looked like a knocked-up Holly Golightly.

"We're four of the hottest babes in all of Northern California," Bea said, giving Ginger a gentle squeeze around her waist as they stood before the mirror.

"Maybe five," Ginger said.

"Whoops! Of course!" Bea bent at the waist and whispered into Ginger's dress. "Sorry, sweet cheeks."

Josie cleared her throat.

"Right," Roxie said, leaning down close to Josie's tummy. "Maybe even six!"

The women laughed and pulled each other tighter. Ginger noticed that tenderhearted Bea was almost ready to burst into tears.

"All right, let's get me married." Ginger held out her hand to Bea, who transferred the bouquet to her grasp.

The women walked to the door, and filed down the guest-house steps. Bea held Ginger's elbow and they hustled her down the covered walkway to the main house. The women stood at the front door, peeking through the window.

Ginger gasped. The great room at Samhain Ranch had been turned into a lovely chapel, decorated with red and white roses and sprays of greenery. A fire roared in the fireplace, sending golden light through the room. Candles were lit everywhere. About forty people were seated in a half circle of chairs.

Ginger peered closer. There were her boys, so handsome and tall in their tuxedos. How proud she was of the men they were becoming! And there was her mother, wearing a dress that advertised her latest boob job, rubbing against the arm of Lucio's father. And there was Larry's latest girlfriend, sitting by herself in the last row. Ginger had met her. She liked her. She was a teacher, with two grown daughters. The woman was forty-seven.

She knew why Larry was not sitting next to his girlfriend—because Lucio had asked him to be a groomsman. He wanted to honor Larry for saving his and Jason's lives, and Larry had agreed.

Will wonders never cease.

Lucio entered the great room. She could barely detect a limp as he strolled between the divided chairs and stood to the left of Mrs. Needleman. He kissed the old woman's hand, which she obviously loved, and then he clasped his hands behind him. Rick, Teeny, and Larry fell into place at his side.

Lucio looked elegant and masculine and just slightly nervous. Ginger felt a sting in her throat at the sight of him, her sexual panther man, her six-alarm lover, a man who had turned out to be as brave and sweet as he was spicy. She thanked God that his arm was completely mended, and it was icing on the wedding cake that Lucio had stopped needing his cane just last week, four months after his gunshot wound. Everyone who had been injured that day had healed fine. And they'd all helped Lucio deal with the suicide of his friend.

Ginger took a deep breath and blew out the sorrow. It did not belong here. This moment was about celebration. It was about hope.

"I've waited my whole life for this," she told her friends. "I don't want to wait another second."

The Spanish guitar soloist paused, and started the melody Lucio and Genevieve had chosen for her walk down the aisle—*Lágrima* by Francisco Tarregá. It was a tender piece of music, simple and romantic.

Lucio's hands fell to his sides. He tried to regulate his breathing, but was failing. Bea came first, taking long strides through the room out of synch with the music, smiling big and winking as she took her spot. The Amazon Woman came next, and Lucio was surprised at how lovely Roxanne looked. She was one of those women whose bitterness could suck the beauty right out of her own skin—but this evening she seemed more relaxed and happy than he'd ever seen her. The red satin suited her as much as the breastplate and spear. Lucio smiled at her and gave her a nod.

Josie came next. She beamed. She glowed. She giggled. It had been a real pleasure getting to know her, and Lucio was grateful that she and Ginger had each other's counsel during their pregnancies. Lucio heard Rick mumble something to himself, and turned to see his friend blinking back tears.

"I told you—no crying," Teeny hissed. "You know I can't handle that shit, man."

Lucio decided to check on his father, who was smiling softly and nodding his approval, not overly concerned with the aggressive advances of Ginger's mother. Lucio had no illusions. Rebuilding a relationship with Isidro Montevez would be a monumental task, but his agreeing to come to San Francisco for the wedding was already a miracle in itself. Now if his papa could only escape the clutches of the glamorous Teresa Barr, former beach-blanket bimbo . . .

For Lucio, everything and everyone else fell away as Genevieve entered the room. Her cheeks were flushed from the cool air. She walked slowly and delicately down the center of the room, the firelight playing on her skin, her smile wide and pure. A collective sigh went through the room. She was radiant. She held the bouquet of roses at her belly, but it did nothing to hide his baby inside. Of all the miracles in that room on that Valentine's Day, his child was the most breathtaking.

After all this time, after all these detours, Lucio was being offered the one assignment he had thought was out of his reach—the chance to be a husband and father.

Genevieve arrived in front of Mrs. Needleman. Lucio moved to her right side and took her soft hand in his. He knew the ceremony would be brief. That had been his only request.

"I know I will forget if there are too many words," he had explained to Genevieve. "My tongue and my brain will be all jumbled." They had agreed to say one simple thing to each other by way of vows.

Mrs. Needleman read a short poem about the mystery of love. Genevieve looked over to Lucio and gave him a crooked smile. He wished they were alone. His bride was so delicious and round that all he wanted was to roll around with her, naked, skin on skin, breathing her and tasting her and singing to their little baby boy or girl. He was so in love with his bride that he didn't know if he could survive the ceremony. He was so in love with his baby that he didn't know if he could survive the three months of waiting.

"I promise to give my heart to you without reservation and without doubt," Genevieve was saying. She'd already handed off the bouquet to Josie and had turned to face him directly. "I promise to believe in you, laugh with you, find the joy in every small thing we experience together. I have been waiting for you forever, Lucio. I am so glad we found each other."

He nodded, painfully aware that it was his turn to speak. *The Host!* He had forgotten what he planned to say!

"Just wing it," Teeny whispered over his shoulder.

Lucio let go with an embarrassed laugh. He took a breath. "So much has happened, my love. Everything that has taken place in my life has led me to you, to this day, to my child, to a world so full of happiness that it sometimes shocks me."

Genevieve's eyes went big.

"I have seen so much of life—the tragedy and the greed and the most spectacular creations of God on earth. But nothing—nothing—has prepared me for what I see today. I have a wife! I have two wonderful young men at my side." Lucio nodded to the boys in the front row, who were grinning shamelessly. "I have a life rich in friendship and laughter, and a sense of belonging."

Lucio felt himself choke up. He decided to let it come. In a broken voice he said, "Even my father is with me today, after a lifetime of . . . of . . . the word . . . ?"

"Alienation?" Teeny offered.

"Separation?" Larry suggested.

"Discord?" Rick asked.

The entire room laughed.

"Anyway, all that matters is that my father agreed to come, and it marks a new beginning." He looked briefly to his father. "*Gracias,* Papa."

After taking a deep breath, Lucio brought both of Genevieve's hands to his lips and pressed them tight with a kiss. "I love you, *pelirroja,*" he whispered. "I will be a good husband to you. I will not let a day go by where you do not know how I treasure you, how I thank God that everything went wrong in my life so that everything could finally be made right."

Mrs. Needleman cleared her throat. "We've rented this joint by the hour," she said, to great laughter.

"Ah, I have said enough, yes?" Lucio released Genevieve's hands and reached behind toward Rick, who handed off the ring.

"Please marry me, Genevieve. Please be my wife."

She smiled. "I will."

Lucio slid the platinum band down her lovely finger. He knew he was smiling like a fool.

"Please marry me, Lucio." She held the ring at the tip of his finger. "Please be my husband."

"Of course! Yes, I will!" he said.

She slid the ring down his finger.

Mrs. Needleman asked them to face her. "Now, I know how it is with this crowd—you're going to want to kiss the bride ASAP, so I'll make it snappy."

The bride and groom exchanged smiles.

"Lucio and Genevieve, you are blessed. You are chosen. You were offered and you accepted the mysterious gift of love. It is now your job to make the world a better place with the light of that love. I now pronounce you husband and wife. You may—"

Lucio had already grabbed Genevieve by the shoulders and pulled her mouth to his. He laughed, he cried, he kissed. He turned to see everyone on their feet, laughing and clapping and smiling.

It was real. It was done. He squeezed Genevieve's hand and they walked through the room as Mr. and Mrs. Lucio Montevez.

Indeed, he was the luckiest man on earth.

"Roxanne, would you mind getting me to my room so I can rest?"

Roxie's eyes went huge. She looked at Bea across the room, who was talking to Teeny and nursing another beer. Roxie waved her arms to get Bea's attention. "Hey! Mrs. Needleman is ready to go to her room," she said, rather loudly. Bea only shrugged, as though it weren't her responsibility.

"But I want *you* to walk me there, dear." Mrs. Needleman grabbed onto Roxanne's arm for support as she pulled herself from the armchair. "A two-hour party is two hours too many for me these days."

Roxanne sighed. She helped the woman through the kitchen and out the back door. They walked down the length of the covered rear patio in silence.

"So what did you think of the ceremony this evening?" Mrs. Needleman asked when they were close to her guest-room door.

A smile slipped by Roxie's guarded expression. "It was really sweet."

"It was, wasn't it?" Mrs. Needleman sighed. "That Lucio is a real hottie. He makes me wish I were forty years younger."

Roxie nearly choked.

"Think about it, Roxanne," the old woman said. "Josie goes out and finds Rick, who is one of the handsomest men I've seen in my eighty-four years. And Ginger comes up with a sexier version of Antonio Banderas, which I didn't even think was possible."

By then, Roxanne was the one who needed help walking. She couldn't believe this old broad! She didn't think little old ladies went around thinking things like that! It was disturbing.

"Do you have your room key?" Roxie asked, trying to change the subject.

"There are no keys here. It's a private home."

"Oh. Right."

"Now, what I was getting at is, I wonder about the man you'll fall for. If he's anything like Rick and Lucio, then, *woo-hoo*! We'd better put on our seat belts!"

"Here you are!" Roxie flung open the door to Mrs. Needleman's room and nearly dragged her across the threshold. "Hurry now. It's pretty cold out here. I wouldn't want you to get chilled."

Mrs. Needleman chuckled. "You're trying to get rid of me."

"Not at all. Good night now. Feel free to call Bea if you need anything."

"Roxanne."

She'd already turned her back to Mrs. Needleman. She stood still, wrapping her arms around herself to stay warm. Roxie looked up to see a few stray snowflakes still falling from the sky.

She turned back toward Mrs. Needleman. "I think we should just be honest, here, Gloria."

The old woman smiled. "You do, do you?"

"Yes."

"Fine by me."

Roxie laughed a little, surprised by the piss and vinegar in this old lady. "Here it is. I'll lay it all out for you. Now listen closely. I . . . do not . . . want . . . a . . . man."

Mrs. Needleman said nothing. She looked almost bored.

"I will not be 'falling for' anyone, as you say. I will never again change my life and myself to please some guy. My life is mine to live. My terms. My dreams. And my dreams do not include a man."

Mrs. Needleman shrugged. "Are you finished?"

Roxie's mouth fell open. This woman was unbelievable! "No. As a matter of fact, I'm not done."

Mrs. Needleman gestured broadly. "Then please continue."

"Okay. Fine. I will." Roxie shifted her weight from foot to foot. "All I'm saying is that I think you're a sweet lady and you mean well, but I won't be sticking around for the mumbo-jumbo lecture about fate and destiny that you used to psych out Josie and Ginger. That kind of crap isn't my thing, okay? I'm thrilled for them, but this is where your fortune-teller gig comes to a screeching halt. I won't be participating. Got it?"

The old woman blinked at her.

"Sorry, but that's how I feel." Roxie crossed her arms over her chest.

"*Now* are you done?" Mrs. Needleman asked.

"Uh, sure."

"Lovely." The old lady smiled briefly. Then she frowned. "You want honesty, my dear girl? I've got some honesty for you." She wagged a finger. "You are the angriest young woman I have ever met. That anger is going to eat you alive unless you face the source of it, name it, and let it go."

Roxie felt as if she'd been punched in the stomach. She could hardly get enough air in her lungs.

"But you will never be able to do that if you continue to run away."

"I've never run away from a damn thing in my life," Roxie said, livid. "You don't know anything about me."

Mrs. Needleman sighed. "I know that you have been badly hurt. I know you are a hard worker and a loyal friend. I know that you are kind and patient, keeping that damaged puppy the way you have. What is her name again?"

Roxie let her arms fall to her sides. "Lilith."

Mrs. Needleman smiled. "Let Lilith show you the way, my dear. I think that if you help Lilith with her anger, you might discover the origin of your own. It's just a suggestion."

"I'm already helping Lilith."

"Then keep at it."

"Fine.".

"Now, was that so terrible? Was my advice—my mumbo jumbo as you call it—so difficult to swallow?"

"I suppose not."

Mrs. Needleman reached for Roxie's hand. "Do you know the one thing you can never run from, Roxanne?"

She shrugged. "Sure. I took Psych 101."

"And?"

"Myself. The one thing I can never run from is myself."

The old lady smiled and gave Roxie's hand a squeeze. "Well, then," Mrs. Needleman said. "My work here is done. Good night."

Then she closed the door in Roxanne's face.

Read on for an excerpt from
Susan Donovan's next book

NOT THAT KIND
OF GIRL

Coming soon from St. Martin's Paperbacks

"Babies, babies, babies, babies, babies . . ."

Roxanne felt free to mutter to herself out here at the paddock, because her only witness was a pretty Appaloosa mare who was loitering about ten feet away, languidly chomping on alfalfa, her big brown eyes looking sympathetic to Roxanne's concerns.

Roxie propped a foot on the lowest rail of the fence and draped her elbows over the highest. "How am I supposed to be a co-godmother?" she asked the horse. "I don't know the first thing about babies. I'm not even sure I like them! Fine, they're important to the continuation of the species and all that, but there are days I'm not sure the human species deserves a pass, you know what I'm saying?"

The horse snorted and twitched her ears as if to agree.

"I mean, why keep adding extra people to the mix when the ones already here can't treat each other decently?"

The horse ambled over to the fence, where she nosed Roxie under the crook of her arm. Roxie stroked the mare's neck. "How did this happen? That's all I'm asking. A year ago we were all perfectly miserable—man-less and about to lose our jobs at the paper. But at least we were a unified front in our misery, you know? We even took a vow to be alone together, just us and our dogs!"

The horse blew air from her nostrils and pawed at the dirt.

"And then, Josie goes out and finds Rick Rousseau, a hunk with a heart bigger than his bank account. And Ginger somehow conjures up Lucio Montevez, a Mediterranean sex god who basically worships her. And suddenly everybody's in a family way and happier than pigs in you-know-what and I'm still . . ." Roxie stopped herself, sighing deeply. The horse moved closer, waiting for her to finish her sentence.

"Oh, never mind," Roxie told her. She let her forehead rest on the broad and smooth plane between the horse's gentle eyes. "I think I've already missed my chance to be a mother. I guess that's what this is all about. I'm probably a little jealous of my friends."

The horse whinnied in protest. "*Fine*," Roxanne said with annoyance. "I realize Bea isn't married and pregnant but, come on, like that's ever going to happen? My point is she's following her dream. Becoming an agility trainer is making her as happy as Ginger and Josie, just in her own way."

Roxie lifted her head and stared off across the miles of rolling vineyard. "What I'm saying is everyone in our little group has moved on—except me. I'm still right where I started."

"Animals are good listeners," a voice said from behind her.

Roxie froze. She knew that voice. It was an irritatingly masculine voice. Annoyingly sexy. She hated the way it flowed, like a slow and deep river sure of its destination. And she really hated the fact that the owner of that voice might have heard even a syllable of her very private musings.

She blew out air, not turning around. So *that man* had suddenly decided she was worth a little of his time? Ha! And he thought it was acceptable to follow her out here without her permission? What a complete *tool* this guy was!

"You and I need to talk," he said, his voice soft and steady. "I promise I will be a good listener, too."

She kept her back to him. He didn't deserve her full attention.

But he moved closer and . . . *dammit!* There it was again, that weird vibration she'd felt the very first time she'd met him, right here at the ranch, the day of Josie and Rick's wedding. She would never forget the instant she noticed him. He was leaning against the stone wall between the garden and the lawn, one knee bent, the heel of one cowboy boot propped against the wall and the toe of the other tapping in the dirt. He'd pushed that stupid black hat back on his blond curls and bit down on the inside of his mouth, like he was trying to keep from laughing. He'd focused his intense green eyes right on her.

Oh, damn, he'd been gorgeous. Big and muscular in his suit. Sun-browned skin. Sensual lips. Graceful hands.

Roxanne didn't want to think about what happened next, but she couldn't stop herself from remembering. The truth was, Eli Gallagher's intense gaze had sliced through her flesh, raced through her blood, and landed with a hot thud right between her legs.

The moment had made such an impression because, embarrassingly enough, that had been the only thing that had landed with a hot thud between her legs in a very long while. And that encounter with Eli had taken place more than *nine months ago!* And there'd certainly been no thudding since. She absolutely refused to do the bigger-picture math.

"I owe you an apology, Roxanne."

"Nope. You don't." She kept her eyes on the vineyards.

"An explanation, then."

"You don't owe me anything." She waited. She strained to hear him let go with an exasperated sigh, or a groan of frustration, or a bitter laugh—anything that would indicate she'd gotten the better of him.

"You are one tough cookie, Ms. Bloom" was what he said.

For just a second, she shut her eyes. She summoned her strength. She knew exactly what she'd see when she turned around—an extremely handsome man, somewhere in his early thirties, with loose blond curls, dusky green eyes accented by smile lines, a set of full lips, an elegant chin, and a tall and fit body tucked inside a pair of worn jeans.

A man that spectacular could have any woman he wanted. And, as he'd made painfully clear a while back, he didn't want *her*.

It was for the best. Roxanne knew she was too much for him to handle. She was too much for any man to handle. That concept had been introduced to her in childhood, with her own father. It was a pattern that would repeat itself through high school, college, then after college, and, most recently, with Raymond Sandberg—the one man she'd convinced herself was mature enough to appreciate everything she brought to the table.

Whoops. She'd been wrong on that one, hadn't she? But it would be the last time she'd ever be wrong about a man, because she understood now. There was no man for her. There never would be. And it didn't matter if two of her best friends had recently been sucked into the vortex of love. She would have to be okay with that. She would have to find her own peace. She was a strong woman, and if anyone could do it, Roxie could.

She shook her hair back over her shoulder, then slowly turned to face him. She crossed her arms over her chest. "Look, Ian—that is your name, right? Did I remember it correctly?"

He offered her a small smile. There wasn't even the slightest flicker of hurt in his green eyes. Her insult seemed to bounce right off of him.

"Elias Jedidiah Gallagher," he said. With dramatic flair, he swept up his hand to pluck his big black cowboy hat off his head. He placed it on his heart and bent at the waist. "At your service," he added.

He was such an ass. Roxanne wanted to grab that ridiculous hat and whack him upside the head with it.

The Appaloosa whinnied loudly in Roxie's ear.

"But you know that, of course," he added, his voice teasing and pleasant. "We talked for a long while at Rick and Josie's wedding, and there was a strong attraction between us. We both felt it. And we discussed how I might help you with your rescue dog's aggression issues."

"She's cured," Roxie said, smiling. "I no longer need your help."

"And I distinctly remember giving you my card."

"I must have thrown it away," she said.

"Before or after I turned you down for that lunch date?"

Roxie enjoyed a bit of clever banter as much as the next girl. In fact, that was something she could never get enough of with Raymond. They would spar, and their words would heat up and the double-entendres would fly, and they'd end up rolling around in bed together, enflamed with desire. Raymond might have been almost thirty years her senior, but the man had been sizzling *hot*. Whoever said the brain was the primary sexual organ knew what they were talking about.

But, since Roxie had no interest in banter with Eli, clever or otherwise, she decided to put an end to the barnyard ambush. One ambush per day was her limit anyway, and Mrs. Needleman had gotten to her first.

"Unfortunately for you, Ian," she said, "cowboys don't do anything for me." She stifled a yawn. "But I do know a girl with a major cowboy fetish. Want her number?"

"The name's Eli."

"Whatever."

Eli nodded broadly. "Right. I think I understand now," he said. "The sheer force of your indifference toward me sent you racing out the kitchen door just a minute ago. Is that it?"

"You flatter yourself," she said, her heart now at a full gallop in her chest. She didn't want any of this. Not the spark. Not the crackling attraction. Not the racing pulse. It had to end. So she delivered what she was sure would be the final blow. "Anyway, you had your chance. You blew it. I don't give second chances."

Now *that* got a flicker out of him. Understanding flashed in his eyes, but disappeared immediately. Eli had no comeback. He returned the hat to his head and tugged at the brim, as if to announce his imminent departure. *Good riddance to him*, she thought.

Suddenly, Roxanne felt something nudge her butt so hard her feet rose above the ground. She flew forward. She slammed right up against the front of Eli's solid body. She screamed. Eli grabbed her by the shoulders and steadied her, her toes just grazing the dirt. She leaned back awkwardly.

"Seems you got goosed," Eli said, smiling.

Roxie whipped her head around in time to see the traitorous horse lope off to the other side of the paddock. When she returned her gaze to Eli, she noticed that his eyelids were heavy and his attention had shifted to her chest, throat, mouth. Then she became agonizingly aware of the touch of his strong fingers on her upper arms. Next she realized their bellies were pressed together. The front of her thighs were smashed right into his hard . . .

Oh, God.

She began to squirm. "Let me go," she said between clenched teeth.

He didn't. His grip on her stayed gentle but seemed to deepen somehow. Roxie kicked but her feet barely skimmed across the dust. His gaze returned to hers and locked in. And that's when the strangest thing happened.

Her body began to flood with a sensation she could only call *ease.* A warm, steady, calming relief that washed through her, softening her and opening her up. Everywhere.

No way was she falling for that shit.

"Settle down, sweet thing."

The words had been delivered in that deep-river voice. His muted green eyes smiled.

Settle? Down? Sweet thing?

Just four little words and it felt like the earth had stopped turning. That comment was condescending, domineering, insulting, and, at the same time, strangely arousing. His hands maintained their grip on her as he lowered her feet to the ground. She became a little lightheaded. She didn't know what was happening. The sensations swirling around inside her were confusing. Scary. Intense. Sexual. She resented all of it.

And if she hadn't despised Eli Gallagher before, she surely did now. How dare he touch her like this? How dare he talk to her with that languid voice? How dare he treat her like a wild stray animal who needed his gentle touch?

And who the hell did he think he was, knocking her off balance this like this? If she'd wanted to experience ease and calm she would have gone out and gotten it the normal way—with a prescription!

"Don't ever put your hands on me again," Roxie managed.

"I won't hurt you, Roxanne."

She felt weak. Way too warm. She wanted to escape his grip but couldn't seem to muster the energy. It took every bit of strength she possessed to shake her head side to side. "No," she whispered.

"You're safe with me."

And that's when it happened. Out of nowhere, for no good reason, a sob erupted from her throat. Before she even realized what was happening, the calm had punched a hole in that giant bubble of rage and grief inside her, and it all came flooding out in one long, searing moan. There was no stopping it. She wanted to die from shame.

Eli kissed her. She knew immediately that the kiss wasn't designed to stop the outburst. Its fierceness only demanded more. The kiss—the heat, the pressure, the need—it wrenched the emotion right of her.

No. This was impossible. This was nuts! She wouldn't allow it. No man would ever again lull her into being a stupid, hopeful, defenseless, emotional, babbling idiot the way she'd been with Raymond. She would never leave herself vulnerable like that again. It had been a sacred promise she'd made to herself. No man—Eli Gallagher included—was worth the loss of her self-respect.

She shoved so hard that he lost his grip on her, with both his hands *and* his lips. Roxie gasped for breath and tried to find her bearings, quite aware of how Eli's eyes had widened with confusion. She turned and ran. Her feet pounded the hard dirt. Within minutes she was in her car heading south on Highway 121, on her way home to San Francisco, where she would undoubtedly shove everything back in its proper place, the way she always did.